THE
SPECTACULAR

ZOE WHITTALL

HODDER

First published in Canada by HarperCollins
First published in the United States of America by Ballantine Books,
an imprint of Random House
First published in Great Britain in 2021 by Hodder & Stoughton
An Hachette UK company

This paperback edition published in 2022

1

Sarah Manguso, excerpt from *300 Arguments: Essays.* Copyright © 2017 by Sarah Manguso.
Excerpt from *Ongoingness: The End of a Diary.* Copyright © 2015 by Sarah Manguso.
Both reprinted with the permission of The Permissions Company, LLC on behalf
of Graywolf Press, Minneapolis, Minnesota, graywolfpress.org.

Book design by Barbara M. Bachman

A CIP catalogue record for this title is available from the British Library

Paperback ISBN 978 1 529 38311 9
eBook ISBN 978 1 529 38310 2

Printed and bound in Great Britain by Clays Ltd, Elcograf S.p.A.

Hodder & Stoughton policy is to use papers that are natural, renewable and
recyclable products and made from wood grown in sustainable forests.
The logging and manufacturing processes are expected to conform to
the environmental regulations of the country of origin.

Hodder & Stoughton Ltd
Carmelite House
50 Victoria Embankment
London EC4Y 0DZ

www.hodder.co.uk

Dedicated to the memory of

ALEXANDRA OLSEN

and to queer femmes everywhere

BOOK ONE

1997

I left home and I faked my ID.
I fucked every man that I wanted to be.

—NEKO CASE

Motherhood is a mental illness.

—RAMONA,
FROM THE MOVIE
HUSTLERS

CHAPTER 1

MISSY

FOUGHT MY WAY through the group of protesters, my eyes liquefied from the cold wind. A gray-haired leviathan, fetus pendant asleep in his chest hair, leaned over me and whispered a guttural *"Slut."* The pink plastic pendant knocked against my forehead. He sank back into their slumpy circle, was made anonymous by the grind of their group shuffle. They chanted. Circled. Chanted some more. When they tried to block me from the door, I lost my shit. A clinic volunteer appeared through the blur and gripped my wrist. *"I don't even want an abortion!"* I shouted above their heads from the top of the steps.

The volunteer ushered me inside, to the near-silent administrative shuffling of any waiting room. Instead of following the volunteer, I turned and reopened the door. I like to have the last word. "But abortions are great! I wish *you'd* been aborted!"

He lunged up the stairs, and I ripped the fetus from his neck.

The volunteer yanked me inside by the back of my jacket,

slamming and locking the door as the old man's full weight came charging up against it.

He reminded me of a horse we had when I was ten, the years we were trying not to use money and barter for everything. My father gave my neighbor an old rifle and in return he gave us Sugar, a palomino with a charcoal heart on her ass. She never acted like her name. She had a mean glare and liked to bite children. She was supposed to be mine, but I wasn't allowed near her. I sat on the top of a manger a good stall away and tried to soothe Sugar with songs from the soundtrack to *Hair.* She kicked at the stall door so hard there were permanent hoofprints, even after we traded her for half a frozen deer and a washing machine that only worked when it rained.

The old man continued to throw his body against the door.

The incantations outside rose in volume.

"That wasn't smart," the clinic volunteer said, sending rolled eyes toward the security guard.

"But it *was* satisfying."

The plastic fetus grew hot in my closed fist. The volunteer wasn't charmed by me.

"Nothing you can say will ever matter," she said, handing me a form to fill out. The pen slipped from my fingers and hung limp from the clipboard string. I dropped the fetus into a nearby garbage can; it stuck to a clump of gum.

Name: *Melissa Wood.* Age: *21.* But soon I would be Missy Alamo, all spring and summer. My fingers were solid calluses from all the rehearsals. I returned the clipboard to the receptionist.

Twenty minutes later I sat in a ripped pleather chair

across from a doctor with a salt-and-pepper crew cut. She seemed amused by me.

"What can I do for you?"

"I would like my tubes tied," I explained, as though ordering something off a menu. When I said the word *tubes* I imagined the black rubber inner tubes inside my bicycle tires. The doctor had feminist watercolors on the wall—all vagina flowers and wispy goddesses. I'd dressed like Julia Roberts in *Pretty Woman*. My skirt was so short I was sure she could glimpse my cervix with a quick pointed downgaze.

"Well, I do not get that request, uh, very often, from someone your age."

I explained my dilemma. She actually listened to me, which I wasn't expecting.

"I don't want to sound condescending, but you're just too young. You may regret it."

"Well, you *do* sound condescending," I said.

Staring contest.

Beat.

Beat.

I won.

She shuffled papers and looked up at the clock.

"Look, I respect your autonomy and your considerable confidence on this issue, but I don't want to be responsible for the implications of this choice when you're older."

She didn't want to be responsible for *future* me being upset, which seemed ridiculous. Current me is *very upset*. Future me doesn't exist yet. She could be hit by a car.

"I'm going to regret a lot of things," I said. "You can't know. What I do know is I don't want to try to get an abortion in Kansas while my bandmates are partying. It's your feminist duty!" I pointed out her *Your Body Is a Battleground* postcard. *"Come on.* I can adopt if I regret it. Biology doesn't matter."

She exhaled upward, stared above my head at the ceiling fan. It clicked in three-quarter time. "Even if I refer you, the doctor won't do it," she said. "I'm sorry. This province wants you to have lots of babies. That's the way it is."

"Isn't this the same country that sterilized poor women of color in jail?"

I'd read that in a women's history course at McGill before I deferred my studies so I could go on tour. She frowned.

"We don't do that anymore," she said, shuffling papers on her desk again and looking like she wished she'd chosen any other profession.

Do you know how hard it is to get sterilized when you're young and conventionally pretty from some angles, when you appear to be middle class even though you've only got seventeen bucks in your savings account, and when all the doctors think you're misguided, because eventually you'll want to blossom, ripen, and suckle?

The doctor continued to stare at me, unmoving. This time I broke her gaze first. I hate losing.

I HAD ALREADY tried several clinics. The male doctors were the worst because you look like the girls they jerk off to, and if they really thought you didn't want their jizz stuck up inside you, they'd have no reason to go on. They'd shrivel up and die, self-immolate from the existential crisis.

I knew the limitations of my body and mind, but no doctor would help me nip my problem in the bud, so to speak.

We were about to be on the road for months, first stop Roch-
ester, last stop Los Angeles. I was getting a tetanus shot,
filling my purse with B vitamins, lip balms, Polysporin, Vi-
sine, and Band-Aids. It seemed prudent, really, to fix a crucial
design flaw in my body, that there was no opting in or out of
its most perilous action, and one I knew I'd never desire. The
tubes tied expression made it seem like a snap, like they could
reach inside and grab your fallopian tubes and do the bunny
ears ritual they teach you in kindergarten. *Bunny ears, bunny
ears, then jump into the hole!*

Do you know how many things I don't need? I have a
closet filled with ten pairs of the same jeans. I have two pairs
of boots, one pair of sneakers, two pairs of army pants. Three
dresses, five of the same hoodie in different colors. That's all
I really need to be a body in the world right now. I don't need
my own eggs, or the useless hollow space designed to house
an invader.

Besides, I was busy. I rehearsed every day. I worked my
last few weeks as a receptionist at the conservatory. I'm a
future-oriented person. When friends were talking to me, I
wasn't really listening that closely. I was thinking about the
day I'd be getting in the van with Tom, Alan, Billy, and Jared,
our new fiddler we'd started calling the Temp. The day I'd
been waiting for since we got signed by a major label, after a
few years of opening for bigger acts. This tour meant hotels,
and a manager taking care of the money, the details, everything that had previously fallen to me. I wasn't going to be
peeing into a Big Gulp cup in the back of the van anymore,
surviving on drink tickets or sleeping four on the floor of
some punk kid's living room that smelled of cat pee and
empty beer cans.

I could think about performance, about the high of playing a really good show, one the bootleggers would brag about having on tape. And I could think about pleasure. Like a reunion with James in Baltimore, Hayden in New Orleans. Hayden could really fuck. He had endurance.

Hmmm, Hayden.

Hay-den.

That was a nice visual.

He asked me to be his one and only, but I couldn't deny other women that kind of devotion, especially since we lived several thousand miles apart. It felt greedy. I had a lover at home in Montreal, but Scott would tell me he was going to come by around ten, and then show up three days later. He really loved me, I knew that, but he liked speed more. I tried it once and I could see his point. I couldn't possibly make him feel like an exploding star or the smartest guy on earth. I could only make him come, but so could anyone. He was twenty-two. He could fuck a hole in the ground and feel pretty good.

When Billy got a vasectomy last year he had no problem with the first doctor he saw. "I told him I was the lead singer in a band. He got it immediately. Isn't that sexist?" he'd said, but he laughed. I've overheard him bragging about it to his future conquests. They think it makes him a considerate person. He just hates condoms because he's watched too many pornos. They don't feel right. He was tired of handing over fistfuls of his father's money for abortions. I advised him to get some antibiotics before we left.

I don't have Billy's familial safety net, nor can I afford the arrogance of assuming everything will work out okay. I was preparing to sublet my room in my shared apartment, teaching my roommate Amita how to water all my high-maintenance plants, getting health insurance, buying a new backpack. Safeguarding my uterus seemed like a logical item to cross off my list. It felt like a good preventative step. Condoms aren't foolproof and the pill made me into a monster. The idea of getting knocked up by accident felt like the plot of a horror movie, yet it was *entirely* possible. Was I supposed to be a nun on tour, while all the guys were having fun? Surely that wasn't the point of the sexual revolution everyone was so nostalgic about lately. There's always a program on TV about the 1960s, about the second wave of feminists. Oh, the nostalgia.

What other choice did I have? I don't like to rely on luck and the stars or whatever. I don't believe in fate. I like to have a *plan*.

I KNEW I had to show up at the next clinic looking self-assured and older than my years. I left mascara from the night before under my eyes to blur and bruise, traded my baggy army pants for some slim-cut, high-waisted pants, the kind that unstylish moms wore. I took the gaudy scarf my granny had given me, which I usually threw over my lamp for ambience, and tied it around my neck. It clashed with the blouse I'd borrowed from Amita for the occasion, trying to look like I was a thoughtful and mature adult. She'd colored in my lips in a neutral pink, took duct tape to the cat hair on my sleeves. She feathered my bangs, turned me around to look in our hallway mirror. "You're so unfuckable right now, you'll surprise them into saying yes."

At the walk-in clinic near my apartment, I was polite and

deferential, calmly explaining that the pill made my moods unmanageable, that filling prescriptions while traveling is next to impossible anyway, that condoms don't work all the time. I explained that I wanted to be responsible. "I'd like a tubal ligation," I said, thinking that using the proper terminology might help.

"You're too young to know the consequences," said a doctor who looked like Wilford Brimley.

I wanted to tell him I wasn't ashamed, that not every slut's origin story evolves from trauma, from lack of or a shifting sense of self. Though of course I was a young girl and had all of those things to deal with, but sex, in comparison, was simpler than anything so thorny. In fact, my problems seemed to stem from too much self. *You're too much* was frequent feedback. At twenty-one, I wanted the richness of the present moment, and that was all. Why not be loud about it? Being demure is for suckers. I'm old enough to join the army and kill people, to have five babies if I feel like it. Why can't I also decide to have *no* babies?

I went home, made a pot of coffee, and drew up a plan. I made more appointments.

I went to a clinic in a wealthy neighborhood next. A middle-aged doctor with long shiny hair and photos of her moronic-looking family all over the office was impatient from the moment I walked in and sat down across from her.

"I need my tubes tied, because any child I'll have is going to inherit my mother's terrible disease."

I was trying to appeal to this doctor's Catholic guilt and ableism.

"What disease does she have?"

"It's rare, and it has a long name, I can never remember it, but it's brutal." I pretended to try to remember it. I hadn't prepared for any follow-up questions, and thus I faltered. I hadn't heard my mother's voice in nearly ten years. I had no idea where she was, or why she had left. My mother's only terrible disease was maternal indifference, and that was something I *knew* I'd inherited.

She tapped her pen on the desk, then curled a shiny piece of hair around it and stared blankly until I was even more uncomfortable.

"I don't believe in abortion, but I want to have sex with my monogamous boyfriend, my fiancé, actually, and I know condoms are only ninety-eight percent effective. I'm a pragmatist," I said. Of course I believed in abortion, but she had a crucifix peeking out of the top of her blouse. She leaned back in exasperation.

Then she narrowed her eyes and said, "Getting sterilized isn't a quick fix so you can run wild and fuck indiscriminately. It's a medical procedure, not a safeguard for sluts."

Damn.

I pointed to her garish wall crucifix. "Your entire religion is obsessed with a whore! The entire culture revolves around the worship of young pussy!"

The doctor stood up, looked me straight in the eye. "You're clearly a smart young girl, but maybe too smart. Maybe think about the future, and what might be important in life besides yourself," she said before leaving the exam room. I was then offered hepatitis vaccines by a stout nurse who smiled, happy to see her boss taken to task by a hysteric dressed like a choir girl.

IT WAS ALL a very stark contrast to the first time I visited an OB/GYN, at fourteen. My cramps had become unbearable, and my father thought I should see a doctor, probably because he had no idea what to say to me. He made the appointment, wrote down the address of the clinic, and told me where to get off the bus.

I hadn't even kissed a boy, but a young doctor thrust a sample pack of birth control pills at me, insisting I take them.

"I don't have a boyfriend," I whispered.

"Ha"—he laughed—"they never do."

I felt like his grin was going to swallow me.

"I don't need them," I insisted.

He held out a bowl of condoms, pressing the lip of the bowl into the waistband of my tights, which had formed an itchy red line across my stomach since homeroom. "Take a bunch of these too. Never trust boys to be responsible."

The condoms felt awful in my hand. I didn't have a purse to put them in. Was I supposed to carry them home in my hands?

I ditched the pills and condoms in the dumpster beside the bus stop, livid. I wasn't the kind of fourteen who wanted to be eighteen. I wanted to be twelve forever. Every change in my body felt aggravating, like I was growing a second skull, like my limbs were out to get me. It's why I chose the cello in orchestra class, because I could hide my body behind it.

But something happened in my first year of university. I looked around at all the formerly repressed kids with their wind instruments and it felt inevitable. It was as though I saw our bodies for the first time, our buttoned-up blouses and awkward knee-length skirts, the boys in shirts their moms had packed in boxes and put in the trunk of their car. I learned to fuck from a tender man named Josh who played the oboe and lived in a shoebox apartment across from the music building where his bed was the only place to sit. We would share one tall can of beer, let it warm beside the bed as we figured out what bodies could do. He was not a good lover, but he was tender, and better than I was. He had, according to him, touched six boobs by that point. By the end of our relationship, I'd figured some things out.

Of course I knew what sex was. I spent my childhood with adults who were stuck in the free-loving 1960s. While sitting on a batik blanket, playing with my Barbie dolls from the church donation box—whose hair had been sheared into tidy gender-neutral bowl cuts before my mother let me play with them—I'd overhear them arguing about monogamy as a tool of the state. When I was a toddler I liked to be as nude as everyone else at Sunflower, but somewhere around six I started wearing full-length overalls every day and pointing to the dangling bits and wayward breasts of the adults around me and saying "Ugh." One thing I understood about adults very young was that they loved to kiss, and not always their own partners. It was gross. I wasn't into it.

So, growing up, sex wasn't something I could use to rebel. I was *expected* to seek it out, to be curious, to experiment. So naturally I didn't want to, until a little later than most. And my body cooperated. It was like I had a defective puberty switch that made me look like a teenager but still feel like a girl. My friends had stories about humping their stuffed animals and playing doctor with the neighbor kids but I never did any of that.

THE LAST DOCTOR I tried was at a private clinic in the West Island near my grandmother's house. You got to the clinic by going around the side of a giant stone house on a residential street near the airport. I used the student Visa card I kept in my freezer for emergencies. It was my last shot at getting a yes. I assumed the doctors would be used to taking demands from rich people who didn't want to use the free and relatively excellent public health system like the rest of us. But that doctor also wasn't having it. "I didn't want kids when I was your age either. Now they're the reason I get up in the morning. You'll regret it, I promise you."

But I knew I wouldn't.

Since I was in the neighborhood, I decided to visit Granny. I got on a bus that took me to the village where she lived. I checked in on her every now and then, made sure she was keeping the place up and doing okay. I brought her a bag of oranges, some tea, a carton of milk, and a fresh loaf of bread from the store at the end of her street. The last time I visited, she'd been using powdered milk for her tea, and I worried she wasn't able to get to the store as easily anymore. She'd never tell me that herself. I pulled a printout of my tour schedule out of my canvas shoulder bag and taped it to her fridge. It was still a month or two away, but I wasn't sure I'd be back to visit her before I left for tour.

We sat in her living room and exchanged our usual ripostes: her in the armchair and me sprawled on the sofa in a way that she used to say was *unbecoming of a lady* when I was a teenager but had since given up commenting on. She asked me a few questions about what I had been up to, about my music, if I "had a boyfriend yet." And, in turn, I informally tried to quiz her to make sure she was remembering things. Are you still teaching the boy with curly red hair, what was his name again? She was, as always, sharp as a tack. Yes, Jonah still comes every week. In a moment of rare straightforwardness, I told her what I was trying to do.

The look on her face told me that was a mistake.

"I don't even understand. That is an operation women get once they've had children already, or because they have cancer. Why would you want it? It just doesn't make sense."

"I'm being practical," I said, a defensive tone coming into my voice before I could stop it. "I don't want any mistakes."

"You'll change your mind! Your generation is just so angry." She laughed. "It's ironic. You have so much freedom, you have no idea. Your feelings on this will change. Wait till you find the right man."

Any time I shared problems with her, she ended her advice with *and then you'll find the right man*, which is sooooo ironic because she never did.

My granny doesn't know what it's like to be twenty-one and unattached on purpose. I've never asked her but if I had to guess, I'd say my grandmother probably never enjoyed sex in her life. I'm not sure if her life in particular looks sad, or if all people have lives that look sad from certain angles, and she's just the only access I have to the really old version of sad. Granny immigrated from Turkey (but she's British/ the whitest person on earth, long story) with a husband who moved his mistress into a house down the block without telling her. Yet she's always telling me that marriage is the only way for a woman to be happy, which seems insane.

And then there's my mother, who thought she was so liberated on the commune, with the lack of conventional expectations, but it was always the women crying in the sunflower patch, and the men shrugging and using words like *We agreed on this, You're so uptight, This was your idea, It didn't mean anything!* They talked a good game, the women on the commune, but I could see that sex wasn't *for* them.

NOW I'M THE age my parents were when they started Sunflower, their intentional community, and I don't want a community at all. I want to cross the country with the freedom of any man my age. I want to experience every spectacular, vivid detail of life on the road, to play our best songs, to jump out into the crowds, to fly on top of their outstretched fingers, to kick one leg in the air during the endless final solos, to be grabbed and kissed by the life of it all, to have a great time.

A GREAT TIME like I'm trying to have *right now*. With Bernie. He plays the bass in our opening band, from the first stretch of the tour. This is his last night with us, so I figured he was fair game.

But it's not working. I'm not going to come thinking about all those doctors, remembering the stressful weeks leading up to the start of the tour. I'm trying. Bernie isn't completely without skill. I close my eyes tight, lean my head back. There's not a lot of room in this tiny bunk and all I can think about is whether Bernie is going to pull out in time.

He fucks like a bass player. He smells like spicy arboreal cologne, and after developing some banter and flirting all day, we'd curled up to watch Talking Heads' *Stop Making Sense* on the little monitor in the back of the bus that had a half-working VHS. The tape kept getting stuck whenever the bus hit a bump. One thing led to another. I like the feeling of the motor under the bunk, the whirring vibration, the feeling of his bare chest against mine.

He's wearing a condom, but I don't like to chance it.

"Are you there yet," he whispers.

Nah, but it's cool.

I've had the same sexual fantasy since I was seventeen or so, when my body finally woke up. By fantasy standards, it is pretty tame. In it a man leans over and kisses my neck, whispers *baby girl*, and then lifts my long skirt up slightly and tugs at my underwear. And that's it. It always stops there. Of course, as I got older I had much more intense daydreams or imaginings, a rotating filmic clip of images or words I responded to in pornography. But I often think of that image right before coming, always works.

I conjure it now, but it doesn't do anything.

I love sex, but I've never come with another person in the room.

Bernie makes the same face when he fucks as he makes when he's playing bass. Up close it is monstrous. He's about to come, his teeth are clenched, his eyes floating off his face. I can see it in his expression, hear it in the speed of his breath, the things he's starting to mumble.

Like most, I can't come just from being pounded, no matter how skillfully, but fucking feels better than a lot of other things I could be doing, and I like the way their faces look when they come, like you're giving them the thing they've been desperate for since they first drew breath.

CHAPTER 2

CAROLA

THE DETECTIVE CALLED, "Carola Neligan?"

I heard his voice like a background beat, a nebulous whir. I was transfixed by the television chained to a high corner of the room, watching my daughter on a late-night variety show. I had not seen her in years. Her face had changed. Contracted. A woman's face.

I kept forgetting about Carola. My name had been Juniper since my early twenties. I was going back to Carola but hadn't acclimated yet. My daughter had scrawled *Pro-Choice* across her midriff. I felt both proud and embarrassed when I saw that. She had a grown-up body to go with her face. The last time I saw her, her limbs were all mismatched sizes. She looked so much like my sister, Marie. She had that Neligan nose. The young receptionist with the eggplant-colored hair was singing along. She knew the song already. She tapped her pencil to the beat against a stack of papers. That Melissa had changed so much in my absence made me feel like I was on drugs, though obviously I knew time couldn't stand still, waiting for me, my slow brain, my anemic heart. The music had no melody I could discern but the volume was low. She stood up from her cello and waved the bow around, and was now shouting into a microphone, touching the side of her head to the lead singer's shoulder. Her hair was blue and white-blond. She had so much energy, I was reminded of when she would jump off the roof of the barn into piles of neglected hay. How she made all the adults watch her dance to Janet Jackson's nasty-boys song over and over in grade five. She sang the chorus with her eyes closed. She was a mess, but so beautiful. The camera kept favoring her. She could really command your gaze. The rest of the band looked like cutouts of the same greasy boy but with differing haircuts.

"Carola Neligan?" This time it registered.

"Yes, sorry, that's me. I usually go by Juniper."

"I'm sure you do," he said, more to his buddy than to me. "But your ID says Carola Neligan."

I WAS PREPARED to be chastened, condescended to. Blue, the one who'd called a lawyer after we all found out about one another, told me they'd taken to calling us "the saggy titty ladies," so this wasn't the worst it could get. Even though Blue is only twenty-five and her breasts point skyward. I didn't think we should involve the police, but the votes went eight to seven in favor. It was the hottest summer in years in New Hampshire. I replaced my sandals that had worn down under the big toe because the concrete was too hot, even for one toe. There was tension between town residents and those of us at the center, sometimes. We had tried for years to build a chimerical peace. All it took was a temperature rise. We couldn't help talking to each other about the heat. This was the kind of town that didn't even have 911 yet; maybe the cops got an overdose, a fight over a stolen tractor, some kid with pot they stole and smoked with the other cops after work. That was it. If anything serious happened, cops came from another town. And this was deemed serious, or at least, noteworthy.

What was happening would make the papers. A reporter had been parked at the gate to the center for the last two days. Blue had given him our group photo from the spring picnic. Most of us didn't read the news every day, trying to avoid the negativity. But this was turning into a big story, the kind of weird headline that made it into the jokes on David Letterman.

But I wasn't sure this was really newsworthy.

If a bunch of people all happened to make the same mistake, whose fault was it? I had a lot to be forgiven for in this life, and I wasn't expecting that to happen until I was in the next one. Who was I to judge? But at the center we believed in consensus, in collective process. I didn't want to hold the group back. Sometimes you have to do what's good for the group, especially if your own feelings flit about like flies, the kind that only live for one day.

I followed the cop into his office. I had said the word *solidarity* and hugged the women who were certain. A fan clicked uselessly. My father had been a cop. I never understood why they were always so angry, when they were quite literally in charge of any room they walked into.

"So, this shaman guy," he said, scrawling my name at the top of a piece of tea-colored loose-leaf paper, stabbing a period at the end before looking up at me, "when did it get, you know, sexual?"

OH, HE WAS ugly. The kind of repulsive that is just factual. I winced at first when I looked too closely at his face. But you can't account for chemistry. It can build between any two people, regardless of how you've been taught to value a certain facial symmetry, to see beauty the way others do. It can change. I didn't know that. So there was one valuable lesson, I suppose. That beauty isn't fixed. It's a comforting thought as one gets older.

When he first touched me, I thought it was an accident. It was an outdoor yoga class in the summer of 1989. There were about twenty of us on the south lawn, and the sun was rising. I'd been at the ashram for a few weeks. It had recently been renovated and it was starting to look less like a ramshackle assembly of old buildings and more like a luxury resort. The staff and volunteers were barely able to handle the numbers of wealthy women coming for retreats. But it was an exciting time. We felt like we were building an empire, and we could see it growing day by day. Because I hadn't packed much, I tended to dress in clothes left behind in the lost and found. I remember that day I was wearing a gaudy hot-pink tie-dyed T-shirt with a silver peace sign decal on the front.

Our toes were wet with dew. My back hurt from the thin mattress in my bunk in the volunteers' cabin. He came over to adjust my pose. Normally he just sat at the front of the class on an oversized pillow looking sleepy and revered, while his helpers demonstrated the poses. Often he gave short talks on the spiritual value of chastity before the class began. I didn't see him as sexual, let alone a prospect. Plus, sex was something I thought I'd left behind when I moved away from the commune. I was at the ashram to be a whole person, to learn about who I could be as more than a body, a mother, a wife.

When I'd first arrived, he seemed just like a normal person, albeit older than everyone else, so it took some time to understand all the small photos of him on the bedside tables of most female volunteers. Some had even set up homemade altars, along with sage and candles and little rocks. A still recovering Catholic, I was skeptical of idols, even ones who are teaching you to slow down, breathe, appreciate both the world and your smallness. I think he liked me because he could see that I didn't glow, open faced and wanting, in his presence. I was a nonbeliever. They can spot you. But I decided to let go and see if he could teach me, the way he seemed to be giving the others a sense of purpose and inner peace. I certainly did not have inner peace. I'd woken up every morning for years feeling like death might be a welcome release. And by the thick of summer, I let go any vituperative feelings about those women and the psychic salve those tiny photos provided. By then, beside my own tidy bed, alongside my book of meditations, my green ceramic bowl of clipped herbs, my growing collection of crystals, was a photo of him. It wasn't a real photo, but a glossy magazine-paper image inside a cheap frame that they sold in the gift shop. Occasionally I would hear Bryce's voice in my head, telling me that Sunflower had been democratic, but where I'd landed now was a cult. *What difference does it make?* I'd ask him in these imagined arguments.

That morning in the yoga class, he put his head close to

my cheek and said, "Let go." His voice was deep and commanding, which surprised me because his body was small and almost feminine. And as he said it, he ran his finger along the inside of my thigh. I shuddered, felt my whole body light up. He looked me in the eye, like a challenge. My body responded like it understood God for the first time.

"You look lost," he said. In any other context that might have felt like a line. But I *was* lost. And so I felt seen.

The other women around me kept their downward dog poses but I knew they were listening. I didn't care. I hadn't felt seen since Missy was born. I was in my thirties then, but still felt physically in my prime. Watching everyone revere him, the corporeal ceased to matter. I suppose it was groupthink, but I desperately needed to be a part of it. I'd been needing it for years, and when I finally found it, I couldn't leave. If you haven't had a complete collapse of exhaustion, if you haven't watched everything around you drain of color and cease to matter, if you haven't felt like slipping off into the chasm of your own pain, then you're not going to understand my choices.

I DIDN'T KNOW how to say that to the cop.

So I said, "I guess the first summer I moved to the center, we became lovers."

He wrote that down, then looked at a photo of him and grimaced.

"You *wanted* to become lovers? With *this* guy?"

"Yes," I said, "I know by looking at him it doesn't make much sense, but I did."

I felt like I was wasting his time.

"Yeah, you're wasting our time here, lady."

But then a cult expert came into the room. Her name was Miranda and she approached me with the gentle, patient demeanor of a kindergarten teacher. Her hair was a mess of grayscale curls, kept in place by a pair of eyeglasses on her head. Clearly, she'd been listening to our conversation from the other room somehow. Was there a microphone in the room? I was feeling a bit spooked.

"Please keep talking. I want to know about how it all began, no judgments." She leaned toward me. "I know this must be hard," she said. It wasn't hard, in fact. I wasn't feeling particularly perturbed or upset by any of it. I was only here because I had made this commitment to the others and I had to honor it.

"I began to look forward to seeing him, and would alter my daily routes to try to catch his eye. When he started paying attention to me, I felt chosen. Then he requested that I join his team of assistants."

"So it was like a promotion?" she asked, writing down something in her notepad before I had a chance to say yes or no. Despite her befuddled style, her nails were a faultless glossy red in uniform ovals.

"Sort of. I mean, we were all volunteers. We brought him dinner at his house sometimes, did the gardening, tidying, ran errands in town, fed and cared for his goats and chickens. I didn't realize right away that there were other women. I thought we had a secret relationship."

"A lot of women have reported that."

"Well, yeah, I know that now," I said.

————

I WAS SUPPOSED to stay for three months, be home in time for Missy to start grade eight, return to life at Sunflower. But after I joined his inner circle, I couldn't imagine leaving. I knew it didn't make logical sense. I knew it was morally reprehensible to leave one's own child. But what about the impact of being around a child when you are a husk? That couldn't be good either.

"Your old life, it wasn't working," he whispered. I couldn't do anything but agree.

He took my clothes off, and then he knelt on the floor in front of the bed. The room smelled of geranium and lemons, faint amber incense. He didn't pull the curtains closed. I think he liked them open. A dare.

One time, when Missy was six or so, I made her some scalloped potatoes for lunch, and then I went outside to get washing off the line. While folding thick towels that had stiffened in the open air, I peeked in the kitchen window to see her at the table. She was looking at the scalloped potatoes with the biggest, most rapturous grin I'd ever seen.

That was how the guru looked at me when I was naked.

The memory made me laugh, out-of-control laughing, which made him laugh, and that was how it was at first with him, a tumbling joy, an erotic escape hatch.

You shouldn't go home. You should stay, he said.

It was as if I could watch myself making those decisions from somewhere across the room, and I knew it was wrong, but it felt right. It felt like I had to stay. A deer was nibbling on grass outside the floor-to-ceiling window of his palatial bedroom. The sky was a soft gray at the edge. We could only make out the shadowy shape of the deer. We watched for so long, silently, that the sky pinkened, and other deer, all clearly defined in rich browns and grays, joined the first one. A flawless tableau. I *didn't* want to go home. I knew that if I were a good person, a good mother, I would want to. It sounds awful, but I didn't miss my family. I didn't miss Bryce. I felt like I'd found my home. Like I could finally breathe.

I padded to the window, slowly, pressed my palms against the glass. They kept eating. I slid open the door, tried to move every isolated muscle in infinitesimal stages so they wouldn't notice. Thanks to daily progressive muscle relaxation exercises, this worked, until all ten toes pressed into the grass, and they were eyes up and then tails retreating, into the woods.

He laughed as I slid the door shut.

You thought you could just join them. Like they wouldn't notice you're not a deer! He kept laughing as he walked into the en suite bathroom, scratching one ass cheek.

Still, I felt like wildlife, like I was free.

I didn't say any of this to Miranda and the cop. I took a deep inhale, counting to four, and exhaled to four. I pressed my hand to my chest. I smelled the lavender oil I'd placed on my wrist that morning.

"He made me feel special," I said, which sounded so elementary, so pedestrian, but I could tell by their expressions this was the kind of thing they expected to hear.

MY PRIMARY JOB that first summer was in the laundry, rows of stainless-steel industrial machines in the basement of the center. It was my self-admonishing cave. The row of rectan-

gular fluorescent light fixtures flickered like TV static. One
row of lights had burned out completely and was never replaced. It felt punishing, the heat and the mounds of linen,
but that was also the point. I deserved hardship, and I needed
to provide service. If every day started down there, my journey would eventually end in some sort of soul healing. I
didn't fully understand the concept of soul healing in an intellectual way, but I felt it. I felt it in the hot cotton sheets
pulled out of the dryers, folded on the long metal table.

Soul healing was the main goal of most of us living at the
center. Everyone walked around like they had done bad
things, or had come here to avoid doing bad things. We
moved around underneath the rich ladies who paid piles of
money to come for silence and meditation, for sweaty yoga
and forest walks. I washed the plain white sheets they slept
under, had soaked with their tears about the husbands who
ignored them or the ones they no longer loved. They'd
screamed into the pillowcases, or rested their heads in bewil-
derment, thinking *Is this all life is?* Everyone spoke to one
another as though life was joyful, as though they were finding simple joy, as though that joy was in the small moments
of life. But their eyes said that malaise was killing them. I
tried every workshop offered at the center, except the one
about laughter. In that workshop the leaders encouraged you
to begin laughing, but not because anything was funny. You
just had to fake it at first, and then eventually everyone truly
started laughing. I found just the sound of it to be heart-
breaking, all that forced boisterous guffawing at nothing.
The facilitator knew I was a skeptic. Linda. Linda cornered
me whenever she saw me, her eyes unnaturally bright. *You
should take my laughter workshop, you look like you need it!*

I worked in the kitchen, too, and we served women who frequently said things like *I really needed this rest* with such sincerity, but they never looked tired. My wrists and hands were covered with tiny moon-shaped burns, my skin puckered from hot water and steam, then flaking and red later as I fell asleep. I rubbed shea balm on them every night but it never quite worked. This was a deep discomfort I deserved.

I ate the plainest of foods, giving up sea salt and tahini and Bragg liquid amino acids, sticking to the end of the buffet with the steamed vegetables, the unadorned brown rice, meant for the residents with allergies or who were undergoing sacred fasts. I did cleanup shifts, standing on top of an old produce box to reach the taps on the giant sinks, and burning myself on Hobee, the Hobart, a dishwasher that sanitized the giant pots and pans. I went to the evening yoga class with parsley in my hair, smelling of the night's meal, hands and arms pink and rubbery from the heat and sweat. I lost weight. I didn't cut my hair. Then I impulsively cut it all off with kitchen shears. I woke up with the sunrise and bathed in the stream on the hill above the center. I was leaving my ego, leaving vanity, behind in the water.

MIRANDA SHUFFLED HER papers. She was beginning to look annoyed, rubbing her eyes so that her eyeliner looked like smudged wings.

"So you left your husband?"

"Yes."

"That must have pissed him off."

"Yes. But we were separated. He'd cheated first."

That wasn't the whole story, but that was the only way square cops would understand the story. I didn't tell them that before I left, our theoretical open relationship had taken a turn for the literal. Bryce had taken up with a new girl at the commune, one barely out of her teens who called everything *the most*. Even lentil stew or carrots pulled from the garden, they were *the most!* I wanted to bash her head in. I couldn't handle the itch of violence she had awoken in me. We always did group conflict mediation sessions, and at the end we hugged and made peace. But I had no peace in my heart. I was acting. Standing in the healing circle, holding hands and discussing conflict resolution and our personal responsibility, I realized Sunflower was a failure. The disintegration of everything we'd hoped it would be. I saw Missy sitting in a tree several yards away, listening to her hot-pink Walkman, aggressively ignoring us. In those days, she listened over and over again to the same song she'd recorded from the radio onto an empty cassette tape in the living room: "Pump Up the Jam." Sometimes she would dance around us in her bright yellow ankle socks, her arms filled with jelly bracelets, and I saw the teenager she was becoming.

She scoffed at everything we said to her.

I drove her to her last day of grade seven the next day, and then I just kept driving.

AFTER I PHONED Bryce from the pay phone in town, telling him I wasn't coming home just yet, he demanded to know where I was, but I wouldn't say. I didn't want him to show up and blue-eyes me back into his arms. There was something about him I could never resist, even when I felt so much anger and resentment I could barely breathe.

I called at night so I wouldn't hear Missy in the background and fall apart.

I truly was trying to find myself, but saying that didn't sound sincere, so I didn't say it.

"Tell Missy I love her and this is better in the long run. It won't be for long, I promise."

"I'm not going to lie to her."

"Do what you think is best, you're the parent now. Say something so she knows she's loved, and that I haven't just walked off a cliff or something. I don't want her to think that."

When I hung up the phone, I felt relief. And then I felt guilt for the relief. I cried through evening yoga. But then at night, there was a quiet. A stillness inside me. I had to press my thumb to my neck to make sure my heart was beating. It was in those moments when I knew I'd made the right decision. A decision that no one would ever likely understand, a decision that would make me an outlaw, a madwoman, a monster to most of society. But it was stillness, and it was freedom, my solitude in a tiny bunk, under stiff white sheets, and it was everything.

AFTER I'D CRIED through several more nights of yoga, the guru led me to his house on the edge of the property. It looked simple from the outside, but inside there was a fire and fresh flowers and an elaborate table of fruits and cheeses. I'd been eating so many plain foods that the berries, peaches, and Brie made me feel alive again. He said he wanted to cleanse my aura while I tore through a handful of grapes like a starving wolf. He laid me down on the softest bed, and moved his hands all over me until I came in waves that seemed endless, and I saw a warm bright light and he held me for hours until I fell asleep. When I woke up he was gone, and one of his handlers was cleaning the room, and she offered me a cup of ginger tea and pressed one palm to my chest and said, *Welcome.*

It sounds so creepy, to recount it, but it was blissful and oddly uncomplicated. And even years later, when we all offered our narratives to the investigators, I told them the truth, that I'd felt loved. When I told him I wanted to leave my husband, he'd put his hands on my heart and said, *Your heart yearns to be free.* He helped me choose myself for the first time in my life, even though soon it felt like I'd chosen him, traded one selfish dreamer for another.

THE ROOM AT the police station was cold, but I was flashing heat from perimenopause. While I explained how I'd given the guru all my money, though I hadn't had much, sweat dripped down my back and then froze. Why couldn't I ever be the same temperature as everyone else? When I described how I felt married to him, it sounded more sordid than it was.

"It was love," I said. The cop gave me a look that said he thought I was a crazy quack, but Miranda just looked down and scribbled another note in her pad. I had felt calm in that love, as I hadn't in years. Not since before Missy was born. And maybe it was crazy to feel that way.

Since the guru's expulsion, everything was chaotic at the center, but we were determined to keep it going. A group of longtime residents decided to take over, and we were in the middle of figuring out how to do this. But instead of asking permission for things, we organized by collective and tried to decide via consensus decision making. We'd been the ones doing the hard work all along, after all. So it wasn't all that different. We replaced any events that had centered on the guru with extra meditation sessions about joy. We brought in a facilitator to teach forgiveness. It was funny that I'd escaped one intentional community only to end up in another, but this time the men were gone.

Sex had always complicated my life. It had almost never made it better, no matter how good it had felt at the time. The acts of devotion, as the guru called it, made me feel closer to the goddess, to the spirit of the world, than anything else ever had. But over time, the sex began to feel a bit like a chore or a habit. I started to see him as ugly and demanding, as any other man. The feelings of transformation were just lies of chemistry and hormones, the alchemy of momentary compatibility, and it was just sex and that was all. Humans are so undone by it, and we are fools.

CHAPTER 3

MISSY

W E ARE DRIPPING in America by the middle of the tour and feeling pretty good about ourselves. I'm in an airfield outside Baltimore, playing my fucking heart out. The crowds are stomping. Hands crushing beer cups. Arms raised in group awe. When the audience is with us, we own them. Their love is embarrassing and beautiful but also crazy to fathom. Here we are, the Swearwolves, a bunch of music-school geeks, but now we're all so fuckable. And I *love* us. My tits through a thin T-shirt that reads THE BITE TOUR are on the cover of *Spin* magazine. I'm not even sick to death of half the new songs yet. When we reach the end of the set and Billy says our names, introducing us one by one, I fall in love with everyone, even when Tom prolongs the drum solo to a masturbatory length.

And there is James. I want James. He's in the front row, which is where I first met him. He's that record store guy at every show, hanging around so much he's genuinely friends with the band. He has an adoring face, a hot interrogation light, but a flattering one. His hair is golden, curled down below his shoulders. But he hasn't been front and center since New York last year.

Near the end of our set, the crowd is a hungry mass and we are feeding them. I'm playing rhythm guitar for this song, and I kick out my leg toward James. He gives me a wink. I can feel the way he likes to wrap one hand around my hair and pull gently, and then with force. As we hold each other's gaze, I'm briefly alight, floating above the sold-out crowd.

The gender split in the major live music scene is a little like the army, a woman here and there, but mostly you are on your own. There's no one to borrow a tampon from, and the girls my bandmates hook up with aren't ever around long enough to get too deep. You have to watch your back, or try to make the most of it. I didn't want to be prey, and so I became a type of predator, a slinking she-wolf bathed in gin and audience adoration with a boy in nearly every port. The boy in Baltimore was James, though he'd been my East Village hookup for about a year and a half. James rips off his T-shirt. He screams the chorus. He bangs his fist on the edge of the stage. The teenage girls in the front row don't know what to make of his frenzy.

I was a shy kid in high school. I didn't even try a sip of beer until after my eighteenth birthday. And here I am, a few years after graduation, taking a full-year break from the conservatory, and there's my photo in *Rolling Stone*, backstage with Kim Deal at a festival. Our first solo tour feels like the endless present. People aren't just recognizing Billy when we pull into rest stops, or in the aisles of CVS picking up hand lotion and condoms. They know who I am. I hear my own voice over the radio sometimes. It's a rush. I get cocky. We all do. It's so easy to see a clear story in retrospect, but in the middle of it, all I feel is hands and mouths, Sharpies thrust forward to sign T-shirts, the sound of applause and the birdlike whoops of those fans in a moment of transcendence, the taste of beer and lemon Snapple, the cold hotel pillow at the end of the night. It's the middle of the orgy, and all we have are feelings, so many feelings, and all of them colossal, creeping through our bodies and messing with our minds.

I play each song without thinking about the notes. Some songs on the cello, others on guitar. I have a tattoo across the knuckles on my left hand that reads MORE. My father told me it was my first word. In these moments onstage, I am more body than brain, and I don't need my brain to play each note flawlessly. My mind is concerned mostly with two things: how many songs are left before I can see James, and the fat crow sitting on the amplifier. The crow is looking at me too intently. I give him a pacifying nod.

Crows will always remember your face. If you throw an empty coffee cup at a crow, it tells its buddies. They look after their own. They can live for a hundred years. I didn't fuck with the crow. Tom did. By accident. Tom's not an asshole; he just didn't see the crow lounging on the rim of the dumpster before he threw the cup. He's got drummer arms, so the cup went too fast, too hard. Surprised them both.

It stopped raining just before our set. A rainbow cradled in thousands of upturned palms. Shirts were stuck to their chests with rainwater and sweat. I look at my left hand. It's moving along the frets again. If you do something a million times you'll just keep doing it. Even when you're gone. Like when you pull up to your house and don't remember driving there.

Billy stands with his arms stretched open, like he's trying to embrace the whole audience, his eyes closed. *Rolling Stone* magazine hailed this song as the "anthem of the year" and I can see hearts swelling. I wrote the song. Billy hates that.

Tom likes it, he says it keeps Billy humble.

Being in a band is kind of like group dating. If everyone is selfish at the same time, it doesn't work. We can't all be the deadbeat dad. I try not to be the mom, just because I'm the girl, and I'd never be able to compete with Tom, who moms us the best. He reminds us to eat dark green vegetables, get at least four hours of sleep a night. Last week in Albany we blanched fists of broccoli in chipped Travelodge coffee mugs with hot water meant for tea, coffee filters tented on top to seal in the heat. I ripped open a small paper packet of salt with my teeth for seasoning. The half-torn packet salted the sweaty change in my back pocket for days.

I COME BACK to the song, now almost over, as my watermelon gum fades of its flavor and goes soft and pink in my mouth. It was great until it wasn't, and I go to spit it out but will it poison the crow? I can't chance it. My T-shirt smells like a gamy blend of sweat and lemon Speed Stick. Touring means bacteria is always at war with heat and fabric. I started the tour with shiny-new pink sneakers, limited edition Converse One Stars, and now they're cracked from overuse, and one heel of my combat boots is worn down so I've been walking with a slight limp from a nail slowly moving up through the sole.

The crowd always grows taller for the final song. Off to the side, on top of the Marshall stacks, three more crows appear. *I didn't throw the cup:* I try to say that with my eyes. Animals can read emotion. The crows' feathers seem to puff up, like a group of guys at last call looking for a fight. Birds make me nervous. So many feathers and tiny bones, nothing of substance. They're a gang. They're after us. It was my job to collect the eggs in the henhouse when I was a kid. They saw my little hands for what they were—perfect for pecking. I never got over it.

Tom catches my eye, gives me a *You okay?* I give my head a nod toward the crows. Now they are six. He laughs.

He mouths, *You're crazy.*

I yell, "You'll see."

I turn back to the crowd. James and I hold eye contact. He rubs one hand against his beard, winks. Bookended by two openhearted girls, singing their guts out. The last time we met up was in New York City last year, opening for another band at the Bowery Ballroom. He'd told me he was moving to Baltimore.

"Baltimore is cheap and full of artists. Houses for sixty thousand dollars!" He yelled this in a triumphant staccato over breakfast at a diner in the East Village where we'd lined up Tylenol, plastic cups of apple juice, and coffee, trying to quell a hangover. I aimed the toe of my right foot toward his lap, a purposeful graze up and down, trying to get him to break. *Show it in your face.* He refused, though I felt precisely how I was affecting him. Instead, a slow sip of his coffee, eyes locked to mine in a dare. James. He would not break. He could meet me.

"Be my girlfriend," he said, ragged breath.

The server was my saving grace, gliding over, coffee pot cocked on one hip.

"Refill?"

"God yes," I said, a little too relieved. "But also no, to answer your question. What we have is great."

"Sure," he said, but I knew he was hurt.

I've always grown bored too quickly. I read the last page of novels first, to know if I should bother. I have a lot of lovers across the country. What's the point of being a touring musician if your bed, in addition to being unpredictable, is also cold?

James knew that. He worked in a record store. He could get any shy, hot pussy in a cardigan with ironic lapel buttons he wanted. For some reason, he wanted me. That day, anyway.

WHAT I LIKE about tour life is how time functions in crescendos and fade-outs. Sunup and sundown don't mean much, nor do squares on paper representing days. The driving, the paying of bills, the organizing of the money and the food, they're like scales, methodical practice, and life continues through the lenses of van windows and into the wide-open eyes of endless teenagers, singing along.

The song ends. We always exit in the same order. Tom goes first. I place my guitar on the stand, glance toward the amps. The crows are gone, probably following Tom. The buzz in my whole body from the noise makes me feel as though I float down the stage stairs and into the performer tent. I grab a handful of frozen grapes, chase them with bottled water and lukewarm beer. The first few nights of tour we'd been excited about the green-room food, the baskets of pretty fruit, small fridges of beer, assortment of cold sodas,

cheap wine in a bucket of ice. We felt like kids in the choco-
late factory. Now we get tired, curl up on the couches, don't
talk, as Billy signs some autographs. I pelt Billy with a few
grapes.

I like to do things to bring his ego down after shows.

"Dudes," he says, mashing the grapes into his chest, then
licking the pulpy slime from his palm. A green-room-wide
groan. The girl with two ponytails shyly leaning against one
of the tent poles giggles. She has a media pass, but that's not
why she's here. I can tell she thinks he's just hilarious and
crazy, a small extension of that audience applause. She averts
her eyes when I peel off my stage T-shirt, pull a tank top
from my purse, rolling it down against my skin that's still
hot even though I'm beginning to shiver. The comedown.
She waves shyly at me when we make a little eye contact. She
could have fit two or three more of her bodies in her giant
pants.

Where's James? He's usually so quick. So obedient. He
knows he's always on the backstage list.

The next band opens their set. The crowd roars.

After the show feels like morning. I go through the motions of waking up, washing under my arms with pink hand
soap from the dispenser, wiping my skin clean with rough
brown paper towel, those private actions in the green room
among the crush of bandmates and their hangers-on. My
jeans are filthy already. You don't really have to wash jeans,
according to Billy. If you don't, they'll last a long time.

This is a lie.

I washed everyone's jeans back in Maine in the middle of
the night. I couldn't take it anymore. *Something's different*,

Tom had said the next day, after he got dressed. *Are my legs bigger? My pants feel weird*. Billy kept asking, *What smells like flowers?* I didn't tell them.

How did Billy always find a girl, no matter what city?

Boys don't line up by the door the ways the girls do. Instead, it's a subtle nod from a cute guy at the soundboard. A proffered beer from the punk kid selling merch for the opening act. You'd miss those cues if you weren't looking for them. For everyone in indie rock, to be seen as wanting was discouraged. Like dancing, it was too overt, beyond a shuffle, a nod, a vigorous nod if it was your favorite song.

So as a girl you get to be aggressive. It's up to you if you want to make sure the venue staff doesn't assume you're a wife or the merch girl, or if you want to get laid, or paid, at the end of the night. When I sent a postcard to Amita back home, I scrawled *You have to act like a predator if you want to be prey later.* From each city, I'd send her the most pornographic postcards I could find, tacky naked girls on the beach with crude messages on the front. She was decorating our fridge with them.

No wonder I fucked it all up. No wonder it all went to shit.

I FINALLY FIND James in the parking lot, leaning against the van. I walked out there on instinct because I'm used to loading gear, forgetting we hired roadies this tour. This was surely a sign of exhaustion. Having a crew made me uncomfortable, though my shoulder didn't crack and smolder every morning the way it used to.

James's vibe is off. When he steps so close I can smell his

aftershave, he offers a rough whisper. "Hey girl, great show, as always." I lean in for a kiss but am denied his lips at the last second—just stubble.

I press my hands against his chest, intentional. I offer him a pull from my flask of whiskey, and when James takes it our fingers touch only briefly. I feel it in my teeth. Still, I'd let him throw me up against the truck. After a show my body is still going going going, the rush like a tornado that lifts me up. I don't want to plummet. James is a way to keep it going.

"I'd love to pick up where we left off," I say. He pauses, steps back slightly. "Billy says there's a good booze can nearby," I continue, reaching out to grab his sweatshirt sleeve in a pinch. "Remember how much fun we had last time?"

Billy and I had been keeping a list of what all the coke dealers look like in each city in a small mint-green notebook, their first name and a pencil sketch of their face. We keep it in the glove compartment of the van with *Bible Verses* scrawled in Sharpie on the front. Baltimore is Kiki, who looks and dresses like a yoga teacher and wrote a master's thesis on Gertrude Stein. *Really clean, no burning*, I'd written underneath a doodle of her sitting on the edge of a pool table, head thrown back, pointed toes, laughing.

I haven't gotten high at all on this tour so far. I've been going back to the hotel with Tom to listen to the set recordings, maybe having a beer or two, but that's it. This is our big shot, and so far we're succeeding. Every crowd has been more invested than the last. Reviews are stellar. But now seems like as good a time as any. It doesn't tire me out if I'm careful. Billy's able to get high more often and still function just fine, but I don't want to tempt fate.

"Missy, Missy, my girl, I swear, you're not going to believe this . . . ," James says, pausing to look back as a girl with thick black bangs and a Hüsker Dü T-shirt stretched over an enormous pregnant stomach comes into focus behind him. She teeters in high-heeled boots, looks at me shyly. James reaches out to her, fingers fluttering. "This is Holly. I'm going to be a dad!" he says. "Isn't that fucking rad? Can you believe *me*, a father?"

Everyone around us, even the roadies who have never met him before, starts congratulating him. It gives me time to hide my immediate response of deep annoyance, both that I'm not getting laid later and also that James joined this new trend of breeding by friends who can barely sustain their own weird lives. James is the kind of guy who sleeps on the old couch in the screened-in porch of a house populated by musicians and fuckups, paying minimal rent. He's the guy who brings scabies to your house and eats all your food, telling you he'll replace it but then he leaves town. I already feel a little sorry for the eventual kid. I was the 1970s and '80s version of that kid. At least I know enough not to have kids. I'd only want to be a parent if I could be a dad in a 1960s sitcom. Come around when I want, tease them and be a hero, and then go live my life. I want to look like a girl, but I want the freedom to act like a guy. This makes me unlikable, but have you ever remembered a likable person? Especially likable, easygoing women. Women who say things like *whatever you want is fine* and agree with everything men say. They're a dime a faceless dozen. They blur together.

How did James, the lovely fuckup, make such a monumental decision when he can barely care for himself? It was probably less an active decision and more a passive broken condom, but still. I'm mad. I snap my gum, long dissolved of flavor, reach my hand out to shake the sweaty hand of his girlfriend. She must be rich. I try to catch a glimpse of her teeth.

"I really love your music," she says, so sweetly, it crushes me.

"Thanks. And that's cool, kid. You'll be a great dad," I tell James, patting his arm in an approximation of platonic.

I turn and begin loading gear, an excuse for James and Preggo to totter off together down the lane half lit by anemic streetlights.

IN THE MOVIES, whenever mothers run away, they always show their abandoned kids wondering and wanting, looking big-eyed and empty, crying in their bedrooms, searching for left-behind clues to their mothers' departure. That was true for a year or two. Then I just stopped. I used to rubberneck at any forty-year-old in a batik dress. Now I don't even see them. But my mother shows up in my dreams.

When I need comfort, I go to Tom. Whenever I don't get laid at the end of the night, I end up with him back at the hotel eating a late dinner and watching movies.

After the gig, Tom and I drive the van back to the Best Western by the freeway, listening to the recording of our set which Tom wants to critique. His biggest fear is that we will plateau and won't keep growing creatively. He shares this ritual with me because he assumes my background in classical music means I'm a perfectionist. I'm not. It is one of the things I like about indie rock, that it's expansive, improvisational, and emotional. We are close to its inception, we invent it as it emerges. But I understand Tom's vision and commitment. I don't want to plateau either, but I want to grow outward, not implode from trying to keep it clean and meticulous.

"Do you agree?" Tom asks, and I nod. I'm not really listening. I'm cradling a lapful of fruit I stole from the green room, am halfway through a second peach even though my mouth stings from the acidity. I'm still feeling agitated about James. I want to put in my Bikini Kill tape and scream along with its brilliant, feral imperfection. I didn't get to where I am without practicing my instrument every day since I was thirteen. If there's one thing I've always understood, it's passion and commitment. But with music, not people.

TOM AND I shuffle to our shared room at the hotel. The ugly paisley-patterned carpets in the hallway draw me downward, the elevator mirrors show us a sloppy picture of ourselves. My arms have tour biceps, my clavicle protrudes. I have pronounced tan lines from my tank top straps, and my wrists are white underneath my sweatbands. At only five foot one, I come up to Tom's midsection. My winter skin is now striped with tan, freckles spread across my cheeks. Tom leans his forehead against the mirror and stares at his reflection as we ascend.

"Am I getting gray in my beard?"

"It's the lighting," I say, though I'm not sure. The elevator takes forever and the post-show crash comes quick, like I've been shot with a cartoon tranquilizing dart.

By the time we discover there's only one bed in our room, we are too tired to go back downstairs to the front desk to request a different room. Once the adrenaline of live performance wears off, it's like being dropped from the sky. We fall asleep holding hands like eight-year-olds while watching a rerun of *Party of Five*. I've spent a lot of my life jealous of people who have brothers—and now I get to have one. He's an oddity among traveling musicians: faithful to his wife at home, insistent on getting at least seven hours of sleep a night. If anyone has temper flare-ups, he hands them fruit leather or granola bars from the front pocket of his hoodie and says *Time out* with a finality no one can dispute, and they go take five minutes.

Tom is married, but I fit well under the crook of his arm, and he gives me shoulder and arm massages that an acupuncturist taught him, and cups of water and fresh fruit, and I'm better on tour with his attention. Tom is both an exceptional father and musician, and aims, as best he can, for balance between the two. The only thing Tom isn't good at, as far as I can tell, is meeting people and being social. Schmoozing. If you catch him at the right time, you can have a really great conversation, but he won't engage in small talk. And that's tricky because the networking thing is real, even if you don't feel like it. Tom usually just hangs in the corner of the room, staring off, replaying the latest set in his head and trying to figure out how it could have been better. But he can get away with this because he's a dude. His gender affords him this luxury. As the only girl in the band, I play some expected roles—I charm reporters, ask strangers for directions, get discounts at hotels, and let everyone feel like they know me a little bit, even if we just met. I get called cute, warm, friendly, lovely, and whenever I do I'm surprised. I'm none of those things. Not really. But I consider it part of the job of being in the world, what you can tolerate and what can get you through it.

I WAKE UP to the sound of a delivery truck backing up outside our window, and I stretch out, longing for James or
Hayden or that soft-faced guy from Albany, accidentally flop-
ping my arm over Tom, who is still in a deep sleep. There is
a knock at the door, first so sotto I dismiss it as ambient
noise, but then it becomes insistent. I stagger to the door and
unhook the chain, and fling it open expecting Billy to push
inside with a coked-up monologue. But it's Tom's wife, Cory.

"Oh hey, Missy, do I have the wrong room?" I understand
immediately that Tom has never told his wife how it's cheaper
for us to double up in rooms, that Tom and I are essentially
roommates. Of course, we hadn't planned the bed-sharing,
the hotel mistake last night, and that we were too heat-
soaked and exhausted to complain. But Cory doesn't know
any of this and I can see I'm being reassessed in these few
seconds.

It is a problem. She folds her arms. Her brow furrows.
Her pupils constrict. I take an instinctive step back. It is also
a problem that I was clearly sleeping in one of Tom's old Sub
Pop T-shirts and not much else. I just shake my head, and
open the door wider.

"No, no, this is his room. We share sometimes, because it's
cheaper, you know. Not for any other reason, of course." I'm
muttering at this point, as her facial expression changes from
assuming the best to assuming the worst. She yells Tom's
name so loud she's probably waking up the entire floor.

"What the *fuck* is going on, Tom? I thought I'd surprise
you. Well, this is certainly a surprise."

"Oh my god, Cory." Tom is wide awake, spine straight,

and rubbing his stubbled face. "It's only Missy. We were tired, the hotel made a mistake with the bed. You know we'd never, ever, come on, it's *Missy*."

I back away into the bathroom, because I can't fully leave the room wearing only a T-shirt. This is when the previously chill tour started to go tits up, when I started making questionable decisions.

IN THE BATHROOM, I want to turn the shower on to drown out their conversation and take a long bath, but there's a disconcerting rustling behind the plastic curtain. I grab the plunger in case it's a rat when I notice a tattered lime-green Converse shoe emerging from the curtain. The name CECILY and a phone number in pen on the white plastic of the sneaker's toe, which definitely belongs to Jared, the fiddler. He is Billy's friend's younger brother, so barely old enough to be on this tour. Maybe eighteen? Seriously irritating kid. I pull back the curtain to see him sleeping soundly in the tub with one hand down his pants, mouth open, drool heavy. A Spider-Man pillow behind his head, hoodie worn backward like a blanket. The tap drips on his shoulder.

I nudge him. "*Dude*, how did you even get in here?"

"You opened the door when I knocked last night," he says, half sitting up, rubbing his eye with a balled fist. "Billy brought a girl home and it was cold in the van."

I remember none of this.

"Well, I need to shower," I say.

He's such a little twit, can't stand up to Billy to save his life. Jared's age and the fact that he never gets laid is an ongoing tour joke. Now he groans, then looks down, embarrassed, quickly pulls his hand out of his pants. He was just waking up, ready to go.

I weigh the options.

He is cute. Ish. I guess? He is a brat. Sometimes that works for me. What *could* happen next would likely be quick. Once I get the idea, I find it hard to let it go. I kneel on the edge of the tub as he blushes, flustered, eyes emptying.

"Do you know that crows always remember your face?"

"Yeah, everyone knows that," he says, cocky. A blush creeps down his neck and he tries to pull his hoodie down to cover himself.

Instead of averting my eyes and giving him privacy, like most friends or like, decent human beings would, I decide to help him out.

"Want me to take care of that?"

His eyes go wide enough with shock that they pull me in, delighted by my own audacious offer. "Yeah, of course." I lick my palm. Unbuckle his belt. His breath catches. I like to watch and hear the way people come. Tom jokes that I have sex the way other people watch TV, to chill out, or for an entertaining story. "No one would think it was weird if I was a man," I'd said to him. He couldn't argue with that, but he still quietly objected to my sexuality somehow, as though he had to because he *cared* about me. If he ever has more than one beer, which is rare, he goes on a paternal rant, which usually ends up being pretty boring and insulting. I would never have sex with Tom. Or Billy. I have boundaries. When I pointed that out to Tom, he'd looked vaguely hurt, then said I wasn't hearing him. He always says I'm not hearing him when what he means is I'm not agreeing with him.

Through the bathroom door I hear Tom defending himself to Cory, as I begin to work Jared slowly with my hand, leaning over the tub. Cory is speaking too low to hear, so I only catch pieces of the conversation. *You have platonic friends, too! What about Bob? You crash at Bob's sometimes. Well, I didn't know he was gay! How was I supposed to know? I am too happy to see you, but you woke me up by yelling at me! How am I supposed to act other than mad? I am not defensive. I have nothing to be defensive about.*

Jared's fast, as expected. While he cleans up I crack the bathroom door open a tiny bit, and see that Cory and Tom have left. I send Jared out to get breakfast downstairs, rip open a pouch of vitamin C powder with my teeth, empty it into a plastic cup, and fill it with tap water. I choke it down. Finger the cellophane wrapper from the cup.

I quickly make myself come twice watching the scrambled porn channel before Jared returns with Styrofoam boxes of eggs and bacon. Bouncing tits, a line of fuzz, some standard in and out. I spread towels at the edge of the bed to put the breakfast down. We turn the TV from porn to *The Great Muppet Caper*, sit cross-legged side by side like children, and tuck in to our food.

DURING A COMMERCIAL break, I call my apartment and check the answering machine. I pull at the yellow threads in the upholstery, always a bit nervous to hear what is or isn't happening at home, where real life resides in a state of suspension. Two messages. The first one from my father.

I'm sorry, bug, I can't come to your show when you're in town. The store is so busy this time of year, and the

> traffic from San Diego is insane that time of day.
> Thanks for mailing the passes though, I'm giving them
> to our babysitter and she's really excited. I wish I
> could come. Rachel can't handle the heat and noise of
> the show right now, you know how it is.

Rachel, my dad's new wife, has a lot of things she's inexplicably, and I imagine selectively, sensitive to. He didn't offer to come up for breakfast the next morning at our hotel, which was my second suggestion. I always provide a backup suggestion.

The second voicemail is from Granny, her nasal British accent cutting through the grimy hotel receiver.

> Melissa, it's your grandmother. *(As if I'd mistake her
> voice for someone else's.)* I'm not sure where you are, but
> I'm calling to tell you I'm taking a trip back to Turkey in
> about two or three weeks. I need to hear from you be-
> fore I leave. *She pauses, and I hear some background noise,
> perhaps a spoon clinking against a cup. And then a loud sigh.*
> I'm old, Melissa. I need to hear from you.

Then some fumbling around with the phone until it eventually reaches the cradle with a resolute click. There are no other messages.

Granny has been announcing that she's old for as long as I can remember. Any time she loses her patience or needs something done, she'll say *I'm old.* She used to say *Just do as you're told* until my father told her that wasn't the way he was raising a kid. He raised me with more of a *do whatever you want as long as you don't hurt anyone* attitude. That also had its downsides.

I push aside the disappointment I feel about my father not coming to the L.A. show, and begin to dial Granny's number. I'm in the middle of keying in the long distance code when I'm interrupted by Billy and Kiki coming through the adjoining door. They look a mess but you can tell they feel like the most beautiful and interesting people on earth.

Billy throws a baggie at me, and I scramble and drop the phone receiver, trying to catch it.

"It's good, Miss. So clean, pure."

"Right, it's basically like doing a half hour of yoga," I say, but I don't throw it back. I flick the tiny baggie back and forth in my hand like it's a developing Polaroid. My mouth tastes of bacon. What does it mean to get high in the morning? I have not been high at all yet this tour. I don't want to be all Sweet Valley High about it but it seems like a sad choice. I watch Billy and Kiki, currently arm wrestling. ("If I win, you have to do a Grateful Dead cover at your next show!" "If I win, you have to walk through the lobby with one tit out of your dress!") I want in on that dumb, all-body joy. I grab the hotel key card from the dresser top and cut a baby line on the room service tray. I throw the bag to Jared, who does the same.

A moment later, Tom and Cory come barreling in. Cory watches, arms crossed, while Tom packs up his green canvas army bag. All four of us become a parody of high people who don't want anyone to know we're high: Jared pretending to read a book, Kiki braiding Billy's hair and pretending to follow the Muppet movie. But it is mostly Tom who's pretending—to not care as we watch him pack.

Cory has cute aqua sneakers I've never seen before. It kills me that I can't tell her how cool she looks, with the baby-blue tank dress, the little star barrettes in her blond bob. There's no way anyone would know she has kids. She looks like she's in a much cooler band than ours. She is close enough to smell, and the smell is like a coconut cream or a berry-heavy shampoo. I want to hug her. I hold out the container of lukewarm home fries. "Want some?"

She turns me down with a curt head shake and glares. She's being so bitchy. I wish she could be my best friend.

"Cory," I say, "sorry if that was surprising. You know Tom's like a brother, no vibes whatsoever." Cory nods, with no smile, which makes me smile even more for the both of us, and descend even deeper into babbling. "Seriously, you have nothing to worry about. I would never think of Tom that way."

"Missy, it's still odd. It's not . . . normal."

"It's the only way we can afford this kind of hotel, plus, you just have to think of me like a guy," I try to explain. Tom looks over at me, a *just shut up* face. "Things in the music scene . . . it's different. The norm is different. It's like a family thing, we're all together. Like, all the time . . ." I forget that coke makes me love talking.

"With the way this band parties," she says, as though *parties* means *has constant orgies*, "I'm just not cool with it. I know it's not cool to ever have serious, adult emotional reactions to things, or to acknowledge when things are dysfunctional, but that's what being an adult is."

"I'm an adult, Cory." Now her bitchiness isn't cute.

"Adults don't have to defend themselves by calling themselves adults, and also, you're what, twenty-one years old?"

"Yes," I say, though when I think about being twenty-one

it feels like a mature kind of age to be. When she says it, it sounds like I'm still in primary school.

Tom hands her one of his bags, and opens the door, urging Cory outside.

"Plus, one of your nipples is just fully hanging out of your tank top right now," she says, before slamming the door.

I look down. Damn. Jared laughs like a stoner, his mouth wide open, little bits of bacon flying everywhere. I pull my shirt up. "Good burn, such a good burn!"

When Jared stops laughing, he grabs my last piece of bacon and asks, "But you *are* fucking him, though?" The sound he makes chewing is revolting. It's so aggravating the way people assume that just because I like having sex with some people, it means I like having sex with *all* people.

I push him, only half kidding, toward the door and then out into the hall. "Get your own room next time. We're not your babysitters."

"What? I can't stay?"

"No!"

I watch as he joins Cory and Tom waiting for the elevator. Cory whispers something to Tom.

I hate her and want to be her friend in equal measure, and the confusing mix of emotions propels me back inside to leave a manic, coke-fueled voicemail for Amita.

Later that night, she leaves me one back that's just *Forget that uptight Cory cunt, I'm proud of your Dicks Across America tour. I love you. You're perfect.*

Sometimes you just need to know that someone loves you, their love like an anchor that will bring you back when your love affair with freedom reaches a tethered end.

CHAPTER 4

CAROLA

T OWARD THE END of the interview the cops brought me a burger, fries, and a Coke. The burger was in a yellow Styrofoam container. The cop poured his fries into the overturned top of his burger container. So I did the same. I hadn't eaten meat or junk food in years. I was about to refuse it, when it began to look like the most delicious thing I had ever seen. It was practically calling out to me. I pulled a leaf of iceberg lettuce from under the saucy bun. It was still crisp. Then I took the plastic fork and dipped it in the ketchup and sucked on the tines. And then I ate it all, even the burger. I ate it too fast to feel the texture on my tongue and be disgusted by the fleshy reality of it. I could barely hear them as I ate. It was as though all my other senses shut down. As I dipped the final fry in the little pond of ketchup, the cops both smiled at each other, like I was a feral child who had just come in from the woods.

Miranda broke my reverie. "Were you raised religious?" she asked. I was beginning to feel like I was part of her research somehow, and I didn't like it. Plus, the answer was complicated. My mother loved Jesus and hated women. Well, most women.

She was always outwardly pleasant, quick to invite a friend in for coffee, but then would ruthlessly pick her apart as we watched her walk down our porch and get into her car. She'd compliment a passerby on her outfit, then mutter under her breath about the gaudiness of it. She knew kindness was a virtue and so she acted kindly, but as I grew older I began to suspect that she didn't feel it. None of this was unusual for her generation, but I found it unnerving.

She didn't like sloppiness. She curled her hair every morning. She polished the baseboards every week. The sink in the bathroom could never be wet after you washed your hands; you had to run a rag over it until it was dry, and then neatly hang the rag on a hook on the back of the sink's cabinet door. She could see a loose thread or a tiny tear on a dress from across the room. She cut the grass with scissors so it was always the same length, even though we only had a small square of grass in the front yard of our small home. During my childhood we lived in the Glebe neighborhood in downtown Ottawa, which was a modest, working-class area. It only became wealthy after my mother's death, which always made me sad. She would have loved to watch it prosper. In my memories of her in the 1960s, my mother simmered with a quiet rage, but it only tipped over and showed itself twice.

I remember sitting in the car outside of the Church of the Blessed Sacrament. It was snowing sideways, wind ripping at the car, while my mother cried in the front seat. My mother rarely cried in public, and this may have been the first time I'd really witnessed her completely let herself go into full-body sobs. Makeup smeared, hair falling into her face. At first, she tried to hide it, but I could hear her sniffling, and then she just seemed to forget I was there. As she cried, the storm outside subsided and the sun peeked through the clouds. The sudden brightness reflected off high walls of snow pushed up in piles at the edge of the church parking lot. I pulled at my itchy brown snowsuit. I tried to reach out from the back seat to give her a hug but she pushed my hands away.

"It's nothing, it's nothing," she said. "I'm overreacting." She used the rearview mirror to press more face powder under her eyes.

Finally, she took a deep breath and said, "Do you know that if I were to ever divorce your daddy—which don't worry, I won't—but if I did, *he* would be allowed to go to church but the priest would not let me in? Can you believe that?"

I'd never heard my mother say one negative word about the church before.

"It's bullshit, is what that is," she muttered, more to herself. I'd never heard her swear. My father and Marie had already gone into the church. But right when we'd pulled into the parking lot, my mother had said she needed a minute. I said I'd stay, too. I didn't want to go in with my father because he smelled bad like he usually did on Sundays. The night before I'd woken up to his yelling. It was around this age that I started to dislike him, even though my love remained firm even as my discomfort grew, these feelings continuing to confuse me until he died. So my father picked up Marie and carried her over his shoulder and I heard her squeal with delight as they crossed the parking lot to the church.

I remember how my mother reached back to unzip my snowsuit and pat my head.

"You're a beautiful girl, you're going to find a good Catholic man to marry someday," she said, "and do it right." She always started sentences so hopefully and then fucked it up by the end. But her heart was in the right place. I would give her that.

The second time my mother got close to self-actualization was on Mother's Day in 1970. When I brought her a bouquet of lilacs at breakfast, she said, "You remember about lunch, right? For Mother's Day, just us girls!" She gave me a look that said I should say yes. It was my last month of high school. I was beginning to see the escape hatch from my childhood. I was like someone who knew they were soon to quit a job they hated and was going through the motions.

But we weren't going to lunch "just us girls." My mother drove right past the restaurant we went to for special occasions and continued up toward Parliament Hill.

"Where are we going?"

"You'll see."

I was nervous in general that weekend because I was covering for Marie, who'd hitchhiked to Toronto to join the antiwar protest for the victims at Kent State. And I'd been avoiding my mom because I was a terrible liar. Marie was supposed to be at her friend Debbie's house in Orleans. I did not want to eat Mother's Day sandwiches without Marie. Marie and my mother were either best friends or enemies, more the latter at that point in their lives. But they were remarkably similar—harsh but nurturing, fierce when crossed. I was the observer, the peacemaker, the wisecracker. I never confided in my mother, she was too Catholic, too afraid of our father.

My mother stopped the car on Parliament Hill. She was

dressed primly as always. She placed her pocketbook in her lap, adjusted her hat in the rearview mirror, and said, "If you tell your father we were here, he won't like it, and it will be your fault. You hear me?"

"What are we doing here?" I craned my head to look around. There was the view of the city behind us, the imposing beauty of the Château Laurier hotel and the canal. But there were also crowds gathering in front of the Parliament Buildings, more than the usual assortment of tourists.

"If we see any police, especially ones we know, we duck and run. We meet back here at the car. Do you hear me? Do not be noticed by any police."

"Mother, you sound insane. I thought we were having lunch."

"I went to a talk," she said, as she pulled her lipstick from her pocketbook and, looking in the rear-view mirror again, swiped it over her lips. "The other night when I said I was baking at Marlene's. I *was* with Marlene, but we went to a talk in a church basement. There were women there from Vancouver who had driven all across the country. I don't necessarily think abortion is right"—she whispered the word *abortion* even though it was just us in the car—"but I went, and the women were very persuasive. I think this is important. But don't tell your father we were here. If you tell him, there will be serious consequences."

"I don't understand," I said.

"You will shortly, just follow me."

We got out of the car and walked up the hill toward the group that had assembled in front of the building. My mother moved so quickly and with such purpose, I stumbled a little trying to keep up. As we got closer, I could see that we were all women, most of whom were chanting.

"Why are they here?" I asked my mother, as she edged into the gathering. I realized she didn't want to be recognized. She shushed me and found her friend Marlene. Someone handed me a mimeographed pamphlet, which listed a set of demands about legalizing abortion.

There was a car with a coffin on top. It was so strange to see my mother standing among these women holding signs that read things like THE STATE HAS NO BUSINESS IN THE WOMBS OF THE NATION!, ABORTION ON DEMAND AND WITHOUT APOLOGY!, and DON'T ROCK THE CRADLE, ROCK THE BOAT! This was the woman who had a portrait of Jesus in literally every room of the house, including a giant crucifix visible from our beds lest we get any funny ideas.

I felt overcome by the spectacle. I'd been to church nearly every Sunday my whole life, but had never felt this feeling, a sense of transcendence, a swelling with divine purpose. Up until that moment, I'd never seen women, in a big group, do anything besides organize bake sales or charity rummage sales, or cook at the Friday night church suppers, catering to the men. I felt the way I did when Marie had taken me to see the Who the year before, like I wanted to be them. Only this time I could conceivably join them. I looked around at the women and memorized their clothes, what they were saying. I wandered away from my mother and took everything in, and chanted so loudly my voice got hoarse.

Later, in the car, I read some of the information on the pamphlets. "Two thousand women die a year from illegal abortions!" I read, astounded.

My mother put the key in the ignition and paused. "Your sister could have been one of them," she said, "last year."

"No, that's impossible. Marie tells me everything."

"Not everything. You were too young. She didn't want to upset you. She was going to go to a place, a dirty apartment with a butcher, basically. I overheard her talking to Debbie on the phone, and I took the money from the savings, and I sent her to some women who know how to do it safely. I told your father it was for a new couch and then I bought a couch from the thrift store. It was the safest option. But still very dangerous."

My mother made the sign of the cross and started the car.

I was in awe of my mother then. And confused.

"But do you think it's wrong?" I asked her.

She fixed her eyes on the pedestrians crossing the street in front of us. "Yes, in a way, but once you're a mother you have a different understanding than a priest, or a man who will never have his own child. My heart led me to that path with your sister, because she is my child and I want to protect her. I don't regret it. Men talk a good game, but they don't have any idea," she said, driving back to our neighborhood. Instead of staring out the window, daydreaming about finally leaving this stuffy city, I stared at my mother as she drove those familiar streets. She was like an alien mother I had never met.

"Don't tell your father, don't tell your cousins—this is our secret. Our shame." Ah, shame. There it was. She pulled into our driveway.

"But why should we be ashamed? None of those women on the hill seemed ashamed."

"Don't ask stupid questions."

My father was painting the porch, a cigarette lolling in his mouth. He turned to wave, and my mother waved back brightly. I raised a limp hand, smiling but more to myself. I had this secret with my mother. It felt grown-up, like I was a part of something bigger.

Then my mother put her hand on my knee, and I expected a wink or a meaningful look, but all she said was, "You should wear a little lipstick, you know—you'll never find a man in those dungarees." And then she leaned in closer to my ear and said, "And I know you're not like your sister. You'll be a good girl until you're married."

She got out of the car before I could say anything back. I *was* the good girl. I was mostly quiet, got good grades, and knew from a young age that complaining yielded more things to complain about. But I was not always going to be a good girl.

I watched my father climb down the ladder, unsteadily, and wished briefly he would fall. Then I felt terrible for that thought and made the sign of the cross.

She kissed my father's cheek on her way into the house.

"How was lunch?"

"Delightful," she said.

AFTER A FEW more minutes of questions, of me being too honest about my conflicted feelings, I could tell I wasn't giving the investigators what they were after.

"So, you gave him all your money, but you don't regret it?" said the one cop.

"Well, it wasn't much. And I don't believe in currency or hoarding wealth to be more powerful."

"Even though you saw him accrue possessions that he preached against?"

"I wouldn't say he preached. I grew up Catholic. He was gentle in his teachings, and he could be reasoned with. He accepted that he had contradictions."

"Did he?" At this point, Miranda couldn't hide her disdain. We had gotten to the point where every question she asked had a tinge of sarcasm or frustration.

Finally, they told me I could leave.

"Thank you for your time, Car—I mean, Juniper," Miranda said, grasping my hand weakly.

A strand of her graying hair was stuck to her glossed lips. I touched my own lip to try to get her attention, but she turned away.

OUTSIDE THE POLICE station, the air was a wall of sponge, humid and unmoving, the hot center of a July afternoon. I stuck my hands inside the pockets of my cotton shift dress, fingertips still sticky with ketchup. I was supposed to meet my friend Sarah for tea, our weekly sharing session, which was basically like agreeing to act as each other's therapist. Lately I'd been talking all about my failure at motherhood. Sarah was gentle, my closest friend at the center for over ten years now, but I could tell she didn't have much patience with me when I brought up my daughter. "I don't judge," she said, but I felt it wasn't true. I wasn't up for it today.

The police precinct was right in the middle of town. I walked a few yards down Main Street, but instead of ascending the gentle S of the curving dirt road that led back up the mountain to the center, I turned up a residential avenue. Sticking to the shade of the overgrown trees, I continued through the neighborhood until I reached the exit for the two-lane highway out of town. I stuck my thumb out and set my gaze on the road.

CHAPTER 5

MISSY

___

WHEN YOU'RE AWAY from friends and family for long stretches, you expect to miss them more than you actually do. By this point in the tour, my life at home seems almost theoretical. I'm beginning to understand why Cory would worry about Tom, because it doesn't seem that we're beholden to norms. It feels like we're in a play: even when we're offstage, we're playing our parts. Everyone else is audience.

But while the everyday people in my life back home have receded, my mother is beginning to feel more present. I'm thinking about her all the time, mistaking women on the street for her, the way I used to when she first left. It's starting to trip me up. Of course, I'm mistaking her for women the age she was when she left. She'd look different now in middle age, but my mind can't reconcile that.

In fact, Cory is probably only a year or two younger than my mother was when she left. No wonder I can't stop thinking about her—Cory. I've been obsessed with her since the run-in at the Baltimore hotel. I just can't get over her unwillingness to be my friend.

After Baltimore, she joins the tour for a week and as soon as she does both she and Tom avoid me. I get it—their kids are with Cory's parents, and they need to rekindle things. But they don't have to *actively* avoid me, and it seems quite apparent that they are. Tom didn't even make eye contact during the last show, or crack any jokes or riff in any way. He played like he was recording a record. I'm beginning to have flashes from high school, that purposeful exclusion that can make you feel like a speck of dirt. And it's beginning to hurt my feelings.

Thus it has become my mission to be likable, fun, and perfectly relaxed, even though I am none of those things. Before sound check a few shows later in Charlotte, North Carolina, I duck out to a small health food store a few blocks away from the venue and buy Cory a soy milk smoothie and some vegan cookies. These are the kind of things that are hard to come by on tour. There were days when Alan, usually our only vegan, had been surviving on Taco Bell bean burritos and plain burger buns with a sloppy center of lettuce, tomato, and ketchup.

I see Cory at sound check, sitting with the band at a cluster of cabaret tables in the middle of the bar. I was right— she only has a sad-looking iceberg lettuce salad. I hand over the gifts, trying to make it seem like I didn't go to the health food store just for her, though it's clear I haven't purchased anything for myself.

"Oh," she says, reluctantly reaching for the bag. "Thanks, Missy." She looks pained to accept the gifts.

"I know we're going to dinner later but thought you might like a snack."

She sniffs at the smoothie. "Does it have honey? Honey

isn't vegan." As if I don't know that. But I keep smiling like an idiot. "No, no, of course no honey. All vegan. I made the woman at the store swear on her life. And I reserved you a good cabaret table on the side stage for the show," I add.

She sips her smoothie, makes an *oh it's delicious* face with a half smile, and then looks away. My cheeks redden. She's a hard nut to crack. Tom leans over and takes a sip of the shake and nods at me.

"Thanks, Missy," he says.

Tom and I are called onstage to check our mics. I hover near him as he tightens his snare drum. He glances up at me, and then toward Cory in the empty venue, who is sitting at the table pretending to read a magazine while surreptitiously surveying us.

"Look, Cory isn't easily won over, once she's decided you aren't trustworthy. It's her thing."

"You know I'm trustworthy!"

"I know, I know. I just don't think she wants to be your friend," Tom says. "I know that's hard since you want everyone to like you."

"What? I don't care about being liked." Why does it sound like a dig?

"It's important to you. To be cool. To be accepted."

"I really don't care that much, and it's so strange that you assume that. I mean, I care that you like me, and that we all get along. Sometimes I feel like the only person who cares that everyone in the band gets along. Also, isn't that just how humans evolved, to need each other, to want to be around each other, for survival? You make it sound like I'm a fucking teenybopper when maybe I'm just a social human being."

Tom appears to think about that, but doesn't respond. He

taps his drum with his brushes, looks toward the sound guy at the boards. He clearly isn't going to explain.

"I don't get girls sometimes," I say, and walk off to get my cello.

That isn't really true. It's just easier to say than to explain why a lot of girls don't like me. Girls resent the ones who like to fuck and don't have hang-ups about it. In high school I remember how Gabby, rumored to be the sluttiest one in our grade, was treated so poorly. She had this gorgeous, long red curly hair and she could swear exquisitely at anyone who crossed her. I secretly admired her, despite my not having grown into my own sexuality until later in the game. Cory's feminist sneers are just another flavor of the same shit.

I sit down in my cello chair, set the mic up, and prepare to do my sound check following Tom. When he's done, I reach out with my bow and tap his arm as he's leaving. "She just thinks I'm a slut, even though she wrote an entire zine called *Slut Bunny* or whatever."

"She was reclaiming the word." He says the word *reclaiming* like he might have to define it for me, even though I am wearing a T-shirt that says BITCH on it and obviously understand the reclaiming concept very well.

"Exactly. So why not, you know, stick up for actual sluts? She should like me."

Tom sighs and I swear he almost rolls his eyes. "Cory is a lot older than you," he says, fishing a granola bar out of his army bag and throwing it my way. "Eat some protein. The gig tonight is important." Sometimes Tom is so very *not* punk rock. "Are you going to forget about Cory and be on your game tonight?"

"Yes, *Dad*," I say.

———

WE DRIVE BACK to the Comfort Inn on the outskirts of town to get dressed and grab dinner, and on the way back to the venue we see a little midway set up in a parking lot. We're in a riverside suburb called Gastonia. I slow down for a jay-walking group of children, faces obscured by cotton candy, bookended by tired-looking parents. The garish lights of the rides, the electronic pings and shouts from the midway games, they call to me. I pull up on the shoulder and order the band out.

"We have time for one or two rides before call time!"

Everyone piles out, except Tom, who checks his wrist-watch. "I don't know. We shouldn't be late. The reps will be there."

Everyone stands awkwardly, arms crossed. Alan lights a cigarette. We all look at Gord, our manager, who is trans-fixed by the Ferris wheel. "All right, kids, let's have a little fun. Half an hour, that's it. Promise to rally back in plenty of time!"

The county fair was my favorite weekend of the year as a kid. The wind in my hair on rides, the livestock in the show barns, playing impossible games to win stuffed animals. Tay-lor (the only kid my age at the commune) and I used to be allowed to run around all afternoon. This parking lot setup was the urban version of a fair, but the blinking lights and the Ferris wheel high in the sky against the setting sun still worked a childlike magic on me.

The band isn't as transformed by it, clumped together and staring at the rides they think are too small and boring.

Passersby stare at Billy's blue hair. Everything about the fair reminds me of my childhood. I look at the band, all city kids, and realize maybe they're all wearing thrift-store clothes but aren't used to being around working-class people. This was the biggest culture shock when I moved to the city from Sunflower. None of the kids from my rural elementary school ever had any money. The fair was our biggest yearly event. Undeterred, I buy us a strip of tickets and convince Cory to ride the Ferris wheel with me. Shockingly, she agrees. It seems like a great idea until we get stuck at the top, when the carny pauses the ride to unload a sick kid. We swing back and forth to the loud, unnerving creaking of the carriage, our sneakers hanging in the air.

"Are you afraid of heights?" I ask, glancing sideways at Cory's hands gripping the safety bar.

"I guess a little." She grips and releases her fingers on the bar. She has a heart tattooed below the knuckle of her middle finger.

"I love it. It feels like flying," I say, swinging my legs a little to make the carriage move even more, but then I stop when Cory lets out an involuntary yelp.

"Sorry," I say.

I look down and find the guys, Alan and Billy getting into a little cage to ride the Zipper, Jared and Tom playing a shooting game, Gord in line for a beer.

"What is it like, being the only girl on tour?" Cory asks. "Like for real. The guys aren't here, so be honest. Is it hard?"

The question feels like a trap, or a test, but I also want to answer properly, to win the game of getting her to like me.

"I guess?"

"How do you deal with harassment? You must be hit on all the time."

I wish it didn't make me so pleased to hear her say that. I hook my ankles together to keep from swinging my legs again.

"I don't know, I'm pretty tough. I can tell someone off pretty well. And also, I usually have to make the overtures. The guys rarely put in the effort."

"No doubt," she says, in a way that is perhaps pejorative. "I just feel like I wouldn't be able to handle it, worrying about my safety all the time. I hate going to shows now because I always get grabbed in the pit. It sucks."

The ride begins to move again, and we make a couple of full rotations without speaking. I enjoy the feel of the wind as we pick up speed. But soon enough, we halt when the attendant starts letting people off and on. We are paused again at the top and I look out at Charlotte.

"Wow, I was just saying this city is such a trash heap, but it's so beautiful from up here."

"It is. So, you *don't* worry about your safety?"

"I guess I'm always onstage so I don't get it too bad."

That isn't entirely true. I'd stopped stage-diving because I was groped too much. The last time it happened, I kicked a guy in the face and it turned into quite an ordeal for the venue. But how was I supposed to be honest in this conversation? I have quick reflexes. I broke a guy's finger once for grabbing my ass. His grimace and girlish screams were so fucking satisfying. I usually tell this story as often as I can, as a brag. But I don't think Cory will buy my bravado.

"I think it's important women stick together, you know," she says.

"I agree. That's why I want to be your friend so badly."

"Right, right."

I glance at her, see her frown. Cory makes me feel like I should be worried, keep my guard up, and the guys make me feel like I'm just one of them. Carefree. Wild. Though that could never be true, either. The Guns N' Roses ballad "Patience" starts to play as our carriage begins to move, then again jolts to a stop.

"Now that I'm a mother, I just feel so much less able to put up with men's bullshit," she says. "It really makes you think about what's important, putting in the work, you know? I don't want my daughter to have to deal with the same shit we do, and that's on *us*."

Cory's number-one annoying quality is when she starts sentences with *Now that I'm a mother*, as though no one else can know or feel anything as profound as she does.

"Is it, on us? Or is it also on men? There's only so much we can do if they don't hear us."

"Well, I'm not going to die waiting for that utopian fantasy to happen," she says.

"I feel like I want to be your friend, and you want me to agree with everything you say."

"Oh, Missy, Missy. Let me give you a little bit of advice," she says, as our carriage jolts its way down to the loading platform. The GN'R guitar solo blankets the lit-up ground below us. "You want everyone to like you so much, all girls do at your age, desperate for approval all the time. But it's such a relief to let go of that. Trust me. Do what you want to do, stop giving a fuck about guys."

"That's literally my whole ethos."

"It's what you say. It's not how you act."

The attendant opens the safety bar, and we slide off the bench. Cory jumps down the rusting metal stairs like she's escaping captivity, and into Tom's arms. He's holding a very flammable-looking hot-pink bunny. The night is cooling off. I feel itchy from Cory's criticisms.

I grab Billy from the beer lineup so we can leave.

"What's the matter? Did you realize Cory's a class-A cunt while stuck on a ride with her?"

"I guess, c'mon let's go."

LATE THAT NIGHT, our post-show binge takes us through the rest of Kiki's stash and every pore in my body feels filthy. I have no patience, no kindness for anyone. I'm feeling homesick. In the hotel all by myself, I pull out my journal and am writing the date when I realize I never called Granny back. I leave a backdoor message on Granny's voicemail. I say in a fake-sober voice, "Granny, yes, I can look after your place when you go on your trip. I can check in and stuff. Water plants. Let's chat about it soon. I'll call back tomorrow. I hope you're okay." I gave her Tom's pager number for emergencies, but knew she probably wouldn't understand how it worked.

I flop back onto the bed, too tired to get up, too wired to sleep. I pull out the green notebook and begin to dial so we'll have a hookup when we get to Nashville tomorrow. It's Conrad, a white guy with dreads who only owns Fishbone T-shirts and talks too much. He'll have to do.

CHAPTER 6

CAROLA

USED TO HITCHHIKE all the time. When we first
started Sunflower, our car worked only half the time
and so hitching was how we got around. One time Bryce and
I even hitchhiked on boats, making our way down from Man-
itoba in the summertime. I had collections of names and faces
in old journals, random people we met along the way.

When I stuck my thumb out now, I felt the wind question
my arm with its strength. It wasn't a day for running away, a
storm about to break. And I wasn't sure what I was going to
do if anyone actually stopped.

I wanted to go to a record store, and there wasn't one in
Mallow, the bucolic little village that ran alongside the river
in the valley below the ashram. There was one small grocery
store, a garage, a restaurant, a few gift shops, and an ice
cream shop for tourist season—and of course the police
station—but that was it. I couldn't remember the last time
I'd left Mallow. That was as good a reason as any to get out.

A pickup truck with chipped paint the color of grass
pulled over. An older man wearing a John Deere cap was at
the wheel.

"Going to Concord?" he said.

"Yes, thank you," I said, stepping up into the passenger seat.

"You're one of the yoga ladies, then?"

"Yes, I am. But I used to be a farmer," I said, as a way to deflect any forthcoming judgment. We made small talk about farming. My knowledge from Sunflower served me well in these moments. But he drove quite fast, and swerved a few times, and I began to clutch the bar above the window.

WHEN I WAS thirteen, I had a friend named Darlene, who lived on a farm outside Ottawa. Once, when picking me up at Darlene's house, Mother came in for a visit while my father stayed in the car smoking. I knew by the way her lips were tight, and by her overbright smile, that my father was *in a mood*. Darlene's mother knew it, too, by the way she glanced outside, and her voice went up at the end of sentences and made one-syllable words into two. "Would you like to invite your husband in for coff-ee-ee? We made a fresh po-ot!"

"Oh, we had so much coffee after church," my mother said.

Darlene and I tumbled in from the garden, still giggling, hands full of carrots and fresh with dirt. But when I saw my mother's face, I quickly washed up and pulled together my overnight bag, saying a quick thank-you to Darlene's parents. I remember seeing them at the kitchen table in that moment, still finishing the last of their late breakfast, and it occurred to me I'd never seen my own parents look so relaxed.

On the way back to the city, I told my parents about helping to milk the cows, and gathering the eggs, and a chicken who had a particularly funny way of walking, but I realized no one was going to engage with me. There wasn't a single word spoken, but my father communicated through his driving. He sped up and swerved around cars, his eyes bulging as he nearly ran a blue van off the road. Cars and trucks honked at us as our car zigzagged around them. At one point, when traffic slowed, he pulled over to the shoulder and raced alongside, as though he were in his cruiser. Why wouldn't we be stopped? We'd been stopped before, but it never mattered. There was a decal from the Ottawa police department on the front windshield of our muddy-brown Pontiac. It absolved him from any violation. I'd been scared before, but this time I really thought he was going to kill us.

I was so sick of my mother's silence in those moments that eventually I yelled, "You're going to kill us!"

"Yeah, that's what you want, isn't it?"

Right then I understood that was what *he* wanted. I was so nauseated by the time we reached the edge of our neighborhood that when he stopped at a red light I jumped out and threw up all over the sidewalk. The light changed. My father's face was still furious.

"Get back in this car this instant!" he said.

I shook my head, clutching my stomach.

My mother implored me with her eyes. Then said urgently, "Get in the car, honey."

I shook my head again. The tires squealed as he pulled away, the passenger door still ajar and swinging open as he drove. I'd been in the car plenty of times when Dad was angry, Marie and I huddled together as he'd threatened to drive off a cliff, as my mother whimpered and screamed *Not with the girls in the car, not with the girls.* She'd even had seat-

belts installed when she took the car in for a tune-up, although he'd scoffed at the extra expense.

Eventually, he would calm down. And late that night we'd
hear him weeping in the living room, and my mother consol-
ing him. Sometimes he would come into my room and sit on
the edge of the bed and apologize. I'd pretend to be asleep.

But by now I was a teenager, buoyed by a new sense of
myself, of confidence and bravado. I went and bought myself
a three-speed bike at a rummage sale with my babysitting
earnings. From then on, I walked or biked anywhere I needed
to go, even on the coldest of winter days. I took it a step further and called the police station from a pay phone. I told
them that my dad was a drunk and that he shouldn't have a
license, spelling out for them his name and address. No one
did anything. But I never drove with him again.

The fall after high school graduation, I went to Oberlin
College on a scholarship for the flute. I'd never been to the
United States, or kissed a boy. Something about the way I
had felt at the pro-choice rally with my mom meant I gravi-
tated toward peace rallies, and consciousness-raising groups,
and beautiful men with shaggy haircuts who carried paperback copies of *The Communist Manifesto* in their pockets. I
lost my virginity with the guy I was handcuffed to at a sit-in.
I read *Sisterhood Is Powerful* and *Sexual Politics*, and in the
summer, my family expected me to come back to Ottawa to
work, but instead I got in a van with a group of friends. We
drove to an intentional community in Virginia called Twin
Oaks, where the lifestyle was based on the writings of Tho-
reau. I volunteered doing gardening and childcare, and that's
where I met Bryce, a handsome man who made me wonder if
I'd finally found the husband my mother had been nattering

on about my entire childhood. I tried to resist his pull, but I failed, and we did get married, in a circle of friends by the sunflower field.

My mother never forgave me for getting married without telling her, and for never going back to school, which had always been her own dream. Instead, we moved to Vermont, bought a broken-down farm, and started our own intentional community, calling it Sunflower. It was started on principles of egalitarianism and humanism, but the worlds in which we were raised still got through.

I called my mother right before our first Sunflower Christmas, asking if she'd like to visit. She said she would, but my father had refused and she couldn't come alone.

"You don't understand what it's been like since you and your sister left," she whispered into the phone.

"Leave him," I said finally. At first very quietly, and then more emphatically.

"You don't understand," she said. "You make it sound easy but it isn't."

"I love you, Mom, but you know you need to leave him."

They were the last words I ever said to her.

On New Year's Day my sister, Marie, called. She was in hysterics. Our phone was a party line, and the other family kept picking up the phone while we were talking. It was a car accident. Dad had been drinking. It was an accident, she said, but we knew it wasn't.

MISSY WAS CONCEIVED a few months after their deaths, during our first lambing season. I remember that time as a kind of haze of grief, but also youthful elation. My parents had lived a life of routine, despair, and escapism, my father with alcohol and my mother with religion. I was going to live with bliss and community, cooperation, and joy. I was going to feel connected with other people. *When we get angry,* I'd say, standing on a chair in a community meeting, *we are going to work through it. We are going to choose peaceful resolution! We are going to love!*

We had a small flock of sheep that we'd purchased with the farm. They were beautiful, innocent animals. Bryce called them simple, which I knew meant dumb, but I saw in their eyes a graceful, peaceful nature. We had brought in a ram for mating, and soon thereafter some of the ewes were pregnant. We had been eagerly awaiting lambing season. I went to the library in town and read all the agricultural magazines. I visited nearby farms and asked questions. It was a time of beginnings.

I was in love with our new community and it loved me back. And there was always so much to do. We were run off our feet, every day, with planting and harvesting, fixing and building, cooking and cleaning, organizing and hoping, hoping, hoping we'd make our small world a better place, and then in time, continue to see it grow.

THE ROLLING, GREEN farms in the valleys outside Mallow were dotted with red barns and bore proud family names. As we reached the outskirts of Concord, the houses were closer together, wild fields giving way to manicured yards. The farmer steadied his speed, and I began to calm down. He had been talking the whole drive, mostly about his son who had just moved to California and become very wealthy on the

World Wide Web. I kept hearing those three words, but I did not hear much else, my mind elsewhere. He dropped me off right in front of the Pitchfork record store.

"Thank you," I said.

"I think you'll get to where you're going, I see things working out for you," he said.

I waved, watching him drive away, and wondered if he was right.

Inside the record shop, I was disoriented. Other than grocery shops and the local Agway, I hadn't been in a retail shop for years. I'd written down the name of Missy's band, the Swearwolves, on the back of an envelope. The store was playing some kind of loud punk music, and the shelves of records were very close together. Several teenagers were crowded around the *S* bin. I began to wonder if this was a bad idea, but then I saw, right there behind the counter, my daughter's band on display. That was my sign. I went up to the cash register.

"Would you like the cassette or CD?" the shopkeeper asked in a listless tone, staring at a spot on the wall behind me. He looked like one of the young men in Missy's band. Despite the heat, he wore a knitted wool hat pulled over a mess of hair, and a flannel shirt hanging loosely over his bony frame.

"Cassette, please," I said.

"They're also on the cover of *Spin* this month," he said, handing me a large glossy magazine with my Missy's face on the cover.

"That's my daughter," I said, pressing my finger to her face. I made a greasy print on her forehead with the ketchup residue.

"No *way*!" he said, the enthusiasm a bolt through his practiced apathy. Then he tried to recover himself. "I mean, that's cool. Why do you have to buy the cassette, then?"

"For a present," I said, "she only sent me one copy." I was lying! He knew I was lying. But why was I lying? I'd given up lying years ago.

"We also have T-shirts," he said, pointing to a rack. I bought one of those as well, pulling it awkwardly over my plain cotton dress. Then I asked him to point me toward the bus station. It occurred to me this record store guy was around the same age Bryce and I had been when we started Sunflower, when we looked at middle-aged people the way he looked at me, which is to say, barely.

BRYCE AND I had never seen a birth before, let alone facilitated one. When the first ewe went into labor, both of us were wide-eyed under thick oatmeal-colored toques, two against one stubborn, scared ewe. It was a deep, cold winter, but that day was unseasonably warm. The birthing ewe did not want us around, but we had the upper hand, with our human fingers, biceps, thoughts of the future. But we didn't know what we were doing. It was four in the morning. We'd been walking over the hill, coming home from a party at the tavern in town, when Bryce went to check on the flock.

"She's coming! Number three is about to pop. The first birth!" he'd yelled across the yard, running and tripping toward me like a little kid. "Should we wake up Chris?"

Chris had passed out on the living room floor before we'd left for the tavern.

"We can do this ourselves," I said, which wasn't in keeping with Sunflower's collective principles, but I felt like Bryce and I were a good team, and this had been our dream, and so I wanted us to share this big moment.

The imminent birth had sobered us both from the mulled wine and generous pours of draft beer. The ewe had a greasy green number 3 painted on her back. The sun had melted some of the snow the day before, and our rubber boots sank into the mossy pathway, making squishy sounds as we tromped between the farmhouse and the barn. I pulled a giant parka close over my thin dress. Bryce had a look of absolute panic and horror in his face when he saw what we were really dealing with.

"Why did I think we could do this? We're not doctors!" he shouted, scaring most of the flock as they moved en masse to the other side of the barn.

"You mean vets?"

"Whatever!"

"It's okay, let me get the book," I said, sitting on the edge of the manger, reading out loud from the chapter on problem birthing from *Storey's Guide to Birthing Sheep*. By the time the sun was coming up, Bryce had stripped down to just his jeans, with sweat-soaked hair. We couldn't figure out what was wrong, why the birth wasn't happening the way we'd assumed it would. Eventually Bryce realized that the lamb was breech.

"Put on the long glove and put your hand inside and turn the lamb around," I said, reading from the book.

He looked at me as though he might faint. "Is that the only possibility?"

I threw him the book, pulled off my coat, rolled up my dress sleeves, and grabbed the gloves. Bryce didn't object. My hand shook inside the glove, but I knew what I had to do.

I pushed one arm deeply inside the ewe, a warmth like nothing I had ever felt before, as I gently pulled the lamb out. It was stunned, silent, and then all at once, bleating, and the mother quickly tried to stand and attend to it. I cradled the lamb and put it next to the mother's nose so she wouldn't have to get up to clean the afterbirth from its tiny, wriggling body.

There was something so primal about it. The sun was coming up as we lay against the stack of hay bales, watching the ewe clean the baby. I started to laugh, relieving the pressure of the past several hours. We had done it. The ewe and her lamb were still alive. We'd triumphed! I was so proud of us.

And looking at Bryce, exhausted and still shirtless, sweating, I felt more attracted to him than ever before. We'd had so many failures: fences that didn't hold back the animals, failed plumbing, not understanding how to manage the crops. I'd lost count of how many times we'd had to go to the neighboring farm to ask very basic questions about how to do something, which I understood to be a source of great amusement for the Hendersons on their dairy farm.

When Chris and Tegan opened the door to do the morning chores, they caught us up against the manger, while the sheep around us did their sheep things. They chuckled and closed the door, smoking hand-rolled cigarettes outside while we finished. We shared a look right after the interruption, one that said *Just this once, just keep going*, and I clutched my legs around him even harder. Bryce had wanted to try, in an official way. This was the first time we weren't careful about it, and it took. I was young. One time was all it took.

LATER, AFTER FALLING back asleep for a few hours in the morning light, I felt like I was sobering up from what had felt like a mystical dream. I looked over at Bryce, who'd begun to snore gently and then emphatically. Who was he? I traced the patchy blond beard, the tan line across his forehead from the hat he wore on the tractor. He looked like an utter stranger. What was I doing with him? But here we were. I'd canned all the vegetables and learned to grow herbs. We'd built several outbuildings, learned to raise chickens and now sheep. I'd put up fences and dug trenches, and learned how and when to plant seeds, till the soil. My favorite thing to do was drive the tractor. Next year we were going to keep bees. Having a baby felt like the next logical step of this constant, generative labor. This experiment was working, however many failures we'd weathered. We had a farm with a group of friends, making all of our decisions as a collective, and for the most part, it was thrilling. So then why did our marriage feel like a game show I'd been tricked into being on?

I crept across the hall to the bathroom. The toilet seat was covered in pee from one of the men who kept forgetting to lift the seat. I'd left several passive-aggressive notes about it, then realized it must be Bryce. Was he really so lazy? The old white sink we'd hauled in from the dump and fixed up was leaking again, a deep rusty stain in the basin. I'd put hooks up for everyone's individual towel, but I suspected both Chris and Bryce grabbed whichever one was closest— always mine. Why was I living with so many men, who didn't know how to make soup stock or wash a dish, and who left an endless trail of dirty coffee cups all over the house? Men who already jokingly called me "Mama" with affection, which was cute at first and now deeply irritating.

I put my head in my hands and sat on the toilet until my feet began to feel numb. I wasn't sure what I was feeling until I heard the sheep outside, the bleating of the baby lamb. Then I felt something click inside me.

I felt a purity of regret I'd never known.

I bore down, trying to force any remaining sperm out of me. Even though I knew the likelihood of being pregnant on the first try was remote, I felt invaded anyway. Something inside me must have known it had taken. I bunched up the skin on my stomach and grabbed it uselessly. How could I have been so stupid? I got in the bathtub, filling it with hot water. The water heater only allowed for one hot bath per day, so we often filled it and bathed one after the other, or just hosed off outside with the cold water in the summer. It was wasteful, but I had to be submerged. I grabbed Bryce's disposable razor from the sink and I shaved my legs for the first time since I'd left my parents' house, then under my arms and my pubic area. The water was hot and now a swamp of blond hair. I ran my fingernail through a white cake of soap, cracked with threaded estuaries of dirt, soaping each toe, every crevice. I stood up, a bit dizzy from the heat, slick and new.

I made a cup of coffee and sat on the steps of our front porch in the white cotton nightgown my mother got me to take to college. It was chaste and white, with lace trim, now frayed at the knee-length hem. I'd defiantly ripped off the puffed sleeves in my dorm at Oberlin, after a girl had made fun of it. I was watching the sun rise, pulling at the stringy lace, breathing in the intoxicating smells of new, wet earth, spring unveiling itself all around me in the flattened grass the color of aged yellow hay, the rivers of runoff from the melting snow. From the porch, I could see clear across to the rest of our little valley, the forest edged around the farm like a painting, the outbuildings closest to us looking like toys on the horizon. We were so isolated there, fenced lines down the driveways, fields of hay and clover, dead trees felled over the tiny, mostly underground river in the middle. You could wander for hours and never see another human being.

I took a last gulp of my coffee. The chores awaited. It was my turn to feed the sheep. I didn't change into my barn clothes, just stuck my bare feet into my black rubber boots and walked across the yard in my nightdress. The lamb looked healthy, bonding with its mother. I leaned against the fence, watching it suckle, oblivious to the feeding-time frenzy in the larger pen beside them.

Afterward, I made another pot of coffee, returning to the edge of the porch, staring out at the horizon. Eventually others joined me; Tegan and Chris smoked a morning joint. I could hear Jeff noodling on the acoustic guitar in the living room. Every muscle in my body was tense, ready to pounce. Bryce was always the last to wake up unless it was his turn for morning chores.

I walked to the edge of the garden, where the chives and carrots would soon grow. I stood at the washing line. When Bryce came up soundlessly behind me, he hooked one arm around my neck in an embrace so quickly that I reflexively elbowed him in the gut. Hard. He doubled over. Normally I would have apologized immediately for such a crazy reaction but instead I yelled, "Don't fucking sneak up on me!" so loud that everyone around looked up. Bryce stared at me, bewildered but grinning. He was wearing dirty white cutoff shorts, and nothing else, and his bemused smile, his arms raised in mock surrender, only made me angrier.

I ran toward the pickup truck. I was in a nightgown, but I got in the cab of the truck, newly stenciled with the word *Sunflower!* on the driver's-side paneling. We always left the keys on the seat. I peeled out on the gravel, speeding off down the dirt driveway, and the road, over the horizon.

It was the first time I had to get away.

And the only time I came back.

CHAPTER 7

MISSY

TUCSON IS SO hot the air is trying to murder you. At this point, I have wicked PMS and I wish everyone harm. *Everyone.* Do you know the sound Alan makes when he's breathing in an otherwise quiet van? Cory went home after Dallas, and I was happy to see her go, not hovering, watching everything we do with a critical eye. The thing about cocaine is that it is a highly personal drug, makes you self-important, the sound of your own voice is a fucking dream, and man, aren't I pretty right now? I'm so pretty right now! That kind of shit. But if you do it too much and then stop, you become as annoying as everything around you. Is that what my voice *sounds* like? Your own weird fingers, the bruises on your legs. Every little thing about yourself is just fucking monstrous.

Coke feels good, until it doesn't. If I don't overdo it, though, a coke hangover is existential, quiet. The world becomes crystallized, cold to the touch. It's not unpleasant, unless you overdo it. The definition of overdoing it changes, subtly, over time.

I don't realize I've been overdoing until we get to Tucson

where I listen to Bailey, the semi-cross-eyed drug dealer, monologue about David Lynch for like, an *hour* while trying to buy drugs. I slip the baggie into the inside compartment of my makeup bag. And then I realize, holy fucking shit, I bought drugs on my own? This was usually Billy's job, and I was the tagalong. It's uncomfortable, this shift. People who actually buy the drugs aren't casual users.

I had to organize everyone who wanted some, and do it surreptitiously so Tom or Gord didn't hear. The other thing about coke is that nobody does it and doesn't like it, but some people can feel ambivalent about it until it is in front of them, and for others it becomes a Thing. Like potheads and people who like to smoke casually when offered. I am always in the latter camp.

Now what am I?

BEFORE SOUND CHECK in the evening, I find Billy chatting up the hot bartender, kneeling on a stool, hunched in a C over the bar, as she leans back against the ice machine, arms crossed and skeptical. She toys with one long strand of red hair, nodding at his monologue, then raises her eyebrows at me in a way that says, *Want a drink?*

"I just need this dork," I say, and drag Billy away, toward the women's bathroom. I sit on the long row of sinks, picking at flecks of minty nail polish, while he taps out some coke onto a paperback copy of *Blue Highways*. I don't like to prepare the bumps or lines. I want to avoid getting too comfortable with it. I want it to remain unnatural in my hands.

"Is it good?" The last bag Billy managed to score had

tasted especially Drano-ish, and burned going down. I'd felt briefly high and then virulently uncomfortable in my skin for the rest of the night.

"Oh yeah, this isn't bad." He leans in to chop it.

Billy snorts a caterpillar rail. I chop up the line he preps for me into one half its size. I don't want to die in a dumb way before I have a chance to write at least one more really good song, just to prove it wasn't dumb luck.

I watched people in the music scene do coke for years before I tried it. I didn't understand what I felt at first; the effects were intangible. "I don't understand it," I told Tom the first time. We were at an industry party and I was depressed because it was November, and I was still in school but had dropped a bunch of classes in order to play some short tours, and we'd just heard that we'd been turned down by the label we'd most wanted. I felt like I'd fucked up school for nothing. Everyone was fighting, and Tom was like a broken record, on a riff about how he had a baby now and didn't want to be in a band that went nowhere. Everyone was a messy combination of drunk and high, and I was tired of feeling bored and sober, so I did a tiny bump off the edge of a house key in the bathroom.

Tom cautioned me against it. "It's stupid, don't even try it once," he said. But he didn't take the bag from me when I grabbed it, and he schooled me in the details. He even did a small bump.

"I don't feel anything," I said later, on the dance floor.

"Missy, it's almost five in the morning, and we're *dancing*."

I looked around and realized it was true.

"Oh, right."

"And are you tired?"

"No, I feel like it's five in the afternoon after a really productive day."

"Well, it's five in the morning in shitty November and stuff actually sucks, so we should go home."

But Tom hasn't done drugs since his second kid was born. He doesn't want his children to know he died in a stupid, preventable way. He says it took a toll on him, too. He did so much MDMA in the rave years he has a hard time making enough serotonin. He takes a cocktail of antidepressants to deal with it. Somehow, this information didn't scare me. If you do something enough it seems normal and safe.

No one knows exactly how much drugs Billy does, but it doesn't seem to affect him. Ever. He's always on time, he never misses a rehearsal. Sometimes I watch him when he's high, and think about all the things I heard about drugs when I was growing up, how they would ruin your entire life: there was no other story about cocaine or other party drugs. What no one tells you in school is that actually so many people are high all the time, or indulge every once in a while, and that most people function just fine. Plus, with Billy, even though he's got a heavier habit, the band is his whole reason for living, so there's not much room for an addiction in the traditional sense of the word.

Twenty-one is a very present-tense age. Addiction is a past-tense problem.

BILLY ROCKS ON his feet, side to side, picking at a zit on his chin. I lean over and snort the smaller line, then apply lip gloss in the mirror, a color that makes them look bruised.

Billy knocks back a second line, then leans against the wall and starts to sweat, inhaling again, rubbing his chest with his hands. Jared walks in and taps his violin bow at my back, trying to unhook my bra strap through my thinning T-shirt. "Sound check, my little babies! Sound. Check. Time. In five."

I follow him into the house, where Tom sits on the edge of the bar talking with his kids on the house phone. The sound guy runs cables across the floor and mutters to himself. Tom holds the phone out. "Guys, it's Missy! Say hi to Missy!" I hear his two kids mumbling hello on the other end of the line. I hand the phone back to Tom and then do a series of handstands and cartwheels across the empty dance floor. I stand up and give a deep bow. The sound guy claps. I hear Tom say, "I love you," and then he laughs loudly and hangs up.

"My four-year-old said, 'I love you too, Daddy, but I love Mommy more,'" he says, laughing, but his eyes flash with fatigue and hurt.

I skip over and hug Tom. "He's four. He doesn't know how to lie yet," I say, rubbing Tom's head and squeezing him to my chest. Because I'm newly high, I turn the hug into a swaying slow dance that he pulls away from. I do a backflip away from him, then another deep bow. He claps.

So Tom and I did kiss once. It was like a moment I plucked from linear memory, extracted and dried out, to live somewhere else. We don't speak of it. It sorted out any attraction we may have had, and put it to rest.

I've kissed a lot of friends, and it doesn't mean anything. I figure that if you don't get that kind of behavior out of your system in your early twenties, you end up having affairs when you're old and boring. And I'm not in any hurry to be either.

THE SHOW IS terrible. It is hard to tell if the audience notices, or sees the looks Tom is giving us. Alan seems tired, and Billy stops three songs in to tell "stories" and the die-hard kids in the front row are loving it at first, like they're getting the real deal instead of just a habitual replaying of the album. But by the third time he does this, they start to look confused. A group of guys are laughing, and I'm wondering if they're laughing *at* us. Is the alt weekly reporter going to trash the show? This is, of course, the point where none of us are really high anymore, and so Tom and I slump into a sort of morose finishing of the set by rote memory. Jared is oblivious, hyping up the audience and dancing, and Billy is just . . . done. He's done before we even get to the encore.

The crowd claps and cheers for us to come back out as we drink water backstage and catch our breath. Tom grabs Billy by the shirt and says, "What the fuck is wrong with you tonight?"

Billy raises his hands in the air, in shock. "What? We were killing it out there!"

"Can you hear? Are you even present?" Tom yells. "We sound like we've never heard music before. Alan, tune your fucking bass, dude!"

"Relax, man," Alan says. "It's fine. Just an off night."

When he first joined the band, I thought that I would bond with Alan more than anyone. In most bands he's been in, he's usually the only gay guy and the only person of color. The band scene is mostly straight white dudes. But Alan mostly keeps to himself. And for some reason, he doesn't love me. He is always putting his hands on my shoulders and looking me in the eye and saying *Shhhh* and *Calm down, Missy, for fuck's sake*. Which makes me like him more. But he's just chill. And so talented. He's been in a million bands, and I feel like if we didn't want him anymore, he'd just sidle up to another band and play bass for them. But for Tom, Billy, and me, this band is our identity.

Tom storms back onstage and starts playing the intro beat to our encore song, as Alan gets his bass back from the sound guy, and joins him. Cheers ensue.

Billy does a quick bump. "I don't know what his fucking problem is," he says. He reaches over and runs his hand along my jaw. I think he might kiss me, and brace myself, but instead he laughs and puts a key under my nose.

The encore is fantastic. Billy looks like he's fucking the entire audience at once. The alt weekly guy is pumping his fist, his face blooming with satisfaction. After the show, I bring him a beer from the backstage green room. He's taking notes in a small notebook leaned up against the stage as the crew is cleaning up. I reach over and give him the set list and the beer, touching his hand a little.

"You better be telling your readers how pretty I am," I say, giving him a little wink. I can see his expression shift with the knowledge that he could probably get laid later. He tries to play it cool, but I can see that perfect combination of nervousness and need.

I love that shift. I reach for his hand and bring him backstage, though unfortunately Tom is raging by the time we reach the green room.

"We have to get it the fuck together!"

No one appears to know what he's talking about. I plunge my hand into the bowl of gummy candies, throw some to the alt weekly guy, who is furiously scribbling and watching us.

Billy tries to keep the peace. "Dude, you're overreacting. So the night wasn't predictable. It got a little unruly, but that's okay! That's rock 'n' roll."

At this, Tom kicks the craft table. A bowl of fruit and a tray of soda and beer tumble to the ground.

I don't know why, but I start to laugh hysterically.

"You're such a fucking baby!" Billy says, laughing.

Alan grabs a broom from nearby and pushes the broken glass aside.

Tom, breathing hard, face flushed, storms off.

LATER THAT NIGHT, I am left with Billy, the bartender, the alt weekly guy, and the rest of the drugs. We end up at an after-hours bar, a blur of karaoke and beer that tastes rusty and watered down. After that, we go back to the bartender's house, a modest bungalow with a red-dirt yard covered in stones, desert flowers, and cacti, with an in-ground pool in the backyard. My memories are point form: I throw the reporter's notebook in the pool; I feel like a wild horse, every step is a gallop; we all peel off our clothes and swim around. I remember I am fearless. I remember feeling like a kid, and like I'm embracing the best moments of life.

Before alt weekly guy sort of half fucks me in a coked-out haze on a chaise longue, I hold his cock in my hand. "Keep these details for your diary, okay?" I make my tone both menacing and then sweet, which I can feel is the perfect combination. This is the moment I enjoy most, when I know that someone will do anything I want them to.

He agrees with a whimper.

The actual sex is unremarkable, physically. There is always a point where my mind wanders and I think, *why do people do this?* I look at whoever I'm with, and I can see in their faces why they do it. It looks like bliss, like they're winning at everything, like they can't believe they are where they are. Even if they're not having the best sex of their lives—how could they, with a half-passed-out girl as dawn nears—they still look complete, content. In those moments, it's as though they're speaking a language I don't speak and I can't think too much about it or I'll get sad.

Later, after the alt weekly guy has scurried home, the sun pinks the edge of the horizon, and I lie awake listening to the insistent pounding of my heart, running in weird little skitter beats. A crow circles my chair. We lock eyes. "I love you," I mutter at the crow. He cocks his head. He eats a cigarette butt. I give him a sparkling bobby pin I'd been using to pin back my too-long bangs. I fall into a minor reverie as the sun comes up.

The sun warms my body like I'm a squirming seedling, bringing me back to life. There's something vaguely holy about a coke hangover. My skin tingles alive, my brain is slower, but then so are my worries.

I stand at the kitchen sink, staring out the window. I don't remember what city I am in. Wherever we are, outside everything is dried by the sun, a splotchy palette of reds and oranges and browns. I drink several cups of water out of a mug with a *Cathy* comics decal on the side. I make a pot of coffee and when I open the fridge for some milk I see the calendar and realize that today is my birthday.

I am twenty-two.

The bathroom door is locked, so I pee outside in a bush, my weak stream pooling in tiny decorative stones.

I touch a cactus. I don't recommend doing that. But it wakes me up.

I peer into the bathroom window, and I can see Billy fucking the bartender from behind, up against the sink. Her ass is just perfect—Billy's hands sink into it as he pounds her. She's quiet but yelping in moments. I turn away and hear him come as I tend to the cactus wound in my finger.

The bartender drives us back to the hotel in time to meet the rest of the band. We have to leave early to be on schedule. I watch blood rise in my fingertip, pressing it into my leg. The cactus meant business.

WHEN WE'RE BACK in the van, I clock that Tom's bad mood has faded, so I cuddle up to him. I feel a slight resistance in his arm, and then he pulls me in closer. He takes a rainbow cupcake out of his knapsack.

"Happy birthday. I can smell that you've already had a birthday party without me?"

The cupcake has a little toothpick with a paper flag in it that says MISSY, and a little cello doodle. I'm so touched that tears come to my eyes, which embarrasses us both. I want to seal it in a bag and never eat it.

"You're the best," I say. "Really. Like, thank you."

The band sings me "Happy Birthday" in five-part harmony, and then we fall back into our own thoughts, watching

the scenery blow by us. I see the northbound signs for Phoe-
nix.

"Oh, we were in Tucson—right!" I accidentally say out
loud.

"Have you been sucking on the tailpipe? What the fuck is
wrong with you?" Tom asks.

"She's been sucking on something!" Billy mutters from
behind us.

Alan turns around from the driver's seat. "Sluts make the
most of life."

Alan barely ever weighs in. Validated, I give him a high
five.

I squeeze my legs together, feel that familiar ache signaling the recent presence of someone else.

Tom doesn't speak to me again until we hit the outskirts
of Las Vegas.

CHAPTER 8

CAROLA

———

I CAUGHT A GREYHOUND bus back from Concord. I
was attempting to make it home in time for the meeting of the women who had been involved with the guru.
Some of them had felt that it needed to happen at night, during the full moon, in a clearing halfway up the hill behind the
center. But I was dreading it. I just no longer felt like engag-
ing, or even being around anybody. The feeling that I required a ring of space around me, and for no one to talk to me
for days, was new and uncomfortable. This was a recent development. For so many years, my life had been about community, making groups of people work together toward a
better good, and lately all I wanted was to go places and have
no one know where I was, to speak to no one for hours and
hours.

I PULLED THE music magazine out of the bag. I stared at the
brash young woman on the cover and tried to reconcile her
with the child I had left behind at Sunflower, blond blunt-cut

bangs and cotton dresses, singing "You Are My Sunshine" and playing the ukulele.

I flipped to the article on the Swearwolves, skimming through to the passages about my daughter:

It's clear from the way she interacts with the rest of the "wolves" that Alamo is the sun they orbit around, even though Billy is the enigmatic front man. "She's a bit of a feral child," says Tom, the drummer. "And he's the dad!" Missy quips, while cartwheeling through the open dance floor during sound check. But the feral child persona holds some truth, as Alamo, née Melissa Wood, was raised on a commune in rural Vermont, where she had more freedom than most in the Reagan era of stranger-danger hysteria and yuppie parenting.

In fact, the one ballad on the album, "Not Looking for You Anymore," is written by Alamo about her mother, who abandoned the family. "No one knows where she is, including Missy," confides Tom, when Missy is out of earshot. "But Missy's not afraid to talk about it, she'll tell anyone if you ask her." He blushes.

And so I do ask her. After the show, I wait for Alamo and newcomer fiddler Jared Keenan to finish playing an extended cover of "Bela Lugosi's Dead" in the parking lot under the full moon as the gear is loaded. Alamo is hyper but charming, the kind of person who, when asked about her missing mother, might look mournful for a few flickers, then jump on your back and demand a piggyback ride around the parking lot instead of answering.

Finally allowing me to put her back on the ground, she puts both hands on my face, looks deep into my eyes in a way that feels moderately discomfiting and certainly unprofessional, and says, "Some people are meant to be mothers, and some people are meant to be free."

I knew I had no right to be hurt by that, but I felt deeply wounded and misunderstood. Maybe she would get it if she ever had her own children. Maybe she said other things, but the writer just emphasized the most salacious bits. And as if she were raised like a feral child—I spent every day of those thirteen years making sure she was safe, warm, fed, and listened to. No parent is perfect. She wasn't wandering the forests with the wolves! But perhaps the reason I felt so wounded by it was because it was true. I wasn't meant to be a mother if I gave up. Even if she didn't remember how I was a good mother for so many years, there's some absolute truth to that, even if I can't bear to look at it.

I thought about how I described my own parents when asked: my mother was remote and demanding; my father, violent and selfish. But they were more than that, too. Of course they were. My mother was smart, cunning, organized. My father could be joyous and impulsive, with a sharp mechanical mind. But in conversation, I always reverted to the short form, the negative. Why do we do that? Why is it important to us to mark our families by their faults? We can't control how our children think of us, how they remember the worst most of the time, how they reflect ourselves back to us in ways that force us to reckon with truths we'd rather push aside. I make a note to introduce this line of inquiry in a future Helping Your Self seminar at the center, one of a few that I lead from time to time.

THAT FIRST TIME I left Sunflower, after elbowing Bryce, I had been so lost, in a state of pure panic and rage. I drove until the anger subsided into a slow, syrupy sadness. I went across the Canadian border, toward my sister, Marie. By then, she lived in a small Quebec town that wasn't a town really, but rather four houses on the side of a two-lane highway, like they all ran out of gas there and just decided to build houses out of detritus lying about. You could easily miss the sign that read SOUTH BROCKTON if you didn't happen to glance up. And there was no Brockton to be south of, but no one seemed to mind. Two of the houses looked as if they were about to fall down, with plastic stapled over windows, tarpaper exposed where pieces of the siding were missing, and like a patchwork quilt on otherwise metal roofs. There were wheel-less cars in the yard, and scatterings of junk, as though maybe no one had cleaned up after a tornado. But people still lived there, you could tell by the signs of life apparent through the mess: the clothes on the line, toys scattered in the grass, rows of ripe tomato plants, kids getting off the school bus and wandering up the drives.

My sister had met a man named Gareth through AA who was born in South Brockton and now managed a small convenience store on the first floor of one of those houses. They lived in the basement apartment below it. It looked like a good place to rob. You could run for miles in any direction and only come across some deer, maybe a farm or two. But Marie seemed happy with Gareth. They'd both spent a year following the Grateful Dead, had done too many drugs and lost themselves in it. They were eccentric in complementary ways, and being away from others kept them from falling off the wagon. She'd planted sunflowers all around the outside of the store, to obscure the crumbling facade. She hauled all the old junk the previous owners had left behind—a children's wagon with one rusted wheel, dented buckets, ancient beer bottles, half-stuffed armchairs, old mayonnaise jars—and piled it neatly on one side. The man who owned the building lived upstairs and was too old to do much physical labor anymore. Gareth was hopeful he might will them the house when he passed. They'd never seen any family around.

The ragged-looking cluster of houses sat among bucolic meadows of wildflowers, rolling hills that seemed to go on forever unless interrupted by equally pastoral forests. I stood beside the truck in the store's tiny parking lot and thought briefly that I could buy some land here, build my own house. I could get a trailer, or build a yurt or a lean-to and live simply. The rain had just stopped, and a mist hovered around my bare feet, soaked into my nightdress, the smell of cedar and rich, wet earth. I could live alone.

Or sort of alone.

If my instincts were right.

I found Marie watching *Days of Our Lives* on the small black-and-white TV behind the counter. I stared at her for a moment before she looked up and noticed me.

"Jesus Christ! Ma belle! You finally left the hippie farm."

She gave me a Styrofoam cup of coffee from the machine by the candy and gum and looked me over. We hadn't seen each other since our parents' funeral. There had been so many cops, and I couldn't handle their show of sorrow. Marie, still pregnant then, had pulled me out of the handshaking line after I kept leaning in to every man in uniform to say, *Thank you, but you know he killed her.*

"They're going to put you in an asylum," she'd said, holding me in a trembling hug in the church hallway. "And what is it going to accomplish? We can't put him in jail, he's dead, too."

We packed up the house and sold it, but there wasn't much left after we paid off my father's substantial debts. Turns out he had taken out a second mortgage and gambled away much of what could have been their nest egg. I was able to buy the secondhand pickup truck for Sunflower, but that was it. My father working his whole life had resulted in this one truck. Marie had paid off Gareth's credit card.

Since then, Marie and I had been talking on the phone more, thwarted attempts to grieve.

"It's good to see you."

She pointed to a door with a sign on it that read NO ENTRY. "Go downstairs and take a nap. The baby should sleep another hour. I'll be off work at three."

I'd never seen her apartment before, and it was so much like our parents' place I felt instantly sleepy. She'd taken most of the furniture from their house. Even the mug I took from the cupboard was once my mother's. As soon as I saw it, the yellow flower decal, I shuddered into a sob. This had happened to me often since their death. An otherwise ordinary day and then a smell, or the sight of someone who looked like her, and my whole body would come undone. It would pass quickly, and then I would feel numb, a sort of ghost of grief following my body for the rest of the day. I buried my nose in the flower mug and took a deep whiff, trying to find anything on the earth that was still of her. Nothing. Lemon-scented Sunlight dish soap, her faithful brand, was a small consolation.

Marie had made every excuse for our father's bad behavior before he died, and her choice of boyfriends usually somewhat resembled him, though Gareth looked like a gentle, shy bear of a man. I hadn't been around long enough to know if he was similar when they were alone.

She had my father's black-and-green standing ashtray and the matching sugar bowl and creamer set that my mother had been so proud of, the overstuffed leather couch scratched along the bottom from two long-haired tabby cats who napped in the shallow windowsills that met the ceiling. Even with all the lights on, I was aware they lived in a basement and what might have felt sad in another moment felt comforting, like a warm cave, a place to fall into.

I peeked at the baby, sleeping in a cradle in the living room. He was so beautiful, peaceful. I wanted to pick him up and hold him to my chest. My heart filled with longing. Perhaps I *could* be a mother. His curled hands, his little sighs. I had the odd urge to put his tiny toes in my mouth and nibble them.

Perhaps it was just Sunflower, the endless collective meetings and ever-evolving dynamics, maybe that was the problem, not having a baby. Maybe it would be okay if we could smooth out the gender dynamics at Sunflower. I stood and watched him for a long time, letting the sight of this new life soothe the grief I felt clawing at my chest. Then I sat down on their couch and considered the future. I stared at the framed photo of my parents on the wall. Bryce was nothing like my father. He couldn't even kill a spider. And his optimism! His hope. That would be a good thing for a child. I felt a little better before I dozed off on the couch.

I WOKE UP when I heard my sister shuffling around in the kitchen area behind the couch. A few minutes later Marie placed a small plate with a piece of raisin toast in front of me, bumps of butter still too cold to melt on either side.

"Did you finally leave Bryce?" she asked, placing a cup of tea beside the toast.

"No, well, not really. It's just—well, it's too soon to really know, but I think I might be pregnant. And I just couldn't stand it. Couldn't stand him," I said.

She picked up the baby and handed him over.

"I'm scared," I said, staring into the baby's eyes. He stared back, which felt both otherworldly and like I was in a horror movie.

"Let's just say, if you are pregnant, it's nothing like you expect. It's both better and worse than everything you can imagine."

I looked into his little face. He was old enough now to hold up his head by himself, and was making a funny little smile. I sat down on the couch and stared at him as he grabbed my hair and necklaces.

"What didn't you expect?"

"Well, I didn't expect my vagina to look like a ripped seam for months. Still can't take a shit without crying."

"Oh my god, that is so gross."

"Yeah, well," Marie said, lighting a cigarette.

"You're still smoking?" I asked. "You know they say that's not good for children."

"Do they now," she said, taking another pull on the ciga-rette. "We survived, didn't we?"

"I guess."

"You'll give up all that hippie bullshit once you have a kid, mark my words," she said. "I use a bottle, and I don't care for the guilt other moms give me. They can fuck right off. You do what feels right, don't listen to everyone else. They don't know. They've all got money, for one. And we don't," she says, gesturing to their modest surroundings. "Well, Bryce does, doesn't he?"

"Not really."

"But his mother does."

"I guess. I just don't know. I don't know about anything. I don't know how I feel, what I want. I was so excited when we talked about building a family, but now that it's maybe hap-pening I'm completely lost."

"That's normal. You're scared. You'll be a great mom. You were a huge pain in my ass growing up but you stopped me from getting killed numerous times. You'll be better than our mom."

"Hey, Mom tried her best, given what she was working with," I said. Back to the normal routine of me defending Mom and her defending Dad. "I know I was always mad at her, but I miss her," I said.

"Do you miss him?"

"I guess I miss Friday night Dad," I said. "Sometimes."

Friday night Dad was always so happy, a six-pack under one arm, and some treats from the corner store. Mint choco-late ice cream in the soup bowls.

"I miss Mom, too," Marie says, stubbing out her smoke after one last puff. "It's hard sometimes, I want to call her when the baby has a fever. And Gareth's mom is a bitch. She'd leave the baby in the yard for hours if I didn't watch her every minute. I don't trust her."

"I'm sorry I haven't visited. You could always come stay with us."

Marie snorted. "I'm not bringing a baby to your lunatic farm."

"But you want me to raise a kid there? It's not a lunatic farm, it's an intentional community. Our principles are based on love, compromise, active listening—"

"Spare me, Carola."

"Juniper."

"Whatever. You hang with hippies and you're weird and all that but underneath you're still the girl that organized all the jars in the pantry alphabetically."

"I object to the word *lunatic* is all. That word would describe our childhood more accurately, wouldn't it?"

"Oh my god, you're so melodramatic. Our family was normal. All families have their issues. People aren't perfect. All fathers drink."

"Normal fathers don't murder their wives. And aren't you an addict?"

"There wasn't a language for it for his generation, is what I'm saying. Men have it harder when they quit. They don't know how to feel their feelings."

The baby started to cry, as if willing us to change the subject.

A few hours later, after we'd been poring over old photos and sitting with the baby, Gareth came down from the store.

"Oh hey," he said, giving me an awkward half hug.

"Hey, Gareth."

He settled into the couch and I realized I'd clearly interrupted their routine. It was close quarters. The baby started to cry again. I handed him back to Marie and decided to go home.

She lent me an old sweatshirt with a Rolling Stones logo on the front, and some flip-flops. As I pulled on the sandals, she presented me with a small velvet box and opened it up like we were on a soap opera. We used to do it as little kids, pretend to propose to each other like we'd seen on TV. It was a necklace I remembered Mom wearing every Christmas.

"You loved this when you were a kid, remember? It's a ruby." Before I could answer, she turned me around and did up the clasp. I touched the stone and remembered how it sparkled when I would fall asleep in Mom's lap at midnight Mass.

"It looks great," she said, nodding. "I think she'd have wanted you to have it."

I GOT BACK in the truck. I turned the engine over, fiddled with the radio dial until I found a clear station. "Love Will Keep Us Together" was playing. I pressed my fingers into the loose tobacco in the ashtray between the seats, a habit, and rolled the window down. Though it was a hit song, and I'd heard it playing almost everywhere, I took it as a sign. I started to feel a rush of love for Bryce, for his calm and consistent love, his excitement about life. I imagined his clear eyes and the way he felt when I cuddled up against him at night. A baby could be good, I thought. This would be great. My sorrow was replaced by a kind of manic energy. I wanted to be home immediately, not in five to six hours' time. I drove over the border as it was getting quite late, and I didn't usually travel the back roads much after dark. I got turned around a few times. At one point, it was too remote for me to get a consistent radio signal, and I stared up at the full moon as I drove, no other cars on the road, absorbing the quiet, the blanket of stars above me.

I reached up to touch the ruby pendant around my neck, and as I did, it fell off the chain and into my lap. I slowed down to find it, and as I gripped it victoriously in one hand, I peered up just in time to see a deer jump over the hood. I slammed on the brakes. If I'd been going slightly faster, the doe certainly could have killed me.

I clutched the stone, breath ragged, and pulled the truck over to the shoulder. I needed to catch my breath. I sat there quietly for long enough that three baby fawns ambled up out of the ditch and crossed the road, over to their mom who was waiting in the first layer of trees. I got out and looked at the hood of the pickup for dent marks; there were none. The mother appeared to be walking fine. A second earlier and this would've all been different.

"Thank you, Mom," I said out loud, and looked up at the knotting of stars where I imagined she'd been watching, finally protecting me.

Now you just stop yer sniveling and go home, she would have said.

A few hours later, I pulled up to Sunflower and parked the truck between the tractor and Chris's beat-up VW van with the perpetual flat tire. I was still wide awake from the near-miss. It was two in the morning and I realized there were lights on in the barn, and so I went to shut them off. When I did I heard Bryce's voice call out, "Hey, I'm still in here!" in the dark. I flipped the lights back on and found him inside the pen.

We regarded each other for a moment, acknowledging that I'd been gone.

"What's wrong with the lamb?" I finally said.

"We have to feed this one, the mother rejected her. I asked Arnie next door what to do." He was holding her in his arms and feeding her with a repurposed beer bottle affixed with a long rubber nipple.

He looked up at me, rubbed his beard. "She's eating again! I think she's going to be fine. I have to get up and do this every three hours or so."

As he rattled off what the farmer next door had advised him to do, I looked at this man, the one I'd always hoped I'd be with forever, as though we were strangers. Sometimes this happened, as though a spotlight shone down from the ceiling to remind me that all our familiarity could distort the beauty that only newness can bring. He had a ring of sweat around the collar of his white T-shirt; his navy blue toque was stuck with hay and half falling off his head. He cradled the lamb as she pulled the milk from the bottle. I could see it reviving her. I realized that maybe this would work, maybe we *could* start a family.

A FEW WEEKS later I went to the local doctor, who had an office in his house and confirmed what I already knew. Bryce honked the horn randomly as we drove back to the farm. *I'm gonna be a dad!* I told Bryce what I'd been thinking since I visited my sister. Maybe we could start over, just the two of us. Sunflower was a fun experiment, and maybe it was best to leave it at that. Bringing a kid into it, how would that even work? This was what my body was telling me, that we had to be a team, a unit. That putting up a fence with fifteen people was easier than with only two, but raising kids that way might be more difficult.

I could tell by the way Bryce kept his eyes on the road that he wasn't in favor of this. But he was also tender, and didn't want to upset me. And he was still thrown by my abrupt departure the previous month. The commune had been his one big dream, and he'd taken all the expectations he'd had to go into business or finance and turned that drive—and inherited money—into making his political ideas a way of life, a working community that was truly equitable. I realized in that moment that he felt as if I was asking him to give up his job, his whole life. And it didn't feel fair.

But I also wanted him to care more about me than about the commune.

To me, starting the commune was more a great experiment, a question. I always thought at some point we would move on. But to Bryce it was an answer. I was drawn to his resolve, his steadiness and sureness. Can you blame me? His vision was exciting, but I have to admit I was never entirely convinced we could pull it off. I knew as little as he did about raising animals, working the land, and keeping an old farmhouse from falling apart even more than it already was. Still, I was delighted to discover that I had some untapped talents, and he couldn't have built the fences, dug the ditches, or put in the new windows without me. My planning, research, and elbow grease made those things happen. I was also better with people—Bryce could talk to anyone about socialism, at great length, in fact, but I was the one who organized meetings and delegated tasks, helped with conflict resolution. I was also the one who could focus on the details: starting a credit account at the feed store, putting tarps over the wood-pile, having the tree branches trimmed before the spring storms. Bryce was the idea person and I was the action person. In that way, we were perfectly matched. The other members of the commune were idealistic dreamers who hadn't found their way in the working world. So while everyone loved being there, very few really embraced the work. In fact I suspected that some of the core members, and the friends who would come to stay periodically—we had an anyone-can-pitch-a-tent rule—liked the commune because it meant they could take a time-out and "work on themselves." Everyone has their own process. So I tried to just go with it when Chris decided to brew beer, decided that this new business venture would make us lots of money. Then three months later, I tripped over the rusting equipment in the basement while going to check the furnace.

After we drove up the driveway, we lingered outside the truck before bringing in the groceries. I wrapped myself around Bryce in a big hug, not sure if I was reassuring him or myself. And to this day, I don't know what switch turned off in me when I said, "Never mind, it's just an idea. I'm just worried about having a baby. What if I'm not a good mother?" Is there a button that makes women do this? A switch in our wiring? Is backpedaling an actual pedal in our makeup? When do we decide that our dreams are not as important as our partners'? That *we* are not as important? So much work in my years since has been trying to solve this riddle.

"Are you kidding? You're going to be amazing," he said, hugging me tightly to him. I looked up at his face and saw how his eyes bore deeply down on me. This man loved me. I also could see that he had relaxed because nothing was going to change. Maybe he thought my idea was a hiccup, a mood swing, but it had been dismissed. I decided to drop it, at least for now.

WHEN WE WALKED into the house it became clear that Chris, who'd decided to take magic mushrooms that morning, had impulsively spray-painted the living room a bright green color. We were supposed to make all major community decisions by collective. We had lengthy meetings every Tuesday and Thursday afternoons.

I stood there, holding my celebratory bottle of apple cider, and saw Chris, naked, huddled in a corner, holding the empty spray-paint can and grinning.

I just lost it. "What the fuck is wrong with you?"

Chris, still quite high, began to giggle in a fit, apologizing but still unable to stop giggling.

"I'm laughing but I'm scared of you, Juniper!" He laughed as if I'd made the funniest joke in the world, gulping, unable to stop. "Trust me, you're terrifying!"

That's when Tegan said, "Guys, guys, I'm pregnant, too! Our kids will be like siblings! Chris and I are pregnant!"

Chris started jumping up and down, covered in green paint.

I wasn't sure what to do with that information. It stopped my tirade. Tegan was wearing her trademark terry-cloth romper, the one that looked like red shorts and tube top with the white piping, that upon closer look was joined together. Her wisps of blond hair escaped a messy ponytail on the top of her head. It seemed impossible that she could be pregnant, being so young and immature herself.

"Are you sure? And you're sure you want to keep it?"

At this Tegan looked offended.

"What, you against abortion or something?"

"No, I just want a baby. I've always wanted a baby," Tegan said, indignant, as if I should have known that.

"Sorry, I'm just tired," I said, and as the rest of the group came inside, celebrating the news and admiring the crazy green wall, I retreated upstairs. I stretched out on the bed and watched the late-afternoon shadows dapple the walls. There was a quiet, mouselike scratch at my door, which turned into an insistent tapping.

"Juniper? Juniper—hi, are you in there?" The door cracked open and Tegan padded into the room, coming to sit on the edge of the bed.

"There you are," she said. She curled around me. I felt hope and exhilaration in Tegan's embrace.

"We'll do this together," she said, combing her fingers through my hair.

But all I felt was uncertainty.

CHAPTER 9

MISSY

YOU ARE SUPPOSED to feel amped in Vegas: fists full of cash, dancing for the groping lights, drawn to the seductive smell of brief, hot luck. The buildings seem blanketed in synthetic fabrics stretched tight, the pavement pulsing. You're supposed to wear a short skirt, to feel like you're perpetually getting finger-banged by a glittering, generous angel you'll never have to see in the daylight. Things like water and fresh air aren't necessary for survival in Vegas; it's all sweat and swagger, booze and amphetamines, coughing up sequins into your morning-after cocktail. If you don't leave Vegas with a UTI, you haven't done it right.

But we're smart about it this tour. The van stops on the outskirts just short of the fantasy. I feel physically depleted, but it's my twenty-second birthday, and the hangover has settled into some serious birthday blues. I want to do *something*. For the first time in ages, I feel a little homesick, probably because I usually wake up on my birthday to a call from my dad singing into the phone. Last year, Amita made me pancakes and we spent the day playing hooky and watching John Hughes movies until we went out dancing. I usually visit my granny at some point close to my birthday, and she makes me a molasses cake in the shape of a bunny, like she did when I was little. But no one can easily phone me here, though Granny and my dad know my tour schedule and have my management's number in case of emergencies. So I am kind of holding out hope, feeling fragile with my coke hangover and needing a nap. The guys want to go gambling, but I don't want to spend my birthday inside a dark casino, surrounded by desperate energy and potentially sketchy buffet food. I tell them to go win me some birthday money.

When I wake up, the room smells musty and I decide it's too nice out to spend the afternoon waiting for a phone call. I debate phoning my dad, just to hear the voice of someone who has known me for longer than a few years, but talking to my dad these days is like reading those free typo-ridden magazines at health food stores that tell you you can avoid cancer by tucking crystal into your pockets. I was used to it; all the parents at Sunflower had been alternative medicine types and free spirits. Taylor's mom, Tegan, for example, wouldn't even look up if Taylor was standing on top of the chicken coop preparing to take flight with wings made out of a gingham tablecloth. She wanted to honor our experiments. My mom was the exception. She was the one who took us to the doctor for actual medicine, not just treating us with essential oils and goldenseal. She noticed when Taylor was just pretending to know how to read, and then sat with her every night practicing her letters. One time, she told everyone we were going to the thrift store for new sneakers, but really we were getting vaccinated. That would have blown shit up had the others found out. In my memories, my mother was always watching over us. So when she left the farm, we knew we were on our own. We knew we could do whatever we wanted to, but we also knew that our only real parent had flown the coop. Our fathers and the other adults felt like taller kids who knew how to fix things.

That was why it was so weird when she left, out of all the adults. Most of them taking off wouldn't have been that strange in the grand scheme of things. But my mom, Juniper, she was the one who knew about the world and seemed to care about our well-being the most. Why would the one who was the most invested drop off the face of the earth and never come back, or call, or write, or somehow check in to see if we were okay? Didn't she ever wonder how we turned out?

Sometimes I fantasized that she had hit her head and had amnesia, like on the soaps I watched with Granny after school in grade eight. Or she had a brain worm and it made her crazy and she thought her name was Brenda and she worked in a shoe store somewhere in Alabama. Maybe she got lost in the woods and became feral.

Then one day in my first year of university I was on the subway, and a kid was screaming and throwing his food on everyone and the mom was shushing uselessly at him, and I thought, *Oh, oh, this is why.* Being a parent is actually a black hole of never-ending sorrow and boredom and maybe that's why she left.

I DECIDE TO at least check my email, so I find an Internet café in a nearby strip mall. I check my inbox about once a month, and while I wait for the dial-up connection to go through, I doodle in my journal and eat a pack of cherry Twizzlers. I am still feeling a bit hungover.

I expect to see a birthday message or two, and I do have one from Amita, who catches me up on all the goings-on back in Montreal. There's another message, from my high school crush Steve—random! *I'm not sure if this is still your email address, but happy birthday. I saw you on SNL!* I press delete.

It's a strange feeling, to be known by strangers, but to feel lonely. I suppose it's a cliché. When we play festivals— which we actually are doing here in Vegas—and I watch some of the bands, how closed off they are from even the other bands, so accustomed to being asked for photos and followed around, it does look lonely. I'm beginning to get a tiny taste of that.

I make my way back to the motel and drag a blue chaise longue beside the pool. Everything about the motel is made to look fancy, but up close everything is totally cheap— plastic flowers, plastic wineglasses, inexpensive wine disguised in champagne bottles, clusters of plastic jewels bedazzled onto the furniture. I massage my sore hip with some Tiger Balm, and pull my gray tube dress a little farther toward my knees.

The pool is the nose in the C-shaped smile of drive-up rooms, and two little girls in matching lime-green bathing suits cannonball into the water while their father sips a take-out cup of coffee on another chaise longue. He is the kind of guy who winks at me when his daughters aren't looking, and I briefly consider how his skin might feel against mine. But then I see a Confederate flag tattoo on the biceps he is faux-casually flexing.

Most depressing birthday ever? I write in my journal.

I draw a sad, wilting flower before I remember this is probably a hangover mood, not real feelings. In reality, my life is pretty great.

These feelings will pass, I write.

I maneuver under a tented motel towel to keep from burning, and try to write some new lyrics, which results in a scrawled list of progressively awful clichés and forced rhymes. I fold the failed pages in the middle and rip them out, stuffing them in a coffee cup. Some musicians can write on tour, but I'm not one of them.

SEVERAL BANDS FROM the festival have also booked the same motel, so when a gangly tomboy walks by with drumsticks in her back pocket, I'm not surprised. She nods at me from behind giant sunglasses and I recognize her as the drummer for a riot grrl band. To best describe her, I'll just say she is often mistaken for David Bowie. Everyone notices her, and by that I mean everyone wants to fuck her. When we crossed paths at a festival in Atlanta earlier on the tour, she flirted with me by the snack table.

She has tattooed arms and wears several bike-chain and leather-band bracelets, and an open plaid shirt over a white tank top that says *Daddy*. I can't remember her name.

"Hi there, Ms. Alamo," she says, stopping to block my sunlight. I peek out at her from under a cupped hand.

"Hey there, where's the rest of your band?"

"Trying to find a macrobiotic food place."

"Good luck to them, this is fucking Vegas. Want some of these?" I proffer a bright green bag of sour cream and onion chips. She nods and reaches in to grab a handful, then offers me a cold can of beer from her canvas army bag.

I take a sip while she settles into the chaise longue next to me, loosening her plaid shirt, then taking it off. The beer helps with my hangover. One of the green-bathing-suited kids turns from the diving board and gives us a semitoothless smile.

"Are you a boy or a girl?" the little girl asks, fixating on Amy? Alissa? Not remembering is going to get embarrassing.

"Neither."

"That makes sense." She jumps off the board. Her father offers us both a scowl.

I laugh, but hope she wasn't uncomfortable. "Does that happen to you a lot?"

"Yeah. Kids say what adults are thinking, but they're usually a lot nicer about it."

I feel like a shy teenager, unsure what to say next. I take a generous sip of the beer that is rapidly warming in the sun.

"So, what are you guys up to today?" I ask.

"I dunno. The band wants to go get their tarot cards read."

"Mine went gambling," I say.

"Ha, so gendered. Is it tough being the only girl in your band?"

"There's more performative farting than I wish, but it's generally not bad. I grew up on a commune so I'm used to being around lots of people. Is it hard to be with all women?"

"Well, there's too much emotional processing and our periods are all synced, but I prefer it to gigging with dudes, which I've done a lot."

We watch the girls in the pool do handstands. I press my fingers into the empty beer can, wishing I had another. I'm not sure that we have much in common, and my high school shyness has returned with a fierceness. Just as I'm about to make an excuse to sneak back to my room, she hands me another beer from her bag and tells me she's rented a car since the band will be here for a few days, then asks me if I want to go to a lake until sound check.

"Fuck yeah, I do."

BY THE TIME we get to Lake Mead I learn her name is Andie. She's older than me, though I would have guessed younger. She has a habit of playing with the little hair she has left on her head, growing out in tiny spikes from a recent shave, running her hands through it to punctuate what she says. A vegan but not an asshole about it, she's been surviving on bean burritos, backstage fruit bowls, and packs of peanuts for the last few months. She's been in bands since the late '80s, when she wasn't even old enough to get into bars, and pretty much lives on the road, but has a steady girlfriend in Los Angeles.

"When I'm home I like to be really domestic. I've started making pickles and jams. Right before we left, my girlfriend and I canned enough tomatoes for like, years." She tells me about how they worked all day putting tomatoes in jars. She felt so fulfilled and tired, and they fell asleep really soundly, and woke up to what they thought were gunshots—they live in L.A., so it isn't inconceivable—and they dove under the bed. Finally they emerged and crept into the kitchen and all the jars had unsealed, and there was tomato and glass everywhere. At first, they wondered if the jars had been shot, but then they realized that they hadn't properly sealed the jars and so the air had tried to escape, causing them all to explode. She still has tomato sauce stains on her sneakers.

I can tell she is the kind of shy I can deal with, relate to, but I know that other musicians think she's snobby and remote, too cool for school. That's notable, since everyone is affecting too cool. "The way I deal with music industry bullshit from dudes is to just keep my head down, play harder, play better. That's what has got me here," she says, "and it's nice to have a break from all that in this new band."

We trek out to a quiet spot away from the tourists. Andie shuffles her motorcycle boots in the sand, like she's trying to figure out how to be at a beach. Everything about her is the opposite of the surroundings: the leather boots, the black jeans, the tank top. We watch some teenagers trying to hide a bong under a beach umbrella as we walk by.

"Were you a skid in high school?" she asks.

"I was in the school orchestra and never had boyfriends."

"That cannot be true! Not with what I've heard about you," she says.

"Band geeks are always the pervs." I shrug.

We find a slightly private spot and I lay one of the towels I swiped from our motel down on the sand.

We drink a few more beers and trade gossip about the bands we both know. The sun and beer have an anesthetizing effect.

"So what have you heard about me?" she says.

"I dunno. Only that you're gay." That really *is* the only

thing I've heard. Most dudes in bands, the same ones who think they're so liberal, reading Malcolm X biographies and wearing pro-choice T-shirts, are so weird about gay people. Usually it's some guy watching Andie walk by who whispers, "She's a dyke," and then seeing my expression, adds quickly, "and a really great drummer."

"Ugh, I hate that that's my only notable tidbit."

"One guy couldn't believe Team Dresch are all dykes. He was like, 'They're too good!'"

"They are the best." She laughs.

"I guess there are few of your people in the indie rock world. But I also heard you banged Courtney."

"She was very drunk. But in my defense, I was much drunker."

"What have you heard about me?"

"That you're some kind of cello prodigy, and that you're, um, pretty wild."

"Wild, eh? Is that a euphemism?"

"Hey, no judgment! I am *very* pro women getting what they want in this life."

"You are, eh? So, what do you want?"

Andie blushes.

"How do you stay faithful on the road?" I ask.

"*Faithful.* What an antiquated word, I love it."

"But for real?"

"We're nonmonogamous, my girlfriend and I. But it's still hard. We write a lot of letters, which is pretty romantic. What about you? Do you have a boyfriend back home who's understanding of, you know, this life?"

"Nope. I'm free to do whatever I please."

"That sounds like a pretty good deal," she says. "I hear you're a heartbreaker, too. That even the most aloof boys kind of follow you around until you ditch them."

"Nah, that's not true. I just meet them where they're at, and then I play to win."

"Win what?"

"The balance of power, I guess." No one has ever asked me to elaborate before.

"I hear James Clark got so tired of you throwing him in the garbage over and over that he hooked up with that girl from that female Megadeth cover band because she'll, quote, 'never leave him.'"

At the mention of James's name, I feel a truly uncomfortable sense of longing.

"Oh my god, that is not true. I don't know where you got your info! He knocked a girl up. He turned *me* down this time around. This world is too small."

"He was in love with you. Everyone teases him about it. He hitchhiked to see you play in cities where he didn't even know anyone!"

I let that sink in. "Nah, that's not true. He just travels a lot. Maybe we should go in the water," I say. Was that actually true? Was I the one to blow it with James? I'm either too attached or not attached enough to people. It feels like a lonely realization, like I am not ever going to get it right. I realize the music world, at this level, even though it is vast and spread across the country, is pretty similar to high school. It is probably a hundred or so people making it big in a given year, and we all encounter one another in festival green rooms and recording studios, at awards shows. It is a small world of sorts.

The heat starts to feel stifling, so I peel off my dress. Andie stares at me brazenly, then looks away as I cross my arms over my bikini top.

"Can you do that again, but slower?"

I throw the dress at her. "Did you bring a suit?"

"This is it," she says, standing, pulling off her jeans—to reveal boxers. She folds her jeans and places them on top of her wallet, and then takes off running.

"Wait!" But she's not running to the water, she's running after something. She catches it and brings it back.

"Someone's beach umbrella, what a score!"

She plants it in the ground and leans it over so it's partial sun coverage and partial block from anyone walking by.

We huddle under the umbrella. A pool of sweat gathers in her collarbone. She smells like some earthy kind of citrus oil.

"Missy Alamo, you're trouble," she whispers, both hands cupping my waist. Our mouths get close.

"I never kissed a girl," I say, as she leans in, then pauses. She turns her head, laughing a little.

"Well, I'm not much of a girl," she says.

And there, on the beach under an umbrella, while a truck speaker blasts all of *Paul's Boutique*, another person makes me come for the first time.

THAT NIGHT, I fuck up the intro to a song I've played a thousand times. I forget to join on the harmony in the finale, and when I do, I flub the lyrics. All these errors are imperceptible to anyone in the audience, but Tom can hear it, can see me glancing toward Andie leaning against a speaker in the wings, arms crossed, smirking, tapping her drumsticks on the wall. Every time I look at her I think I might come again, just from the way she's looking at me. Looking at other lovers I'd always felt like they were conquests, to be tackled and climbed. When Andie looks at me I'm the one caught in a net, wishing she'd throw me over her shoulder and run away. *This must be what they felt*, I think, remembering the way I studied my lovers' faces in those moments. *This is it. I am feeling that.* Holy shit. I look at Andie again. She bites her lip and nods my way. I feel a deep longing in my chest, and also a hesitancy that turns quickly to annoyance with every mistake I make.

After our set, I pour a bottle of water all over myself before I've even changed clothes. It's hot, but more than that, I'm irritated. Irritated for fucking up so much, irritated by this flush of emotions I can't handle.

I duck out early, even though I promised Andie I'd stay for her set. She wanted to take me out somewhere for a late-night special in Vegas, some secret spot with incredible food where real mobsters used to eat. But by the time I get to the green room, it's the last thing I want to do. Tom and I are jumping in the motel pool before she's even done her set.

"What was it like?" Tom asks, floating on his back as I crouch under the lip of the diving board.

"I dunno, I guess she's really skilled." I shrug. I don't know why I'm downplaying it, but it feels like the right option. What am I supposed to say—*It was the best sexual experience of my life and the way she circled my clit with her tongue without actually touching it until I wanted to die, was, like, expert-level moves?* But also, *I really hope she moves to Mars?*

"Yeah, my roommate in college used to blow me sometimes when we were drunk. It was the best head I ever got, but I never, like, had romantic feelings for him."

"Did you hurt his feelings?"

"No. Guys don't really work that way. I mean, I don't think so. He never said anything."

"I feel more like a guy in that way," I say. "So, don't tell anyone about it, okay?"

"Girl, I don't think anyone's gonna think you're gay with all the dick you suck."

I kick water in his face until he ducks under. I'm already trying not to compare the sex between Andie and me, and men in general. I suppose she was more attentive, slower, than most guys. But I didn't touch Andie after she'd fucked me. I followed her cues that the sex was over. She'd gotten dressed, smoked a cigarette. Maybe that's just what happens? I have no frame of reference. It was nothing like lesbian porn. But it was hard to discount the Only Orgasm Of My Life While Someone Else Was Present.

WE DRINK BEER around the pool until most of the bands return. Tom indulges more than usual, and by the end of the night we are curled in a pool floatie writing a song we insist is our next single. Of course, it's garbage, but it feels like the best thing we've ever written. I am happy Tom and I are cool again.

When Andie and her girls walk by us on the way to their rooms, the singer waves and raises a beer toward us. Andie looks down, casually aloof, doesn't even glance in my direction. A part of me feels like I should climb out of the pool and follow her, should explain, but I have no idea how. So I shove my guilt aside, as I'd be doing all tour, and flip out of our floatie, staying under the water until I know they're gone. I tell myself, *Just pretend you're a dude and only your own feelings matter.* So far, it has been working for me. But this time, it doesn't feel totally right.

MY BANDMATES ORDER pizza and before we dig in poolside, they stick a fat birthday candle in the middle. I blow it out just as the singer from Andie's band emerges from her room, barefoot in a yellow sundress. She nods at us from a chaise longue across the pool, drinks an entire beer, burps, and puts the bottle down before pulling off her dress and jumping into the pool completely naked. She swims toward where we are sitting, pops her head up out of the water, mascara running all over her face like a candle melting.

"Hey, I'm Agatha," she says to me, not Tom, though we both say *hey* back.

"You know, no one ever rejects Andie. I've never seen it. It's like science fiction, basically. Anyway, respect," she says, laughing and swimming back to the other side of the pool.

We watch her stand up, squeeze the water from her hair, and saunter back to her room with her dress in her hands. Sometimes I have a knowing feeling when I meet someone new. I had it with Tom. With Amita when I walked into first-year composition class.

I turn to Tom and say, "She's going to be my best friend."

"Yeah, sure. She's way too cool."

"I'm cool!"

"You are not. *We* are not. We're just having a cool phase right now. It's not permanent."

I FINALLY HEAD to my room. I save a message from my father playing "Happy Birthday" on the ukulele. I listen to it three times. I lie back and listen to the click-click of the overhead fan. I think about knocking on Andie's door. I get up and go outside onto the landing. I flash on the afternoon at the beach. It's so late but it's still just as hot out. I grip the railing, second-guessing my desire. I want to see her, but I also want to never see her again, with equal intensity. A crow bops around on a lawn chair below.

"Hey pretty," I call out. "What should I do?"

I used to ask the sheep questions every night when I was a kid, after they came in from pasture. The crow looks up, cocks its head. We are making what feels like fairly meaningful interspecies eye contact when out of nowhere another crow swoops down and starts attacking it.

"Stop!" I yell uselessly. I clap my hands. I yell again. He doesn't stop.

I run back into the room and grab a can of Coke from the mini-bar and throw it toward the attacking crow, trying to stop him. But it's already done. It's like a horror movie. I run down the steps, slipping on the bottom one and scraping up my leg. The crow's body is still and bloodied. The murderer is squawking and strutting.

I start to cry, so hard I feel like the full-body shuddering might never stop.

"Hey, hey, what's wrong, girl? You hurt?" I look up and see Agatha, holding a bucket of ice from the ice machine.

When I explain what happened she gives me a big hug and says, "Sometimes crows are territorial. They'll kill other threatening males."

"That's so crazy, I thought they were smart. And loving!"

She shrugs. "Why don't I walk you back to your room?"

We sit on my bed and she paints my nails silver as we watch *Desperately Seeking Susan* on TV, our mutual favorite childhood movie.

"We have another gig together in Los Angeles in a few weeks," she says, blowing on my thumbnail. "We should write each other postcards until we see each other again. We could even compile them in a zine or something?"

"I love that idea." I lean back against the pillow, debating asking her when she knew she was gay. I rehearse a number of ways to bring it up that would sound natural. But instead I take a hit of a joint she offers, and fall asleep.

CHAPTER 10

CAROLA

THE BUS LET me off in front of the post office in Mallow as the sun was setting. I walked up the hill to the center.

Since I was a long-term resident, I had my own small cabin up in the woods behind the main buildings. Nothing more than the essentials—it was pretty much a studio with a kitchenette, a bathroom. I had furnished it with nothing more than a futon, a bookshelf, and a single dresser for my few belongings, mostly loose clothing for yoga, thick oatmeal-colored sweaters for the winter. Living without excess was an essential part of my life here, and I couldn't imagine padding on the layers that most people live with, photographs, knickknacks, or god forbid a television. Other than a few candles and books, feathers or stones I'd found while hiking, my shelves were bare.

When it was time for the meeting, I hiked up to the springs. The moon was bright enough to see through even the thickest parts of the forest path. I'd gotten used to everything at the center, but I was still taken by the beauty of the springs every time I visited, the silvery mossy rocks and the sound of the water trickling. Though technically a mineral bath, there was no unpleasant sulfur smell. One time I saw a bear lolling about in the water when I arrived just before dawn.

A few other women had already gathered and were taking off their clothes and getting into the water, or rolling up pant legs and dipping their feet in while perched on the low rocks that bordered the pool.

I took off my outer clothes, kicked off my sandals, and put my feet into the springs, sitting away from a few other women who were speaking in a familiar rapid hush. The oldest woman was Ocean, whose face was freckled and bronzed, framed by a slick silver bob. Most of us were in our forties, and then several of the women who had been involved with the guru more recently seemed to be in their late twenties to midthirties or so, if I had to guess.

Blue had anointed herself our leader for the evening. We went around the circle and began to talk about our relationships with the guru, about whether they were right. I didn't say much. It had been so long ago. We'd had an amicable split after about five years on and off. I wasn't one of them anymore, but it felt important to them that I joined their ranks, so I just kept my story at a minimum.

Rose, an ebullient redhead who still looked like a teenager, spoke next. Was she even eighteen yet when she met him? Could she be younger than my daughter? She had been a volunteer in the gift shop. She talked about how she'd gotten pregnant, and he had made it clear that she had to have an abortion or leave the ashram.

"He gave me some herbs, and I had to be rushed to the

hospital. I almost died. He didn't care. He said something about the universe taking care of us."

I pulled my feet out of the water, slowly drying them off with a scarf. I wanted to reach out to Rose and comfort her, but she was across the pool. Everyone was murmuring consolations, before a pause so long I thought I might have to take over facilitating.

But Blue brought us back to the task at hand. "Juniper, do you think the community should hold him accountable?"

"Yes," I said. "He should be held accountable."

"I think so, too," Sarah said. "He's not who you think he is. He has this whole thing about condoms, right? He won't use them. He says they're unnatural." Sarah had always been my closest person at the center, but we had not confided in each other about our relationships with the guru.

"I tried to avoid certain acts with him, avoid him when I knew I was ovulating. Eventually he started to figure it out. I think it was his *kink* in a way, to try to get women pregnant, though he'd panic when women actually did."

Half the group looked at me, alarmed, but others nodded in agreement.

I didn't tell the group that the month before we officially broke it off, he'd discerned that I was avoiding him and why. He had me summoned over the intercom to come help him in the garden. I already knew I was pregnant. My breasts were tender again, in the way they had been with Missy. I'd felt them when I was raking leaves.

He'd given me the herbs in a purple cloth bag. But instead I had it done at a proper clinic.

When I came back, I avoided the guru, but I hardly had

to. There was no tenderness in his looks my way, no invitations or overtures. I had been spoiled for him somehow. And
it started to make sense, how some women had left the center
abruptly and sometimes in distress, over the years. They all
thought they were chosen.

"You didn't warn anyone about him?" said Jaya.

"Honestly, I thought I was his only partner at the time.
And any women that came after, well, we're adults. We can
negotiate our own terms."

Jaya looked at me, puzzled.

"You have to remember that we all worshipped him. No
one wants to hear anything bad about any boyfriend, let
alone a guru."

I remembered that after I'd returned from having the
abortion, he'd kept me behind after a class. He asked, and I
was honest, about where I'd been.

"You didn't trust the herbs, you didn't trust the natural
solution, and you endangered the reputation of the center by
going outside the walls."

At the time, I'd been defensive, then felt guilty. But revis-
iting it now, years later, I realized what a scammer he was.

"I'll help," I told Blue. "I know a lot of what you need to
know."

"Thanks, Juniper. That's brave of you," Blue said, satis-
fied, evidently ready to move on to someone else.

No one has ever told me I was brave during a time when
I actually felt that way, but I would take it.

AN HOUR OR so later, we sat in a circle, our blankets spread
over the grass in the meadow by the spring. The moon was

so bright it might as well have been a spotlight. Blue lifted her hands in the air and led us in a full-moon ritual.

"As you all know, the full moon is a nourishing time, her light upon us, let us soak it in right now," she said.

After connecting us to the four elements, leading us in some chanting and dancing, during which my mind never stopped racing with what we should do about the guru and the future of the ashram, Blue brought us back to a discussion of resolution. What were we to do? How had our discussions with the police been? We went around in a circle, passing a talking stick made of an old wooden recorder that had rope braided at the top like a wig. The more recent partners felt the most betrayed and wanted him to go to jail. One woman said she was still in love with him, and that he would be punished in the next life and that was enough for her. Another said she felt that if she didn't have our sisterhood, she would have burned the ashram to the ground by now. But most of us didn't know what we should do. We had all these feelings, but what should our *actions* be?

The police had become involved initially because of the ashram's assets, because Ocean, as his longest companion, considered by many to be his wife, knew he was going to try to take it all once the trouble started. She called a lawyer. The ball was in motion before we really knew what was happening.

We were letting the moon touch our skin. Bathing in its light was supposed to energize us.

"No one should be caged," I said, "even if they hurt you."

I thought of my father, how many people he helped put in cages, how I'd often wished he could have been restrained. But what would it do to the guru? His health would fail him sooner rather than later, and we were literally running him out of town. The thing we all wanted, the one thing we agreed on, was that we wished we'd seen even one speck of his shame, even a shadow across his face, any kind of sense of culpability. So far he'd only met all the accusations with defiance and mockery. And that was why some of us wanted the police involved, to execute the consequences we could not, but it wouldn't do us any good.

Ocean explained that with the threat of a lawsuit, of exposure, we could fight in civil court to keep the money and the center. We could become a business. We were rich in land, and in heart, she said. This made the most sense. What we wanted more than anything was for the center to be ours. I had built a life here, one that mattered to me. I was teaching women, helping women. And when I thought about it, that was what had kept me going at Sunflower—not building a community per se, but, especially, raising our girls with Tegan, finding the strength in numbers when women work together. But did I have the right to it? To help other women, when the most important one in my life was the one I had left behind: my own daughter?

WHEN I FINALLY left Bryce for good I reminded him of the day we found out I was pregnant. He had no memory of it. "I knew it then," I said. "I knew it was a bad deal for me, and that you didn't care, and that you wouldn't really be there for me, for us. I've tried to tell you so many times over the years, I've explained it a hundred times, and you never take it seriously. You always laugh it off and forget about it. Well, now I'm just done."

I wanted to say to Bryce that leaving was better than the alternative, but it wouldn't have made sense to him. I loved him, and I still love him. I still think he's the love of my life, and I feel intense rage and jealousy when I picture him with his new wife, but if I'd stayed that love would have died. I didn't want it to. Leaving was the only way to preserve it.

What I understood about myself was that the feeling of regret that happened after conception never fully left. Sometimes it felt strong enough that I assumed I would miscarry, that my mind and body were connected enough to sabotage it all. It receded for long stretches, and I acclimated to life as a mother, but I never felt an ecstasy or even just a comfort in the role. The feeling came back strongly sometimes. For me, everything about motherhood felt practiced. I always paid attention, was nurturing and loving and consistent. I did all the things I wished my mother had done—listened to my daughter, valued her opinions and autonomy, didn't force her to act just like me—and I read all the books about being a good parent. But there was something I always knew I wasn't feeling. It was like committing to playing an instrument, and playing it well, but not quite making music.

No one at Sunflower noticed this ambivalence, except occasionally Missy would give me a look and I knew she knew it. She sensed my difference. It was the source of most of my shame, and I wished I could change, but I had no idea how.

I kept on for years—I'm surprised how long I lasted, quite frankly. But eventually, I had nothing left. I felt like a shell. So I got back into the Sunflower truck, thinking I was just going on a yoga retreat to recharge, to reinvest in myself. I'd be back before they knew it. But I wouldn't.

CHAPTER 11

Missy

W E LEAVE VEGAS, all a little bit depleted, and head toward San Francisco. Even the van sounds a little tuckered out. By the time we are twenty miles out of the city, Alan and I have started coughing, and then by the first gas station, Billy is sniffling. Tom insists he won't get it. He has it under control. He's been strengthening his immune system with astragalus and goldenseal and this will prove it.

But by the time we are in Fresno's traffic, even Tom has a killer headache. We are hitting the last leg of the tour: San Fran, Portland, Seattle, and Vancouver. Our final date is in L.A.: a festival and a TV show appearance.

The illness feels like a physical manifestation of the emotional tensions between us, though I hate to think of it like that. Reminds me of my mother and all the other hippies and New Agers I grew up with. Whenever I had a sore throat as a kid, my mom would ask if there was anything I wasn't saying, if I was holding in feelings. I used to try to figure that out, in case it would help my sore throat. *I guess I'm mad that Taylor stole my pink sandals?* If the cold turned to strep, I'd probably *really* done something wrong. Later I was like, duh, it was a virus. I always thought my mother didn't really believe all that, either. She wanted to, but she took us to regular doctors in town whenever we were really sick. My mother could never really commit, I guess, to being as countercultural as everyone else.

I think of my mom now, as each of us goes down physically, just as our emotional bonds have totally frayed. Or maybe I think about her because it was my birthday. On the drive, Billy forces us to listen to a book on tape by the Dalai Lama, and I fantasize about just punching him in his fucking face as the audio voice drones on in a monotone.

I'm sitting next to Alan, and we both suck on ginger candies and drink from a liter of cranberry juice. Every time I close my eyes I shudder, remembering Andie's hands, the way she kissed my neck, her smirk. Then I try to push the images away.

"When did you know you were gay?" I ask him, as I rub Tiger Balm on my neck and stare out at the side of the highway.

"I always knew, as far back as about five. Everyone else knew, too."

"You always knew?"

"Always. Why?"

"No reason."

He smirks and grabs the Tiger Balm, rubbing it into his shoulder.

"I heard about you and Andie. She's fiiiine. She looks like Bowie but more butch. Hot."

I blush.

"I have never seen you blush, *never*! Oh my god, you are

like, the most shameless in the best way, but *this* makes you shy?"

I bury myself under my sweatshirt and he gives me a side squeeze. "You can be like Anne Heche, or one of those Calvin Klein models."

"Right. Maybe I'm bi?" I say, but I don't quite believe it.

"Have you ever heard of the Kinsey scale? Maybe you're just a little more toward the middle than you thought. It doesn't have to be a big deal."

I put my headphones on and lean against the window as Alan continues to tease me. I definitely never even thought about a girl sexually until one was kissing me on the mouth. So I must not really be gay. She was just skilled, it was simple friction and beer and horniness. I take the truth I know from that moment, and I lay back my head and close my eyes, willing myself to sleep.

I wake up when we stop for gas. When I get out to stretch, I go into the convenience store and buy Granny a postcard. *The people out west are so friendly, it's hard to get used to, but ultimately a welcome change from the stand-off attitudes on the East Coast. I hope choir is going well. I'll call you from Vancouver to check in? Love, Melissa.*

WE ALL SLEEP most of the way to San Francisco, roll into our hotel and sleep more until sound check, all of us pale and weak. I feel my fever break while onstage, sweating it out. Being close to the end of tour makes us adventurous. My voice is low and raspy, so I do a cover of "Fogtown" by Michelle Shocked on the acoustic guitar, all by myself, while the rest of the band re-ups their B12s backstage. The crowd loves it. For some reason, the Bay Area loves us in general. We sell more merch there than in any other city. We feel as if we can do anything and be appreciated, and we get our groove back, literally. We all sleep again until the second San Fran gig, and everyone starts to feel better.

"Our groove hasn't just returned by osmosis," insists Tom, as we sit in a diner having an afternoon breakfast. "It's because you ran out of coke." He looks pointedly at Billy, with a glance at me. Billy declines a response, spearing his avocado and singing along with the Clash.

"The Bay Area is not magical," Tom insists, but everyone digs into their giant Mexican breakfasts. Except me, I'm struggling to get down a yogurt and juice, my throat still raw.

Tom is right. There is no one in our *Bible Verses* notebook to call in San Francisco. But that's okay. It feels good to take a break. As a result, we play a second awesome show in San Francisco. Tom even begins to smile at me again, offer me snacks and compliments, encourages me to work on some new songs.

DURING THE DRIVE to Portland the next morning, Billy becomes increasingly upset that no one is laughing at his jokes and stories, and I wonder if maybe *he* hasn't run out of drugs. Sometimes you can tell right away when someone is high, but Billy is such a regular user—and such a chatty spark plug anyway—it's hard to tell.

"What is the thing you're most afraid to say out loud?" Billy asks, slapping the steering wheel as punctuation.

I shift the lavender oil–soaked tissues I'd stuffed in my bra and avoid his searching glances in the rearview mirror. By the final leg of the tour, I've taken to experimenting with ways to mask the musk of masculine bodily neglect; the lavender oil does a decent job. Then there's Alan, who sprays his whole body in a sexy cologne that stays on you if you hug him, which makes me wonder if cleanliness is less to do with gender than with sexual orientation.

But I'm hardly one to judge. My own hair is coated in a neglected, waxy sheen. I run my fingers across my dirty scalp, pressing the strands between the pads of my fingers, while Billy continues to monologue.

"I'm afraid I'll never really be free," he says to no one in particular.

Alan looks at me and rolls his eyes. Billy is the freest person I've ever known. He'd take his clothes off in front of anyone. He is never devastated if he sings a bar or two off-key. He is the son of a judge, has never had a job besides music. How much freer could a person get?

"I'm the only one in this van who knows what it's like not to be free, for real," says Alan. "So maybe shut up and put on some Fugazi."

"I don't mean like literally not free . . . not like when you were a kid or whatever," Billy says, shaking his head, as if Alan just didn't get him.

Alan and his mom had been refugees when they came to Canada in the 1980s. This comment angers Alan even more.

"You think I'm free now? You know what happens when cops pull us over, or when they raid a gay bar? You think I'm free then?"

"No, man. That's not the kind of free I mean. I'm talking, like, spiritually."

"Just shut up, Billy. Let's all be quiet for a bit," says Tom.

Alan puts on his headphones and rolls his hoodie up against the window. I expect that he and Billy will come to actual blows at some point on this tour. It happened last year at a roadside stop in Michigan, where Alan drove away in the van and left us nursing terrible coffees for an hour before he returned.

"I'm afraid of mice," pipes up Jared. No one is listening.

I guess if I had to answer, I'm afraid of what happened with Andie. I try not to think of how she smirked and looked at me, like she could devour me. The way she pulled off her plaid shirt, and those drummer arms. How there was no point in our encounter where I wished she'd hurry up or say something different, do something different.

I haven't even really thought about James since we left Baltimore, and we actually *had* a relationship of sorts. Andie lurks, and the more I try to stop thinking about her, there she is, sifting in and out of my thoughts. Unwelcome and welcome at the same time. And I've started seeing lesbians everywhere, like when you think you're pregnant and see pregnant ladies everywhere.

"Come on, assholes, play the game! Tell me your fears!" Billy yells, after trying to find a radio station and coming up with only static.

"I'm afraid we'll never have another great album," says Tom.

This gets our attention.

"Oh that's nice, Tom. Real nice," says Alan.

"And that you're all going to fuck it up while I put every ounce of myself into making something excellent, and you guys aren't even aiming for excellence." He stares straight into the rearview mirror, so he can catch Billy's eye.

"I'm afraid of Tom stabbing me in my sleep if I fuck up," says Jared.

"I'm afraid this conversation is never going to be over," said Alan, punching the ceiling of the van.

I reach between the seats and squeeze Tom's shoulder. "Sorry, buddy," I say. "We'll do better, right, guys? We'll focus. We won't fuck it up!"

There were murmurs of *yeah, of course, for sure.*

I squeeze Tom's shoulder again but he jerks away from me.

THE PROBLEM WITH touring is how it becomes difficult to discern what is normal. Most of us in the band do things to try to feel like a regular person. I practice scales every morning, even if I'm hungover. I do stretches, arching my body up toward the sun. We all drink Throat Comfort tea and suck on slippery elm tablets, especially Billy, so we won't lose our voices. Tom likes to get out and jog around the van ten times every time we stop for food or gas. Which is ridiculous and admirable. Alan carries his own pillowcase in his knapsack, to put over hotel pillows. And no matter where we are or what we're doing, Billy takes a nap at one o'clock in the afternoon for exactly one hour, even if we're just sitting in a Denny's. (That's how you get kicked out of a Denny's.)

I also try to journal every day, with a pack of drawing pens and several black hardcover notebooks. When I fill one, I mail it home to myself. The ritual feels important. But I can't write about Andie. I have one page with her name written on it and a thousand doodles of flowers and trees. Will I forget Andie if I don't document the experience?

———

IN PORTLAND, WE have a whole day off. My plan is to hit Powell's and some record shops, maybe eat at a restaurant where I'll have time to linger and relax. But I barely have the chance to look around my hotel room before Tom summons us all to the lobby.

When I get downstairs, all I find is Tom, wearing a track suit, sitting on an oversized green velvet chair.

"What's up?" I say.

"Go back upstairs and put on comfortable shoes. I'm taking us on a group outing."

"This whole tour *is* a group outing. I think we need to un-group. Plus, the nail fully went through my boot sole, so these *are* my comfortable shoes," I say, re-strapping my platform sandal. He frowns. Everyone else slowly gathers around us.

"We need to regroup!" he says in his best dad-voice. "I promise it will be good."

We get back into the van and Tom drives across the bridge and north on the interstate, over the Washington border and through several small towns until Alan says, "Are you taking us driving on our day off from driving?"

Tom ignores our complaining as we wind around several dirt roads that feel as though we are slowly tunneling to a center point. Instead we arrive at a trailhead.

"There are hot springs two miles into the forest," he says, jumping out and stretching.

We continue to grumble as we get out of the van, but there is no denying that we are into it. We need to feel like characters in a children's storybook, wandering down dirt paths, breathing in the wet, lush air, touching moss so bright green it looks like paint and seems to breathe. The scale of beauty on the West Coast is immense.

My body is still exhausted from being sick, and I do that Canadian thing where I heard Tom say miles but understood kilometers, and keep expecting to arrive when we've barely gotten anywhere. I trail behind the group lazily, stopping to smell and touch and take it all in. I get caught up in the small-ness of my body as I walk away from the city, from the pulse of audiences, their blazing attention, and the repetitive rhythm of each show ritual, the endless driving. This break is welcome.

I fall further behind, sit on a rock, and scribble down some notes for lyrics. My imagination unlocks, away from the chaos.

I sit for a long while, until I see that Jared has circled back. He hasn't shaved for a few days. His dyed mop of hair is a disgusting shade of green that blends into the trees. He borrowed my terry-cloth sundress a few days back and is still wearing it, with his tallest blue Doc Martens.

"I was worried about you," he says, holding out his hand to help me up and then kissing me. His kissing has improved. We've found a groove. Sex with Jared is fine. I can take it or leave it, but I always choose to take it when offered. Because why not?

Jared and I climb a few meters away from the path, up into where the trees thicken. He ties my arms in my sweat-shirt sleeves around a thin tree. "Let's pretend I found you here," he whispers. It's a lovely fantasy to get lost in, until I open my eyes to see, between a break in the leaves, a line of sun across Tom's stunned face.

"Shit," I say. "Stop! Tom's here," I whisper in his ear.

"He'll leave," Jared says, barely pausing. And he does. But now I am out of the moment, out of the magical forest space, and grumpy as Jared finishes. I tell him to continue on ahead, saying I need to be alone for a while. After he comes, Jared is unbearable to look at. As he walks away, he looks like a weird, oversized pink-and-green Muppet. I pee behind a rock, then climb back down to the path, clinging to errant branches to steady myself. Even so, I slip right and my ankle goes left.

I can do nothing but lie on the forest floor, cursing my footwear and looking up at the slice of sky between the trees. My foot screams with pain, as I curse Jared and Tom and every tree in the forest. This will be a verse in the song Tom will insist we write later, the bright white breaking through the trees as I will myself to not pass out. I start to see crows circling, but maybe it's a hallucination.

I END UP in an emergency room in Portland, where I am relieved to find out it's just a bad sprain, nothing broken. Plus some cuts from the fall, which need stitches. The nurses give me some painkillers, and I sink into an imagined softness.

A kind doctor pulls the curtain around my bed a little tighter, then lowers his voice.

"You told the nurse there was no way this could be true, but we did some routine bloodwork, and you are pregnant, Melissa."

His face begins to shine. He is half smiling, like this is good news.

"That's impossible. I'm careful, like so careful. You don't understand how careful."

"Well," he says, "you'll have to see your family doctor when you get back home. Maybe it will feel like a happier surprise then."

Loneliness is loud inside my chest. My ankle's throbbing pain subsides as whatever they've given me begins to take hold. The bandages are itchy, but I'm also getting really drowsy. As I drift to sleep, I think, *I knew this would happen. I fucking knew it.*

SEATTLE IS A blur. Having a team of people insist on taking your photo while all you can think about is hurling yourself down flights of stairs is a real trip. And a bad one at that. Sitting in some giant warehouse getting primped for a shoot, while a journalist pushes a recorder in front of my mouth, barking, "Tell us how the tour is going, Missy Alamo!"

I pull handfuls of decorative parsley off the craft services trays and munch it down, because didn't some hippie witch once tell me it can cause abortions? I'll try anything. But what I try most is drinking. I drink and I drink and I drink.

AND THEN I look up and we are in Vancouver. Tom tries to take the drinks away from me—he doesn't know I'm pregnant; he is just worried in general.

But I hate Vancouver.

I don't know why, really. It's objectively beautiful. Maybe because everyone I meet eventually starts talking to me about hiking. Maybe because they don't get pissy when it rains all the time. Maybe because, for me, the West Coast of Canada takes a puritanical turn, with people wearing windbreakers and eating too many protein bars. Maybe because I'm pregnant.

Billy loves it, though. When we cross the border into British Columbia and stop to get gas, he gets out of the van and humps the ground yelling, *"I love Canada!"*

Billy grew up in Vancouver, and like most West Coast kids with rich and inattentive parents, he partied too hard. It's partly why Billy ended up leaving. His father got him out of doing time for heroin possession, got him in rehab, and pulled some strings to get him into McGill in the music program. He dropped out in the first month, but he stayed in Montreal.

Though he's never gone back to heroin, Billy's end-of-tour debauchery is legendary. And pretty much everyone joins him, except Tom. There is a big party planned after the show, and everyone except Tom is game. When we get to the hotel, Tom grabs his overnight pack and gives a wave.

"See y'all at sound check! Cory's parents live in Kitsilano, so I'm going to crash there," he says.

"Can I stay with you? Do they have an extra bed or anything?" I ask. We have a free day before tomorrow night's show, so this means I won't see him for nearly twenty-four hours. We've been together for so many consecutive weeks that the thought of this suddenly terrifies me. Plus, I am more tired than I've ever been in my life. I feel as though I won't be able to even crawl onto the stage.

"I don't know, Missy. I kind of need solitude right now, like some space," he says.

"I thought we were supposed to be a group! Regroup!" I come back at him.

"No, we're good." He laughs. "It's just too much, you

know, the end of tour. I just need some silence. And if you
come with me, it's like bringing the noise with me."

"I'm *noise*?"

"You know what I mean."

"I won't party, I swear, I'll just read quietly, alone, like the
beginning of tour. We can do yoga. Or not! You won't even
know I'm there."

He shakes his head.

"Don't leave me with them," I say, motioning to the guys
who are draped across the hotel lobby furniture.

"See you later, Missy," Tom says, and walks out the re-
volving doors.

THE NEXT MORNING, I try for a healthy day on my own.
Maybe I'm trying to prove something to Tom. I go to a record store and walk to Granville Market and buy fresh fruit,
then sit on a bench spearing orange slices with a toothpick.

THE DAY OF healthy perspective is short-lived. I'm feeling
bored when Billy knocks on my door that night before sound
check. He, Jared, and Alan want to get high. I'm all in.

Tom is distant at sound check. I don't look at him, just
grind my jaw, looking at the floor, sawing away. The songs
start to blend and blur. Why am I even doing this? I am
going through the motions of playing my cello, the most
beautiful sidekick in my life, and not even appreciating it. I'm
not even hearing the melody, feeling the magical high I get
from knowing I am playing well. I can't get up and dance
because of my ankle, and a stagehand has to bring my instru-

ments to me when I switch from cello to guitar. I am phoning it in.

The show isn't our best, but it's not our worst either. Tom is pissed, but I don't care. I keep partying after the show, eventually blacking out.

When I wake up, I'm outside, lying on grass. I can hear an acoustic guitar, and some early-morning birdsongs.

"You waking up? You would *not* let me move you."

It's *Tom's* voice.

I try to stand but forget my ankle, and the pain is so intense I fall right over and throw up on the grass.

"Where are we?" I ask, looking around. It is almost dawn, we are in the backyard of a suburban house somewhere.

"Cory's parents' place. They're actually away. I told you this already."

"Oh, right," I say, trying to recover. This is my blackout recovery routine, playing along until I start to remember. "Look, I need to lie down."

"Let's get you some water."

Tom walks me inside an immense house that looks like every suburban 1970s house—shag carpet, avocado fridge and stove. He leads me to the bathroom and I drink a cup of water from a paper cup, throw it up, and lean my head against the coolness of a shower stall. Tom occasionally knocks on the door.

"Just fuck off," I whisper.

When I finally open the door, he is sitting in the hallway outside, looking concerned. He leads me to a guest bed, tucks me in, then crawls in beside me. I feel myself dropping off into sleep as he runs his fingers through my hair until I push away his hand.

THE VAN COMES to pick us up a few hours later. No matter what I do I cannot remember anything from the night before.

"You looked like you were asleep onstage last night," Alan says as I climb into my spot and pull my sweatshirt into a pillow.

"Well, I can't stand up, so I'm going to look a little less active than normal."

I drink a bottle of peach Snapple, close my eyes, put on my headphones. I don't wake up when everyone else does the pre-border cleanup. I don't even know where my passport is when Tom shakes me awake and says, "Get out your ID, we're at the border." We have a few cars to go, are moving quite slowly, and it takes me a while to find it stuffed in my army bag with crumples of receipts and wrappers. When I hand it up to Billy, who is driving, he gives it to the bored-looking customs agent. When he opens it, a forgotten flap of cocaine falls out.

In my defense, there isn't actually any cocaine left in it, but it isn't the world's smallest bag of flour. The customs agent sighs. Tom mutters, "Fuck you, Missy. Just fuck you."

THE BORDER GUARD hands me a cup of coffee in a paper cup, the kind they have in police stations in the movies. I take a sip. Calling it coffee is generous, more a halfhearted scoop from a lukewarm puddle. He smells like the drugstore cologne a lover of mine in New Mexico used to swipe from CVS. Cheap. The kind you wouldn't want to light a match around. I imagine his apartment, navy-blue sheets on his bed, never washed enough. Sweat socks bought in bulk with red, black, or blue stripes. First-person-shooter video games, canned pasta, Dave Matthews or Hootie & the Blowfish CDs, a girlfriend he once punched in high school that he still talks about as his true love when he gets wasted with his buddies.

It feels wrong when he speaks with authority knowing all I know from just looking at him.

"We can't let you back into the United States, Melissa. That's the bottom line."

He drums his fingers on the fake wood desk. I know he isn't the guy at the top, or even the middle. He has a ruddy glow, too many pimples, to be deciding my fate. I blink. His zits get bigger. I saucer my eyes to keep the zits from taking over his face.

"I have official invitations from music festivals and a live TV taping to attend." I start rummaging in my backpack and pulling out papers: an itinerary listing our venues, the official invitation to appear on the late-night show, the financial details that management had typed up in case we were asked at the border. I can't believe Gord went ahead on a plane, and isn't here to be the business guy, the smooth-things-over guy. Gord makes people do things they don't want to do. But what would he say? *I'm not your babysitter*, Gord often sighed, pulling me toward my room some nights.

I can't convince the agent that the baggie contained traces of aspirin or a crushed-up vitamin C tablet. It is stamped with a juvenile skull-and-bones design on the outside; the dealer felt the need to brand his product in a way. Plus, the agent found a second baggie in a pile of bow resin, loose change, and hair elastics in my cello case. Now agent number two has joined us; seems like we've hit the next level.

"Your band will have to continue their tour without you," he says, affecting the tone of a child playing the role of vice principal. He slides some paperwork across the desk and gives me a dismissive look.

"You didn't actually find any drugs on me. You can't arrest me for *memories* of cocaine."

"I can do a lot of things," he says, purposely fondling the gun on his hip.

I can't hold back my scoff.

"Do you want to make your life even harder, Ms. Wood? I can put you in jail. I have that authority."

I don't want to be Melissa Wood. I am Missy Alamo. I've been Missy Alamo for months. Melissa Wood used to skip social studies class in grade seven and once walked into the police station near her high school and sat across from a lady with a patient smile who said there was no way to find my mom if she didn't want to be found. That happened more than once.

"Answer me," says the second agent.

"No, I don't wish things to be harder," I say, in a clipped, chirpy tone.

The reality of what this border guard is saying starts to seep in. This isn't something I'll be able to talk my way out of and tell as a funny story to the guys later today.

"We were on *SNL* last month. Did you see us?"

He looks vaguely impressed, but suppresses it.

"Oh, I've heard of you guys. Your singer is the faggot with the long hair?"

"Well, Billy gets more pussy than God if you want to get technical, but you're probably picturing our band, yeah."

He starts humming the chorus to our most famous song.

I nod because I think he wants confirmation that it's the right song, but he doesn't. He hums an entire verse and chorus. It is very uncomfortable to watch and listen to him do this, he holds eye contact the entire time, and it makes me wonder if he's a sociopath. After the final note, he stands up and they both leave me in the tiny office room. I'm never going to be able to play that song again.

After what feels like an hour, but is probably only about ten minutes, he returns.

"You can go, we aren't going to hold you. But you can't cross the border. You have to go home."

"Right," I say.

As I leave the office, I see his co-workers gathered around a screen.

Outside, the van has been thoroughly dismantled, doors off the hinges. It looks torn open, bleeding out with opened suitcases, cracked CD and cassette tapes, packets of guitar strings. I run to my cello case as though it is sentient and possibly bruised, but because it's mine they'd carefully searched it, it isn't as banged up as the rest.

Billy rages.

"They broke my guitar!"

Most of the instruments were with the gear in the van with the road crew, but some of us travel with what's most precious to us. I hold my cello case and my army bag and backpack as I stand there, watching Billy lose it over his guitar.

I sit down on the curb. The band gathers around me for an explanation.

"I have to stay here, in Canada," I say, as I start to cry.

Billy punches the side of the van, even though the border guards are eyeing us warily.

"This is going to fuck up our L.A. gig and it's the most important one!" he yells. "Our appearance on the late show! I can't believe it. We need a girl onstage, people want someone to look at."

"Fuck off, Billy," says Tom.

"Oh, what? You just hate that anyone *else* stares at her."

"Now you can really fuck off." Tom goes after Billy then, so quick I don't see it start, he suddenly has Billy pinned with one arm against the van. They huff at each other, then Tom drops him and storms off.

"Where the fuck is Alan?" Billy says, turning back to the shards of his broken Les Paul. I shrug, shoulders like wet towels, face hot with regret.

Finally, Alan emerges from the screening area, scowling. It happens every time we cross a border—he always gets pulled away from the group for extra screening. He had not wanted to go to Vancouver for this reason alone. Customs agents always act as if it's a big favor, letting him in the country, even though he's been a citizen since he was a toddler.

Billy quickly fills him in. Alan starts laughing. "I'm sorry, but it's funny. I can't believe it's happening to *you*, you're the whitest girl on the planet. Was there someone you couldn't flirt with to get out of it? You must have like, *tried* to get banned. Did you punch a guard? Come *on*."

I can't laugh about it. If I fly back to Montreal, I have nowhere to go. My room in my apartment with Amita is sublet until the end of the tour. I could go to my grand-mother's house in the suburbs, but that feels incredibly de-pressing, like those dreams where you have to go back to high school.

I stand beside Billy at the pay phone, on a call with our management office to ask if they can do anything, but no one is answering. Rows of cars line up at the border, families on vacation in minivans. They look so normal. Their lives make sense. It's like I'm watching my possible unwanted futures whiz by.

"No luck," says Billy.

"Could you call your dad?" I ask.

Billy frowns, but shrugs. "Couldn't hurt to ask, but he's an asshole." He dials a number. His dad is a judge, and he always gets Billy out of jams. But I hear him laughing through the phone, saying, "Look, son, I don't even know this girl."

"Dad, this is my career! Did you even watch us on *SNL*?"

"If *you* were in trouble it would be a different story."

They exchange a few more heated words and Billy hangs up the phone, resting his head against the receiver for a moment. Then he straightens up, pulls out a cigarette. "Sorry, I told you. He sucks."

I follow him back to the van, where the guys are trying to salvage the scene, pack everything up, and it dawns on me that I am going to be left behind. The show will go on with-out me. Jared offers a "Sorry dude, that really sucks," and I can't believe I ever had sex with him. Or that I might be knocked up by him, that I didn't watch him put on the con-dom every single time.

I approach Tom, who pulls me into a hug and lets me cry. He finds me a power bar and a lemon Snapple from his stash.

I desperately want him to stay with me, not let me be left behind.

"What do you need?" Tom asks. It is such a simple question, but I can't answer him. It feels too vulnerable to say.

"I'm okay," I say. "I'm just so shocked and disappointed." And I start crying into his flannel shirt that mysteriously smells freshly laundered.

I look at him, trying to beam my thoughts into his mind. *Stay with me. Stay with me. Stay with me. Don't leave me here.*

"I wish I could stay with you," he says. "But you'll be okay. We'll call management again, see if they can't book you a hotel and a plane ticket home. We'll meet up in a month to start recording. It will be okay."

"What if you stayed and flew to L.A. tomorrow?"

"Oh man, sorry. I can't do that. You know, because of Cory."

I give him a look and he follows with, "It was your mistake, Missy. You're lucky he's letting us go ahead. You're lucky we're not all arrested and having cavity searches right now."

"Sure," I say.

But Tom keeps talking. "You're not a child. You guys all take risks. It sucks and it's not generally fair, but you should at the very least feel a bit responsible," he says.

"Maybe now's not the time to be a moralist," I snap, pushing a finger into his chest over and over. He turns away from me, climbs back into the van, and slams the door.

CHAPTER 12

CAROLA

—

T HE DAY AFTER our moonlight meeting, I was exhausted. Depleted. I hadn't gotten home until the sun was beginning to come up. Some of the women probably could have talked until the next night's moonrise, jonesing off one another's energy and trauma. But I had had enough. So had Ocean, who finally said, "So here's what we're going to do. We will give him the option to go and we don't press charges. But he leaves us everything." We all agreed it was the right plan.

I made myself a cup of porridge, some tea, and sat cross-legged on my bed. Instead of my morning stretches—because who was I kidding, it was hardly morning any longer—I was starting my day with the Swearwolves. I placed the cassette in my little bedside player, which I mostly used to listen to guided meditations before going to sleep.

I was not surprised that Melissa ended up a musician. I knew her grandmother had started her on cello lessons the moment they moved in with her. But this kind of musician . . . I couldn't say I understood it. I liked the energy sometimes, and of course the rebelliousness. She had so much freedom. To know herself. And I suppose, reading the article, that she had those things. But did she?

I slid a fingernail through the cellophane seal and pulled out the liner notes of the cassette. The Swearwolves—*Claws Out*. As you accordioned out the insert, there was a full photo of the band looking very serious, and then on the other side, one where they were goofing around. In that photo Missy was standing up on a BMX bike wearing big chains around her neck. I didn't even really see the other members of the band. I examined her expressions, her shoelaces, her stance, her tongue piercing. I looked at the credits for each song, impressed by how many my daughter wrote. The design, the song titles—everything was so aggressive.

I put the cassette into the player and clicked forward to Melissa's ballad, "Not Looking for You Anymore"—the one that's supposed to be "about her mother." But I pressed stop at the chorus.

It was too much.

Shouldn't I be glad that she stopped looking for me, stopped wondering, that her pain stopped? I had to leave. It would have been worse if I hadn't. But she would never get that.

I left the cassette in the tape player, placing it on the window ledge, perhaps hoping an errant bird might come and spirit it away. I was due to lead a guided meditation for the new volunteers in an hour, so I began to gather my things and re-center myself. I find that when my own emotions are overwhelming, it helps to give back to others. Just the other day, one of the new arrivals cried through her whole first practice. She reminded me of myself the summer I first arrived. The bafflement of why I was there, the release, the sorrow of what I had left behind, the emptiness. It's taken all these years to fill myself back up.

After class, I approached her.

"Are you okay?" I asked. "The first time can be intense, I know."

She sniffed, gathering up her mat and water bottle.

"I'm fine. But thanks."

Later, after lunch, I saw the same woman rolling a suitcase out to a car.

"Leaving so soon?" I asked.

"Yeah," she said, opening her trunk. She had a bumper sticker that read *A Woman Needs a Man Like a Fish Needs a Bicycle.*

"Can I ask why?"

She looked uncomfortable.

"I guess I just needed a moment to myself, you know. Time away from my kids, my husband. But there's so much pain in there, it was overwhelming. I'm not as lost as I thought I was. So I need to go home."

I was stunned by this answer. I read the evaluation forms when residents left; they were always effusive. They wrote about reconnecting with joy, finding resilience, self-actualization, independence.

"It takes courage to stay and really look at yourself, to do that true soul searching," I offered.

"You don't know me," the woman said, and shut the door.

I watched her drive away and I felt anger flood my entire body.

OVER THE NEXT few days I listened to all of Missy's songs, over and over. The music sounded grating at first, and then it became catchier, and I found myself singing along and humming some of the poppier selections from memory while gardening, and minding the gift shop, while doing the dishes. I drove the ashram truck into Concord to pick up supplies and stopped at the library. I looked up newspapers from across the country, finding and photocopying every bit of press I could about her band. One of them had an advertise-ment for the entire tour, so I knew where she was almost every night. I took my bank book out of my dresser drawer and looked at my balance. I'd been saving my weekly volun-teer stipend for years. I had a little something there. I had made up my mind: I wanted to see her.

CHAPTER 13

MISSY

THERE IS ALWAYS a comedown when touring ends, but usually it coincides with going home and seeing friends and family, writing music again, tilling the creative soil. I am completely unprepared to be in Vancouver, alone, pregnant, and with only one good leg. I realize that I've never traveled by myself before. I wasn't like the other kids in the conservatory, who grew up traveling around the world. I've never left North America, and I've never been in a hotel alone—I never even went to the airport by myself! The only traveling I did as a kid was camping. Another thing to thank my parents for.

But here I am, stuck in a Vancouver hotel room until our manager can book me a flight back to Montreal. I can't go for a walk because at this point my ankle is throbbing. I certainly don't feel like writing music and everything on television—even the porn—feels achingly pointless.

I realize I haven't eaten anything in nearly twenty-four hours, but I'm also hardly hungry, the combination of hangover, sadness, anger, and probably some alien fetus making my stomach roil. But nonetheless, I go down to the lobby to

seek out a smoothie or salad. I find a place next to the hotel
and settle down at a table by the window and grab the abandoned newspaper on the table next to me. I skip the head-
lines, turning a straw in my smoothie, since it's all mostly
about Princess Diana and the horrible tunnel car crash. I remember watching the wedding of Charles and Diana with
my granny when I was a kid. She got so into it. She must be
so sad about how it ended.

I fish out the back pages and do the crossword, read my
horoscope, skim the comics. I'm just about to ditch the paper
when a headline catches my eye: *Sex Scandal at Ashram.* There
is a photo of a bunch of smiling hippie ladies of various ages.
I feel a strange uneasiness come over me as I scan the names
under the photo, confirming my suspicion, my sixth sense,
that my mother is in that photo.

A group of residents at a New Hampshire ashram have
accused the former guru of sexual misconduct.

"It's difficult to think of him as guilty, since we regarded him as our guide. But we had, and still have, a
spiritual study. We are still on that journey, with or
without his dishonesty," said Juniper Neligan.

She has the exact same hair: blunt bangs, straight sides to
her shoulders; everyone used to say she looked like Joni
Mitchell. A beautiful, deadbeat-mom kind of Joni Mitchell.

There is a photo of the guru, too, and I can't believe that
my mother left us for this guy who looks like someone's
pervy grandpa. He is so shriveled up, with the glassy eyes of
a creeper. Did she seriously not know what she was getting
into?

And then it dawns on me. New Hampshire. I know where she is. I. Know. Where. My. Mom. Lives. I have wanted to know for so long, and now I just don't know what to do with it. I read the entire article over and over until I've basically memorized it. Then I go back upstairs to my hotel room and try to dial my dad's number. It takes three tries because my hands are shaking so much.

"I found Mom," I say into the machine. "She's at a yoga center in New Hampshire. She left us for . . . yoga."

I'm about to pick up the phone to call Granny when Gord calls. They've arranged a ticket back home and a cab to the airport for a red-eye.

I hang up the phone and slide off the bed, and begin to cry. Pain is everywhere. I am sore and nauseated, throbbing inside and out. My body that has held me in a state of suspended pleasure for months is betraying me, and my spirit is slowly eroding.

RUTH

Perfect happiness is the privilege
of deciding when things end.

—SARAH MANGUSO,
300 ARGUMENTS:
ESSAYS

1.

Having a mother who is cold to you as a child never leaves you. A ceaseless inner chill. In my first childhood memory, my mother is saving my life. Corralling my sister Gail, our nurse Greta, and me into a rowboat. We watch my mother's pale arms, unused to hard work, row us across several miles of the rough Aegean Sea toward the burning port. Greta, who had been caring for us since birth, stretches her jumper around both of us and whispers soothing thoughts. As we approach, the city of Smyrna is awash in gray smoke. It is on fire. Our father never arrived on the sailboat to fetch us from the vacation house on the island, where we'd fled from our home on the mainland to escape the simmering conflict in the city.

2.

Greta taught me how to love. I begin to cry, afraid of the deep, roiling water around us, the splashes that fall across our faces from the slash of the oars. It is a sunny day, but the smoke drains the blue from the sky. As we progress, the chaos of the warring port ahead gets closer. *Stop sniveling!* Mum says, rowing harder. Greta squeezes me in a one-armed embrace. *It's okay to be frightened*, she says. We all fall silent, except for Mum's breathing, the occasional whimpers from the dog curled at Gail's feet. I try not to look at the glow of the city on fire. I feel for the first time the precariousness of life, which is perhaps why I remember that day, and no other days from when I was seven. I know for certain how quickly it could all be over. But when it really is over, I'll ask my son to scatter my ashes next to Greta's headstone in the family plot in Bornova.

3.

The thing about traveling in a rowboat toward a burning city, worrying that your father is dead, worrying the dog won't make it onto the next rescue boat—and he won't—is that it turns into a story that almost feels like a fiction, but one you can't shake. The further you are from being a child, the more your childhood self will feel like a character in a fable. I will feel irritable in Canada when everyone insists on canoeing for a good time. I'll tell my friends that campfires are a filthy business. Why would we purposely sleep outside in the cold? Any wild wind will set my heart racing. I will keep a box of emergency supplies in the basement: sealed brown paper envelopes of cash, drinking water, Aspirin, tins of beans and fish. But I know we were lucky in 1922. Later I learned that my parents were also lucky in the First World War, escaping internment despite their British passports. That my family's wealth and foreign passports got us from our own rickety rowboat onto an actual rescue boat once we reached Smyrna, ahead of less fortunate families on the beach. And that my luck in life was a balm to my bad luck in love. I may not be happy, but I am always safe.

Later in life, I will remember Turkey as a paradise—I'll skirt over the burning, the wars, the loss, and remember the heat, the way my family moved as though one unit. But when I eventually go back, I'll surprise myself by wishing to be home in Canada. A place I had always considered rather cold. A home will be the thing I'm always looking for but never able to pin down.

4.

When I meet my husband, Frank, we exchange our stories of September 1922. How, at the same time I was in the rowboat, Frank, also the child of Levantines in our village, was in Bornova crouching outside a window of my house, watching while a Turkish soldier got drunk on my grandfather's liquor and then danced with one of the taxidermy bear heads in our sitting room. Dishes smashed, jewelry thieved, the inhabitants fled and scattered. Some left days earlier on boats back to England and Italy and France, and others, like my family, were in the vacation houses on the islands. Frank's father had refused to leave, stubborn, convinced the conflict would soon blow over. When it didn't, he led Frank and his mother to a drainpipe some yards away from our house, where they hid. Frank crouched behind his father, who held a rifle with two bullets—enough for just two soldiers, at close range. Then they moved stealthily in the shadows behind walls and shrubbery, and into the church up the road. They hid under a quilt in the back by the pulpit, listening to the sounds of gunshots and explosions. My great-great-grandfather had built the church after arriving from Liverpool in the 1700s. Frank hid under the heavy quilt clutching his mother as the soldiers arrived. They smashed the stained-glass windows, destroyed the pews, even poked a bayonet under the blanket, but his family remained undiscovered, unhurt. A miracle.

5.

I thought I loved Frank when we met, but I didn't know love until very recently. It's funny how love can be any new feeling. Until you really know it, you're just guessing. My mother, who never thought much of me to begin with, called me weak that day, with my tears, my helplessness. Years later, my husband would betray me; Frank was the weak one. But he gave me my son, Bryce, and my granddaughter, Melissa. I'll always thank him for those two blessings.

6.

In 1997, I'll stand in that church again, trying to feel something momentous. I'll know I'm the oldest I will ever be, in the oldest city in the world. I was born here. I'm going to die here. For the first time in my eighty-plus years of life, I'm not afraid.

1.

Most people wouldn't choose to move 3,139 nautical miles across an ocean to a country they'd never visited with a four-year-old and a marriage that was less than solid. At the time, it felt like the bravest and sanest solution to our problems. We boarded the *Empress of France* and as Frank put our suitcases into the shelf above our small bunk, all the anxiety about leaving began to dissolve. We were on the boat, on our way to a new life in Canada.

2.

Little Bryce was interested in three-syllable words—the meaning didn't matter. So to him, everything was *elegant*. Elegant. Elegant. Elegant. Before we left, he would pick things up from the ground and say, *This is elegant, Mum!*, even if it was just a dirty feather. At dinner on the ship, I gave him a buttered roll. He held it in his chubby hands and gnawed it, grinning around the large formal dining room. I sipped my soup and blanched—the broth was metallic. Oh no. Just like the last time with Bryce. I was pregnant. Everyone else was murmuring about how delicious it was. I discreetly pushed my plate aside. Bryce chewed his bread, openmouthed and with abandon, then threw it to the ground and laughed. And that was when I saw her. Of course. I bent down to retrieve the discarded roll, and before lifting my head back up, I glimpsed Frank across the room, standing at the bar. His face bright and engaged, and I knew before I saw her. I couldn't even see her face, but I'd memorized that reddish-blond hair, the shape of the curls that fell below her neck. I wanted to lie down on the ground. And I would have if Bryce hadn't begun to wail.

3.

I had left Smyrna, left my entire family, to get rid of this thin childless woman whom my husband was so taken with. And so, when Frank suggested this journey, I was all for it. An ocean wasn't big enough to put between us, but it was the best I could do. And there she was again, trailing my life like a barnacle. I stood up from the dinner table and went out to the deck, leaving my son wailing. Surely Frank would tend to him if an entire dining room was watching. The boat was in the middle of nowhere. The water stretched out in all directions for farther than I could conceive. The sky was black. The wind pushed me about. It was so windy that no one else was on the deck. Gail had hated the boat. She had gone to Canada first, and wrote letters from her bunk below, where she had curled up, saying the upper deck made her dizzy. I leaned against the railing and threw up. The woman's perfect curl, the way everyone remarked that she was just so clever, clever like a man! I felt a depth of sadness as long and wide as the sea before me. I put one foot up on the railing. The ocean below so rough, I felt like I belonged down there in the chaotic swirl. I could dip out and over and this feeling would stop. The feeling of being on fire and drowning at the same time. I put a second foot up, testing. Yes, relief. And then I heard a voice. *Mum, Mum?* Bryce was behind me, had followed me out. The boat rocked, knocking him to his bum, and he began to cry. Out of instinct, I put both feet back on the deck and went to him. I pressed him to my heart and began to cry, the two of us sobbing together. For the rest of my life I will think of it as the time my son saved my life.

4.

Later that night, I would ask Frank, *Did I see Frances in the dining room?* He said, *Quite a coincidence, isn't it? The steak was just lovely. You wouldn't think they could cook a steak this lovely on a boat.* We left it at that. But I developed a simmering rage that would not leave me for many, many years. I remember when Carola, Bryce's first wife, used to caution me by saying, *All that anger is going to turn to cancer.* I told her feelings don't give you cancer.

Feelings are everything, she said.

1.

In Canada, I was weak. Or afraid. Or just overwhelmed. My feelings shifted depending on the day. It was hard enough to know how to find garden shears or proper olives, let alone figure out how to acquire an abortion. But in those first two liquid weeks, I didn't feel pregnant. I wasn't sick. I didn't notice my body at all. That night on the ship, I hadn't told Frank and I continued to keep my silence. Imagine if I had just let myself grow bigger to see if he'd notice? He mostly looked at me—or through me—as though I were a piece of our new furniture set. When we went to church, I'd hover at the top of the steps and wonder if I could slip forward and tumble down. But I could never bring myself to do it. There are moments in my life where I can look back and say I was brave, but this was not one of them.

2.

Bryce turned five, finally old enough for kindergarten. Gail and I walked our children to school every day that first month. Once, Bryce saw a man in a light suit walking a small gray poodle, and gripped my hand tightly, tried to hide in my skirt. He thought the man a soldier. We rarely just walked down the street in Turkey. I had memories from occasionally living in London and Vienna as a girl, but this was Bryce's first time anywhere outside Bornova. The new sounds and sights alarmed him in ways I couldn't have anticipated. And this was his first time at a real school, not just a handful of cousins taught by a hired instructor. After we dropped off the children, Gail talked about renovating her house and I watched her lips move but couldn't hear a thing. I finally just told her. Gail didn't hug me, or whoop with congratulations the way she had with the news of Bryce. She could see it in my face. *Well, this isn't like home*, she said. *You can have it taken care of.*

3.

I discovered how much I loved walking. The freedom of movement, down to the lake, and north beyond Gail's house into the farmers' fields. This was the freedom of living in this new country. Here, I could just walk for miles, and no uncle walking home for lunch would see me and scold me, or go tell my parents. No one would kidnap me for a ransom, as had happened to one of my cousins. Sometimes I walked to the water, where I'd dip my toes, and it was always in the water where I'd step out of my denial. And make plans. I knew that I wasn't attached to this baby. I knew I would need a few hundred dollars. I had some money my father had given me upon leaving Turkey, but it wasn't enough. But I would ask Frank. I would say it was for a new oven. He never touched the oven. We were eating bread that had just been baked in it, but I don't think he thought about it too much. Or he didn't want to know. He just left the bills on the bedside table, in the copper tray with the loose change, matches, and rings. So he knew without having to know. He got away with everything, even the burden of emotion.

4.

The woman didn't go away. Whenever Frank went away on "business," which seemed implausible for someone at his relatively low level at the insurance company, he was at her house. I discovered where she lived one day while walking home from my sister's house. Frances was standing in her yard, picking crabapples from the tree, not six blocks from my own house. Brazen. We stared at each other. I held her gaze. She offered a weak wave. After that, I often peered into Frances's backyard when walking down the dirt-packed alleyway between our streets. Once I saw that Frank's car was parked there. He was five minutes away, though he had told me he was going to Philadelphia. It dawned on me that Frank wouldn't stay with us forever. If I had the baby, maybe he would. Or I could at least prolong things. Without him, I'd have only a little money from my savings, no way to support Bryce. Again, I felt my weakness banging around in my chest. Amongst the Levantine families in Turkey, men stepped out on their wives all the time, it was almost condoned, but none of them ever left for good. I had watched my parents go through the same thing. That was probably why my mother had been so remote, so unkind. I didn't want to be like that. Every night, I wrapped myself around Bryce, making sure he felt safe and warm, loved. Thinking about Bryce, a bravery rose up in me.

5.

The procedure itself was less daunting than the arrangements. Gail and I had to construct a whole scheme to get to the hospital, complain of false symptoms, and check in under a pseudonym. We found the nurse with the sparkling flowered brooch on her uniform and, as we had been instructed, handed her an envelope of cash, tucked into a thank-you card with a picture of a smiling fox on the front. I was not used to hospitals. Back home, our family doctor made home visits. We had both been born on the kitchen table. Or so we were told. There was a thin curtain between my bed and that of a young woman, far too young to be in the same situation. The girl whimpered. She was frightened. Next to her bedside sat her stern-looking mother, who was also very young and held a baby in her arms. She kept telling her daughter in harsh whispers how ashamed she was. The French in Quebec was quite different from the French I had learned at boarding school, the accent indecipherable, but I could pick out enough words.

6.

I woke up after it was over, and was instructed to remain at the hospital for a while and rest. A nurse with a pretty pink scarf around her neck gave me a small green pill and a paper cup of water. I fell into a deep sleep but then woke in a fog, hearing screaming from the bed next to mine. I looked to Gail, who was sitting next to me, a grim look on her face. *Time to go*, she said. Later in the taxi home, I said, *I think the girl in the bed next to me, she was so young, I think she may have died in the procedure. I heard her mother sobbing.* Gail whispered, *No, she didn't die. That was the girl crying. You know it's very rare for women to die in that situation when you know how to do it correctly.* Gail sighed and explained that she had asked the desk clerk the same thing—what had happened to the girl. She said the girl's mother had a change of heart, had called the doctor. But they'd already started the procedure, they had to lie that she'd started to miscarry, but he knew. He intervened to save the pregnancy and the girl was quite distraught. She was crying because they had saved her baby. *Judge not lest ye be judged*, Gail said. *Especially in this situation. And I think it was likely someone messing with her, don't you think?* I looked out the window, my face burning. My marriage was over, and maybe I'd just done something unforgivable. That young girl had so few choices, and here I was with a comfortable life, and I could have made do. I'd made a selfish choice. Gail squeezed my hand. *Don't go feeling bad about this. You know if men carried the babies they'd have shops on every corner like the dentist offices for this very purpose.*

1.

My granddaughter, Melissa, grew up with too much freedom. But freedom was the whole point, Bryce said, of this living experiment. Sunflower Commune. Somehow autonomy and community were the two most important values, but all I could see was how those values were often in opposition to each other. You can't spend a whole life being yourself without ruining someone else. Gail and I were visiting for Melissa's twelfth birthday. I knew I probably wouldn't be able to make the trip much longer, even with Gail, who made everything seem easy. Sunflower was several miles outside of a small village that was several miles outside of a slightly bigger town. Towns were clumped like birds in a nest in the small valleys' clearings, with one gas station, a store, and a handful of modern homes beside a river, and then a continual rural void. Gail loved not knowing where she was. I hated the remoteness. By the time you arrived near the commune there was a feeling of lawlessness, a sense that families fended for themselves in this area. It reminded me of Turkey in that way. Some people feel protected by open space; I am unraveled by it. But in late summer Vermont was so green, rich with growth and promise. It was impossible not to feel alive. Gail pointed at a swooping hawk, which made her swerve the car toward the ditch and then right herself, heavy on the gas. The older Gail got, the more she leaned into living life like an outlaw. Sometimes she inspired this in me. When we pulled over at a gas station, I overheard the attendant tell the cashier, *Looks like the cast of* Cocoon *just pulled up.* He was talking about us! So when I paid for the gas, I slipped a packet of orange Trident gum into my purse without paying. We drove on until we saw the hand-painted sign on the thin lip of the highway: SUNFLOWER—THIS WAY. Behind us in the back-seat were two blue hard-shell suitcases. Between us a cooler with cucumber sandwiches, slices of cheese, apples, and a Thermos of coffee. I held my pocketbook in my lap for most of the ride until Gail said, *Are you expecting to have to make a run for it?*

2.

We were halfway up the winding dirt driveway when we came across a woman in a white cotton dress wielding a chainsaw. Gail couldn't help but stop the car and watch. The woman sawed off a giant branch as though it took no effort, bits of smaller branches and wood chips raining onto the ground, before the tree limb fell with a thump we could feel beneath us. The woman put the chainsaw down, pulled up her safety glasses, and waved, walking toward the car. Up close, I realized it was Tegan, whom I'd met on a previous visit. *Ruth!* she said, pressing one hand to her chest, soaked in sweat. *Welcome to Sunflower again! It's nice to see you!* I waved and Gail roared with laughter as we drove away. *Imagine that. It's kind of brilliant. Imagine!* I knew Gail would be impressed with the commune, and it would drive me crazy. But that was why I brought her along. A buffer. We parked under a lilac tree in the gravel lot beside a tractor that looked like it hadn't moved in a while. I greeted the dog, some sort of collie mix. I cradled his head in my lap as I swung my legs out onto the ground. The farmhouse was made of red brick, with a wooden addition built out from the side. The forest crept up behind it, and beyond the barn were acres of fields that went up the hill and down again. In front of the house were the gardens, and another few hayfields that were mostly cut back for the visitors to place their tents when it got busy. There were several small lean-tos and cabins here and there, people who came every summer and went back to the cities during the winters. *It's so pretty here*, Gail said, stretching her arms up in the air and doing some hip twists with the driver's-side door still ajar. I looked toward the house. Normally Melissa sat in the living room window waiting for my arrival and ran out to greet me.

3.

There was an odd silence before the door popped open, revealing Carola. She, however, did not look excited to see us. I didn't always like Carola, but I had to admit that she was the one who made an effort while everyone else at Sunflower tended to dance to the beat of their own drum. Carola pulled me into a hug, kissed my cheek. I noticed she had aged since the last visit; she looked tired. As I watched her bend down to embrace Gail, her clavicle was visible, her cheeks drawn, and she was quite pale against a bright purple terry-cloth sundress, with a clashing plaid shirt over top and white-rimmed glasses. She needed a proper haircut.

She invited us inside. *It's harvesting season, so most people are in the garden right now, but I've been trying to set up the house for you guys, come on in.* She opened up the first door, which led into an unlit woodshed with a perpetually damp smell. *Mind the floor. It's a bit messy here in the dark and Bryce has been meaning to put in a new lightbulb.* She tried to open the second door but it stuck, and then sprung wide with the force of her shoulder, unearthing another faunal smell.

Keep your shoes on, the floor's been splintering lately, she said, walking ahead with the suitcases and putting them at the bottom of the staircase. In these moments I could see remnants of how Carola was raised. She slipped into a polite hostess role, even if, like now, she wore men's black rubber boots and had leg hair long enough to braid. I sat down at the dining table while Gail picked up a fat cat that was winding around her legs. *What's its name?* she asked. *That's Che, but he's a biter,* Carola said, stirring a wooden spoon in a glass pitcher of iced tea. She pulled down several plastic cups from the cupboard above the sink. The cupboard door had one dislodged hinge and so hung on an awkward angle after she closed it. She tried to shut it properly, but it kept slipping down. She offered us some of the tea, and then I asked, *Where are Bryce and Melissa?* Carola poured two glasses and brought them over to the table. *I have no idea where either of them is, actually. Taylor, do you know?* she said, addressing a teenager I'd just noticed, who had been sitting on the old hardwood floor under the window playing solitaire. The girl shrugged. *She's mad at you,* the girl said. *She thinks you forgot her birthday. You know, you usually make those bunny pancakes and wake her up with them.* Carola said, frowning, *Oh. I figured she was too old for that. You remember Missy's granny Ruth, and this is her sister,*

Gail. Taylor suddenly looked shy. *Did you bring us any candy?* she asked, and I laughed. *Taylor, that's rude!* Carola said, but couldn't hide a slight smile. *What, last time she brought chocolates!*

I fished the Trident gum I'd stolen from the gas station out of my pocketbook and handed it to her. Taylor pumped her fist and grinned with an *Awesome! Thanks!* and ran off. We sipped tea, trying to figure out why things felt so ill at ease. Gail noticed a fat housefly floating in her glass and fished it out of her cup, then fed it to the cat.

4.

Carola opened the door to the guest room, and there was my son, fast asleep on the guest bed, the bedside table cluttered with beer bottles. *Bryce!* I shouted, as if he were still a teenager, and not nearing his forties. Carola slammed open the window, kicked at the metal bed frame, grabbed a handful of the empties, and left Gail and me standing there, staring at a shirtless Bryce, skinnier than I'd ever seen him, his beard so long it could have been a nest for birds. *Useless,* Carola whispered under her breath before exiting. He opened his eyes and groaned, *Mom, oh my gosh, what time is it?* I told him, *It is afternoon.* He sprang up and embraced us. His arms were like thin branches but felt substantial, muscles still firm. It was still the best feeling in the world, to hug my son. *You've lost weight,* I said. *I just finished a cleanse. It was transcendent.* Then he went on to tell us that he had had a few beers to celebrate the end of his cleanse. Then was up late making a present for Melissa. A large painting of bright primary colors in a swirl leaned against the wall. I couldn't make heads or tails of it, but according to him it was a field of unicorns. Then he had started to prepare our room and fell asleep. A giant white cat jumped over the windowsill from a tree branch outside and dropped a mouse at Bryce's feet. They had so many cats I never knew what their names were. *Ah, you shouldn't have, Snowflake*, Bryce said, picking the mouse up by its tail and flinging it back outside. The cat licked its paw, briefly pleased with itself, then followed the mouse out the window. *Is everything well, Bryce?* I asked. *Yeah, yeah. Why wouldn't it be?* He grabbed at the bedsheet and balled it up with the quilt, bringing it across the hall to the bathroom and throwing it inside. *You know how it is around here, always something going on! The washing machine broke, we've been doing laundry in the tub.* He was yelling then, like a manic child, over the sound of water flowing from the tap. Later Gail would complain about how we never taught our sons any house skills and for the first time I would agree.

5.

I decided to go find Melissa myself. Carola gave me a pair of rubber boots in my size. She explained how they would be better than my loafers in the mud, if I had to go searching in the fields. I took a boot from Carola, and just as I was about to put my foot inside, I glimpsed a flicker of movement in the heel. I turned the boot over and a mouse ran out, over my socked foot. I yelped. Carola nodded her head and said, *Oh yes, sorry, you have to check your boots. The mice are really into the house this year. The indoor cats aren't interested and Bryce doesn't want to kill them.* She shook the boot out and handed it back to me. It fit. *That's absurd*, Gail said, whose sneakers were good enough for the back fields. *So where might I find my granddaughter?* I asked Carola, hand on the front doorknob. *Honestly, I'm not sure. She likes the pond, and the big boulder on the top of the hill. She likes to sit with the sheep when they come in before supper.* And so we set off into the wilds, Gail laughing and miming me finding the mouse in my boot all the way up the hill. If I'd known then how little time we had left, I'd have laughed along with her.

6.

We found Melissa swinging from a tree branch, singing to herself, kicking her feet in the air. Her back was to us so we got to witness her unfiltered exuberance. I was relieved to see that she looked more like a child than Taylor did, though they were the same age. We called out to her, then stood under the tree as Melissa dismounted in one final swoop from the branch and settled into a cross-legged position below. She was wearing green overalls and a ripped white undershirt. Her hair, cut shaggy and short, stuck up in the air. She was filthy. She wasn't wearing shoes. She broke into a toothy smile. *Hi Granny! Hi Auntie Gail!* I said, *Happy birthday, Melissa. What are you doing out here by yourself?* She told us that she had decided to make the tree her new home. I looked around at the flattened area under the tree's shelter. She'd carefully cleared all the brush and made an ad hoc fence from a variety of sticks and fallen branches. She'd arranged a sleeping bag, a pillow, a teddy bear, a few mason jars of nuts and dried fruit, and an old army canteen. *And why are you going to live here?* I asked. *Everyone's annoying. Tegan's decided that we have to have okra with every meal. My mom has had the flu for like, two months. Chris won't stop playing the banjo. And all the summer people have stuck around longer than usual, ugh. And Dad is trying to write a play with Susannah who is like, crazy. She has long blond hair and she's always smiling.* Susannah? Before I could ask more questions, she jumped back up on the branch, swung a bit, and then back down to the ground. I caught her for a hug. *Let's go back to the house, your mom is making a cake,* I told her. *We brought presents for you.* Her eyes briefly lit up at the mention of presents but then a stubbornness returned. The same face Bryce used to make as a child. *I'm not going back. I live here now.* I didn't quite know what to say to that. *Come on now, we traveled a long way to visit, just to see you.* Missy shrugged. *So stay here with me.* I looked to Gail for backup, but my sister was grinning. *You've got an independent spirit!* she said, which Missy recognized as praise. Then Gail started walking toward the house.

For a moment, I thought Melissa would follow. Her face was inscrutable, and I couldn't tell if she was twelve or six or sixteen. Regression and maturity at battle in this girl. Then suddenly she put two fingers in her mouth and let loose an extremely loud whistle. *Baileeeeeeee!* she yelled. Sure enough, the sheepdog came bounding over the hill and toward Melissa. They collapsed like two long-lost lovers. She pulled treats out of her overalls pocket and led him toward the tree. *Bailey will stay with me,* she said. I wasn't sure if this was the saddest birthday I'd ever seen, or the sweetest.

7.

We ate supper with Bryce and Carola in the kitchen. The other commune residents roamed in and out, helping themselves to the stew and pot of rice on the old cast-iron stove, or heaped their plates with salad made from leafy romaine and dotted with sunflower seeds and apple slices. All of the chairs around the oval kitchen table were mismatched, and Carola sat at the end, high up on a stool, with her legs crossed, eating stew from a bowl. *This is Missy's favorite, I don't know why she doesn't want any,* Carola said. *Maybe you should bring her some,* I suggested. I had the strong suspicion that Melissa would welcome her mother's company in her tree. *Well, I suppose if she doesn't come back soon, I will walk a plate out to her and try to see what's what,* she said, *but I don't appreciate the manipulation.* Gail piped in, *It's not manipulative if you're trying to get your needs met.* Carola scoffed, *Children can be manipulative. They're human.* Bryce sat at the other end of the table, drinking golden cans of beer and thanking Carola so profusely every few minutes for cooking that she finally stood up and slammed her bowl down on the table. *Enough, Bryce!* It was clear we'd arrived in the middle of a war, and it had something to do with Susannah who was out in the yard doing some sort of spinning dance by herself in the clover. Both Carola and Bryce kept glancing out the window at her. When we finished eating, Carola cleared everyone's plates and brought out a homemade birthday cake. It was very pretty, with white icing and Melissa's name spelled in rainbow jelly beans. Carola said, *I'm really tired. You can bring this out to her.* She headed up the stairs, with Bryce trailing her. Gail and I made our way across the fields, carrying the cake. We took turns holding it, each nervous to drop it. Melissa saw us coming and lit our final march with a flashlight. The three of us sat under the tree, digging into the cake with our forks. *Why didn't my mom come and get me?* said

Melissa. *She made the cake, didn't she? Is she mad?* I told Melissa that her mother was not mad, but just tired. She'd had a long day, taking care of everyone. I tried to be gentle, to weigh my words. *A pretty cake for a pretty girl. Your mother loves you very much.* My body was so uncomfortable under the tree, sitting on the hard ground. I worried I wouldn't be able to stand up if I didn't do it soon, when at last Carola and Bryce ducked their heads under the tree boughs. Missy's face lit up. We piled everything into the wagon, and Bryce carried a sleepy Missy on his back over the hill like a child, even though her longer limbs and her arm of bright red jelly bracelets were a whisper of what was to come.

8.

The next day I drove Melissa into town and let her pick out a birthday present: a Sony Walkman. I don't think I'd ever seen Melissa so happy. I also let her pick some new clothes from the small selection inside the one department store, which seemed to specialize in power tools and cases of discount beer but had a small aisle of cheap clothing. *Mom is going to be so mad,* she said, giggling with delight, as she admired her red stirrup pants in the store's mirror. I had not planned to buy her an extravagant present, but she smiled so wide as she sorted through a bin of plastic shoes with silver stars on the toe, looking for her size, that I had to do it. In fact, I'd brought a gift for her, Bryce's old violin, still in excellent condition. When I gave her the violin she'd looked confused, and then remembered her manners and said, *Thank you very much, Granny.* We had lunch at the diner, plates of burgers and fries, washing it all down with soda. All forbidden food back at Sunflower, but I didn't care. This was my day with my granddaughter. I tried to ask her if she was happy, if she liked the farm, if her parents fought all the time, but she didn't want to talk about any of it. *What do you want to do when you grow up?* I finally asked. *I don't know, but I'd like to be rich.* Gail snorted. Melissa asked her why that was funny. *It's less funny than it is ironic. You'll understand when you're older.*

9.

The following spring, Bryce and Melissa showed up on my doorstep, a truck packed with their belongings, the old white farm cat, Snowflake, in Melissa's lap and Bailey squished between them. Carola was not with them. Someone had been injured on the farm and the family of the young person was suing them. They'd lost everything. And Carola had already gone. I didn't know how to talk with Melissa about what had happened, so I taught her how to play the violin. She was so good at it, so intuitive, a natural. I had been teaching music lessons to children for so many years and I'd never seen anyone take to an instrument the way my own granddaughter did. In a way, music saved her. Of course, she didn't stick with the violin. Once she tried cello in the high school orchestra, there was no turning back. Her life's course was set, but, as with everything, Melissa had her own set of plans.

1.

I am lucky to have lived as long as I have. Most people I have known and loved have already passed. After Gail died, I kept her ashes in an Ovaltine tin from the 1970s. The funeral home suggested a brass urn, but Gail wouldn't have cared. She'd worn corduroys with ink stains on both pockets for the last two decades of her life. I intend to bring the tin back to Turkey and lay her ashes in the family cemetery. I can't put it off anymore, not with what Dr. Lebel said so nonchalantly this morning. Four to six months. Try treatment, which will be hard on a woman of your advanced age, or do the things you've always wanted to do. What are the things I've always wanted to do? I always do the same things, I suppose. I go to church. I teach violin. I have lunch with friends. I call Bryce on Tuesdays. Life has had the same shape for as far back as I can remember, up until I met Cy six months ago. What I wanted was to be able to rewind time and meet a young Cy and marry him. Life's cruel like that.

2.

Cy usually stops by in the mornings at half past eleven. We were introduced by Marlene, my preferred teller at the bank.

I was next in line and an older gentleman was just finishing his transaction with her, when Marlene said, in her busybody way, *Ruth, this is Mr. Acropolis.* She winked. He looked at me, quite startled it seemed, and the skin above his white-and-gray beard reddened. Marlene suggested we drink coffee together at the café across the street, and he mumbled, yes, that would be nice. I was so surprised by this interruption to my daily routine, I didn't quite know what to say. I followed him out the door, cautious but charmed. I liked that Cy didn't immediately start talking, the way most men do. And I knew it could have felt embarrassing to be set up by your bank teller. But I was lonely, so why not? I used to be so shy. Not anymore. Who has the time at this age? You can get so accustomed to being by yourself that loneliness is not even noticeable, and the idea of conversation and company feels too effortful. You begin to wear solitude like a comfortable coat. But it's an illusion, getting so used to being alone that it feels pleasant. Cy helped me remember that other people weren't always bothersome.

3.

Looking back on marriage from the other end of life, it seems altogether a strange and desperate custom. I was married to Frank, someone who, in the grand scope of things, was ultimately insignificant to me emotionally, with the exception of our shared child. When Frank died, I felt a twinge for our former life, but it passed in less than an hour. Relatives called to soothe me and I had to pretend I had a depth of feeling I didn't have. I have the kind of feelings for Cy that are meant for marriage. That is a cruel irony. The way he smells, a cologne that makes me think of the spring, of new life. Oh, we would have had such a life together! I love how strong he is, even at his age. I can feel it, the way he holds me. And his gentleness, the way he is sincere in wanting to hear about my life, my whole life, when most of it is behind us. This feels important. To know the before, and to experience what feels like an endless erotic presence whenever he is near. God is giving me one last gift. And it is precious. Dutiful, doting Cy. If I could have designed a man to come to life, it would be him.

4.

Cy spent his young adulthood along the same stretch of the Aegean Sea that I did as a child and, for some reason, landed in the same area outside of Montreal in the 1950s when we both had young families. He managed to get on a boat to Athens with his father while Smyrna was burning and Turkish soldiers slaughtered most of the people he knew. He's never asked the details of how my family escaped; it would have been a difference that kept us apart, knowing that my family's money bought us escape on a boat, while everyone he loved died. But now my passport and privileges don't matter. We are simply Canadians now, and he has far more financial security than I do. Cy and I share memories of the same cypress trees, the same green-blue sea, the intensities of the climate and the people. We laugh together at the contrast in Canada: the gray swaths of seasons, and the mild-mannered people. Now, the semirural village of Beaurepaire we immigrated to in the '50s has become a thriving suburb, and we've grown old as the houses bloomed around us.

5.

Since Melissa and Bryce left, and since my sister died, I have been pretty much on my own. Bryce calls for distant conversations about nothing much, and my granddaughter comes to visit every few months for dinner, always makes a stop when she is home from touring with her band. I never ask directly, but I get the sense the two of them don't talk to each other all that often. Melissa can be difficult. A shy girl who grew into one of those brash women who says things just to provoke a response. She's not the same girl who used to sit at the window and give the sparrows names and character traits as she watched them bop around the feeder. I have to do something for Melissa before it's time for me to go. It's not her fault her mother left and she didn't have any role models. Who is she supposed to become, if she spends all her time with men in a van traipsing all over the country? When Melissa told me over the phone that she was quitting school to be in a rock group I took it quite personally. It was the same feeling I'd had when Bryce decided to quit pursuing business and instead become a full-time idealist. Only I'm more forgiving of Bryce. He was such a sensitive child, and I appreciated his sense of wonder at the universe. It's ill advised to be that way as a woman. The world will eat you up.

6.

It is odd, I suppose, that I discovered sex so late in life. Before, it was like a hobby other people had that I didn't quite understand. But the chemistry between Cy and me was a revelation. Romance, touch, connection. I'd never known it.

My wife, she didn't like it like you do, Cy said, after our third post-church encounter. He was stretching carefully on the side of the bed, arms pressing against the wall, wearing white cotton boxer shorts with a red waistband. Years ago, a comment like this would have made me horrified with shame, but now I didn't care. He clearly meant it as a compliment. *When you get to be my age, you have to give up all the hang-ups. We have bodies for a reason and we don't have them for very long.* Cy laughed, rubbing the spot on his neck that always aches. *Besides, my husband took a mistress soon after we were married. He even moved her here from Turkey and bought her a house down the road. For years he kept up a double life. So I'm making up for lost time.* Cy often leaves some time in the evening, so he can be home for his daughter's weekly phone call from Kansas. He walks up the street and turns right, through the garden he still keeps immaculate, and into his little brick bungalow. He tells me that it feels too empty now that he has the pleasure of my company. Before, his life was just his life. Now his solitude feels magnified. He once tried to explain this, suggested we move in together. But I just said, *Oh, Cy! You're such a romantic. We're just having a little fling.* He didn't come to church the week after I said that. I had to show up at his house with a tray of homemade baklava. After that, I understood that he was tenderhearted, and acted accordingly. I told Melissa that if you want to have a boyfriend, you have to learn how to lie, but kindly. Everyone just needs to hear what they're obviously yearning for. What's the harm? It doesn't cost you anything.

7.

When the gravity of my diagnosis hit me, I spent a day having what felt like an anxiety attack, immobilized with an infuriating fear. And then as quickly as it came, it receded. I decided a few things in a very short period of time. I will not get treatment. I will call Melissa and her mother and reunite them, no matter what Bryce wants—which is to punish his ex-wife till the end of time. They both have to figure out their lives, and they are going to need each other. And I have known where Carola was for years. Bryce told me, when Carola had contacted him, but he made me swear I would never tell Melissa. It seemed quite important to him, though I was never sure if we were protecting her or playing out his own personal revenge. I will go back to Turkey with Gail's ashes. I will set my old body free in the ocean that had once tried to take my young body—my final victory.

1.

My granddaughter and her mother sit across from each other at my dining room table. I brought them here as a final gift. I laid the table with the beautiful white linens I only use for the most special occasions. I put out the real silverware. I have high hopes. Missy sips from a can of ginger ale. She tears off the metal pull tab, stuffs her pinkie finger into the hole, then drums it on the table. She glares at Carola. Her mother looks out the window at the bird feeder, remarking on the size of the hummingbirds, *Nearly insects they are.* I've been humming with anticipation all week, like when you have a lightning bolt solution for a problem. Now that we are all here, I don't know what I want from them precisely, but I'd like for them to stop being ridiculous. Dying lends perspective to absurdity. I want to say, *Do you know these days are finite?* But instead, I take another sip of my wine. I was so hopeful when Carola first arrived. Missy has been marinating in her room for a week and I was at my wits' end. Maybe her mother could shake her out of it, even though they haven't seen each other for years. A mother's still a mother. But now I feel like a director who has forgotten the script. Maybe I forgot all the effort required to admit your mistakes, to be open to forgiveness. Those things seem easy when you're dying.

2.

When the roast is ready, I go to remove it from the oven, but Missy follows me to the kitchen and shoulders me aside, insisting on doing the lifting. The smell of the meat hits her and she turns her head. My granddaughter is pale, paler than when she had mononucleosis in high school, like the girl who was kept underground by a madman in a recent TV movie-of-the-week. Only instead of a bonnet Missy wears a toque, pants that appear big enough to house her cello, as big as her T-shirt is small, which seems made for a doll, with the words FREE KITTEN scrawled in marker across the bosom. I tell her to go sit back down, offer her the bottle of Aspirin I keep in the cupboard with the tea and biscuits. Missy has appeared hungover since she returned, but I have yet to see her drink. Carola helps me bring the food to the table. I take stock of the bounty before us. I have spent the previous several days planning and executing. But what have I done with my life? It comes in waves, that question. I spoon out roasted potatoes onto our plates, a sprig of crisped rosemary on each. Sliced carrots, scoops of gravy on slabs of beef. *Ruth, you didn't have to go to all this trouble*, Carola says. But she seems grateful, either for the food or simply to have something to say. Everything tastes incredible, knowing I only have so many more moments left to taste. Missy twirls a carrot on her fork.

So you left us for a cult, is that it?

It's not a cult. It's a retreat.

Oh, that makes it much *better. If it was a cult you could blame someone else.*

It's okay if you want to blame me.

Oh, is it okay?

The conversation escalates, but we don't stop eating. The clang of silverware, the airing of grievances. I can't remember the last time I made a roast. I get lost in the flesh of it all. I put my fork down. I ask everyone to think about what they are grateful for. Cy does this at every meal. It seems sentimental, but it's been making me feel more grateful anyway. *For example,* I say, *I am grateful to have you both here.* I reach for their hands. They are both warm.

3.

I can see their twinned cheekbones, matching eyelashes, the same filial yearning in their face. Unmistakably mother and daughter, but essentially strangers.

I've been listening to your band, Carola says. *The song about me was hard to listen to.*

It's not about you. The line between art and life might be thin but it is there, Mother.

I don't want to be here any longer. I get up and walk to the window and look out at the garden. I think about making a plan for the beds next season, choose which flowers, which vegetables, but decide not to. Let everything die. Return to the earth. The perennials will come up if they choose to. I feel invisible, like I'm already physically disappearing. The dinner conversation continues without me. Missy tells her mother how she used to go to the police station, asking them to look for her.

I'm so sorry. Your father knew where I was, but I suppose he didn't want you to know.

Don't blame Dad. He was basically insane with grief.

I return to the table. It's my turn, but it's increasingly clear that they may not listen. I reach for the ceramic serving spoon and tap it against the crystal water pitcher. *I have an announcement.* Their heads swivel. *I'm going to Turkey. And I wanted you two to reunite before I leave. It's time.* I don't say I'm dying, even though I had planned to. Instead, I say that Missy is clearly not doing well, and she needs a mother. Let bygones be bygones. At that, my granddaughter pouts. The phone rings. *That will be Bryce,* I say, excusing myself from the table, and they turn their heads at the mention of his name. Even after everything, Bryce will always be blameless, the most beloved. I pick up the receiver on the kitchen phone. My son's voice fills my heart. He knows I'm sick, and he has been trying to sell me on treatment. He tells me his travel schedule, the details for his flight to Montreal, where we will meet. *Write this down. Are you writing this down?* His concern makes my chest feel warm as I scribble notes on the back of a Hydro bill. Only when I tell him that his ex-wife and daughter are in the next room does he stop talking. *Oh,* he says. *Oh, wow.* When I return to the table, Carola is crying, and Missy looks even more ill. She stands up suddenly, and then falls over, collapsing onto the floor. Carola gasps, palms the ice from the water pitcher, and rushes to Missy's side. She draws the wet cubes across Missy's face until she wakes up. Carola holds her wrist, takes her pulse.

Fuck, Missy says. *Fuck fuck fuck.*

Are you sick? Carola and I ask at the same time.

Missy's head is cradled in her mother's lap. I stand over them, clutching the table's edge, feeling weak myself. *No, I need an abortion.*

4.

Missy sits on a stool, taking occasional sips of water. I offer the strawberry rhubarb pie I bought from the bakery down the road. A rectangular block of vanilla ice cream. Carola says, *Ice cream is all I wanted when I was pregnant with you.* Missy refuses the ice cream but allows me to cut her a slice of pie. Handing her the plate, I say, *Perhaps now is not an ideal time, but you will make a wonderful mother.* Missy looks at me as though I've suggested she fly a pony to the moon.

Don't be ridiculous, Granny. I'm still a kid, basically.

You're basically the same age your mother was when you were born.

And look how well that worked out.

Who is the father? I ask.

There is no mother. There is no father. There is a clump of cells.

Exactly, exactly, says Carola. *This is Missy's choice, Ruth. Don't pressure her.*

Missy screws up her face. She doesn't want her mother's support. For a brief moment I see Missy contemplating motherhood just to spite her own mother. She crosses her arms. Perhaps she is still a kid.

5.

I am feeling done. And suddenly desperate to see Cy. I tell Missy and Carola that I'm going out for a walk, might stop by a friend's house. Might, in fact, stay there overnight. Carola grins. *Good for you, Ruth!* Missy doesn't follow. She cannot comprehend that I'm a woman, just like her, capable of having a lover. I enjoy her look of puzzlement.

Don't run the bath and forget about it, I say.

That happened once, Granny. Once. *Jeez.*

I put on my coat and I look at them. Then I cross to the couch, stepping on the carpet wearing my outdoor shoes because I don't care anymore. I kiss Missy's forehead. *Good night, my dear. When I was pregnant I had the most vivid dreams. Maybe you will, too.*

6.

When I get to Cy's he is so delighted to see me that he throws his arms up in the air like a happy child. I lead him to the bedroom and hours later when I fall asleep in his arms, a part of me hopes that I won't wake up, because that would be a storybook ending.

1.

What do you do when you are not coming back? You make lists. You write letters. Things you want to say. You tell people you love them. You apologize. You get your affairs in order, as they say. See your banker, check your insurance papers. And Cy. Oh, Cy. I know, the way you can know something that's so true and so difficult at the same time, that I have no other choice. I write him a long love letter. I tell him he was a gift from God at the end of a long, hard road. *You renewed my belief in love, in this one life. No one loves like you.*

2.

My suitcase is too light to be logical but no one questions it. Gail's ashes are tucked in there, beside my good pair of shoes, a bathing suit, two cotton dresses, several scarves. The airport in Izmir is smoky and Bryce and I have to slip the officials one hundred American dollars to get visitor's visas. My grandnephew, Christian, is waiting outside. His car is quite old and disheveled but thankfully has air conditioning. I sense he was being punished by being asked to run this errand. The last time I saw him he was a toddler. Out the window, the city

of Izmir—the Smyrna of my childhood—sprawls before me.
I marvel as we drive and drive, unable to tear my eyes from
the red, endless desert on the left and the modern city on the
right. And then I glimpse the sea. It's a cloudless day, and
though we could have been at the house in Bornova in half an
hour, Christian is taking us to his mother's summer house near
Cesme, a one-hour drive away.

3.

When we arrive in the pastoral seaside town of my childhood, I find it has grown gaudy, its solitary charm gone, replaced by chaotic, slapdash housing, a luxury hotel, surf
shops, and crowds. All the people are unnerving. The noise
of Turkey is overwhelming, but it is an answer of sorts. I'd
thought of returning for so many years. The last time I went
home was before my divorce, when Bryce was still a teenager, in the 1960s. And now here I am. The village had always been barely a village at all, just a sparsely populated
beach escape. Now, it is bustling, with paved roads clogged
with cars, plus the usual donkeys, packs of roving dogs, and
families walking about. But behind the white gate of our
small family compound, everything is familiar, as if it has
been frozen in time. An outdoor kitchen with a roof attached
to a master bedroom, a living area outside with two enclosed
rooms on the other side, each big enough for a bed, a dresser,
and en suite bathroom. Bryce and I are given these guest
bedrooms. We unpack and go out to the courtyard for iced
tea and platters of fruit, cheese, and olives. I forgot the way
food tastes here. There's never a tremendous amount of vari-

ety but everything is perfect for the heat. For the first hour it is peaceful, and then the new nightclub next door begins to play loud music and doesn't stop until after midnight.

4.

I did not anticipate that coming to Turkey would bring a new wave of grief for my sister. Aren't I here to mourn my own departure? She has been dead for almost ten years, but I still see her everywhere as I walk the narrow streets to the village, test my toes in the sand at the water's edge, order a coffee from the vendor by the beach. I think of things to say to her all the time, memories from when we were kids I want to share. While I've missed Turkey for all these years, for Gail, it was the opposite. Gail never wanted to come back here. *Good riddance,* she would say. *It's a backward country and we're lucky we escaped—in every sense of the word.* Gail loved Canada. In the 1960s, she became obsessed with Prime Minister Pierre Trudeau and with the Kennedys. Her house was a chaotic mess of art supplies, afghans, and tchotchkes, all things our parents would have loathed. She only visited Turkey with me once, and had to be dragged. Frank and I had brought Bryce back every five years or so, and Gail refused, except for that one time. I thought once about moving home to Turkey, but I was comfortable in Canada, especially with Gail living right down the street. Gail did not indulge in nostalgia. For a while I was made up almost entirely of nostalgia. But still, I don't feel like she minds—it feels like the right thing—when Bryce and I drive to Bornova and we bury her ashes in the cemetery next to my parents.

5.

Bringing Bryce back to Turkey is like bringing a celebrity to town. The American! Of course, he brought a suitcase full of treats. Dinners late on the patio with the cousins, he is the life of the party, cracking them up with his stories. Finally, I get him to myself. We drive to the house in Bornova and sit in the garden. We only have a short time because now that the family fabric business has shuttered, they've begun to rent out the yard for the weddings of Turkish celebrities. Bryce's beard has grown silver, but I still see the little boy he once was, the one who was born in this very house. I can see his boyishness in the shape of his face, the mischievous glint in his eyes. The love I feel for him is almost unendurable. But I am tired. It is difficult to walk up a flight of stairs. My brain is cloudy—well, more so than usual. We have two days left in Turkey. I say to Bryce, *You used to love playing hide-and-seek around here, do you remember?* He looks at me funny, then says, *I do, Mom. Sure, I do.* My son always wants to talk about my illness, but I want to talk about the past. I tell him, *You were my shining star, you know that.* He looks at me again, as if I might be losing it, and says, *Yes, Mom, I know that, too.* I see that this nostalgia is mine alone. Bryce has years to think back on these memories, to remember. I have less time. *Bryce,* I say, *you know Melissa is not in a good place. You need to pay more attention when I'm gone. Don't let her drift away from you.* He denies this, saying she's doing great, her band is nearly famous, she makes more money than he does! So I simply make him promise that he'll check in more, make sure his daughter knows that he is there for her. And if he doesn't hear from her for a while, that he will follow up. And he promises. *I will, Mom.* Then he turns his gaze to the gardens before us. I follow my son's eyes. Inhale the garden air deeply into my lungs. My weak lungs. It's such a trip to be back here. *Do you ever think about who we would have become if we'd stayed here?* he asks. *All the time,* I say.

6.

On the day before Bryce and I are to leave, we are going sailing. I had asked for this, asked my cousins if they would take us out. We drop the anchor in the bay. It is beautifully sunny. Cloudless blue. We eat a little lunch of melon, white cheese, and fresh bread, pass around some wine. I drink two glasses. We spread our towels on the bow and watch the kids jump into the water. I watch Bryce and the other adults jump off the boat, joining the kids. I am still astonished that my own child is a middle-aged man, with a soft paunch, wiry hairs on his legs turning gray. He splashes about. He really knows how to connect with children. So why is it so hard with his own daughter? Because she is a woman now? They all swam away from the boat, leaving me alone on the deck. When they come back, I will be gone. I have had a wonderful life. I say a prayer of thanks to God, and I ask Him for forgiveness. And to watch over my loved ones in my absence. I slip into the water and begin to swim away from the boat. As I tire, the swirls that once tried to envelop my young body now embrace me. I offer myself back. I am not afraid.

Book Two

2013

[A] friend wrote to ask all the desperate questions I used to ask before I became a mother. How old were you? How long were you married? How long did it take? I wrote back, one of the great solaces of my life is that I no longer need to wonder whether I'll have children.

—SARAH MANGUSO,
*ONGOINGNESS:
THE END OF A DIARY*

I'm just another lady without a baby

—JENNY LEWIS,
"JUST ONE OF
THE GUYS"

CHAPTER 1

MISSY

I SAW THEM THROUGH the cottage's bay window. It was dusk, so the light was diffuse and I wasn't sure what I was seeing at first. I could hear the ocean below, down the steep and winding stone path on the other side of the pool. I'd gotten out of the car and stretched toward the failing sun, while Penelope ran around sniffing the dirt before rolling over onto her back and kicking her legs in the spasmodic frenzy of the recently unbound. I kicked at the gumnuts under the eucalyptus tree. Everything smelled so rich when I was away from the city. I took three slow deep breaths, then got a moldy box out of the trunk, filled with Granny's china my dad had shipped me from Canada in a recent cleaning frenzy. I was preparing to get the key from under the oddly menacing bunny sculpture we bought as a joke and that was now just one of the many inside jokes that make up a marriage. But I saw that the door was already ajar. Had we been robbed? Then I noticed an unfamiliar car at the far side of the house.

I was surprised Navid could get hard again. That was my first thought, as though I were watching my husband complete a simple athletic task I'd assumed he'd aged out of. A floral saucer slipped through a rip in the damp cardboard and smashed on one of the granite stones of the walkway. I kept watching. The box on the ground, arms crossed around a squirming Penelope, as though it were a show I'd paid admission to. I couldn't speak. Could hear only the steady beat of my heart breaking in my own ears. Then a soft rage. I don't know why I waited. It wasn't turning me on. Her hands were up against the wall above the couch, his hands curled around her wrists. I was concerned she might knock down the framed gold record that was my most prized possession. She was pretty quiet for such a small girl getting railed like that. The last time Navid had fucked me he was half hard, and he got tired. It was as though we were both determined to finish a project neither cared about anymore, and I remember thinking I was trying to work a battered baby bird in my palms, revive it with my efforts.

But watching him fuck her, I remembered how he used to have to *own me*. He'd been breaking off his first marriage at the time. He made it sound as if it was already over, but later I learned she didn't feel that way. Of course this was how it would end with us. If you begin as the beloved, passionate affair, you'll end as the one who is forsaken. Why should I be surprised that it would end in such a tawdry and ultimately banal way?

I couldn't turn away. It wasn't a half-bad show, for amateur porn. She had no body hair, two big leg tattoos, like all young chicks have now.

A FEW DAYS earlier, Navid had tapped me on the shoulder while I was mixing a song in the studio. Light was drifting in through a gap in the curtains, dust floating around in the beams. I pulled off my headphones. I hoped he was going to suggest dinner, or a walk, something that might involve us actually hanging out. Instead he told me he was going to attend a last-minute conference over the weekend. Even though I'd been craving connection, I was relieved to spend some time alone. It was our wedding anniversary the following week and I was dreading it. Would we sit through a dull dinner, wishing to be elsewhere? Every year I made him a gift, usually something that took months to complete. This year I was scrambling. The year had been difficult. A memento wouldn't cut it. I didn't mention that I was planning to come up to the cottage in Half Moon Bay. I needed the solitude and space, so I could really think, so I could *finally make a fucking decision.*

Well, here was the decision, made for me.

THAT MORNING I had gone to the thirty-second floor of a high-rise in downtown San Francisco to have my blood drawn by a perky fertility doctor. Because I'm a fainter, she told me to lie down on a leather chaise longue. I turned away from the needle and stared out at the cityscape. "This test is going to give us a snapshot of your ovarian reserve," she said. "Every day after thirty-five, your fertility declines."

"My life isn't really set up well for kids right now," I admitted, watching the tiny antlike cars driving up and down Potrero, "but I'm afraid it might be too late."

"No one ever really feels like they're ready!" she said, pressing a spot of gauze to my arm and handing me a Band-Aid. I blanched at the carefully labeled tubes of blood on the steel tray. How would I give birth, if I hate imagining what's under my skin? I stood up slowly and followed her back to her desk.

She sipped from a rainbow mug that read BE STILL. Her hair was very shiny, a deep walnut brown, and I squinted at her until she appeared to slip into the sun's glaring whiteness outside the window. She set up an ultrasound appointment so they could take a closer look at my ovaries.

"You know, parenting is hard, but it's the best thing I've ever done," she said. People always said that. I remembered doctors telling me similar things when I was young and definitely never wanted kids. But things were different now. For one, I thought about the future now. And I was less easily entertained. I'd done years of therapy. I was less angry. I'd already achieved the kind of success in my career that I wanted, so having a kid wouldn't keep me from any goals.

"Thank you," I said, and walked back into the waiting room, where anxious people waited for early-morning ultrasounds.

Maybe I could do this. I could join them. I'd assumed that she was going to tell me I was too old. But I wouldn't know until we got the test results. Part of me was thrilled about the possibility that I could still conceive, while another part was hoping my body would make the decision for me. If my egg count turned out to be too low, I could walk into the midlife I'd always planned without kids. I could see that child-free future clearly, and it looked like happiness and freedom, songwriting, and movie scores, friendships, travel, independence. I liked my life the way it was, mostly, didn't I? Lately, I was never sure how to answer that question.

I'd checked my phone, looking for a text from Navid, wishing he had remembered about the appointment, had checked in to ask how I was. No message. I figured he was in conference mode, phone turned off in his pocket. But it would have taken so little to remember and send a short *hope your appointment goes well!* text. He used to be so considerate, more present than anyone I'd ever been with. The slow unraveling of those daily thoughtful habits, the ease with which we took each other for granted, it was both mundane and crushing.

Last month, we'd gone to a record release party our old friend Peter was hosting. Peter had recently divorced and taken up with a younger woman, and begun throwing elaborate parties at his big house in the Presidio. He posted photos of himself on Instagram skateboarding and posing in Joshua Tree, shirtless, with this tiny woman making peace signs in every photo.

I'd lost the enthusiasm for that scene. It bored me, since I didn't get high or really drink more than a glass of wine. But this party energized Navid. He hadn't wanted to leave. I had some fun in the earlier part of the evening talking shop with a guitar player I hadn't seen in a while. I picked up a violin and we jammed a little and it lifted my spirits, but soon I was tired. The people I knew began to leave to relieve their babysitters or be up for work in the morning, and so I sought out Navid. For a half hour or so I couldn't find him, until I went down into the basement where I found him hovering over a Stooges record doing a line of blow with several young techie kids, something he hadn't done since he was young. He looked up at me and grinned, offered me the long golden straw. Do kids carry their own fancy reusable straws now? It was so insensitive of him to offer it to me like that. He knew my history. He just didn't care. I stared at him in amazement, as though we'd never met before, let alone were married.

"Does no one carry bills and you can't snort coke with your fuckin' Bitcoins or whatever?"

I thought it was funny. No one else did. It was a deflection of my hurt. That was all that mattered to me. They gave me the up-and-down look of people who didn't like to get high in front of people who aren't also partying. I remembered that look. It looked like scorn but it was shame.

"You're Missy Alamo," said a thin guy wearing an old Mudhoney T-shirt who probably would have been four years old when their first album came out.

"Yup, thanks for entertaining my husband," I said, pulling Navid up. "Come on, we should get going."

He looked at me as if I'd suggested we burn a pile of money, like why would he ever want to leave this basement full of strangers, who were now dancing ironically to the music we'd helped make famous?

I was done with getting high. I wanted to be doing something else. Navid was genuinely confused by this feeling, when I tried to explain it on the drive home. The streets were filled with partying kids, jaywalking erratically, ping-ponging about. I nearly missed a kid on a skateboard flying down a hill, skirting the front of the car and then hollering into the night.

"You could have just done one line. It's been long enough now. What could be more fun than this kind of night?" he asked me. His pupils were saucers. I could tell he was rolling in that euphoric way I used to *love*. I felt a brief pang of nostalgia. I would have loved that party if I'd gotten high, too—it made everyone interesting, and me interesting to myself. The way you hear music when you're standing in a crowd when you're high, there's nothing like it. For a second, I missed that feeling. I thought about going back to the party. But then I looked at my husband again, in the glow of the traffic light. His face appeared to be rapidly aging in time lapse. He *knew* I wasn't capable of doing just one line. That there were people who could do that, and people for whom that could easily ruin their life. I was in the latter camp. And if he loved me, he wouldn't even joke like that.

Suddenly the feelings of malaise cemented into definitive disgust. He said it again, that this was the best kind of fun night. He was being sincere. I didn't know how to answer him. When I pulled the car into the driveway, I asked him, "Don't you want to grow up, though?"

"If you think having a baby will make you grow up, that's kind of sad, Missy. We're grown up. This is our adult life. Now. We're not waiting for it to begin—we're here! It doesn't have to be a drag, changing diapers and watching TV at night, like, I didn't sign up for that shit."

"What's a *drag* is you doing blow with kids you are old enough to have sired, Navid."

The fight ended in tears, in him going back out to the party, and me ordering several memoirs about single parenthood from Amazon.

STANDING OUTSIDE THE fertility clinic after my appointment, I unlocked my bike, the sturdy baby-blue commuter with the white wicker basket that could hold a week's worth of groceries. I had bought it a few weeks back, trading in my sleek fixed-gear for a soft seat. I realized I'd purchased a parent's bicycle. I leaned it against a post—while trying to force my rusty bike lock back together. I'd been meaning to grease it for months and hadn't. Now it only worked periodically. I could not picture my life without Navid. We were going to grow old together, that was the plan. It felt like a certainty, despite how hard things had been. I was so frustrated with the U-lock not clicking into place that I wanted to throw it into the street, but all around me were young tech workers rushing to work, or standing in a long loping lineup for butter coffee, or almond milk lattes. Around them were flitting spark plugs of desperate people, a man with a ripped white T-shirt and a beard gunked in neglect, muttering about algebra and the coming world war.

A woman walked toward me, a baby wrapped around her chest, a leash attached to a German shepherd. She was the only one who didn't avoid the homeless guy, so certain in her gait, the dog jaunty yet dangerously loyal. This woman could climb a mountain with that baby snug against her, the dog at her side, solid and competent and like she knew how to rewire a house or defend her family against a bear. I felt briefly filled with promise. *I could do that!* I watched her cruise up the block, striding up the steep ascent, and then I caught a reflection of myself in the window of the café—I was a thirty-seven-year-old woman wearing an old KILL ROCK STARS sweatshirt with holes in the wrists for my thumbs; my half-blond hair was unbrushed, growing out an awkward ombre experiment and twisted in a flaccid topknot; an old Tupac song blared in a background whisper from my headphones, the tick-tick of the beat. My nail polish was chipped. I had a bruise on my leg right below my cutoff shorts from where my cello case always bumped when I walked. I did not look like anyone's mother. I barely looked like I could keep an aloe plant alive.

But Navid was skilled at nurturing plants. Our home was a greenhouse and I rarely watered any of the plants. When he left town he had to write out painfully specific instructions and still I often killed something if he was gone longer than a week. He had three siblings he'd helped raise, and was the favorite uncle to his nieces and nephews. In fact, he was far more comfortable with children than I was. He was a natural—people often remarked on it. As I pedaled away from the fertility clinic, the U-lock atop a mountain of take-out coffee cups in a bin, it occurred to me, why couldn't that be the solution? I hadn't always wanted a kid, and that had shifted. Perhaps it could for him? Maybe his vehemence the other night was just coke talk. It could reinvigorate us. But Navid didn't have the looming deadline of turning forty, this dark gate closing in under two years. He was forty-five.

WE GOT MARRIED when I was thirty-two, when I had so much more money than I'd ever had before, and I finally felt capable of making a mature decision. We'd been together for almost five years. Agatha, who became my best friend after we moved to the Bay, who quit music to become an astrologer, said it was the decision typical of someone on the tail end of their Saturn return. Usually I just smiled and nodded at her star-talk, but she'd been right. It felt like a period of rebirth.

I had just bought the cottage in Half Moon Bay. Agatha officiated the ceremony in the yard. She brought Finch as her date, back when they were just newly courting. We invited a few friends and our families—it was the first time my parents had been in the same place since Granny died—but it wasn't a huge event. Tom, Billy, and Alan played some acoustic songs, Alan's husband DJ'd a little dance party. Tom's kids were teenagers, gangly and lost-looking, sneaking joints behind the cars, as Tom and Cory were in the final season of pretending their marriage wasn't perpetually on the rocks. My mother had invited Tegan, who had been a sort of aunt figure to me as a child at Sunflower, but who I had barely known for nearly twenty years. When Navid and I left for our honeymoon in Mexico, my mother and Tegan stayed in the cottage, painting the walls and starting a little garden. In the years since, I'd let them visit any time they wanted. Neither of them had any money to vacation, so every now and then they'd come and spend a few weeks there. Originally a rough, slapdash log cabin, we'd modernized it over the years, insulating it properly, adding a new bathroom and a black-bottomed pool. It was our oasis.

The wedding weekend felt like a merging of my childhood and adulthood, a ceremonial push into the next phase of my life.

BUT NOW NAVID was forty-five, and forty loomed for me, daring us to look at ourselves, decide what was important to us. It was the first time—in a long time—that I had envied men. I was deeply jealous that Navid could wait another decade to have children, if he even wanted to.

"Wait until we're midforties, then maybe we can adopt or foster," he'd once said, as though adopting a child were as easy as rescuing a shelter dog. We were standing at the market, shucking corn in front of a big bin.

"You're not understanding how disorienting it feels. It's an embodied experience, this yearning. It's not intellectual at all. It is physical craving," I said, shucking the corn so fiercely the cob went flying into a display of oranges.

The only thing I could compare it to was how I felt at twenty-one, the reverse of the feeling that I didn't want a baby, ever. It was that definitive.

Navid rescued the cob of corn, putting it far too calmly into our grocery cart with the others, in the nest of bitter lettuce, frozen slabs of salmon, cans of cold-brew coffee. "I just think you might be confusing societal pressure and marketing with something physical happening in your body," he said. "You don't need to be a mom to have meaning in your life, that's just the messaging all around you. I know you, you're romantic and impulsive. This is just a midlife-crisis thing, and it will pass."

A woman holding a toddler in her arms walked between us, muttering "Excuse me," but she gave me a look that said *Forget this guy.* Or maybe I was imagining it, the signs from the universe telling me what to do.

"Well, I hardly think you're unbiased in that observation," I said.

But some days I thought he had a point. There weren't many women without children at my age. Or at least we didn't know many. Most of my peers were now parents. Was I mistaken and this feeling of peer pressure was just a run-of-the-mill midlife crisis? Was I just bored and unimaginative?

Agatha told me it was very typical for a Virgo with

Aquarius rising to flip from believing one thing to the exact opposite. But I wondered: if my conviction was so change-able, would I ever be able to believe in anything absolutely? I wanted a solid core. I wished for the fuck-you-all certainty I had had as a younger woman. She was a fucking asshole, self-centered, acting out, and confusing vulnerability with weak-ness, but at least she had a strong sense of self.

So, for a while, I let it go.

AFTER THE FERTILITY clinic, I went to see Judy, my therapist. I ran my fingers along the flat leaves of the ponytail palm in the corner, and explained, as I always did, the pros and cons of having a baby. Judy had endless patience. Her office was a jun-gle of well-cared-for plants and meticulously chosen soothing decor. But this time, after my rant, she said, "You don't sound like you have a baby-decision problem. You sound like you have a should-you-leave-your-bad-relationship problem."

She usually just asked questions, so I was startled by her assertion. Was that what it sounded like, that my relation-ship was the real issue?

"Navid and I are solid. The only real problem at hand is the ticking clock of my dying ovaries. All relationships have ups and downs."

"I wonder if you might reflect on that, though. It's been a while since you've been happy with Navid."

This observation nagged me on the drive up to the cot-tage. What gave her the right to say that? But it bothered me because she was right. Standing outside, being an accidental voyeur to my husband's affair, she had a real point. Fucking Judy. I hate when she's right.

After staring at their vulgar, unruly display, my thoughts became unstuck—this was *my* fucking cottage, the one I bought with the money I made from the song that won an Oscar. That was the wall my mother painted antique sea blue, the couch where Agatha and I sat singing Violent Femmes classics at the top of our lungs, before running down the rocky path to the ocean. This was where the band had retreated when our beloved manager died of cancer, spending the summer lying in the grass, eating elaborate meals on the long wooden table on the deck, remembering our early days together. That was the quilt I hand-sewed while my back was out a few summers ago, and that was *my* regularly half-hard cock, driving into this little baby thing right now. I could tell she had breasts that still pointed upward, because he'd turned her around and was now pounding her still, with even *more* vigor I hadn't seen in years; this girl, whose lips were now curled in a gross monstrous shape, eyes rolled back in her head, screeching, was someone who appeared to have left a University of California–Berkeley denim bag strewn on the doorstep, a loaf of bread now being pawed at by a fearless chipmunk, the door half ajar. They hadn't even waited to unpack. Or close the blinds. That was how desperate they'd been. She was a student, no doubt, from his Intro to Film Studies course. A teaching job I got Navid because I made Tom feel sorry for him, about how little he'd accomplished in the last ten years. How he fucked around teaching yoga and making birdhouses and researching for a documentary he never shot any footage for. Or was she one of the girls from Pete's party with the gold straw?

I got my phone out and texted Agatha a barely decipherable *Navid is cheating on me. I think we're over.*

Then I put Penelope in the car with the window cracked, and heard the buzz of Agatha replying to me over and over in my pocket as I went into the cottage and began to yell at them, throw whatever I could find at their heads as they struggled to dress.

"This is my house!" I screamed like an idiot. "I bought this house!" She grabbed my quilt to cover herself, but I pulled it away from her.

"I made this quilt! I own this house!"

I had never in my life cared that I bought the house; I'd never cared that I was the one who made more money, who floated us in the lean years, whose royalties and residuals kept us housed in the Bay Area when everyone else besides the tech assholes had fled. I'd never felt an ounce of resentment until that moment, and I unleashed it. Every horrible thing I knew he probably thought about himself, I was happy to confirm it.

I made this poor girl cry from fright, gripping the quilt she'd covered herself with. She ran to the rental car, got in, and locked the door. Was I more jealous of those tits, the way they were perfect and taut, than I was of the cock inside her, or any other part of Navid?

Maybe I hadn't truly wanted him in years?

Though some fucked-up animalistic misfiring made me want him right then.

Or maybe I just knew I was ovulating. Lately whenever I was ovulating I noticed men everywhere. I stared back at them when they lingered on the edge of condo construction sites, beat them to the punch. They would see something in my stare that stopped them from hollering. The way I appraised their biceps, strong hands, stamina, and softness of stubble. Then I would go home and put my groceries away and watch them through the curtains and daydream about one of them coming in and just taking me on the kitchen floor. It felt disgusting to feel connected to this biological mess, these urges.

I YELLED AT Navid about how he was free to go live in some dorm room with this skank. Even as the words came out of my mouth, I knew I was being horrible. I was turning into a monster.

I threw his laptop onto the driveway. It was amazing how easy it was to hurt someone you love. I didn't think I could ever stop loving Navid, but I didn't respect him anymore, or trust him. I'd never felt so betrayed, and in such a humiliating, predictable way.

He stood there, taking it, completely naked, still half hard.

I was actually yelling about my youth, my wasting time with him because marriage was something you stick out, commit to, something you work at, even when you're miserable every day for years, even when you avoid going to bed, watch reruns of inane shows while claiming to be "working," just so you don't have to see them clip their toenails at the edge of the bed, or hear them complain about the thing they'd do anything to change.

The girl, tired of being locked in the car, turned the ignition on and drove away.

"Is she even old enough to drive?" I yelled.

When I ran out of insults, when I had said all the things

I regretted later but that felt satisfying in the moment, he sat by the edge of our pool, head in his hands. He didn't fight me. He mumbled weak apologies. They weren't enough.

"How could you do this to me?" I asked. I walked back inside, trying to still the heaving sobs that were painful now but felt unstoppable. I took the wedding photo from the mantel, gripping it as though my hands were claws, went back outside, and threw it in the pool in front of him.

"You don't want me anymore, Missy!" he yelled, standing up. "You cringe when I touch you!"

I was about to launch into a monologue about his fragile ego, his male insecurity, but I knew he was right. I had already left him. Years ago.

"And *now* you want to have a baby, when you can barely look at me when we fuck? Why? Why now? It's not just because I'm forty-five that I couldn't get it up—it's the visible disdain in your face! You can't hide that shit, Missy. You can't."

"There isn't much time left!" As I blurted it out I realized how awful it sounded, but it was true.

"I never wanted to be a dad. You knew that when we got married. You were always telling me that story about trying to get sterilized, how mad you were about how patriarchal those doctors were, but now they were right, huh?"

"Shut up! I didn't want to be a mom, either! But now I can't stop thinking about it! I don't know what's wrong with me."

"Go to a sperm bank, Missy. I'm not going to have a baby with you when we're in such a bad place. You know I still love you, you know I want to make it work. But it can't keep going the way it was."

"Are you in love with her?" It sounded pathetic coming out of my mouth.

"No," he said, but his face said he was. "I like the way she looks at me, she thinks I'm *cool*. The way you used to look at me when we first met."

"Am I so easily replaced by a younger, prettier face?"

"Of course not, I wasn't trying to replace you, Missy. Seriously, it's just dumb. Dumb infatuation! It's just lust."

But lust is a lot. It was the whole reason he divorced his first wife, that feeling between us. That wasn't nothing, and this probably wasn't either. But it was what you're supposed to say, what you're supposed to feel, in these moments. As if the new person is just an accident, a phase, everything to avoid saying you're newly in love, and you aren't in love with your partner anymore.

He pulled me close and into a kiss that was more electric than any kiss we'd shared in years. I'd forgotten about kissing, how good it could feel. After a few moments, I remembered why it felt that way, and retreated, dizzy, and jumped in the pool with all my clothes on. The weight of them pulled me down. He jumped in, too. We stared at our weird watery bodies, me in jeans and a blouse, him completely naked. We didn't have to say anything else.

When we surfaced, we were over.

CHAPTER 2

CAROLA

———

L ARRY WAS TEACHING me how to shoot. And it was all I could think about. Like the time I got addicted to playing Tetris on the iPad. I loved the satisfying ping of the bullets as they hit tin cans hanging from the tree out back behind the house. I didn't want to kill anything. Neither did Larry. But we wanted to scare off the bears from the compost. They were getting too comfortable this year. We couldn't let the cats out anymore. Rufus did fine on the one front leg. But still.

It's a strange thing to be thinking about while leading a meditation group in a meadow, high up the hill beyond the center, on a late-spring afternoon. Bucolic. The kind of new-earth smells that made you want to burrow in the mud like a worm. But it was so quiet I thought I could hear the ping of Larry's shots in the distance. Sounds traveled far in the valley. It could surprise you.

The Inner Quest was one of our most requested wellness retreats. I had created it about ten years ago when the center was close to bankruptcy and we had to find a way to get more people to stay for longer periods of time. It lasted a full week, and necessitated that you hike up into the forest and commit to self-work the entire time. There was a two-acre meadow where we had built ten yurts in a circle around the clearing for the purposes of our weeklong retreats. The plan worked. After a few bumpy encounters with the IRS, we hired some business folks and then officially became a corporation. Not something we advertised, but it was easier to run that way. Now everything ran pretty smoothly. Especially the retreat. I could lead it in my sleep.

I sat among the clusters of clover and buttercups, some flattened under yoga mats. It was our heavy season; spring always was, Everyone wanted renewal. New divorces, people who got through winter but weren't totally fine, anyone who needed a rest, a new direction. The group in front of me were the usual suspects—recovering drinkers, newly single, depressed, and oh, the anxiety was everywhere. In all of them. Despite their money. They all had to have a lot of money to attend the weeklong workshops. We used to accept anyone who could do workshare, but less so now. It was partly why I had moved off the campus and into a larger cabin a few miles away. With Larry and the dogs and the bears in the compost and the beehives in the front yard. Larry, who said things like *I reckon it's going to be a wet one.* Who always left me the big umbrella by the door whenever there were clouds overhead, looming above our cluster of dense hugging trees.

I was sitting cross-legged on a small woven mat, teaching a group of women about the importance of adopting a healing breathwork practice. It was the final day, and therefore *the day of sacred silence.*

An ant crawled over the exposed skin of my ankle, using it as a bridge to the other side, and continued on its way. I'd always been able to rely on my body. My spirit was the thing that could falter, be lazy. That was why it was my life project, I suppose, to remedy that schism in myself and others.

I'd sent my sister, Marie, our catalog once. Later when we spoke on the phone she said it was ironic that I was teaching others how to be more self-actualized. *No one in our family can talk about emotions. No one has ever been taught to have that kind of emotional intimacy with ourselves or other people.* I took her off the mailing list and didn't answer her calls for several weeks. Which I can see now was playing right into her narrative.

I RAISED MY right arm, signaling that the group should inhale. I counted to seven, lowered my arm as they exhaled. I walked them through each breath cycle using only my hands and facial expressions. The truth was, I had instituted the final day of silence only recently, because I had been so tired of the pleasantries and requests for insights by day five.

"That sounds like self-care," said Blue sarcastically, when we were sitting in the mineral springs on our day off, exchanging foot massages, leaning our heads on carefully folded stacks of white towels. We were always joking about the things we wanted to do but couldn't justify as actual self-care. Like in the summer when we sometimes rode bicycles down to the ice cream shop in town on Sundays. The last time we did that we hid behind the dumpster while Blue smoked a single American Spirit and talked about applying to grad school.

"Do you think I should?" she asked.

"How should I know?"

"You have wisdom, you're twenty years older than me! Tell me what to do."

"What would your mother say?"

"She'd say I should find a rich husband."

"Definitely don't do that," I said.

"See? You're like the mom I wish I had," she said, stubbing her cigarette out on the side of the dumpster.

"I was not a great mom," I admitted.

Blue looked at me curiously. "That seems impossible. You're the first person from the center I think of calling when I'm having a problem."

"Huh," I said, thinking that was possibly a sad sign for her life, and not a compliment to me, but I gave her a side hug as we walked toward our bikes to ascend the hill back to work.

But Blue was right that making the last day of the retreat a silent one was, in a way, self-care. It conserved my energy so I could keep giving it to others. I cared about everyone who took my workshops, even if I didn't like some of them. I wanted them to benefit from it. I had never in my life been able to find the right balance, giving people I cared about too much, burning out, and being unable to give anymore. It was my life's work, to let go of wanting everyone to like me.

A squirrel came close to my mat. I was sitting so still, I don't think it knew I was sentient. We held eye contact, and when it realized I was a giant living, breathing thing, it scurried off up a tree. This was the moment I normally said, *Sit with your thoughts, watch them float by you, like a cloud.* This was their fifth session, so they knew to do this already.

I'd been running the workshop for years and had trained others to lead it, but there was a bit of the cult of celebrity about mine. The grayer my hair got, the longer I was with the center, the more respect I garnered. There were waiting lists of hundreds who wanted to attend. We were booked solid for the next two years. Every day I received more emails and even paper letters from women who swore the workshop had changed their lives. I couldn't even read them all to respond.

I held out my hand in the air, a flat palm, emphasizing my five fingers. Then I touched my right eye with my pointer finger and mimed shutting my eyes. Five minutes within yourself.

When I glimpsed their eyes closed, I pulled a lime-flavored lip balm from my fanny pack and applied it to my dry lips, then took a long drink of lukewarm water from my canteen. It's not that I didn't believe in what I taught. If I wasn't able to ground myself in my breath, contextualize the chaos of daily life, be in my body, I didn't know where I would be, probably floating in space, untethered, I suppose.

I hadn't been all that present in my joy lately, but I tried to show up for myself and be grounded as I led the women through their journeys. It was usually this time of the retreat that I started to feel solid, grounded, present in the world. I loved to see the group transform from harried city folks to women more in touch with their bodies and the natural world, who tapped into the inner selves they'd been ignoring for years. It was fulfilling to see, especially the one skeptic who had been dragged here by a friend. There was always one in every group. On the day of silence, they loosened their crossed arms, they finally managed to do some of the yoga poses they had previously assumed were too difficult, and they looked up at the stars at night and breathed deeply. I heard the whispers shift from *I'd kill for a latte and a scotch and soda* to *I haven't felt this calm in years.*

The bright spring sun was shifting behind the clouds as I rang the bell to signal that they should open their eyes. I led the group into Savasana. A group of chickadees chirped in the bushes, and I watched them jump and thrive. A squirrel made a sound like static feedback from high atop a maple tree. I was so transfixed by the sound that I startled when a volunteer came through the bramble and tapped me on the shoulder. She ushered me into a nearby huddle of maple trees. I knew immediately that something was wrong. She mouthed, *I'm so sorry,* and handed me a message from the reception desk. *Tegan called. Chris died. There is a memorial next month. She wants everyone from Sunflower to be there. Says Chris would have wanted that.*

I hadn't seen Chris in years, but I was overwhelmed by grief as I read it, crying out and startling the attendees, who lifted their heads from their resting poses. The volunteer opened her arms and held me there, sobbing so unexpectedly. I'm not sure why the news hit me the way it did, given our somewhat accidental estrangement, the way lots of friends move apart as they age. I knew he'd been sick. I'd been planning a visit the next time I took some time off.

"Would you like me to ask Aruni to come take over for this evening?" she whispered.

"No, I'm okay. I'll be okay. This is what I'm teaching, right? To be present for our emotions as they come."

She nodded at me.

I got through the evening meal and twilight nature walk. I stared up at the full moon. I remembered how at Sunflower, when the moon was full, we would build a bonfire and bring out all the instruments and play our hearts out, a clanging rock opera. Chris would stand on one of the nearby boulders, naked if it was summer, and howl up at the moon while beating his chest. He always acted as though he'd just been set free from some enclosure, running his body and his mouth, singing and jumping, twirling and pounding the ground.

I LEFT EVERYONE around the fire to retire to my yurt alone. Sometimes I snuck my phone on these retreats, so I could text with Larry at night, but this time I'd forgotten it. I read and reread the note. I thought about how terrible Tegan must feel, though she'd had so much anger toward him at the end of their marriage. And of course I wondered how Bryce was doing with this news. His life had grown far more conventional with age, but the last time we spoke, I could tell Bryce admired the sustained wildness of Chris's life.

I heard a rustling outside and grabbed my flashlight, preparing to tap the metal side of the bunk to prevent a raccoon from nosing under the canvas and stealing my toothpaste. But then I heard my name, softly called by my favorite voice.

"Carola, it's Larry. Can I come in?"

Larry had never once come up here, except for walks sometimes with the dogs when the camp wasn't in use. "I brought you your phone, it's been ringing off the hook."

He came into the yurt and sat on the bunk. He was so tall and hulking, with his fluffy graying beard and giant work boots, looking at odds on the tiny cot. I scrolled through, mostly Tegan and old Sunflower friends. I slipped it into my pocket and curled up beside him, laying my head in Larry's lap while he ran his fingers through my hair.

I got my phone out again and scrolled the texts.

"Chris died, one of the four founders of Sunflower," I said.

"Oh, Carola, I'm so sorry."

"I'm sad," I said, like a child pointing to a sad face on a mood board. But it felt that simple.

"Oh, of course you are." He kissed my forehead and took a deep breath, then asked the question he'd learned to ask me in these kinds of moments. "What do you need?"

"Nothing. I'm going to call Tegan and make some arrangements to go to the memorial—it's just outside of Burlington."

"Okay."

"You don't need to come along."

I could feel his body relax.

"You sure?"

"Yes."

"Do you want to come back early? I'm sure someone could come up from the center and take your place for the morning goodbye circle tomorrow," he said.

I shook my head.

THE SMALL LOG cabin Larry and I shared sat on ten acres of property. Our dogs, a collie named Pepper and a German shepherd named Saturday, bounded up to the car as I drove up the winding lane, shaded on either side with brush and tall trees. When I reached the house, I crouched down to embrace them. They pummeled me with their big paws on both shoulders, licked at my tears. "I've missed you, too," I said. Pepper backed away and leaped into the air in a spiral shape, the way she does when she's overwhelmed with excitement, and then barked. If she could talk she'd be like one of those kids who says *Mommy, Mommy, Mommy* nonstop morning to night. It had been a long week away from them.

Larry was on the roof of the bunkhouse he was building for his grandkids, just to the right of the house, where he had cleared the brush. The inside was a mess of plywood scraps and sawdust, but it was starting to shape up. He had accomplished a lot in my absence.

"What's all the fuss?" he said, which was a quintessential Larry question. Larry never fussed. He actually barely spoke. He was like one of the maples that surrounded the house. He made me feel safe. There weren't any butterflies or passionate arguments, just a consistent warmth between us and it was everything I'd ever needed. Something I realized once I stopped expecting him to blossom into a conversationalist. He spoke rarely, but he listened. When Missy met him, she said, *Is he conscious? Does he grow moss?*

"I just missed them is all," I said to Larry, while giving the dogs a thorough ear scratch. "I wish you wouldn't be up on the roof without someone here in case you fall."

"Don't you worry," he said.

"I'm going inside to make some calls."

I left my bags by the door and pulled on my plaid house slippers. The cabin was mostly one open room, with a kitchen on one side, a living room on the other, and a bedroom in a lofted area above. A large bay window opened out onto the backyard, where there was a clearing for our garden. Beyond that it was just abundant forest. Larry had put a fire on in the woodstove, the coffeepot was full, the glass bowl on the kitchen island was full of green apples, bananas, plums, and cherries. The way Larry loved me was to pay attention to the small details. I poured a mug of coffee, pulled my feet up under me, and called everyone I needed to call. I dialed Missy first and got her voicemail. I called everyone else and then tried her again. The coffee warmed my chest, and I got settled into the couch under the quilt, Saturday warming my feet and Pepper curled around him. Rufus hopped up and joined them. This time, Missy picked up and I told her the news.

"Oh, that's sad. I remember him. He was, uh, kinda nuts, right?" she said.

"I suppose he was eccentric," I said.

"No, for sure. I remember he tried to teach me about the Illuminati when I was like, seven. I had nightmares for weeks."

Missy hadn't seen him since childhood, and she spoke of Sunflower with a certain animosity that was always hard for me. But fair, in a way, too. But still I wanted her there at the memorial. "Will you come out for it? You could fly into Burlington and I could pick you up at the airport."

"Oh gosh, Mom, I don't think I can."

"I think you should be there. Chris was a big part of your childhood."

"Was he, though? I mean Taylor was my best friend. But her dad wasn't, like, my friend. From what I remember, he was always off somewhere, doing crazy shit."

I realized this wasn't a conversation I could have right now, especially since it was turning into a confrontation. So I let the silence sit between us. This was the strategy I felt worked the best. But I could hear Missy's breathing, her rising impatience. Her dog barked. She had a fat pug she doted on that always looked on the brink of death. I inhaled again.

"Look, there's stuff going on here. Navid and I are separating. He found an apartment today, actually."

"Oh my lord. Melissa, why haven't you told me?"

"Oh, I don't know. I have support. I'm fine. It's not like we weren't having problems, but it feels like a failure, I guess."

"You were together more than ten years, Missy. That's a success in itself."

"I haven't thought about it that way," she said.

"We have a great grieving-through-divorce retreat at the center. I can get you in for free. Come for a break."

"That sounds like my literal nightmare, Mom."

"Just think about it."

I heard my daughter sigh dramatically. This was the moment we always reached, if I ever tried to offer her advice. And if I continued, she shut down even further.

"I have to go. I'm sorry about Chris, Mom. That must be hard."

"It's fine. We're all getting older."

"Right."

"Right."

Larry walked by with the dog food, and the dogs jumped up and followed him into the kitchen. Outside the cicadas roared.

Missy said, "Bye, Mom."

"I love you," I said.

"Bye."

I got up and took the .22 off the gun rack by the back door, loaded it, and went outside. After the first shot, where

I hit the tree instead of the can, the family of raccoons who were tumbling around the compost ran off. The sun was going down, but I hit the can a few times. Larry came out and watched from the porch, amused.

"I think it might be too windy out to be practicing."

"Okay, then," I said, and brought the gun back in, took the bullets out, and put it back on the rack.

"Talking with Missy?"

"Yeah."

"Hard?"

"Yeah."

Larry brought me a cup of mint tea, placing it on the end table and then squeezing my shoulder as I sat on the couch, troubled. Missy and I had a history of stops and starts, long stretches of estrangement over the years. Our relationship was pretty good these days, but we never quite got to great. She had decided not to speak to me for most of her twenties, even after we were reunited by Ruth, but then invited me to her wedding. I couldn't predict how things would ever be between us, but I'd learned to be grateful for what I could get.

Larry settled in his chair beside the fireplace and picked up his latest book on boatbuilding. I thought about Larry coming with me to the memorial, and meeting Bryce, who was his opposite in every sense. Larry had a low tolerance for socializing.

"I really am happy to go alone, to the memorial," I said.

Larry looked up, nodded.

"That's fine with me."

This man was a balm against my chaos. All of the emotions that came up at my retreats, and in my other relationships, they all found a safe place with him. Not to mention my own sensitivities, being a Pisces with Cancer rising. All feeling.

After some time, he took my hand and brought me to bed. We made love for the first time in a while, and I fell asleep with his arms around me, a sharp wind rattling the windows.

CHAPTER 3

MISSY

———

D AVID MOVED OUT exactly one month after I caught him cheating. I wanted him to leave, but I was also insulted by how quickly he found a new place; the rental market in San Francisco was a nightmare compared to when we'd arrived. Now it was a city where only millionaires could afford a small apartment, especially anywhere near our house in Noe Valley. Of course, he could only find a place in Oakland, where nearly everyone we knew lived now. I wanted him gone, but not too far. Oakland felt far.

While he packed, I took to my bed like a Victorian-era heroine. When I got up, I wrote discursive songs on the electric guitar, real indulgent Sonic Youth noise-type songs with no beginnings or ends.

The day after he signed the lease, he walked into the bedroom holding a rose-gold ceramic bird. It had hung from a short length of twine looped around a nail on the front door.

"You cool with me taking this?" he said. The bird was wrapped in his fist, sharp beak poking out as if he were squeezing it to death.

"I want it." I got out from under the covers, then crossed

my arms tight. I stank like neglect and sorrow, after three days in a blue silk nightgown, picking at the frayed hem, a coffee stain on the heart.

"I bought it!" he argued.

"No. We bought it in Petaluma, together. That garage sale on the side of the road. The religious kids in the ankle-length dresses." I wasn't sure. But I knew the detail would sound convincing.

"No, that's where we bought the rose-gold lamp. I got this at that pawnshop outside of Vegas with Dave."

"That's an utterly fabricated memory," I said. "We got it together, right before we got the house. It was the first thing we put up."

"You can't take everything," he said, defeated, dropping the bird onto my dresser.

I followed him into the kitchen, where he was packing up the porcelain espresso cups. He was just tossing them into a box, with no protective wrapping. He'd taped the stainless-steel toaster oven shut and left it unboxed, like he didn't care if it broke in the moving truck. Both of us could afford to buy another one, but I grabbed it, electrical cord trailing, pushed the door open with my foot, and dropped it onto the decorative stones of the patio.

"You don't even make toast!" I screamed, taking the base-ball bat I'd hidden inside the barbecue and bashing the toaster with it.

Navid began to laugh hysterically, raising his arms up like *What the fuck is happening*, which made me bash the toaster harder. It was so satisfying, watching it buckle with dents. Jackie, the neighbor next door, opened her window and peered out at the commotion. She squinted down at us, then put on her giant glasses. I was wearing my nightie and one gray wool sock, that's it. My hair was a mop of greasy, mashed curls.

"You okay out there?" she yelled.

"Yeah," I said, pausing with the bat aloft.

"Then shut up, for god's sake!"

Navid's laughter turned to crying.

THE DAY NAVID finished moving out, I went downtown to the fertility clinic to discuss options and the results of the ultrasound tests I'd had done earlier. I could have a baby. I wasn't in a reasonable state of mind, but I felt a sudden razor focus about having a baby. I mean, why not now? But filling out forms in the waiting room, I began to fall apart. Who would I put for my emergency contact number? Agatha? Tom? My mother? Then I accidentally checked the *No* box next to the question *Have you ever been pregnant before?* It took me a minute to remember. It felt like a lifetime ago, going to that clinic in Lachine with Amita, driving back to my granny's house to recover.

The day after my abortion, I found out Granny had died in Turkey, fallen from a boat unnoticed. It was also the first day my mother and I had an honest moment together as two adults. We'd walked down to the water together, the way I used to after dinner as a teenager. I was in shock that I would never see Granny again, feeling terrible about how we'd left things. Thinking of her in the water by herself, it made me curl up in her bathtub inhaling the smell of her awful overly scented soaps, weeping in a way that felt unhinged, helped by the still-lingering pregnancy hormones. Grandparents are supposed to pass quietly, in bed, surrounded by loved ones. That she'd gone alone, struggling, it was too much to bear.

When I got out of the bath, my mother was there, holding out a spoon of blackstrap molasses, the kind we used to feed the sheep at Sunflower. "You need iron," she said, putting the spoon in my mouth like I was a baby bird. It was cold and I was wrapped in a towel, like a child after a bath. We both thought it would be good to take a walk, even though I was still bleeding and cramping. The house felt as if it were closing in on me.

We walked slowly, my hands jammed in the pockets of the old jeans I'd left behind from high school. My mother was gesticulating while she talked, and the loud jangle of her dozen or so thin copper bracelets punctuated her small-talk nattering. Eventually she was quiet for a few moments, and then turned to me as though just realizing I was there.

"How are you feeling? This is your first death. I know how hard it can be."

"My first death was Taylor."

"Oh, of course, of course."

She got quiet for a block or two. I was expecting her to talk about it, but she didn't. Taylor died at sixteen, a blood clot from the birth control pill. That Mom forgot was so telling. There hadn't been a funeral. My dad had mumbled something about being sad about it over dinner that night and we never talked about it again.

I hooked my thumbs through the belt loops of my jeans to keep them from falling down. They'd built more houses by the lake. The street had been a dirt road when Granny moved here. There had been farms. Now it looked as if it could be any 1990s suburb.

"I go from feeling overwhelmingly sad, to feeling nothing. Like right now, is it strange that I don't feel anything?"

"No, no, it's common to feel numb at first. It's shock."

"I know she wanted me to have the baby, she was so Christian and everything. But it's weird timing, don't you think, that she'd die while I was pregnant?"

"Did she tell you straight out not to have an abortion?"

"Yes."

"Well, that's a bit rich. Your grandmother had one. She told me about it for some reason, never told Bryce."

"Are you sure? That sounds out of character."

"No, when she first arrived in Canada. She was pregnant, but she found out your grandfather was cheating, and he'd actually brought his affair from Turkey over with them on the boat. He thought your grandmother didn't know, but she did. Women always know. That man was a dog."

I'd met my grandfather once when he visited Sunflower and he didn't make much of an impression, except he drank this thick Turkish liquor that tasted of black licorice and tried to teach me to play chess. I knew Granny and he had split but she never talked about why.

I was still trying to accept Granny's death, and here was a whole new story of her life. I never really thought about her at my age, or at any age other than old, or as being someone who had a life outside of being in our family.

My mother continued, "Back then it wasn't legal. She had to pay a lot of money to get it taken care of. She said she wasn't sure Grandad was going to stay, and she didn't want to have a baby all by herself."

"But she said motherhood was the only thing that made her happy, that saved her."

"She lied. She wanted you to have a kid."

"Even when I'm still basically a kid."

"I had you when I was around your age."

"Look how well that turned out."

She jangled ahead a little faster so I had to jog to keep up.

"So, who was the father?" she asked.

"Father?" I said.

"Well, not father, really. Who knocked you up, Melissa?"

"Honestly, I'm not sure."

"Really?" I expected her to look vaguely amused. She was the one who told me marriage was a conformist farce when I was eight years old. We reached the edge of the water at the public boat launch and dock. I picked up a few flat stones and skimmed them along the top of the lake.

Instead, she looked oddly concerned. "I understand you're young, and it's a time for parties and celebrating and rock 'n' roll and all that."

"It's punk rock."

"Yeah, yeah. I know. Remember, I bought your record, not really my thing. But the lyrics, Melissa. *Your* lyrics . . ." Her voice cracked a little. "Well, they were revealing, I guess."

My mother waved her hand, like she was pushing that thought away. "But what I'm trying to tell you—what I want to talk about—is that I'm worried that you have a problem. The drugs, Melissa. You almost got arrested. I think I've told you that my father was an alcoholic. He used to drink from the minute he woke up in the morning. It ruined him, it ruined my mother. Killed them both. They say it can be genetic . . . addiction. That's all I'm saying."

"I don't think I've got an issue."

"You've been shaking, you're pale and sweating. I know the signs."

"I went too hard in Vancouver. It's not always a thing."

"I just want you to be aware is all, of the genetic predisposition."

"Okay, well, just letting you know it's fine."

It wasn't fine, obviously, but I also wasn't half mad and wandering into traffic. I was just having a shitty month.

But her concern felt like a drug. It made me want to grab both of her hands and confess everything about the tour—getting high, having a boy in every port, about Andie. All of it. But I stopped myself. I was getting giddy from our closeness. I grinned, looked down at the pavement, trying to contain myself.

"You know, to your granny, the abortion probably meant a moral failure. But it was also a failure to be a single woman with a baby, and that was public. She was always concerned with what people thought. She never acted as if she regretted it. That said, it was always hard to tell what she was ever really feeling or thinking, her being so brutally British and all."

"Totally. She had such a poker face about everything."

"But so many women have abortions. If you're a woman who hasn't, you're likely the exception. Most people never regret it," she said.

Though it would be years before she told me about her own abortion. That was how she was, wanting to be close but never wanting to risk any of her own secrets that might help foster that elusive intimacy.

I watched my mother staring out at the horizon across

Lac St-Louis. *But do* you *regret having* me? I was too afraid to ask.

My mother turned to me abruptly and put both her hands on my shoulders.

"I know this is a hard time for you," she started. I braced myself then, for some maternal wisdom, or an apology, something meaningful that I could hold on to. Her bracelets jangled against my shoulders. "And I guess I just really need to go do some walking meditation by myself right now."

I was a bit stunned by this sudden turn, but it was also familiar. She used to do this when I was a kid, abruptly need to escape from me. Now that I wasn't a child, if I kept her in my life, every time I got a flicker of potential reconciliation between us, would she always choose herself?

"Okay, sure," I said, and started walking up the sloping pavement of the beach's parking lot. When I reached the street, I turned back, ambling down the gravel as I watched her walk out onto the long dock, doing some sort of movement with her hands, like a bird trying to fly. When I jumped up on the first plank, the dock swayed a little.

"Mom!"

She had a look on her face so irritated I had the answer already. When I opened my mouth the question came out differently.

"Do you consider it a moral failing, to have left me?"

She closed her eyes as if my face was too bright to look at.

"Oh, I don't know. I wasn't prepared to have this conversation right now. Please, I just need quiet."

She turned and went back down the dock. I watched her. If I sat down on the beach, would she drop off the end to avoid coming back to me?

———

THE REST OF that time is a bit of a blur. My father moved back into Granny's house. I moved to California. I didn't speak to my mother again for a number of years. I almost never thought about having been pregnant.

EXCEPT NOW. WHILE cycling to the clinic, I had been filled with purpose and excitement. But the fertility doctor was less perky, full of warnings, gloom and doom. I found myself gripping my purse in my hands as she spoke.

"Even though your eggs are viable, at your age it could be difficult to get pregnant. Especially since you are now single, yes? But it's possible. Here are some pamphlets about IVF, pay attention to all the tips on how to prepare. Have you thought about a donor?"

"No. I mean, not yet. Just trying to narrow down my list." But of course I thought of Tom. He was my list.

We went through the costs, the schedule, the details of every potential procedure. It was a lot to take in.

When I got home, Agatha was sitting on my front stoop wearing a mint sweater dress and giant sunglasses. I settled in beside her and cradled her legs dramatically.

"Welcome to your new life, babe," she said. "How was the egg doctor?"

"I feel like having a baby will bankrupt me."

"It probably will, but then you'll have a baby. Babies are amazing."

"Oh, really?" I said. "I thought Finch wanted a new one and you were against it!"

"*Babies* are great. Toddlers are the devil. I'm hiding from mine right now," she said, arranging her thick, glossy braid up in a bun on top of her head. "This morning I was so annoyed at Emily I had to leave the room to save myself from turning into a monster," she said. "She was lying on the floor crying and claiming that she couldn't walk. Of course she could walk! She just didn't want to put her shoes on. I tried to reason with her, but she doesn't understand that kind of complicated thinking yet. I lost it. I've tried being patient with her when she gets in these moods, but I can't. I just can't. I just slammed my bedroom door and punched my pillow and took deep breaths until the rage subsided. I actually had to give myself a time-out! When I came back out, she was walking around just fine, like nothing had happened, with one shoe on. She looked so cute, but like, minutes earlier, I hated her. I can't describe it any other way, I hated my own child."

"It will get easier when she's older. Three is hard," I offered, but I didn't know anything, really, about three. Four. Fourteen. I'd been reading so many parenting books, but the more I read, the less confident I felt. "Did you know that they did a study with world-class athletes, and had them mimic the exact movements of a toddler, and they couldn't do it for very long, they were too exhausted? It's a lot. You'll get through it."

"I believe that study. Man, I think every age is kind of cool but also awful," she said. "You know, if I had to go back in time and decide all over again, I don't know if I'd do it. But Finch would. She loves every minute of it. She doesn't even notice that we haven't fucked in months. She is so fulfilled it makes me sick. By the way, she signed you up for softball. She thinks it will help you through the divorce."

"That's insane. Who actually likes softball?"

"Dykes, historically. But you could be the token straight."

"I'm bi. You always forget that."

"I think *you* always forget that. I think your membership expires after a while."

"So, did you come over to get me drunk?"

"Nope, I'm going to turn Navid's old studio into an oasis for you."

"I thought you were joking about that. I have a whole house of my own now. I was just going to let it be the room where the dog throws up and I don't find it for weeks."

"Missy, trust me. You are going to need a place. A special room for playing music, meditating." At this, I raise my eyebrows. "For whatever," she said. "It's already soundproof. I have a whole plan."

"I want to go to sleep. For a year."

"Come on, you can lie on the couch while I get to work."

AGATHA CLEANED OUT Navid's old studio room and redesigned the space. She brought in a soft throw rug and a standing lamp that emitted a calming light, and placed several large ficus and cactus plants in front of the window. She set up a songwriting notebook on a music stand and placed my cello beside it. She adorned the walls with a framed poster from the Swearwolves' first tour and a photo of Agatha and me in our twenties when she was in that all-dyke band from Portland; we were both onstage about to jump into a crowd, wearing lacy baby-doll dresses and boots bigger than our skulls. On the end table, she placed some smaller plants, a crystal that was supposed to be "cleansing"—I'd really try anything at this point—a book of illustrated birds and a well-thumbed copy of *When Things Fall Apart* by Pema Chödrön.

I stayed on the couch, dozing with the dog, staring at the TV in blinks, not really absorbing anything, feeling guilty every time she popped in to bring me a glass of water or carrot sticks, slices of peach that lost their vibrancy, easing into yellow bruised sponges. She touched her hand to my forehead. She looked alive and sweating with purpose. I couldn't remember how that felt.

"I'm sorry," I whispered on occasion. "I'm an adult, you shouldn't have to do this for me."

"I don't mind," she insisted. She put a few big crystals on the windowsill, even though I thought they were silly. Slowly, in my thirties, I had watched all my peers take one of two different routes, loosely described: they'd either become New Age—going to silent retreats, learning tarot, spending the money they used to spend on beer on hiking equipment and do-it-yourself kombucha kits—or they went full-tilt into the oblivion of their jobs, parenting, or substance recovery. Just as we were beginning to see the fruits of our labor, to see our dreams unfold, and to feel okay about where we'd come from, about how our childhoods had spit us out into our twenties, that was when the cancer started circling us, then miscarriages and car accidents. Time sped up as we attended fortieth-birthday parties and ten-year wedding anniversaries. And of course, divorces.

Agatha let herself out when she was done, during one of

my deeper moments of sleep. I walked into the room and it was beautiful. It was all mine. I sat down with the cello and played for a few minutes, but couldn't feel it. Someday I would really appreciate it, but not quite yet.

She had left me a note on the back of an unpaid bill on the kitchen table. It read: *I'm giving you a couple weeks of mourning but then I'm taking you out to the Lexington and getting you drunk. You're not dead yet and you need some joy! Plus, I have a plan for a new band and you are going to FREAK OUT. Call any time of day/night. You WILL be ok, I promise. xox*

A new band? Agatha and I hadn't been onstage in years. I wrote and recorded music for a living, but I hadn't been in a band since the Swearwolves disbanded, unless you counted the community orchestra I played in on occasion for fun. I ached for it sometimes. But this wasn't the time.

I WOKE UP the next morning to a text message from Tom. *Good morning! Life isn't over! Soon it will feel like one of those weighted X-ray blankets lifting off your body, every decision will only be your own, and it will feel beautiful!* He never said *At least you don't have kids*, which was what everyone else said when they heard the news, like somehow the divorce should be a snap, with no strings.

Forty-five minutes later, there was a knock on my living room window. I was listening to the Mountain Goats' "No Children" on too high a volume to hear the knock, but Penny was standing on the top of the couch, barking and scratching at the window. I popped my head up.

"Penny, it's Tom!" said a voice outside. "Tell your mom to let me in."

I got up and opened the front door. "Happy divorce, doll. I think divorce should always come with some celebration, so—" He reached into his bag and handed me a small assortment of semicrushed tulips.

"Ah, yes, tulips, the official flower of romantic disentanglements."

Then he handed me a baseball cap and a hoodie.

"Put these on, we're going to have coffee outside of the house," he instructed.

"I can't. I'm not wearing, uh"—I looked down—"pants."

"That looks like a dress."

"It's a nightgown."

"No one can tell the difference. We'll scare the gentrifiers."

I put the cap on, wrapped myself in the hoodie, put the tulips in a beer mug of water, and put a leash on Penny, then followed Tom out the door.

We made for an awkward threesome ambling down the street. There was a new SoulCycle across from my house and I hadn't even noticed. A spinning class was jammed into one room, visible from the street, going hard and nowhere like a tangible metaphor for the way I was feeling.

I hadn't seen Tom in person in a while, because he'd moved north of the city to a small house near Petaluma, only coming into the city to visit the kids. The youngest was now in college, something I found impossible to believe. The first few minutes of being alone together in person were a bit strange, like we had to remember how to speak in full sentences instead of quippy, infrequent texts. We walked two blocks to a café at Church and 30th. Penelope was so happy to be outside, she stopped to smell everything. Tom was mostly quiet, occasionally squeezing my arm affectionately.

"I'm not a kid with cancer, it's just divorce. Shit happens."

"Still, I know it's hard. Even though we've all been expecting it for years, you know. Navid was never good enough for you."

"I never understand why people say that. He was a great partner."

"Was he?"

"I guess I don't have anyone to compare him to. He was the first person I settled down with. I just think it's weird when people take sides."

"When I got divorced you confessed that you thought Cory was slow and unevolved as a woman."

"Oof, I shouldn't have said that."

"It felt good at the time, though. I was so shocked when she left. I would have stayed forever. But I know better now, she was right. Plus, he cheated on you."

I hated when people brought that up. Made me feel like the righteous protagonist in a rom-com.

We sat down at a sidewalk table, and Penny settled at our feet. Tom went inside and returned with coffees and smoothie bowls. I dipped a spoon into my bowl, revolted.

"It looks like a pile of something someone already ate."

"I'm assuming you're not eating much. I don't have that problem," he said, rubbing his ample stomach. "Remember I used to have well-defined abs back in the day?"

"I still have a few outfits from the Lollapalooza summer that I keep for nostalgia but I can basically fit the skirt on one leg."

"We're still cute, right?"

"You are," I said. He really was more handsome as a bear type. We both paused, watching a young hipster couple at a nearby table get up to leave, their perfect skin, their shiny hair.

"Billy looks the same, doesn't he?"

"Yeah, he's got some freakish ageless thing going on."

"Maybe if you're not prone to self-reflection you don't get as many wrinkles."

"Yeah, maybe we just don't have time for massages every day with all the time we spend caring about people outside ourselves."

"Good to know you guys still get along."

It felt like old times, ragging on Billy together. The café music switched abruptly to "Untied." This used to happen when servers would notice us, they'd put our music on. But it hadn't happened in years. The song was nearly twenty years old, but because it got played in a 1990s nostalgia movie recently, I'd been getting bigger royalty checks and I'd heard it in a CVS recently.

"This is so weird."

"Totally weird."

"That bridge still bugs me."

"Me too."

Tom lifted up his coffee in a cheers.

"I swear, divorce was the best thing to ever happen to Cory and me. Now I love the shit out of her and she's my best friend. We're better parents now. I love her new husband."

I've heard this all before. And it did help. I didn't remind Tom that he'd bottomed out after the divorce, and ended up in the hospital after a suicide attempt. He didn't like to talk about it, but sometimes I remembered how helpless I felt visiting him in the ward. How he looked like all the life was just gone from his eyes, and there was nothing I could do but remind him he was loved, he was talented, he would get through it. Eventually, he did, and he had been doing well for the past few years.

"But I like having a partner," I said. "It's grounding. And I want a baby. I've been seeing a fertility specialist."

He narrowed his eyes. "Remember when you hated relationships? When you broke hearts all across America? Like, literally."

"I think the band functioned like a relationship did back then, it was anchoring. Now I feel like a relationship acts as the same anchor. I like sharing my life with someone intentionally," I said.

"I don't miss it at all," Tom said. Tom was resolutely single. He had an occasional lover here and there, but he'd crafted this loner identity.

"I doubt I'll ever fall in love again," he went on. "I know what I like. I don't want anyone intruding on that. I have good friends, the kids. Didn't Aristotle say something about platonic love being the ideal? I have you, I have Cory. I can have sex any time I want, basically. It's not that hard."

I wasn't sure how to respond to that. To me, Tom seemed lonely. He was the epitome of someone who could use a partner. He could wander off into the depths somewhere and never return. I thought that a partner might ground him, but I didn't share this. No one wants to hear their obvious vulnerabilities exposed when they've crafted such safe narratives to oppose them.

"So," he said, changing the subject, "tell me more about this baby goal of yours."

"Well, I want a kid. I'm thirty-seven. I have no time to waste if I want to find someone to do that with."

"Yeah, don't lead with that on Tinder."

"I know, I know."

"I don't think you want a kid, Missy. You're just at loose ends. You're not a mom type, you never have been. You'll always put your music first and you can't do that with a kid around. You'll resent the kid. I'm just saying. I know you."

You'll resent the kid. He said it so casually, forgetting I had a mother who ran away from home for that exact reason. But he kept going, and the more he emphasized my worst, most selfish qualities, the more I was certain that Tom didn't know me at all. He knew my life history, he knew my talents and flaws, but he didn't know where I was at in that moment. He was my music friend. Agatha was the person who knew me.

I was pretty much done with this conversation, and I didn't want to invite even more lectures from Tom, especially since he was my only shot at a donor at this point. Convincing him of that was going to take some time. We sipped our coffees in silence, and then he walked me home.

He dropped me off as if I were a child, making me promise to eat some food, to text him if I felt sad.

"Come up to Petaluma. Billy and Alan are coming to stay next week. We can record some songs," he said.

"Agatha wants me to join a new band with her, too."

"Oh, we could do a seven-inch together, two side projects. Remember side-project bands?"

"It's actually not a bad idea," I said.

"I heard about Agatha's band idea, everyone's talking about it."

"Everyone? Well, I guess that would make sense. She's reached out to, like, every girl from every band from back in the day. I think she sees it as a sort of supergroup reunion."

"Join that band, you need a new thing."

Penny scratched at the front door, wanting to be inside. I pulled Tom into a hug.

"You're going to be fine," he said while walking away, "eventually."

"I know," I said, but when I got inside, and watched Penny circle her dog bed three times, the way she always did, before falling asleep, I felt strangled by the silence of my empty house.

CHAPTER 4

CAROLA

THE NIGHT BEFORE the memorial, I couldn't sleep. It had been several weeks since I'd heard the news of Chris's death, and I thought I had been processing it, but there I was at dawn, standing at the bay window and watching the bears be thwarted by Larry's new locking system on the compost bin. They tumbled around. Frustrated, they came close to the porch to see if we might have left anything edible about, but they triggered the security floodlights— also a new addition by Larry—and ambled away. He was always one step ahead of whatever calamity might befall us.

The day before any kind of trip anywhere, I always wanted to cancel. The thought that I could just stay home was soothing. I found the routines of my life with Larry and my work comforting to the extent that any interruptions threw me. I pulled my dusty plaid suitcase out from where it lived in the storage area in the rafters above the loft, vacuuming the outside before unzipping it and praying it didn't house a family of mice. What would I even pack? I sat on the edge of our bed and stared into my closet.

I hadn't seen most of my Sunflower friends for over two

decades, with the exception of Tegan. We all sort of reunited on Facebook, and I knew some of them judged me for leaving the way I did, especially since the commune was dismantled only a few months after I left. Tegan had long forgiven me, though. We didn't speak for the first three years, but she showed up at the ashram one day in late summer. Taylor had died so unexpectedly earlier that year. I didn't even know. I was so isolated there, and only Bryce knew where I was. I was so angry he hadn't phoned me to let me know. We spent a week sharing my volunteer's bunk. She was manic with plans, having just left Chris. She wanted to start an all-women's commune on some land she'd leased in Quebec. She wanted me to come. I'd wanted her to stay at the ashram. But from then, Tegan and I kept in loose touch. She'd remarried— a woman this time; they owned a farmhouse in Vermont and ran a small press that published books about women's health and feminism.

THE MEMORIAL WAS held at Tegan and Karen's farmhouse on the lawn out back. Their two youngest kids were living with them at the moment: a daughter who was in high school, and a college student who'd come home for the memorial. I was one of the last to arrive, because even though I'd been up at dawn, I'd fretted about what to wear, what to pack, where to get gas, what snacks to bring. I parked on the lawn, among so many cars; I was surprised to see such a big crowd, people of all ages. I'm not sure why I expected it to be smaller. Tegan had made it sound like Chris was very lonely at the end.

Bryce was there, thankfully without his wife, Rachel. The

last time Bryce and I had seen each other was Missy's wedding to Navid years earlier. It had been a bit of a disaster, at first, and then we'd slowly become friends again. I wondered if Missy had told him she and Navid were separated. I hoped she would talk to him about it. Bryce could actually be quite sensitive. He listened very intensely and took your feelings seriously without trying to fix everything. There was still so much shorthand between us. It was nice to know someone who had known me so long ago. I would always feel close to him, but the key to that closeness was the fact that we didn't see each other often.

We stood in a circle and listened to Chris's closest family and friends eulogize him, and then Karen set out a large buffet lunch and we mingled until the sun set behind the trees, and Chris's kids lit a giant bonfire. I could see Chris in their faces at certain angles. He used to love the bonfire at Sunflower. Just the smell of wood burning in the air reminded me of him. The crowd got smaller and smaller until it was just us old-timers.

I told the story of how Chris had spray-painted the living room green when I was pregnant. Tegan had forgotten all about it. She told the story about how when they were teenagers, he'd come into the grocery store where she worked and picked her up and threw her over his shoulder, brought her into the lemon-yellow Volkswagen he powered with vegetable oil, and they did doughnuts in the parking lot for five minutes. Then he carried her back inside to work.

"That's what it was like with Chris. You'd be doing something mundane, like unpacking a box of canned peas, and then you'd be twirling around in circles, half sick and half elated."

Chris had lived a hard life. The unpredictable nature that made him popular and enigmatic at twenty-one had made him unemployable and difficult in middle age. His freedom of expression, the self-actualized glow, hardened into *poor boundaries.* The fun nature that drew everyone to him became a *drinking problem.*

His second wife, Lilith, had tried hard to keep him together, but eventually she left with their two sons in the early aughts. She stood stone-faced around the fire, not laughing when everyone else laughed. She didn't speak at the earlier part of the evening.

We'd all quietly wondered how he even made it to sixty. After Taylor died, he'd gone deep into a strange cult that was paranoid in its distrust of the world. Then in the last few years he'd switched from collective living to being mostly a hermit, working odd jobs at farms near where Sunflower had been, and living in a converted shed on the edge of town. In the end, it was Tegan who came back to nurse him, even though they hadn't been together in years.

"Don't even think about asking me to do that," I whispered to Bryce.

"Oh come on, Carola. You were always so good at taking care of me," he said with a wink.

I rolled my eyes and gave him a playful shove. We were sipping bottles of beer, sitting at the edge of the bonfire, occasionally fanning flames away.

"Have you talked to Missy lately?" he asked.

"Just email. Last I heard she was doing another soundtrack for a show on HBO," I said.

"Yes, yes, I heard that."

"The end-of-the-world show?"

"No, the one about the rich family with the secret. Sometimes it surprises me, how capable Missy is," Bryce said.

"She was always independent."

"Remember when she tried to run away on the pony when she was six and she made it all the way into town?"

"I do, I do."

"Were we terrible parents, though?"

"Well, we're not going to win any awards, that's for sure."

"But she turned out okay, she did. She did."

It sounded like a question when he said it like that.

"She did, yes. Not that I really know. She talks to me now, but she has put up so many walls. She probably doesn't do that with you."

Bryce shrugged. "I think she got fed up with me. I made a lot of mistakes, too."

I'd been waiting decades to hear him say that, and for whatever reason, tears began to well up in my eyes. To hide them, I took a long sip from my beer.

"She and Navid are getting a divorce, you know."

"No shit. Ah, I never liked him."

"I loved him! Are you crazy? He was so present."

"He was self-centered. She did all the emotional work. He coasted on charm."

I didn't mention the irony of Bryce saying that.

"Did you ever tell her the truth about your mother?"

"No, no. I don't want her to remember Mum that way."

"But you did want her to think I'd abandoned her. You were fine with that being her memory of me."

"Well, you did abandon us."

"You're oversimplifying."

"I think that was more to punish you, it wasn't so much about Missy. But my mom . . . I want Missy to remember her the way she was. My mother was stubborn. She wanted to go out with some agency. I only realize now how little she'd had in life."

"Listen to you, using words like *agency*."

"We weren't much older than them," Bryce said, pointing to Chris's kids, "when we bought a farm and we were going to live outside of capitalism. Look how young they are!"

"I remember feeling old."

"I remember feeling like I knew everything."

"Funny how that shifts."

"It sure does." Bryce put down his beer. "Should we get high?" he asked, pulling a joint out of his fanny pack.

"I haven't gotten high in years," I confessed. "A little CBD tea at night, but that's it."

Bryce sparked the joint. His hands were swollen a bit around the knuckles, freckled with age spots. This would always surprise me. The Bryce of my imagination would always be twenty-five.

I watched the fire and took a small drag on the joint. I leaned back against Bryce, who was leaning against the log bench. As the dope took hold I felt my muscles relaxing. I moved my feet back and forth like windshield wipers.

"I feel twenty-one again," I said. "My body feels young."

Bryce laughed and he ran his fingers through my hair. It sent shivers down my arms and into my fingertips. Some things don't fade in your body, even if they've long left your heart and mind.

"Remember how beautiful my hair used to be?"

"It's still beautiful," he said, continuing to comb through it with his fingers. I knew it wasn't, nothing could make it luscious and shiny again. He proffered the joint.

"I'm good, that's enough for me," I said.

We watched the fire crackle, as the night grew colder. Tegan brought out a guitar and we sang some old songs, including some of Chris's favorites, like "Tangled Up in Blue," "Four Strong Winds," "Our House." I remembered the first verse or two, and then hummed along. I felt nostalgic and wistful in one moment, filled with gratitude for still being around in the next.

Eventually the guests peeled off, in ones and twos. Most of them were camping out on the property, but a few of us had rooms in the house. Bryce kissed my head softly before he stumbled off to his own one-person tent.

In the end, it was just Tegan and me, passing a bottle of wine back and forth, an old wool blanket wrapped around us. She poked at the fire with a long stick one of the kids had been using to roast marshmallows. We had often ended nights together at Sunflower like this. Only it was watching the sun rise, not the midnight moon, while blinking away the last sparkles of acid trips. We hadn't spent much time in person for over a decade.

"So, Karen's really great. So relaxed about having everyone here like this. I'm glad I finally got to meet her."

"Karen *is* great," she said. "We've been together for almost twenty years now. She puts up with a lot. She can roll with anything. Like we used to, you know? And how's Larry?"

"Same, same as always."

"You and Bryce seem fine, no drama, as the kids say."

"It's been too long for all that to matter now."

"Do you think he knows?"

"Knows what?"

"About how close we were at Sunflower."

"Everyone was close at Sunflower."

"Don't do that."

"What?"

"Make light of it."

I poked the stick at the ashes, embarrassed.

"All our old friends, they give me these looks like Chris was my first big love, but you know he wasn't."

"He wasn't?" I pulled my side of the blanket a little closer. I'm not sure why I was pretending not to understand. Tegan took a long swig of the wine. I didn't like it when she got sloppy and tried to process old memories. What was the point? We couldn't go back now. I only ever answered her phone calls before sundown. If she called after dinner she might be slurry and accusatory.

"You're gaslighting me," she said, standing up, blocking the light of the fire. "You're so afraid of conflict. We could have resolved it."

"Didn't we resolve it at the ashram a few years later?"

"I barely remember that week, Taylor had just died."

"That week changed everything for me," I said.

We were both going to stick to our stories, our version of events.

IT WAS MY third year at the ashram, 1992. I was working in the laundry when Blue came to tell me I had a visitor. "She's, uh, a real hippie. Like, I don't think she has shoes. She seems . . . possibly not quite right," she said, leading me up-stairs.

I didn't recognize Tegan at first because she'd cut her hair and permed it. But as I got closer, it was unmistakable. She was wearing a T-shirt dress tie-dyed in blues and purples with a dolphin decal jumping across it. I got her a cup of green tea from the lobby's refreshments table and took her outside to sit on the lawn.

"How did you know where to find me?"

"I called Bryce."

"Oh."

"This place doesn't look like I thought it would, it's so institutional."

"It used to be a Jesuit monastery. How did you get here?"

"I hitchhiked. It's harder now. People are so suspicious. But I got a nice trucker who tried to get me to accept Jesus into my heart."

"Well, you do look like you might have just escaped an asylum."

Tegan laughed and pulled her knees up to her chest and burst into tears. I remember thinking that I couldn't believe we were almost forty.

She explained that she and Chris had split, that it was too hard after Taylor's death. I sat with the shock of the news, that such a vibrant girl was no longer with us, the one who sat on my lap and who I'd taught how to read.

Tegan slowly filled me in on everything that had hap-pened after Sunflower disbanded—the property was auc-tioned off after the courts settled with the family of the girl who'd been injured when she fell down the well while on magic mushrooms. Chris and Tegan moved into an apartment in the town nearest to Sunflower. Chris wasn't happy living in two rooms, started spending every night at the local bar, working seasonal jobs on farms while Tegan worked part-time at a daycare. She pulled a small photo out of her wallet—Taylor, with bright red teased bangs and black lipstick. "She was going through a wild period, I guess. She had a boyfriend we just hated. He was goth. They used to wander around town like ghouls. The school only had about six kids in her high school class. I didn't want her getting pregnant and having to be stuck there. You know? So I made sure she was on the pill. So ironic that the thing that was supposed to keep her free caused her death. You're not really supposed to smoke on them, and she loved smoking because she knew we hated it. Remember how we used to keep them from eating sugar? The last year of her life she just drank Tab and smoked and ate Doritos. She just didn't wake up one morning. An aneurysm in her sleep."

I remembered her under the table when she was a kid, pretending to be a dog, those buck teeth from sucking on her middle two fingers all the time.

"It was only then that I was starting to feel like a good mom. As though I could finally pay attention when it was just us in that apartment. And of course she hated that."

I MOVED TEGAN into my little cabin—extremely close quarters. It was jarring to see two toothbrushes in the beer mug I stole from the pub in Mallow sitting on the little window ledge in the bathroom, next to the Dr. Bronner's lavender soap I used for my body, hair, and to wash dishes in the tiny sink with the rusted-out basin. You could stand in the middle of the cabin's only room, reach out your arms, and touch both walls. We spent most of our time in two lawn chairs outside, except when we slept in the single bed, waking to sore necks and limbs gone numb.

I didn't tell her about the guru. Tegan was weirded out by him, the photos and the altars. I took her to a talk he was giving and she left halfway through. I came back from sunrise yoga on the first day and she'd brought me coffee from the village, with lots of cream, the way I'd loved it before giving up coffee. I drank the whole thing anyway, and felt hyper all day. I had forgotten what it felt like to feel known. Even though I had friendships at the ashram, they were all very present-tense. They didn't know where I came from.

On the third night, she brought a bottle of wine back from her walk into town and we walked up to the springs.

"I must confess I have an ulterior motive for this visit," she said, lowering herself into the water. "I leased some land and I'm starting an all-women's commune."

"Why all women?"

"Why not? Wouldn't it be more efficient that way?"

"I guess it depends on the women."

"Also, I'm a lesbian now."

"Really? There are quite a few lesbians here, you know. Some couples."

"And you're cool with that?"

"Of course."

"You weren't always so cool."

"What do you mean?" I knew what she meant.

"We used to sleep together! For years. Everyone knew."

"That wasn't a big deal, that was just youth, partying too much."

"It's just us, right here. You can be honest."

"I am being honest. I've hardly ever thought about it since." That part was true. I'd placed those memories in a box and labeled it irrelevant. I wasn't ever attracted to any other women around me.

But she looked devastated.

"I came to rescue you," she said. "So we could finally just be together."

"Oh," I said, absolutely shocked. "That's a lot for me to take in right now."

She dunked underwater and reemerged, changing the subject. Tegan was in the deep stage of grieving where the only thing getting her through was big plans. The commune's philosophy, the buildings they were going to build, the horse barns, the playground, the outdoor kitchen. She monologued about it, like a manic salesperson, all the way back to the cabin. We stood farther apart, the awkwardness of her confession like an object between us.

That night Tegan went to sleep on the floor, and I stayed awake, trying to think of a way to apologize, to explain my feelings. Right before dawn I knew she was still awake, too, and I invited her back to the bunk. "We have a chance to start over again," she whispered, before kissing me. It was such a familiar kiss. And this time, with none of the chaos of Sunflower and husbands and children around us, with only us, I could release all my fears and just be with her.

I went to morning yoga, leaving her asleep. I was grinning and feeling a euphoria I hadn't felt in years. *I'm in love, too!* I realized, as I stretched up to greet the rising sun. I ran back to the cabin after class, so excited to tell her. But she had left, scrawled a postal box address in the town nearest the new commune. I felt an odd mix of relief and sorrow. I wrote her long letters, confessing my love, but could never bring myself to send them. Eventually she sent me a letter. She'd met Karen. *Finally*, she wrote, *I have met someone who really sees me.*

And now, over twenty years later, here we were, trying to talk about it.

"I was in love with you, too," I finally said. "I realized it the morning you left the cabin. I wrote you a long letter about it. It was a revelation for me. You were right. And then you sent me a letter that you'd met Karen, and soon after I met Larry, so I just let it be."

"You loved me, too?"

"I did. Of course I did. We could both feel it. It was part of why I left Sunflower."

"That means a lot, to hear that, from you." She grabbed my hand.

"Everything all right out here?" Karen called from the doorway. "I was just about to bring a pitcher out to drown the fire."

Tegan jumped up.

"Thanks, honey, we were just going to bed. Good night, Juniper."

"It's Carola now," I said.

She walked inside, leaving me wrapped in the wool blanket, watching Karen pour water on the fire.

CHAPTER 5

MISSY

WHEN AGATHA ORGANIZED a meeting about the new band, she knew there was a fifty-fifty chance I might not show up. So she invited everyone to *my* house for it, and showed up early with iced lattes. I wandered around tidying up. Was I going to have strangers in my house? Had I become a hermit, that this concept of visitors was so uncomfortable? Was I becoming too used to my own company? I'd been composing for so many years by myself. But I did miss collaboration, and I certainly missed performing.

Agatha sliced up raw vegetables on the kitchen table as I reswept the floor. She told me about how, after the meeting, everyone was going to the Lexington, a dyke bar that was closing. Every night for two weeks they were having a good-bye party for it.

"I don't get it. Why is everyone so attached to a bar?" I asked Agatha.

"You straight people have a million bars. This is literally the only dyke bar in this city! I met Finch there. I spent my youth there. Have some respect."

"Sorry, babe. Sounds good."

I was mostly just nervous because I hadn't socialized in so long. I wasn't sure I remembered how to do it. I'd looked at all the shoes and boots in my closet. How could I choose which ones to wear? I'd opened my medicine cabinet and scanned the nail polish for a color that said *awake human woman*. I'd pulled out one of my old dresses from the band days, the kind that used to be baggy and '90s style and was now a tight bodycon number.

"You look perfect," Agatha said.

"Ugh, no, I look ancient." I touched the deepening wrinkle between my eyes. It was all I could see when I looked at my face.

"We're all ancient now. Embrace it! The alternative is worse," she said, bringing a few music stands from the studio into the living room and arranging some chairs.

Slowly, everyone arrived. Linda, the bass player from King Pussy; Debbie, lead guitarist from the Debbies. Agatha was going to sing, and I was going to play rhythm guitar, maybe cello if it made sense. I sat with my acoustic in my lap as everyone settled in.

"We just need a drummer," Linda said.

"I'm working on that," said Agatha, passing around the bowl of pretzels.

"What about Tom?" I asked.

"He actually said no," Agatha said.

"He said no? He's been trying to get the Swearwolves to reunite! He's making new music right now."

She shrugged. "It would be better to have a woman," she said.

"Or at least someone queer," said Debbie.

"What about Andie?" Linda asked. Even just hearing Andie's name made me flushed and sweaty. It was so funny that

I could barely remember the names of some of the guys I slept with back then, but I remembered every detail of that day on the beach.

"Life is too messy for Andie right now," Debbie said, and everyone nodded.

"I'll ask Tom. He might say yes to me," I said, trying to camouflage the disappointment about Andie.

By the end of the meeting, we had a rehearsal schedule, the start of a marketing plan, a tour to five or six major cities, and an idea to make a documentary about the tour. I was filled with purpose and it felt good. Really good. So when everyone was ready to head out to the bar, I went along.

THE LEXINGTON WAS tiny and packed, but somehow Finch had gotten there early and settled into one of the few booths. I said no to proffered shots, sipped my ginger ale, and began to feel bored. Then someone put a beer in front of me, which led to one shot, which led to sinking into the seat leather and feeling like *This is the best feeling in the world, that three-drink feeling!*

"You're loaded." Agatha laughed. "Now, don't start crying."

I started crying.

"This is a celebration night only!"

"Other people are crying," I pointed out.

The vibe was definitely a funeral for our revolutionary youth. I don't think I'd been fully drunk in years. I watched, daze-eyed, as a group of friends who'd grown up in this bar reminisced and caught up. A butch with a salt-and-pepper crew cut sat beside me. "This is Angus! Angus, Missy!" Finch yelled across the table, introducing us.

"Hey," they said, taking a sip of beer and nodding at me.

Our thighs were touching. I didn't want our thighs to ever not be touching. Back in the day, I would have considered this many drinks to be relative sobriety. I scanned the room: How did it just never occur to me that maybe I was queer? I contemplated what my life might look like if that were true. I was nervously peeling the label off a bottle in front of me, trying to think of something to say to Angus, when Agatha pulled me outside so she could smoke in secret.

I grilled her about Angus—what's their pronoun? (They/them.) Who were they into? (Femmes.) Were they single? (Sort of.) Should I ask to buy them a drink? (Bring them a whiskey.)

"I love it when you're drunk and bi," said Agatha, laughing.

"That feels dismissive!"

"Sorry, feel free to come out now. We've all been waiting."

"Like who?"

"I don't know, everyone in the band when you went to the bathroom today was like, is she finally going to realize she's queer?"

"Stop it! Really?"

I sat with that for a minute, leaning against the brick, watching Agatha revel in the cigarette Finch was going to yell at her about later.

When we went back inside, I went to the bar and bought Angus the whiskey. My heart was pounding, I was feeling so enamored by this new possibility, but when I got back to the booth, Angus was making out with the woman next to them, a femme with a tattoo of swans across her clavicle.

The amount of rejection I felt in that moment was completely out of proportion. I'd just met Angus twenty minutes ago, but suddenly I felt old and awful. I drank the whiskey myself and began to notice, as though a spotlight from the ceiling shone down, who was probably high on coke. That was what I wanted. It was what I always wanted if I had more than two drinks, which was why I rarely did. I needed to go home. But first I needed to pee, and the line to the bathroom was a mile long. I stumbled outside, thinking I'd just go in the alleyway. I was aiming for the ripped condom wrapper and pile of pebbles, but instead I peed down the side of my leg, my shoes, and the panties I'd tried to gracefully move aside. These are the things I used to be able to do when I was younger, but now not so much. I decided to just take my panties off, ball them up, and throw them in a dumpster.

"Classy," I heard a male voice say through the din of the music from the bar. A guy was smoking and leaning against the alley wall near the entrance. A skinny hipster in a plaid shirt with a beard, the kind of guy who drank craft beer and sought out yuppie hot dog restaurants, the very places that made it so this historic dyke bar couldn't afford the rent anymore. *Dick*, I wanted to reply but wasn't quite that drunk.

"Yeah, yeah. Well, the trouble with dyke bars is if there's only one bathroom, you always have to wait for chicks to stop fucking in it to piss," I said.

He shrugged, took another drag.

Whatever, asshole. He was standing in the middle of the alley now, making it so I had to walk around him to get back to the bar entrance. When he saw my face, his eyes lit up. I was not in the mood for this kind of shit today. And he was grinning, which only irritated me more.

"Missy Alamo. You don't remember me, do you?"

I regarded him a bit closer. I definitely had never seen this dude before. If I asked *Bass player or sound tech?* I'd probably have a good chance of being right on one of the two. He was too skinny to be a drummer. He looked way too young to have been on the road with me sixteen years ago.

"No, sorry. I don't remember," I said, as I moved to go around him in a slow, purposeful, don't-fuck-with-me walk.

"We hung around one summer during the Lollapalooza era," he said.

"Yeah, I hung around a lot of dudes during that time." I laughed, taking a bottle of sanitizer out of my purse and cleaning off my hands and leg.

He gave me a curious look.

"Damn, I thought I'd be memorable," he said. He shook his head, then dropped his cigarette quickly and stubbed it out as a tall woman in high boots approached him. Her thighs were covered in flower tattoos, someone I'd seen at Agatha's parties sometimes but I couldn't remember her name. Chelsea. Courtney. Coral. None of those.

"Where the fuck have you been?! You know the babysitter needs to be home by eleven," she said, giving me the side-eye and walking away briskly.

"Sorry, babe," he said, rushing to catch up with her. I watched them walk up the street, both somewhat stumbling, voices rising in a fight. One of those dumb married fights I wouldn't have to worry about anymore but in that moment almost missed.

I CALLED AN Uber and left. My driver was cute and laid it on thick from the moment I got in the car. "You're really pretty," he said. "Sorry, I don't mean to be creepy. I'm not a creep!"

He began flirting in a not entirely awful way, but definitely a persistent *bro* kind of way. I'd forgotten what it was like to wear a barely-there dress out at night. He was a guy I would have affectionately called a "pounder" back in the day.

"Want to have a drink with me?"

"I'm going home, no thanks." I crossed my arms over my chest, and looked out the window.

"Come on. One drink . . ."

I would normally have cut him off curtly, told him I was married. But tonight, buoyed by my depression and the whiskey, I leaned toward him between the two front seats and caressed the slight stubble on his young face and said, "Oh honey. I'm too old for you."

"I'm not that young! I'm twenty-six. I've got stamina and you're an angel," he said.

I thought about when I was young, and how I was so capable of transactional sex. It felt freeing, didn't it? I couldn't really remember. It wasn't a feeling you could always get to when sober. But I saw the way the next few minutes would unfold, maybe straddling this guy in the parking lot down the street, my ass bumping against the steering wheel, the shiver of terrifying possibility that he could reach up and choke me to death. As I contemplated taking him up on the offer, a part of me knew it was so reckless, possibly suicidal. Maybe that was the gift of this loneliness.

I was the kind of sort-of drunk that turned my depression into an ache in my chest, something that could go from vaguely self-destructive, like trying to find drugs or texting Navid, to something benign, like really, really wanting pizza.

The driver put on a slow jam and upped the volume,

glancing at me in the rearview mirror. The song reminded me of high school, when I would daydream about being the kind of girl men would sing to.

He *was* really handsome. We had some more banter, and I texted Agatha his name and Uber info in case I wasn't heard from again.

When we got to my house, I invited him in. I handed him a beer, but I really didn't want to prolong any conversation. He didn't need much persuading. This was the moment I used to excel at, would flip a guy on his back, put my tits in his face, and get a condom out of my purse in ten seconds. But in this moment, a whiskey-and-desperation-soaked moment, I realized I was being given an opportunity on my own living room sofa. Had God or whoever sent a virile, handsome young man to knock me up? A careless, dangerous chance, but also one that could work out. I was debating all the possibilities as he pumped into me roughly. Would he stop before he came? He was staring at my pussy, getting off on watching, mumbling, "Yeah, yeah, yeah." Maybe he was young enough I could whisper something so filthy that he'd come before thinking about it.

"You . . . on . . . the pill?"

I closed my eyes and nodded.

"Yeah, come inside me."

He looked shocked, then really, really psyched. I felt him get even harder, start pumping faster.

Though the lead-in could have been something from an erotic, true-stories website, the sex was not as hot as I anticipated. I thought at least the novelty of a stranger would bring something to the table, but the thrill wasn't there. The thought of my thighs pressed against Angus in the bar felt more electric than this. It felt vaguely good, but it wasn't that desperate attraction that really gets me there. Perhaps it was the guilt that I'd just lied to him and crossed a serious ethical line. There was that.

Or maybe I was a bit broken. Maybe I hadn't waited long enough, mourned, grieved Navid.

Why did lust happen so quickly for him?

When the guy left, I watched his car retreat down the block through my front window. I deadbolted the door and I got in the shower. I could not believe I just *did* that. I started to cry. Clearly I could not just casually drink, or fuck, the same way I used to.

I CALLED AGATHA the next morning. She was in bed nursing a hangover, while Finch had taken their daughter, Emily, to a sing-along class.

"Wait, tell me the story again," she said. "Because I think I heard you wrong. I think you just told me that you fucked your barely legal Uber driver without a condom in your own home. Are you fucking insane? When I got that text from you last night, I thought it was a joke."

"You would have literally high-fived me ten years ago."

"I know, but you're in a vulnerable place right now."

"You sent me a text last week that said I needed to go get some strange dick."

"Yes, but not Uber dick!"

"This is a class thing!" I said. "You think it's weird I fucked my Uber driver, and not some fucking tech guy. If we were in our twenties now we'd probably be Uber drivers."

"And you didn't use a condom, Missy. Like, seriously? What

about STIs? Birth control? Because shriveled as they may be, I believe we still have viable eggs. What if he got you pregnant?"

I could be pregnant. I. Could. Be. Pregnant.

"Do you really think I could be pregnant?" I said. I didn't tell her that was the whole reason I didn't insist on a condom in the first place.

"Missy! C'mon, be serious. No, probably not. It's pretty hard to get pregnant at our age. Maybe if you'd had some marathon sex session for like, two days you'd have a shot, but I don't think the Uber bang would do it. But Missy . . ."

"Yeah," I said, absently, still stuck on the Could. Be. Pregnant.

"You need to get out there and meet people you want to date."

FOR THE REST of the day, I couldn't stop thinking *I could be pregnant.* I looked at my cycle app, and it had been the day before ovulation, so it was possible. I called the doctor and booked an appointment to get an STI check. I went to the gym, did some stretches in the mirror, tried to imagine my midsection swelling. I went to Whole Foods and bought a bunch of vitamins, a big smoothie, some kale. I was going to make this happen, I was thrilled, this could happen. It just made sense that all of it—Navid cheating, our separation, Agatha's new band, the night at the bar—had happened so that I could have this baby. I was throwing myself on the mercy of the universe.

CHAPTER 6

CAROLA

I WAS DOING A volunteer shift at the center's front desk when the doctor called. I couldn't hear him very well because there was an a cappella workshop happening in the auditorium and they were very spirited. "Your mammogram results were inconclusive and we're not sure why. We will have to do some follow-up testing."

Sing out! Sing out loud, the spirit within you! the group sang.

"All right, then," I said, thinking it was a rare thing when Western medicine practitioners admit they don't know something. And in this case, it didn't seem good.

"Are you free tomorrow?"

"Tomorrow?" It had taken months to get the original appointment, and then I had nearly forgotten to go to it. I didn't think it was necessary anyway, but when Larry found the lump he made me promise to get it checked out. I was fairly certain it was just a cyst, an aging thing. I'd had a benign one before. No use getting all worked up.

"Yes, I hope it's okay. I've arranged for you to have all the follow-up tests right away. Time is of the essence."

I wrote down the time and location, but wasn't sure if I would tell Larry. Why worry him?

After my shift, I walked the dogs up the mountain and around the pond, letting them run off the morning they'd spent cooped up in the house. I met so many breast cancer survivors in my workshops. Of all the types of people who frequented the weeklong joy retreats, they were the ones who often had something to teach me, about the weight of time, about truly being present. While the dogs ran, I did a series of stretches and then lunges across one field and back. I did the plank pose for as long as I could, until the dogs came and tried to crawl under me. Eventually I relaxed into a dogpile cuddle, staring up at the sky while they licked my face.

I'd been eating organic and restricting sugar for decades. I took an immune-boosting supplement every day, drank turmeric tea in the afternoons, and took a spoonful of apple cider vinegar every evening after supper. When I told people my age, they often didn't believe me. I walked the fundraising 10K for the center almost every year. I ticked off this inventory of my behaviors all the way home. Usually people got cancer and then changed their diets and routines to be more like mine. How could I possibly be the one to get sick?

I TOOK THE anti-inflammatory cookbook from the bookshelf and made us a soup for dinner. I decided to tell Larry about the tests after he grimaced from one spoonful, getting up to make himself some baked beans on toast.

"These tests, they're inconclusive all the time," Larry said. "The ultrasound technology, for example, the machines have gotten so much more sophisticated but the way the doctors read them hasn't changed. Sometimes they aren't sure what they're seeing. Likely the same for mammograms." I smiled at him gratefully. Larry's encyclopedic knowledge of nearly everything scientific was reassuring.

"And whatever happens, we'll be fine. I'm right here."

I sipped my soup and changed the subject.

BEFORE I WENT to the follow-up tests at the hospital in Concord it was as though my nervous system kicked in and did not allow me to feel anxiety. I slept through the night, woke to Rufus making one-pawed cat biscuits on my back and purring. He held oddly consistent eye contact with me as I scratched his ears, listening to Larry putting wood on the fire below. I was going to be fine. Larry offered to drive me, but I waved his concern away. Perhaps I'd do some shopping afterward.

When I arrived at the lab, I produced my forms for the receptionist, offering chipper small talk, but once I shed my street clothes and hiking boots, trying to fit them into a tiny locker while wearing a humbling blue paper gown, I could hear my heartbeat in my ear. Then I was tapping my fingers against a magazine, unable to take in the text of an article about menopause. The tests were numerous. The doctor was clearly concerned. I had a full MRI and so much blood taken I wasn't sure they'd left me enough to live on. I sat in the car afterward, picking through the stale trail mix I'd left in the glove compartment, sipping from my Thermos of lemon water. I nearly choked on a lemon seed and wished I didn't have to drive myself home.

———

A FEW DAYS later, I was in the garden harvesting some of the earliest carrots and radishes when the house phone rang. And then my cell. And the house phone again.

"We've caught it early," said my GP. "You'll need a minimally invasive surgery, then just four weeks or so of chemotherapy. I'm referring you to an oncologist, she's fantastic."

I wrote down everything, feeling strangely detached.

"You're in great shape, you're only fifty-nine, still young. You can beat this, Carola," he said.

I wondered how many times a day he said this kind of thing and how often it was true.

Larry was off with the dogs. I wasn't sure what to do. I dialed Tegan's number but hung up before it rang. I started a text to her, and then erased it. I went and took the rifle down, loaded it, and lined up all the wine bottles I'd been saving to take into town, took a few shots but missed.

It had been so long since my life truly involved other people in an intimate way. It was Larry and me on a raft with our dogs and cats and bears, and my work life involved so many other people that I couldn't imagine doing that much socializing when I got home. But Larry wasn't going to be enough right now, with this news.

I put the rifle strap around my shoulder and went back inside, being careful to pick up Rufus when I opened the door only slightly. He'd been dying to go outside again but it was too dangerous. It was cruel in a way, to keep him in this tiny space, but I couldn't imagine him being truly safe outside these days. I gave him a cuddle, which he squirmed against, scratching my arm and running off.

I pressed a cold cloth to my bleeding skin, cradled the landline, and called Missy.

It felt like a first step toward . . . well, *something*. I didn't want to ask her for anything. And this felt like, perhaps, a way of carving out an opening.

When I dialed her number, I expected to get her voicemail, but she picked up on the second ring. We exchanged the usual pleasantries about my garden and she told me that Agatha had recruited her for a new all-female band.

"That's wonderful!" I said. "I'm so happy to hear you'll be playing again with a group. And how extraordinary to be in an all-female ensemble."

"It's not really an *ensemble*, Mom. It's a punk band."

"Yes, but still."

"So, what's new with you? How's Larry?"

"Larry's fine. Things have been . . . well, you know I went to Chris's funeral and caught up with Tegan."

"How are they all doing?" Missy asked.

"Sad," I said. "But it was good to celebrate Chris's life together. You know I saw your dad there—"

"You *did*? I thought he might be there. How did that go?"

"It was good, it was . . . good. It gets easier every time. We talked about you, mostly," I said.

"He told me he never liked Navid, last time he called."

"Well, he's protective that way. But listen, Miss, I wanted to talk to you about something. Tegan and I got to talking—about you. She says you guys talk on the phone sometimes, and she couldn't understand why we weren't closer."

"Huh," said Missy. "There's no confusing reason, Mom. You know why."

"There are so many things I wish I could have done differently back then. But Bryce and I are fine now. Tegan and I are fine. I really want it to be fine with us, Missy. I want to figure out how to try and start knocking down some of these barriers between us."

"Well, how do you suppose we do that, Mom?"

"I thought," I began, "that sharing what's going on in our lives more might be a start. Not just the small talk, but the in-depth things."

Missy was silent for a moment. Then she said, "And what do you think gives you the right to know the 'in depth' parts of my life?"

"Because I'm your mother?" I said quietly.

"Okay, well, it's not something I'm completely sure about, but it's the most 'in-depth' thing I've got going right now: I think I might be pregnant."

I was briefly shocked into silence, but quickly recovered.

"Oh, Missy, that's wonderful! Really? Who's the—oh, that's so, so wonderful."

"There is no father," Missy said. "I'm going to do this on my own. If it happens. I've been thinking about it for a long time. It was a thing between me and Navid, to be honest. Me wanting a baby and him not. But now I have the time and freedom to make it happen. Well, if it happens."

"So you don't know for sure?"

"Not yet," she said. "But I'll let you know."

"Well, I think it's a great idea."

"You *do*? Are you serious, or are you being sarcastic?"

"Melissa, I'm not a sarcastic person. I genuinely think this is a great idea. You already have such a successful career, you don't have a man weighing you down. Go to it, sister!"

"You think that I can do it? On my own?"

"Missy, you're literally the strongest woman I've ever known."

Missy was silent again and I wondered whether I had said the wrong thing again.

"Missy, I'll come and help you with the birth. I can stay with you until you're on your feet again."

"No, you don't have to do that," she said.

"Why wouldn't I? What better way to spend my time?"

"Okay, okay, Mom. But listen, it's not for sure. It's not real yet. But if it's not this time, well, it's something I'm working on and thinking about. And it's really cool that you want to be there for me."

I heard a catch in Missy's voice and felt tears welling up in my own eyes.

"Well, you just let me know," I said, my voice cracking. "I'm here."

I didn't want to share my news of the diagnosis after that. I wanted to leave it on a high note and not burden her. But I did share news of my illness with others. I told Marie right away, and Tegan. And eventually, I would tell Missy. But not now, when she was dealing with so much. Pregnant! Maybe I could kick this thing before I'd have to tell her. After all, now I might be a grandmother. A potential do-over of sorts. And that wasn't something I planned to miss.

CHAPTER 7

MISSY

———

WOKE UP ONE morning like that scene in *My So-Called Life* when Angela is finally over Jordan Catalano and she dances around the room to the Violent Femmes. If you don't know it, look it up. It will help you if you're heartbroken. I was over Navid. And I needed a new lover. Agatha took a series of almost duplicitously flattering photos of me and showed me how Tinder works. (She and Finch were in a new nonmonogamous phase and she was all over the apps.)

The thrill of finding a new lover was different this time. I found myself mindlessly swiping at my device. All lefts, until I glimpsed a familiar-looking guy, one I had a few friends in common with, all mostly lesbians. If his community was queer, I figured he must be a cool-enough dude. He looked young but he was thirty-nine. In one of his photos he was wearing a T-shirt that looked like the Black Flag design, but it said CAT FLAG and had black cats in the shape of the flag. At least he liked good music and didn't have any photos of himself holding a fish, or standing on a yacht. He suggested we meet at Dolores Park.

"Just see what happens," Agatha said. "You deserve some happiness, or at least, some good sex. This is San Francisco, you're supposed to be able to fuck in the park here. I'm not going to stand for you being celibate."

"Maybe I had all the sex I'm meant to have in my twenties," I said.

"Don't be ridiculous. Clean your room before you go out, shave your legs, take Penny on a long walk. Be prepared to have some fun."

TWO DAYS LATER, I left the apartment with no expectations, except that after this date inevitably didn't work out, I was going to go find a nice gay man to have a baby with. It had taken me forever to get dressed. All my clothes looked wrong, but I wasn't sure what "right" would look like to meet a complete stranger. Finally, I decided on a denim dress, standing in front of the long hallway mirror, pulling down the top of it to inspect my nipples. The Internet said they would change color, get bigger, that it's one of the first signs. Trouble was I'd never scrutinized them enough to know what they looked like before. Were they always this big? I pulled on some black tights, stretching out the waistband and contemplating whether it was snug. I enjoyed the fantasy of a changing body. I was wrapped up in this potential journey, just me and whoever might grow inside me, and I hardly cared what happened on this date.

He was already there when I arrived, sitting on a bench and leaning over his phone. Lanky, Converse sneakers, a plaid button-up, black baseball cap. He looked like almost every white guy his age, stylewise, but then he looked up, revealing a face so handsome I wanted to immediately turn around and run home. But instead, I screwed up my courage. I leaned my bike up against a tree and locked it to itself before joining him. What was the worst that could happen?

"Hey . . . Andy? I'm Missy," I said, feigning self-confidence, and then immediately dropped my bike helmet, tripping over myself to chase it as it rolled down the grass. I finally retrieved it and hooked the helmet through the strap of my purse, my arm falling around it like I was cradling a weird globe. So, so awkward. Damn.

Andy stood up, pretending not to notice my dishevelment. He was *too* handsome. He looked like he should be trying to sell me an Apple device.

"Hey, Missy, so good to see you," he said, though he was looking over my shoulder, then at my boots, wiping his hands on the legs of his jeans. His eyes were like a fluttering bird. Was he going to bolt? We half hugged. Suddenly I cared very much about being there.

He motioned to a bench, and we both sat down. I tucked my purse between my feet and tried to remember how to be articulate and funny.

"It's like we're sitting beside each other in a car?" I laughed.

"Do you want to go somewhere else?"

He was nervous, too, I realized. What if he was disappointed? Aging was really teaching me something about humility. Maybe I wasn't as cute in real life and that was why he was giving me a strange look, couldn't quite meet my eye. Should I throw myself down the hill into obscure spinsterhood? We cleared about four minutes of small talk, most of which was a rehash of our pre-date messaging, flirty, factual.

Testing the waters. But then he cleared his throat for what felt like the fiftieth time and blushed, before saying, "So, Missy. I need to tell you something."

Oh no, I thought, it felt too soon for bad news. Because I wanted this. I really liked him, and not just because he looked like Ryan Gosling. He made me feel like a giggly teenager, which, at my age, I didn't think was possible. I don't think I felt that way even when I *was* a teenager.

"We've actually met before. I saw you at the closing of the Lexington Club, outside in the alley?" He rubbed a hand against his beard, then opened both palms up at me, like he'd just thrown me a ball. I remembered his soft lean in the alley, our brief exchange.

"Right, well, we didn't really meet then," I said. "It's more like you watched me pee?"

"Right, right, thanks for the free show." He laughed. But then he went on. "But also in Las Vegas, in the nineties. I used to be Andie with an *ie*, you know. Now I'm Andy with a *y*."

He unbuttoned his plaid shirt to reveal an old shirt that said *Daddy* across the front. "I still have this shirt, one of the only old things I kept from that tour," he said.

To be honest, it took me a few minutes to understand what he was saying. Eventually, it clicked.

"Wow, from Agatha's old band," I said, and I could see vaguely, in his eyes, the shape of his face under his full beard, the person I shared that scorching day with, the beer by the pool, the hookup under the beach umbrella. I was shocked, but I tried not to show it. Agatha hadn't mentioned that he'd transitioned—but they'd had a falling-out years ago. No wonder I felt such immediate chemistry. He'd been the one person from that tour who'd managed to break through to me, that whirlwind body bedding anyone I felt like in a series of tornadoes, but he'd been the one who'd kept me in the air for years.

I tried to recover and be cool. "I thought you lived in Los Angeles."

"We moved here a year ago, my ex got a job at Pinterest. I work freelance, so it was easy enough to move. I don't do music anymore. Maybe Agatha told you that."

"No, she hasn't mentioned you." I didn't mention that his name had come up in our band meeting. "Listen, I know it was a hundred years ago, but I'm sorry that I was an asshole to you, in Vegas," I said.

"Were you? It was so long ago." He shrugged.

"We were supposed to meet up after the show. I was a real love-'em-and-leave-'em type back then," I mumbled. I knew my whole face was red. I could feel the heat spreading across my skin. I remembered every detail about our encounter. Of course, he wouldn't.

"No, of course I remember that, I was just trying to be cool." He laughed.

He crossed his arms and looked out across the grass, at clumps of people lying out on blankets, dogs tangling in their leashes. I followed his gaze, for something to do. A man with a radio on the front of his bike played an old disco classic, yelling out that he was selling pot brownies.

"Okay, yeah, I guess when I saw your profile, I thought it would be a chance to at least ask you what had happened. I wasn't used to rejection back then. You shattered me!"

"Did I?"

"No, of course not. Well, maybe you bummed me out for a night. The road was full of hookups, so I got over it quick. But I was depressed in L.A. when you didn't show up for that final festival date. I've often thought about how, if it had been a few years later and we'd had cellphones or Facebook, we'd probably have reunited and kept in touch. Back then it was possible to disappear so easily. I knew once I moved back to the Bay that you and Agatha had gotten tight. But I didn't think of looking you up until I saw you at the Lex and then on Tinder."

"I've thought about that, too. I've searched for you on Facebook, now I know why I didn't find you!"

"It's funny, that night in L.A. when you didn't show up, I got drunk with a girl backstage and we ended up getting married. Well, then divorced obviously, a few months ago."

"Ah, well, then it was fate!" I laughed, pulling at the edge of my dress nervously. "I know the divorce train. I know it well. But wow, your relationship lasted a long time. I feel like I am a different person from the kid I was back then."

"You were fantastic back then," he said. "You were the wildest girl I'd ever met. I swear, I was sure you were going to come out. Remember that time you punched a roadie in the nuts for grabbing that young fan's tit?"

"I will admit to not remembering that at all. And you know, I don't think it occurred to me to come out back then in any official way. When we hooked up, I mean, I'd had lots of lovers on that tour, but what happened between us felt more significant."

"It did?" He looked pleased, started buttoning up his shirt. He unzipped the small backpack between us and showed me an array of beverages—LaCroix, kombucha, juice. "I usually don't seek out dates with straight women, but I was still curious about you, I guess."

I was too nervous to read the labels carefully and ended up grabbing a truly foul-tasting kombucha.

"That is, uh, certainly fermented," I said, trying to hide a wince.

"I'll drink it if it doesn't suit," he said, taking it back and handing me a lemon soda water.

"I'm not totally straight," I said. "I'm figuring that out, right now."

"So, do you still want to have this date? I mean, I chose the park so it wouldn't be too awkward if you didn't," he said.

"Why wouldn't I?"

"Well, because of the trans thing," he said, as though I'd asked a really stupid question.

"No, no, of course not. I live in San Francisco. Most of the butch lesbians I knew in my twenties are all men now, it's no big deal. I date men, so this is obviously cool." But I was speaking fast, maybe not quite as confident as I was trying to seem. I gulped the water, spilling some down my dress. "Sorry, was that offensive?"

"How could it be offensive?"

Oh shit, maybe *asking* that was offensive. I felt like an idiot.

"Oh, you mean that all the butch dykes are men now. Nah, it's mostly true," he said, laughing. Dolores Park was now buzzing with laughter, shouting, crowds had formed, the way they normally do on a Sunday afternoon. But then a drum circle got louder, the insistent beat of their instruments drowning us out.

"Oh no," I whispered, and he laughed.

"Should we go get a drink or some food?" I asked.

"Well, I'm sober now. I'm a man *and* I'm boring, ha ha. Bet you're psyched about both."

"Well, I don't do drugs anymore, or drink much either. I got tired of waking up feeling like I had the flu. And I don't think I'm my best self when I drink."

We got up and gathered our things. I pushed my bike along the sidewalk as we walked to a nearby bakery.

"Do women really bolt when they find out you're trans?"

"Not often, no. But I'm also new to dating. I've never been single as a guy before, except for the last year or so when my ex and I were poly. But I don't know, I guess I always wondered if you didn't, you know, enjoy yourself when we hooked up last time. When you ditched me, I figured I was a bad lay."

"Oh my god, *no*," I said, probably too emphatically. "I don't know what it was, but I think it was the opposite. I think I couldn't handle it. Like I said, it felt significant in a way that kind of threw me off."

"So, sexual orientation panic?"

"Yeah, probably," I said, smiling sheepishly. I stole a glance at him and saw that Andy was smiling, too, though he kept his gaze on the sidewalk as we walked.

"It's so different now," he said. "The kids are all bisexual and nonbinary and whatever. I have a thirteen-year-old and all her—sorry, all of *their*—friends think I'm boring for being a man. They say I'm *too binary*. Like, this is my dad, he's 'binary trans' and then they laugh."

"That is very funny. I saw a documentary about nonbinary kids, and there were some femmes, you know, talking. I realized that if the option had been around for me at twenty-two, that's probably how I would have identified."

"Not now?"

I shrugged. "I'm pretty okay being this person. Agatha calls me a low femme. I suppose kids are luckier these days." The more I talked, the more square and ancient I sounded. "So, you have a kid?"

"Three actually. The thirteen-year-old is my stepkid, and then my ex and I had two, they're seven and three."

We reached the bakery and there was a lineup outside. We decided to hang out and wait.

"How did they take the divorce?"

"We haven't told them yet, actually. I'm still living at the house. I'll probably stay until we figure out all the details and let them adjust."

"Are you and your ex getting along?"

"We have to, because of the kids. It's odd that way." He took out his phone and showed me photos.

"Getting divorced was hard enough for me—and it was just me. I can't imagine what it would be like with kids. But I guess it's good that you're doing it?"

"Yeah, it's good," he said.

I wished I could've gone back in time and not fucked up our first meeting. Was this one of those fateful moments I could put in a hack love song, about getting a second chance?

When we finally got a table, we stayed for hours, nibbling pastries and sipping our coffees. The time unraveled easily as we spoke excitedly, like kids who had just met at the playground, delighted to have found a friend.

The chemistry between us was so present I felt like it had to have a color. We should have been able to hold it in our hands. I had so many questions for him. Was he just looking for casual hookups? Was he the kind of post-divorce dude who wanted to never get married again? Was he cynical about love? But I stopped myself. Agatha had made me promise not to babble. "You're intense right now, just try to tamp that down a bit when you meet new people," she'd said. "You used to fuck too quickly, and now you talk too much."

"Balance has never been my strong suit," I told her.

So I tried, pretty hard, to keep my interrogation at a minimum.

Andy had given up music and become a graphic designer, but had started playing the drums with old friends in the last few years. We talked about making music together. He seemed really excited about that.

"It's part of this new post-breakup life. I could start drumming again. Ceci didn't like my touring, especially after we had kids. Now I have some more freedom, when the kids are with her, anyway."

"But you said no to joining the new supergroup!"

"Right. Because it's a girl band."

"Ah, of course."

"I know, it's just weird. Doesn't feel right. Plus, I just want to play for fun. I see the potential for it to get complicated, with egos and such. Agatha and I had a falling-out, as you know."

"Sorry, I just got excited because I wanted to be in a band with you."

"Let's write some duets, then?"

He reached out and grabbed my hand across the table. His hands were so sexy.

"So, what is it like to be a dad? I've been thinking about becoming a single mom, considering the option, anyway."

"For me it was really, really difficult sometimes, especially at first," he said. He was the first person who didn't automatically add *But it's the best thing I ever did, and you should do it, too!* Instead, he spoke honestly about the positives and negatives, the things most parents don't talk about.

The conversation turned to dogs (he loves them, but never had one), gardening (his passion), and cooking (his bane). We ordered a second round of cappuccinos, still jittery from the first. We edged closer together, our knees touching under the small table.

"I guess we don't have the awkwardness of the first kiss, since we've already kissed before," I said. "This is our second date."

"I guess it is," he said.

He reached across the table, touched my face, and I put my hand against the soft flannel of his shirt, and then he kissed me. It couldn't have been more than three seconds. But it was the most exhilarating three seconds I'd experienced in years. I looked around the room after, embarrassed, as though the café patrons could see how a relatively chaste kiss felt more erotic to me than the entire encounter with the Uber driver, or the last few years of married sex.

When we pulled away, he looked at me and smirked. "You're trouble, Missy. You're real, serious trouble."

LATER THAT NIGHT, I woke up in bed to a jolt of pain in my abdomen. I stumbled to the bathroom and sat on the toilet, assuming it was my period. There was so much blood. I was almost four days late and still hadn't taken the pregnancy test that sat by the sink. But here was the answer.

I pressed my hands against the back of the bathroom

door, running a finger along the grooves, as another wave of pain tore through my uterus. Eventually, I crawled back to bed and tried to sleep, though it was fitful, as I kept waking up with cramps.

In the morning, I called Agatha.

"I feel awful and I'm bleeding kind of heavily. Do you think I should go to the hospital?"

"Sounds like you might have had a chemical pregnancy—it's a very early miscarriage—or maybe it's perimenopause," she said. "Everything gets heavier and weird around our age."

An early miscarriage? The pregnancy had never been quite real, so I wasn't sure this could be, either. I put her on speaker and googled it.

"I guess either way, the pregnancy dream is over." I put my cheek against the bathroom wall, feeling more disappointed than I'd expected to.

"Well, if you're sad about it then you know your true feelings."

"I guess."

"So, how was your Tinder date?"

"It was kind of amazing. And you know him," I said.

"What? Who is it?" asked Agatha.

"Andy, from your old band!"

Silence on the other end of the phone, then a sigh.

"Oh girl, Andy? He's great, but he's complicated."

"Why? He seems literally perfect, like God created the perfect date for me."

"Nah, no, of course. He's an incredible person."

There was a bit of an edge in her voice, but I couldn't decipher it.

"Did you hook up?"

"No, he had to go pick up his kids, but we had so much chemistry. He said he'd call."

"Well, great. I'm happy for you."

We talked a little more, mostly about the new band and when we would meet up next, and then she had to go because she was taking Emily to a swim class.

I hung up the phone and wandered into the living room. I looked around my house with new eyes. It was all mine. There was a vase of wildflowers on the coffee table, my red Converse by the front door, Penny was sleeping on the living room couch, and my cello was leaning against the fireplace. I sank into an armchair and got out my phone, looked more closely at the results for *chemical pregnancy*. I'd had the symptoms, but maybe I wouldn't ever know for sure.

CHAPTER 8

CAROLA

I HAVE NEVER BEEN good at sitting still. Of course I practice meditation and have for decades, but I am not a natural. I have built a muscle, and it is useful. Cancer reduces you to your earliest self. Every day I wore my softest, loosest clothing and woke up feeling like a cranky newborn. And for the first few weeks post-diagnosis, when I wasn't asleep, I was moving around, trying to get away from my body. I set the timer to do my morning sit, and ended up bolting upright after five minutes, unable to breathe deeply or just observe my thoughts. I was pulled to reorganize the house, scrubbing every sliver of discolored grout between the bathroom floor tiles with a toothbrush. I fell asleep with my cheek against the wall of the shower stall, woken up by Saturday's cold nose and a lick across my face, worried I'd lost consciousness.

A lot of the work of having cancer is administrative. I had readied myself for the spiritual work of being sick, the necessary introspection and self-care rituals I thought would be required. I booked vitamin C IVs and afternoons at the sauna, lymphatic massages. I started a new journal and sketched out

an elaborate wellness plan, complete with charts and illus-
trations. But very quickly, every day was subsumed by the
endless river of forms to fill out, calls to my insurance pro-
vider, the doctors who didn't talk to the other doctors, the
labs who forgot to call the doctors, the doctors who forgot to
order the labs. I routinely paced the living room with the
cordless phone on speaker, listening to hold music, spelling
out my last name and date of birth—again—saying the
words *You told me to call back, so I'm calling back* until I would
begin to cry. Again.

I was lucky that they caught it early enough that I had
only minimally invasive surgery to remove the lump, and
four weeks of chemo afterward. I knew I was lucky. The
treatments were brutal, but more or less what I expected. I
went in with such a positive attitude, but over the first few
weeks I felt demoralized. Larry was my rock, but there was
only so much he could do.

AND IN THE middle of a particularly bad day during the week
off between treatments—often when I felt the worst physical
symptoms—I realized that I hadn't seen Rufus in a while. I
looked everywhere in the house. I couldn't hear his gentle
snoring, or the tap tap tap of his limping jump with his single
front paw. I went out to the bunkhouse, where Larry was
painting the walls, the final step before it could house visitors.

"I can't find Rufus," I said, a rising panic in my voice. He
steadied himself on the stepladder and dipped the brush back
into the paint can.

"Oh, I let him out yesterday. He's probably just enjoying his freedom."

He ran the brush up and down, slopping blue over the masking-tape border, so carelessly I wanted to reach up and redo it immediately.

"How could you do this, after he lost the paw, after the trauma of the surgery? We decided he was an indoor cat now."

Larry put the brush down in the paint tray. "No Carola, you decided that. He's a cat. He deserves to be outside. We haven't seen the bears in a long while."

"How could you make this decision without me?"

I was livid. I circled the house and went into the forest paths holding a bowl of kibble and shaking it, calling his name over and over. I walked across the road and up the long driveway of our neighbors, to ask if they'd seen a three-legged black-and-white cat. No luck. I wandered their fields, calling his name. I gave up after a few hours. He was gone.

I caught a chill outside that felt as if it was eating into my chest. "I don't know why you keep pushing yourself. You shouldn't be wandering outside for hours. You are sick," Larry said, pushing the buttons on the microwave as I shivered under the couch blanket. He brought me a bowl of broth and set it on the coffee table.

"Carola, I used to let him out while you were at work. We had a whole ritual. Cats like rituals. I don't know why he isn't coming back around by five, it's a mystery. But I mean, ultimately, he has had a good life, hasn't he? Most cats don't get to murder that many creatures, that was his whole passion in life."

"Leave me alone," I mumbled into the bowl.

I emailed the center's discussion list about Rufus being missing, to look out for him, that he was microchipped and very friendly. Blue responded right away saying she'd make posters. I missed being at work. I missed people who wouldn't just shrug like Larry would shrug. A week went by, and everyone at the center looked for Rufus on their walks around. Someone emailed to say they thought they saw him in the forest. I brought the cat treats out to shake every afternoon when I walked the dogs. No luck.

I wanted to be well enough to work. No one could teach my particular brand of workshop, especially when women signed up to come and learn from *me.* I tried to train some of the volunteers, talk them through it, but it felt like more work to explain the work than to just do it myself. I had been a pillar of strength for the women who attended my retreats, an example of success in conquering my mind and building a strong, clean body. But now I was not strong. My body was not clean. I thought about all the times I had had cancer survivors in my workshops, how much I thought I could help them. The hubris! I had truly had no idea. What would I even say to them now? In moments of clarity, I wrote notes toward a workshop for cancer survivors. One that could have helped me right now, or after this was over. But mostly my mind felt fried from the chemo. I was lucky to make it through the day remembering where I kept my shoes and who I was supposed to call for what. Most nights I gratefully collapsed in front of episodes of *Murder, She Wrote,* until I fell asleep. By the time the break between treatments was over, I would have started to feel normal again and I'd be loath to start over. I felt so heavy even as I knew I was getting lighter.

Blue was trying very hard to be a support person. A few weeks after Rufus disappeared she showed up for her weekly Sunday drop-off of the meal-train lunches. As I was placing the neatly labeled Tupperware in the fridge, I said to her, "It's funny, the wellness industry is for people who are already well, isn't it?"

"You're just tired," she said, "but you're a fighter. You're going to fight this and you're going to win. You know, I heard about a guy who was stage four and cured his cancer with qigong."

I couldn't look at her after she said that. I'm not sure why I felt such rage. I handed her a bag of cat treats and told her where to go and look for Rufus. She nodded. I crawled up to bed for a nap and heard her through the windows of the loft calling Rufus's name.

I felt more tired than I thought possible. Even more than when I was pregnant with Missy.

TEGAN WOULD CALL every few days.

"I'm so tired. I can't teach, I can't inspire. I have one week left of treatment. What is my purpose here?" I moaned into the phone, the TV on mute, a plate of sprouted toast untouched.

"Your purpose? Jesus, Carola. You don't have to do anything but rest. You don't owe anyone any lessons, or any positivity. You can be mad every day. Maybe it would help? But even if it doesn't, you're allowed to complain."

"I don't want to lose hope, it could make things worse."

"Okay, okay. What do you need?"

"I don't know. I've been thinking about the old days at

Sunflower a lot, why everything went wrong. Did you know that Bryce's mom killed herself instead of doing chemo?"

"But wasn't she already a hundred years old?"

"I'm just saying, I used to think it was a bit of a selfish choice. Or weak. But now I get it."

"You are not going to do that, though? I thought you had stage one. You can kick stage one, babe."

"No, of course not."

"It wouldn't be fair to Missy, to leave twice."

"Ouch."

"Sorry, but you have a second chance with her now, and I'm glad you're taking advantage of that."

"Not really. I don't have time for relationships that require much work right now."

I could hear her breathing, but she didn't respond.

"Look, she doesn't actually know."

"Doesn't know what?"

"That I'm sick. I haven't told her."

"Holy shit, Carola. You love your secrets. Jesus. You need to tell her."

"Every time I'm about to, I just feel a rush of guilt, like I can't put this on her. Asking her for anything feels like too much."

BEFORE RUTH DIED, I failed Missy again. Ruth invited me to Beaurepaire to reconcile with her and Missy, and I'd arrived keen and hopeful, and every day that hope had slowly withered. Those few days with Ruth and Missy were intolerable, and things got worse after Ruth left for Turkey. I tried not to think of it much, how I'd failed that reunion. I'd promised Ruth I wouldn't leave before Missy did, that I wouldn't re-traumatize her. But it was a shock to see her as an adult, as though we were in a science fiction film and she was regress-ing before my eyes. I could barely make sense of what I should do, how I could help her. She wanted the abortion and I could support that, but her problems went deeper. I almost felt like *I* was her biggest problem, so how could I possibly help? But I stayed through her abortion, through her recov-ery even though she would barely speak to me. I brought her soup. I kept the house clean, watered the plants until Ruth was due to return from her trip.

But then Bryce returned alone, grieving over the aston-ishing loss of Ruth.

So I stayed even longer. I helped Bryce pack up Ruth's house. Missy skulked around us, shooting me mean looks, then rushing in to hug Bryce every chance she got. That was fair. I deserved it, but also Bryce was just a mess. The dy-namic felt familiar, though. Back at Sunflower, everyone else was allowed to have big emotions and act on them, but I was never seen or heard. I just kept on keeping on. Bryce had his big dreams and big plans, while Missy ran wild, and I washed the pots, fed the animals, and led the meetings. I sorted through Ruth's belongings, a life's worth of things, while Bryce collapsed into sobs and Missy raged. My feelings would get sorted out later, by myself, since no one there was interested in them.

The last thing I did before I left was to try to gently coax Missy to talk about her addiction issue. I was told, quite vo-ciferously, that it was none of my business. My offerings were left untouched and I was getting nowhere. If anything, our relationship was getting worse, a mash-up of grief, anger, and withdrawal. I didn't know what else to do, so I decided it was time to return to my own life. Melissa was an adult, and she had a right to be angry with me, but I couldn't be her punching bag.

The morning of my departure, Bryce crept into the living room, where I had been sleeping on the pullout couch, and gently shook me awake.

"Carola, she did it on purpose. She killed herself," he said.

"What?" I said, bolting up. I thought he was talking about Missy. "What happened? Where is she?"

"My *mother*," he said. "She killed herself."

"Bryce, what are you talking about? You aren't making sense."

"On the boat. My mother killed herself," he said, his voice catching. "It was suicide. But we can't tell Missy."

He held out three envelopes. One had his name on it. The others said *Missy* and *Cy*.

"Who's Cy?" I asked.

"The neighbor down the street," Bryce said, smiling a little. "I guess he was Mom's boyfriend."

I stared at him, openmouthed.

"I can't believe it," I said. "What do the letters say?"

"Mine is saying goodbye," he said, his voice cracking as he fought another wave of tears. "I am guessing Missy's and Cy's letters are the same, but we can't give Missy the letter."

"Why not? We have to, Bryce. It's not our decision to make. Those were Ruth's last wishes," I said.

"No," he said. "Missy is too vulnerable right now. You've seen her. She'll get better, she'll get over this and then maybe

I'll show her the letter. But not now. She's not strong enough."

I didn't argue. I couldn't imagine what I could say to convince Bryce, plus I had given up fighting with him years ago. Moreover, I didn't feel like I had the right. When it came to Missy, Bryce was the parent, wasn't he? I had given up that privilege, so how could I claim it then?

TO THIS DAY, I hadn't told Missy about her grandmother's letter. And to my knowledge, Bryce never shared it with her. So here I was, undergoing cancer treatments and still keeping secrets from my daughter. None of it was lost on me—in fact, I was reflecting on my mistakes near constantly—but I couldn't see my way clear to make any of it better.

I told Tegan everything, tearing at the now-dry toast in front of me, trying to take a small bite. "So, what should I do?"

"I don't know, Carola. I think you might want to make a list of things you want to make right, and when you're well enough, start working through them. But it's a two-way thing. You can't control how Missy reacts. For now, just let other people take care of you. I know that's hard for you."

"It's literally all I've wanted, to be cared for, protected."

Tegan didn't say anything. I felt embarrassed by my candor and ended the call.

I went outside and walked the trail behind the house that goes into the woods. Larry had strung up a hammock between two trees so I could get time in the woods without walking all the way to the riverbed if I was having a very difficult day with no energy. I curled up in it and stared at the fluttering leaves, at the chickadees popping from branch to branch, a curious fat squirrel unnerved by my presence. I closed my eyes and tried to take three cleansing breaths.

I cannot control my body, inhale.

But I can calm myself down, exhale.

The air got very still, and the squirrel stopped vocalizing, as though accepting my presence.

I fell into a light sleep, and when I woke up, Rufus was asleep on my chest.

Because I'd assumed he'd been taken by a coyote or another predator, I briefly wondered if I'd died, and I was encountering him in the afterlife. I petted him gently, trying to puzzle it out.

I felt at peace either way, I realized. No panic. Just a deep purring acceptance.

Then I heard Larry calling my name from the porch, and I grabbed Rufus by the scruff of his neck, cursed into his ear while cradling him like a baby, both of us unambiguously alive.

CHAPTER 9

MISSY

ANDY AND I went on three dates before we slept together. On the second one we went for a long dinner I barely tasted, so consumed with sharing our childhood stories. He'd grown up with a lesbian mom who started a cooperative dairy farm in the Midwest, so we had some similar experiences—from embarrassing tempeh sandwiches at school to dealing with groups of adults beyond a nuclear family. By dessert we were deep into relationship histories, and then of course, sex. Talking about it without jumping into bed right away made for some epic tension. In between dates, we exchanged new compositions, favorite poems, revealing photos, and endless quippy texts. There was so much lead-up to our first tryst I felt like I was in junior high for every awkward, sweet moment. He was smart and handsome and funny, and he listened so well. After three dates I felt as if he knew me better than Navid ever had.

It was a weeknight and I had been getting ready for bed, sporting an old Vision Street Wear T-shirt and yoga pants, when my doorbell rang. It was Andy, leaning against the doorframe in another soft flannel shirt and jeans, smirking at me.

"Is it okay that I'm just . . . here?" he asked, pacing in the front entranceway. "I can leave, it's weird that I'm here, isn't it? You weren't expecting anyone else?"

"Ha, no, no, come in. I love it. I'm happy to see you," I said, trying to catch my reflection in the toaster oven. I made us some tea, while he sweet-talked Penny and walked around looking at the art and photos on my walls. The framed cover of *Spin* magazine, some group shots from Sunflower, some beautiful gig posters from the early aughts. Then we sat beside each other on my couch and I tried to work up my nerve, quiet the insecurities tumbling around in my head. I finally leaned over and put my face close to his. I thought about what I would have done at twenty-two, and I kissed him, then pulled back. He looked captivated enough by the kiss, so I took off my shirt. "Wow," he said, and pulled me on top of him.

FOR THE FIRST couple of months of our relationship, I walked around in a desperate erotic stupor. I walked out of dinner with an important producer before the meal came because Andy texted me that he'd rented a hotel room and had to fuck me that instant and for the rest of the night. I couldn't sit and watch TV without my mind wandering to every moment of our last encounter. I missed deadlines because I spent three hours trying to send him a photo of my tits with the right lighting and angle. Every other priority vanished. I was only a body, waiting for a quick tryst when he could stop by between work and going home to the kids. I didn't even need foreplay, he could just breathe on my neck and reach under my skirt and go. He could look at me from across the room and I'd feel close to coming. He could wrap one hand around both of my wrists and make me feel a type of divine completeness that was filthy, ecstatic, and beautifully obscene, and in those moments I felt more alive, more free, than I ever had.

I'd had so much sex in my life, but this was the first time I felt like I truly understood the power it had to transform you. And that power was frightening, too, because I was so attached to him, right away, because of it. I couldn't dismiss what was happening. I would nod when friends would laugh that I was having a *hot rebound*. But it was more than a story to tell a friend later, it was more than an interesting challenge, it was more than something to give me an ego boost, or a way to pass the time. It was transformative.

The first night he dropped by, he had to be home by midnight. He hadn't told his ex about me yet, though he'd been living on the basement couch. He put his coat and shoes on at eleven forty-five but kept running back into my room to kiss me again.

"I want you to be mine, all mine. Is that ridiculous? I know, you probably have other dates, but I just wanted to say it. I know it's so soon."

"It is really soon, but I like it. Do you mean like, be monogamous?"

He looked sheepish at this, but nodded enthusiastically while putting one of my breasts in his mouth.

"Are you sure? This is a big deal. You just got divorced."

He looked up at me, his grin mirroring mine. "I'm sure. I don't know why, I just am."

He didn't leave until four-thirty, and later in the morning, when I was stumbling around the block with Penny, under-slept and sore, he sent me a text that read: *I love being your boyfriend.*

You better, I replied.

I was fucking done for, and only one week in.

EVENTUALLY WE FELL into a ritual where every second night or so Andy would come to my house after the kids were in bed. We'd make snacks and start watching a movie and then have sex almost all night. He would leave at five-thirty in the morning so he could sneak home before the kids realized he'd been gone and wonder why.

He and his ex decided to tell the kids about their divorce. Although it would take some time to work out the details, for Andy to move out and find a new place, at least now we could spend time together for real, in the daytime. No more sneaking around, which felt significant somehow.

Our bond felt unquestionable. We started writing songs together, taking weekend trips away. I had more fun with him in the first few months than I'd had in years. Andy was like a bus heading straight for me, and I was standing in the road just waiting for the rush of impact.

ANDY AND I waited four months before he introduced me to his kids. The first time, we took the two youngest ones for a hike north of the city. I came prepared. I had packed Band-Aids, granola bars, mixed nuts, and a flap of My Little Pony stickers. Ayden was a surly seven and Harlon was three, with a blond skater haircut that won me over. That, plus his chubby legs sticking out of mismatched socks. Ayden grabbed the walking stick from Andy and powered ahead of the rest of us, forging ahead so fast that I had to double-step to keep up. Andy picked up Harlon and we took turns carrying him piggyback. Every now and then Ayden would look back at us with a devilish laugh, and I imagined myself growing to love the sparkle of mischief in his bright eyes.

"I'm going to catch up with him," Andy said.

I had Harlon on my back, and he brought his little face around to look at mine every so often, as if to say, *Who are you again?*

I held Harlon's legs firmly against me, as the trail was increasingly steep, but he started to squirm. I put him down but watched him like a hawk, wondering why no one had put a railing on the outer side of this trail, wishing Andy and Harlon would stop and let us catch up. The world with a toddler in your care looked like an elaborate set of ways they could injure themselves.

"Would you like a granola bar? It has almond butter," I said quickly, trying to get him to slow down.

He paused a moment and stared back at me, then took the bar with a raised eyebrow, unwrapped it happily, and lumbered on.

"Where's Daddy?" he said, with an edge of worry in his voice. Three and a half was a terrifying age emotionally, as far as I could tell.

"It's okay, they're not far. Let's speed up, okay?"

He let me put him on my back again and I lumbered up the trail as quickly as I could, a half gallop, half run.

"Don't you worry, we're close behind," I said, though perhaps I said it more for me as I hoped we were still on the right path. On our right was a steep, unpredictable landscape of rocks and bramble, and a rushing stream about ten feet below. As Harlon gripped my neck with his small, sweaty arms, it occurred to me just how precious and vulnerable this little guy was, and I was filled with a fear I'd never known. I slowed down and stepped carefully, mumbling soothing things.

"Where's Daddy?" he asked again, and started to cry.

"It's okay, he's just up ahead."

I was beginning to really worry I'd gone off the trail when we turned around a bend and the landscape flattened out. Andy was standing at the bottom of a tree that Ayden was trying to climb. Harlon stopped crying.

"Oh hey," Andy said, smiling at me. Harlon leaned his arms out for his dad, nearly bringing me down with him.

"Here you go, Harlon," Andy said, pulling him off my back and lifting him onto a low branch of the tree, so he could "climb" like his sibling, though Andy kept a firm hand on his waist.

I felt an overwhelming sense of relief. Of course, nothing bad had happened, but my heart was pounding and I was covered in sweat. "You good?" Andy asked, curiously. I nodded. I'd only just realized that when kids get upset it's not always an emergency—often it's frustrated feelings.

I knew so much about music, about how to keep a band together, how to write a song with someone, how to compose a musical score. How did I learn so much about one thing and know so very little about children? I had once been a child. Surely that had to count for something?

We followed the trail a little farther until we arrived at

a small beach along a river. I shook out the blanket Andy had brought, while he unpacked Tupperware containers of cheese, apples, carrot sticks, and crackers, a plastic bag of green grapes. As we laid the food out, the kids took off their shoes and waded in the water, shrieking from the icy cold. I sat back and sipped my Thermos of coffee and tried to take it all in, to relax in it, to listen to the birds and feel the soft wind against my face. The stress seemed at odds with the desperation I felt to have my own child. This was what my life would be like, I realized, but with no one to lay out the snacks with me. With Harlon, you couldn't look away for even half a minute. The kid had no instinct for self-preservation. Yet I watched as Andy, looking calm as ever, picked both kids up and swung them around over the water while they squealed in delight. I pulled one of the *Star Wars* Band-Aids out of my purse to apply to a fresh blister on my ankle from the hiking boots I'd purchased for this day. Would I feel differently if this were my own kid? Would I be less afraid, or more? The feeling of being responsible for some-one so small, someone I loved so much. Poking at the red, ripping skin, I wondered if this was some kind of metaphor, that I wasn't prepared to care for children, that I wasn't ready and it was too late. I'd been with Andy and the kids for barely over an hour and I was exhausted. I wanted a nap.

I wondered if my relationship with Andy's kids would ever feel authentic. They would always be his, so how would I slot in? I was beginning to realize that my own childhood had left me totally insecure about parenting. I was so free-range, my dad off trying to build his commune world and my mom, well, just off. Gone. What did I really know about how parents were supposed to be? What if I made a mistake, wasn't paying attention, and Harlon stumbled off the trail and down the cliff? You have to be so on it as a parent. Before she left, I guess my mom really had a lot on her plate. Managing the commune, but also making sure I had everything I needed, and Taylor, too, sometimes, when Tegan was off having a solitary walkabout in the woods. It gave me a new perspective on how much stress my mother must have been under. How alone she must have felt. How idealistic the commune had been, and how positively insane it seemed now, with real kids in front of me, awash in wild energy and needs and emotions.

As we drove back to the Bay, both kids fell asleep. Harlon was adorable with his head tucked into his T-shirt, a collage of melted chocolate ice cream and dirt.

Andy looked over at me as he drove, and said, "You were good with them today. I like to watch you guys together."

I turned toward the passenger window, not wanting him to see the sudden tears in my eyes that I couldn't account for. I liked being a guest star in his family, but was this what I wanted? Bringing the kids into what was happening between us was a giant step, and I didn't feel like Andy was taking it quite seriously enough. When he'd suggested the hike, we'd talked about it at length. I was worried whether the timing was right, since the divorce was still so fresh. I'd asked him if it was too early.

"You're part of my life," he said. "I want you to be a part of theirs."

When he pulled up in front of my house, Andy glanced to the back seat to make sure the kids were still passed out, then grabbed my hand and looked at me intensely.

"What?" I said.

"I'm really grateful for you. I really love you."

I loved him, too. I knew I did. I'd felt it during the last few months, but the words felt strange in my mouth. He put his hands on my face and kissed me.

"I love you, too," I whispered into his ear.

I was happier than I'd ever been before, possibly in my whole life. Whatever love I'd known before, this felt like a new level.

LATER THAT NIGHT, I was still swooning when I took Penny for a walk. I texted Andy to say thank you for the day, that it had been so meaningful. He didn't text back, but I figured he was putting the kids to bed, cleaning up from dinner. Or maybe he was already asleep. After all, now I understood how exhausting kids could be.

But the next day he didn't text either. We hadn't made plans, so I didn't have an excuse to check in. Still no text that night. We'd established a pattern of good-night and good-morning texts, even when we were busy with work or family. I had a feeling in my gut not to text him until he contacted me, but I wasn't sure why.

I had lots of work to do, some catch-up plans with friends I'd been ignoring to spend time with Andy, but for three days my phone was always in my bag, heavy and weighing me down. Finally, on Wednesday morning, the longest we'd ever gone without contact, I texted to ask if he wanted to join me at a friend's art opening. He didn't answer. I broke and checked social media, and saw he was updating his Facebook. He'd posted a new photo of his cat.

I went over and over the day of the hike—I've not historically been the most self-aware person—wondering if maybe I'd said or done something wrong. But then what was that in the car when he said he loved me?

I texted *Are we good? No big deal if you're busy!* Then immediately felt like digging a hole in the backyard and lying in it until I died of humiliation or starved to death.

On Thursday, I turned my phone off entirely and made myself very busy. I went to a spin class, walked Penny by the ocean, finished a score I'd been too absent from myself to finish, practiced my cello, cleaned out the fridge, answered every email owed in my inbox. I called the fertility clinic. I might as well get this show on the road!

And then I brought in Agatha. Over tacos in the Mission, I spilled it all. The hike, the declaration of love, the sudden silence.

"You can't lose yourself in this," she said. "Don't forget your own priorities. You need to be careful. Andy just got divorced and so did you, quite frankly. You guys have been super hot and heavy, so just take it easy for a bit. Maybe this was just a rebound for him."

My stomach dropped at that.

"It's true we should slow down," I said. I actually really liked my independence. My life had started to feel mine again. "I know I should just chill," I said, chewing on my straw and staring out the window.

"You really should. But also, be a bit careful with him."

"Is he fragile in some way?"

"No, no. I mean you. Be careful of your own heart."

"Why, is he a cheater? Did you hear something bad?"

"No, he's just unpredictable. We were in a band together,

remember? That's kind of like dating. He had to call the shots all the time. He would promise things and then just ghost. I went along with it until it got to be a bum deal. But he's older now."

"Yeah, well, we all are. We all have our things. I'm no picnic."

"No, you're not, girl."

"Hey!"

She gave me a big hug before we parted ways and I turned my phone on again walking back up the hill to Noe Valley, listening to the new Neko Case record and feeling fine for the first time in days. If he'd changed his mind about us, then I couldn't do anything about it. Maybe it was just a short-lived love affair.

Suddenly my phone buzzed to life with texts, mostly from friends and work stuff. But then one from Andy: several heart emojis. That was it.

"We are nearly forty," I yelled at my phone. But there were bubbles underneath the text, and soon: *I HAVE A PLAN.*

ANDY'S PLAN WAS a mini-vacation. He wanted us to go away that weekend to a spa north of the city, near where Tom lived. I tried to play it cool. He wrote, *Are you free this weekend? Could Navid take Penny?* I replied, *Yeah, probably. What's your plan?* He answered by sending me links to mineral baths, hiking trails, cute cottages.

Looks beautiful.

I just booked us a cabin.

That seemed presumptuous, but it was a quiet thought that I couldn't hear over the pounding of my thrilled, in-love heart. I wanted to ask him, *Where have you been?* But I didn't.

Instead, I drove Penny to Navid's and stopped at a lingerie store on the way home and bought something flimsy and memorable. I asked the band to push our weekend rehearsal ahead a week. I baked us some cookies for the ride. I put an auto-responder on my work email. I knew as I was doing these things that I was dropping my life to accommodate his whims, but I felt okay with it. This kind of connection doesn't come along very often, right?

The next afternoon, Andy pulled up in front of my house, car packed for adventure. I got in, threw my overnight bag into the back seat. Andy leaned over and kissed me. From the moment he put the car in gear, one of his hands was always on me, and I never wanted to come back home.

CHAPTER 10

CAROLA

MISSY AND I sometimes went stretches without talking, but she hadn't called me in months, just a text to say she wasn't pregnant. A text! I had a nagging worry that she was falling into a depression after her split with Navid, maybe even using again, but even so, I couldn't make myself pick up the phone. I had too much to explain.

But now I knew that the worst of my treatment was over, I had to check in.

"Hi, stranger," she said. She was bubbly, in a way I hadn't heard for years. I wondered if she was high.

"Ha, you're the stranger," I said. "What have you been doing with yourself lately?"

"You know, same same. You?" She sounded distracted.

"Really?"

"Well, actually, Mom, I met someone."

"Really? Who is he?"

"His name is Andy. I guess the short version is that I'm really in love. I feel crazy all the time, but like, good crazy! He's so smart, Mom, and handsome. I feel like he really sees me, I know that's a corny thing to say, but it's true. It feels different than any other relationship."

"That's wonderful, I can't wait to meet him," I said. "What does he do for a living?"

"He's a musician, too, but does graphic design for a day job. He's a single dad, recently divorced. He lives in North Beach. We met on Tinder but we actually met a long time ago in the nineties. And he knows Agatha. It's all kind of crazy, how small the world is. But I'm happy."

"I'm so glad to hear that. You sound happy. I mean, I guess the last time we spoke Navid hadn't moved out yet."

"Yeah, it was rough for a few months but so much better now. How have you been? I was just thinking that in the spring you're going to be sixty. That's wild."

"It is. It is."

"What are you going to do for it?"

"Oh, nothing. Too old to make a fuss."

"No way, it's a big one!"

"Well, maybe I could come for a visit!" I'd never just invited myself before. I felt nervous suggesting it.

"Well, Andy and I were talking about how it would be cool to know each other's families. Maybe we could all meet up at Half Moon Bay and have a real party. Why not? I could invite Aunt Marie, too. Maybe Larry—"

"Oh, honey, you know Larry won't get on a plane."

"Right. Metal not meant to fly and all that."

I looked around the camper van, how it was its own tiny house on wheels.

"I have an idea," I said, "let me figure it out."

I wanted to keep this positive vibe going, so I didn't tell

her about the cancer. Why not just wait until I got the next news? Why worry her when she was in such a good place? By the end of the weekend, I'd found a place where I could rent a bigger RV, one that could fit Larry, Tegan, and Karen. I had a few months to work on Larry and his homebody ways.

Tegan was immediately on board when I told her about it. But she wasn't sure she could convince Karen.

"She's a bit jealous sometimes, you know, my first love and all."

"That's ridiculous," I said, laughing, but was secretly touched to be someone's *first love*. And even more grateful that someone who loved me that much could evolve so seamlessly into a friend I could count on, even at the lowest moments of my life.

A WEEK LATER my oncologist called to tell me the news. They had got it all. I was officially in remission. I went back to work the following Monday for the weekly staff meeting, where I was greeted with balloons and cupcakes. I was thrilled to go back to regular workdays. They had a sheen to them now, and I appreciated every ordinary, comfortable moment. Surviving made me grateful for everything I already had—the sound of Larry making porridge in the morning that used to drive me crazy, Rufus bringing me half-dead prey gifts, the dogs jumping up with muddy paws, the ladies who got angry when they weren't immediately self-actualized on day two of a retreat, I loved all those moments.

When Larry asked me what I wanted for Christmas I told

him I wanted him to join Tegan and Karen and me in an RV and drive to California to see Missy for my birthday. "You have months to prepare. No flying, I promise."

He agreed, somewhat unenthusiastically. I let him research all the RVs and choose the one with the best mileage and safety rating and then he became excited, buying a map book of America and drawing out possible routes. As we were lying in bed the week before we left, he said, "You know, I've only ever been to Florida, once when I was a kid. It's about time I saw some things." All five of Larry's older brothers had gone to Vietnam. Three came home. As an anxious child, he'd developed an ulcer, which kept him from being drafted. I think this was why he liked to stick close to home. Everyone he knew as a kid who left came back different or not at all. I loved Larry so much in that moment, hearing the sweet, curious little-boy voice come out of a six-foot-tall gray-bearded man of few words.

CHAPTER 11

MISSY

___

AFTER A WHILE, I began to understand the rhythms of my relationship with Andy. I understood that sometimes he wanted to see me every day, and other times he had to disappear for long spells. As my mother's birthday party in Half Moon Bay approached, we were deep into a hot-and-heavy stretch and had just returned from a whirl-wind last-minute trip to Hawaii. It had felt like a honeymoon, as we eschewed hikes and beach days and hardly left our little beach rental. We just had sex and more sex, and eventually I had to lock him out of the bathroom, laughing, so I could shower and drink water and not get a permanent UTI.

And when the airport taxi pulled up in front of my house, he surprised me by getting out. "I don't want to leave you yet, and I don't have the kids until tomorrow."

"Oh, okay," I said, ushering him inside. The next morning, we were sipping coffee in the backyard, being leisurely, but I didn't trust it. I knew it was just a matter of time before he got antsy, would need his space and his freedom. He would leave and then I might not see him again for a few days, or even a few weeks. I'd learned to accept Andy's disappearing acts, though they still unnerved me. At least he'd agreed to send me a heads-up when he was going AWOL, and I'd agreed I wouldn't respond. I would wait it out and be there when he came back. But for the last few months we'd been on a high, and our relationship was almost starting to feel normal, like we'd balanced things out.

I'd packed him up a bit of leftovers from dinner, brought them out to the patio table. "If you want to take them home?"

"Oh, I don't have to leave yet," he said, "if you don't want me to."

I never wanted him to. Which was in itself an odd feeling.

He looked up from his datebook. "So I have an idea for the food for the party for your mom. How about this cake?" He passed me his phone, a series of recipes. A bird landed on the patio table and started pecking at crumbs from our muffins. "Man," Andy said, "your garden is like a little Eden. This place is just perfect, you are so lucky."

"It's a good house," I said. "I was lucky to get it in the divorce." I was feeling so comfortable, so happy, that I took a risk.

"My mom says you should move in here, that it's a big-enough house. She's such a hippie," I said.

"Well." He sat up, put his phone down. "She might be right, huh?"

"Andy, we've been dating for like, barely a year."

"Well, we could take some time to get used to the idea, see how it feels?"

"Are you sure we're not both still too fragile from our divorces?"

Honestly, I wasn't that fragile. Navid and I had become

friends again. I looked at him and couldn't imagine being a couple anymore, but he felt like family.

"I don't know, it might be nice, though?" Andy said, looking at me with shining eyes.

"It could be nice, I guess?"

So we began to plot it out, a possible domestic future together. We spent the next several weeks describing a joint household that began to feel less like fantasy and more like a real life. We talked schedules and schools, bedrooms and closets. We might need to build a new bathroom in the basement. We might need additional parking space. By the time we got to furniture, my head was beginning to spin, overwhelmed with elation or just overwhelmed, I wasn't sure.

I'm so excited about this. I can't wait to tell them. I think it's such a good idea, he texted me from the furniture store where he was pricing kids' beds.

FOR THE NEXT few weeks, I read everything I could get my hands on about blended families. What I should and shouldn't do to make kids feel welcome, the role of a good step-parent, how to adjust to the expected bumps. Andy texted me photos of furniture. I sent him articles about how to introduce children to pets, so Harlon would warm up to Penny. I went up to Petaluma for a few nights to record some songs with the new band. Andy had the kids for a few days, and he drove them up to hang out on the last day.

We rehearsed a few songs we'd be playing at our first show. The kids looked alternately entranced and bored. I'd been staying with Tom for the band's rehearsals and he had said that Andy and the kids could crash for a night, too. When we got there, Tom already had the grill going for burgers. Tom and Andy got along like a house on fire, talking about the dad life and drumming. They had a lot in common.

By the time we finished eating, Harlon was sleepy, and cranky from all the adult conversation. I offered to take him for a walk, asking if he'd like to go find the bunnies that lived out in the meadow behind Tom's house. It was so beautifully quiet outside, and the sun was about to disappear. Harlon often got quiet when we were alone. He was a thoughtful kid. His hair was white-blond from the California sun, and he wore a soccer uniform basically every day. The pathway took us along a grouping of sunflowers twice as tall as he was, and as we got close to the patch of grass where I usually saw the bunnies, I whispered that we had to be extra quiet.

We sat on the ground and watched as the mama bunny emerged from the warren, and then several little kits. Harlon's eyes got wide, and I pulled some carrots from my pocket and handed him one. We crept forward slowly, and then Harlon got too boisterous and the rabbits ran back into their hole.

"It's okay, we can leave the carrots on the ground and when the bunnies come out again, they can have their dinner."

Harlon carefully placed his carrot on the ground and looked at me solemnly. "They probably don't want to be fed by giants. I mean, I wouldn't want a giant to feed me."

"You're so funny," I said, laughing. He grinned.

We lay on our stomachs, trying to make ourselves small, and silently waited until the rabbits returned. Eventually, they did, and Harlon's face lit up as the mama rabbit grabbed a carrot and scurried back into her hole with it. As we walked back to the house he said, "You know, if the end of the world comes and I have to build a hole in the ground for my family, you could come, too."

"Oh wow, thank you, Harlon," I said. It was a pretty good offer. I was overwhelmed by the feeling that he wanted me in his life, and was trying to say so using this imaginative example.

We went inside and I offered to read him a bedtime story while Andy and Tom were excitedly playing records for each other, and Ayden and Harriet, Andy's oldest, sat on the couch glued to a video game on their iPads. Harriet was quite indifferent to me. I was reading all I could about teen development in hopes we could connect before they moved into the house.

THE NEXT DAY Tom and I watched as Andy and the kids drove off down his long driveway. "He's so good," Tom said.

"Isn't he?"

"I love how happy you are with him," he said.

"Aw, thanks."

"But be careful, he seems . . . complicated."

"Agatha said the same thing."

THE FOLLOWING WEEK Andy and I met for breakfast on the Friday before we were to drive down to Half Moon Bay. He was late and I sat in our usual booth by the window, people-watching and sipping coffee. I was so lost in my reverie I didn't notice that a toddler had sidled up to me and was pulling at my dress.

"Oh, no, don't bother the lady, Semi," a mom said, rushing up and grabbing her.

"Oh, it's okay."

The mom also had a baby strapped to her chest, barely out of the oven.

I watched them go back to their table and started to cry. I hadn't had a baby craving in months! I was so awash in everything-Andy, the sex, the idea of moving in together, having a blended family with him, the romantic getaways, all this stuff I couldn't do if I had a baby. I guess I thought I had moved on, had realized that there was a lot I could enjoy with my freedom, and I'd found someone to do it with, which felt meaningful on a whole new level. But seeing this woman brought it all back. Even how tired she looked, how her shoulders sagged. I wanted it. I was overwhelmed by a feeling of *I can do that*.

I quickly swiped at my tears when I saw Andy step into the café. He apologized and ordered a coffee, diving into a rapid monologue of his crazy morning. Then he noticed my splotchy face and red nose, which I kept surreptitiously dabbing.

"Is everything okay?"

"I think I must be premenstrual. I just saw a really cute baby. Sometimes I still really want one."

He grabbed my hands and squeezed them across the table.

"I don't want to stop you, you know. I've already said this, but if it's what you want, you should do it."

But he didn't want another baby. We both knew that.

"It's fine, I don't even know if I could be a single parent. That I'd be capable."

"You'd be capable, you'd figure it out," he said. I'd never wanted to change a subject so desperately before.

"Anyway, I was looking at loft beds today, I think if we build one in the study, Ayden would love it and it would make the room much bigger." I pulled my phone out to show him the design. "And Harriet could have the other room all to themself."

"Right, right."

There was a long pause.

"Look, I've been thinking and my friend has a place in North Beach he's leaving for a year while he's on sabbatical. He said I could have it. It's only a two-bedroom, but I could stay on the couch when the kids are there. It's ideal, actually."

"Oh." I looked down. The tears started again—I couldn't control them. I was so angry at myself for being surprised by this.

"And I'm not sure I can make it up to the cottage this weekend after all. I want to meet your mom and be there, but there's so much going on."

"Oh," I said again. Suddenly not able to say anything else. What was happening? He had planned the menu, he was supposed to pick up Marie from the airport. The party was *tomorrow*.

The waitress came, and I ordered my breakfast.

"I'll just have this coffee," he said. "I have to get going actually."

"Oh, then never mind, I'm good," I said. "Guess I have a lot to figure out for the party now." I added a bite to my tone, hoping he would respond, apologize, change his mind. But he just looked at his phone as it blinked with incoming texts, then keyed in a response, looking up and mouthing *sorry*.

"I'm going to go," I said.

"You're upset."

"Yes, I mean, you practically initiated this weekend. It meant a lot to me, that you'd want to meet my mom. Now you just can't come?"

"I'm sorry, I've just been so disorganized. It *is* important to me, I do want to meet your mom. I just can't."

When we left he stood up to give me a strange half hug and avoided my eyes before I turned and slammed out the door.

THERE WASN'T MUCH I could do. I didn't have time to wallow. I ran around doing last-minute prep for the party—half of it stuff Andy was supposed to cover—then raced to the cottage. They'd called from Las Vegas a few days ago, where it sounded like they were having an amazing time. When they pulled the hulking RV up the winding driveway and got out they looked so much older; it always took me a second now to recognize them. I hadn't seen my mom since Navid and I had visited her and Larry for Christmas one year. She looked so strange, though. She was usually fit, but she was downright skinny and it made her look even older. She had lost tone and color. It made me worried, but I filed this away as something to ask her about later. There was too much to do to get into it now. And she had cut her hair into a bob, which was maybe not the best choice. She pulled me into a massive bear hug.

"Oh, Missy, you look wonderful. It's so good to see you! How I've missed you," she said.

I had to bite my tongue not to point out how she clearly didn't miss me when she went so many months without calling. But whatever, I hadn't exactly been calling her either much this past year.

She held on to my arm and kept patting it as she spoke until finally Tegan shouldered her way in for a hug.

"Oh, look at you!" she said. "Divorce agrees with you, you're just gorgeous! Just so . . . healthy now!" she grabbed at my hips, pinching them. One thing I did love about hippies was that they understood gaining weight to mean growing healthier.

I groaned and pushed her away playfully. It was hard in those moments not to say things like *It's incredible what not doing cocaine and actually eating regular healthy meals does to a body!* But instead I just hefted her carry-on onto my shoulder and started directing them toward the parking lot.

Larry was busying himself bringing a cooler into the house, but mumbled a sweet and soft hello.

Tegan loomed in my childhood memories as a sort of Chrissy-from–*Three's Company* type, but a hippie Chrissy. Always bleached blond or bright red curls, dripping with silver and turquoise jewelry, carrying the scent of sandalwood and amber oil. I hadn't seen her in a long time, but we'd always kept in touch over the phone and email. Sometimes she would call to talk about Taylor, share memories from when we were kids. I was always game. It made me sad, but also happy to think about Taylor. That frizzy-haired kid was my first best friend. I still couldn't believe she was gone.

It was a bit of a shock to see Tegan in her sixties. She

looked as though she'd been out in the sun for years, and her hair was in a sensible short style. The more Mom and Tegan aged the more they looked like butch farmers, in a way. Except Tegan wore feminine earrings. If I'd passed the two of them in public, I'd have assumed they were regular older ladies, heading to a book club, instead of women who used to organize magic mushroom weekends where women looked at their vaginas with hand mirrors and sang Joan Baez songs under a full moon. But they looked like they did not give a fuck about men anymore.

"So how's Andy? Looking forward to meeting him this weekend," my mom said.

"I don't think he can make it, actually."

"Oh no, that's too bad!" Tegan said, giving Mom the side-eye. "I have to say, Missy, you seem happier without Navid. I never liked him."

"That is such a lie, you loved him!" I said.

"All right, I loved him. He was very handsome. But you do seem calmer now, more peaceful, grounded. I always noticed how you were very different people."

I SETTLED MY mom and Larry in the guest room. Tegan was going to stay in the RV. Then I went to the market in town to buy fresh vegetables. I filled the trunk with herbs, apples to make a pie, an array of meats and cheeses. I sat in the parking lot, taking a moment to try to get myself together. I couldn't stop thinking about how Andy and I had planned so much of this weekend together, and now he was suddenly absent. I felt mad, and moreover, let down. And then I wondered if I had a right to feel so let down. I felt like I was dating two different people, the one who literally couldn't stand to be away from me for even ten minutes and the one who stayed away for days on end and had just evaporated in front of me earlier today at the diner. We'd been dating long enough for me to realize we had a pattern, but bailing on the party felt like a new level. I didn't understand the rules anymore. I decided that when I got back to the city, I would tell Andy that I couldn't deal anymore. It was making me crazy and it was depleting my self-esteem. *Go be single, and then figure out what you want, and if it's me, you can let me know.* I imagined saying it in such a self-assured, confident way and then walking away. Even though I couldn't even say it to myself in my head without crying.

I DROVE THE five miles back up the hill to the cottage, and when I got there, Andy's car was in the driveway. I looked in the window and saw him holding Penny and chatting amiably with my mom. He was charming her. When I stepped inside, I tried to not look as surprised as I felt, and realized that in the time I'd been gone, he'd already made some salads and taken Penelope on a walk. He had put cut flowers in vases around the house and stocked the wine rack with fresh bottles. He even had Bob Dylan's greatest hits playing in the background. Wow, he was really working it. And the older ladies were enamored.

We all made dinner. While chopping veggies for a salad, Andy grilled chicken breasts and tofu patties for my mom and Tegan.

We built a fire in the fireplace and stayed up talking, Andy telling stories about Harlon's latest daycare adventures and my mom and Tegan reminiscing about the Sunflower days.

"I cannot picture Missy as a tomboy," said Andy, laughing. "Now, that's something I would like to see!"

"Yeah, yeah," I said, beginning to clear our glasses. My mom got up to join me. I tried to shoo her away, she looked so tired, but she insisted. In the kitchen, she leaned in and said in a low voice, "He's so right for you."

"We're taking it slow," I said, though that was hardly true. I was happy she wasn't being weird about him being trans. I'd let her know ahead of time to thwart any potential issues so it wouldn't impact Andy at all. But they were all being cool. Tegan's wife, Karen, had a nonbinary grandkid and she was prone to talking about it too enthusiastically around Andy, but that was it.

"I can tell he makes you happy. He's just so thoughtful, so sweet," she said. She rarely offered many opinions about my life, and it was a bit startling to hear her be so definitive on Andy.

"Mom, are you sure you're okay? You seem—I don't know—you seem kind of off."

"Just the wine, honey," she said, "but I was thinking that it might be time to tell you about why I left."

"Mom, you don't have to . . . I already know, mostly. You explained it when Ruth died." I wanted to stop her, the words coming from her mouth. I just couldn't take another confrontation today.

"I didn't do a good job of it back then. But you know, women today have far more choices than my generation had, than my mother's generation had. A woman deciding to leave her child, that's not something a lot of people will be on board for, but it was the only choice I could make at the time."

"Or you could have made the choice to stay. That's a choice," I said, my voice wavering as I tried to tamp down the anger. Not now. Not now.

"Not really," she said. "Remember how my dad and mom died? Driving in a car? My dad held anger and he didn't know what to do with it. He had run out of choices, so driving off in that car was the choice he made when he couldn't see anything else clearly."

"So staying would mean killing yourself?"

"Not exactly. But then, I don't know. I had hit bottom, Missy. We had a very complicated life at Sunflower. You probably didn't understand it, but there were a lot of complicated relationships and fractures. When you get pregnant and you're not ready, you have to roll with it, or decide, as you did, that it isn't the right time. You know what that feels like, to make the right decision. Sometimes I wasn't sure I made the right decision, frankly. But I loved you. I always loved you."

I was speechless. The grown-up me understood this intellectually; the kid part of me wanted to stamp my feet.

"Missy."

The tears were streaming down my face now.

"What? What do you want?" I said.

"More than anything," she said, "I want you to know how much I love you. How much it hurt to leave you. Even though it didn't feel like a choice—I actually thought I was saving you somehow by leaving, saving you from *me*—I still loved you. And I do now. I'm so proud of you, of who you've become, the life you've built, the music . . ."

"The life I've built? I'm a divorced ex–rock star with ge-
riatric ovaries! It's not exactly the stuff of storybooks. I'm in
love with someone who sometimes loves me back and sometimes looks at me like I'm an irritant, and I never know what
I'm going to get, you know? Remember when I left Navid,
how sure I was that I wanted a baby? Sometimes I still want
that."

"Well, you can do that. You can leave. I didn't mean to
cheerlead too hard for Andy if you can't work out your issues. But I do think every couple has issues, and you just have
to love each other enough to want to figure them out."

"Okay," I said. "Okay, Mom. I'm really, really tired. It's
been a long day."

"Okay, so good night, then," she said, leaning over and
kissing me gently on the cheek, lingering.

I went through the house turning off lights, then went to
the bedroom. Andy was already asleep. I curled up in bed
beside him, and he put his head against my breasts and began
to cry. I held him close and asked why he was upset.

"I'm not sure," he said, but kept crying.

"It's okay, it's okay," I said, soothing him until he fell asleep.

I WOKE UP early, before anyone else, and I took Penny for a
walk, trying to turn over everything my mom had said to me
the night before. If anyone else had told me those things, I'd
have sympathized. But with my mom . . . I don't know, I still
couldn't get past her selfishness. How could she make her
leaving about me? She had to leave to save me? When all I
needed was *her*? We all make choices to stay or to go. I knew I
had to make one about Andy. It wasn't hard to leave Navid and

we had been married for years. Why was this harder? I bent over and bagged Penny's last offerings, then headed for home.

THE PARTY WAS wonderful, there was no way else to describe it. When my aunt Marie showed up, my mom burst out in tears. "You're here! You're actually here, you're all here!" she kept saying, hugging and kissing us all. It was pretty awesome. My heart was full, more than I'd felt it in a long time. Tom and his kids had driven down, and Agatha, Finch, and Emily as well. All of our people were here, gathered. I'd been so consumed with the practical details of shopping, cooking, and arranging everyone's sleeping situations that I had nearly forgotten what we were celebrating.

Andy remained by me the whole night, taking every opportunity to squeeze my arm, compliment me, kiss my cheek. He was, once again, the perfect boyfriend.

When I was clearing the plates after dessert, Tegan joined me in the kitchen, filling up the sink with soapy water.

"You don't have to do that," I said.

"I want to," she insisted. "You know, your mom and I, we were really young when we had you and Taylor. We didn't always know what we were doing."

"I know, I know," I said. She always talked like this when we were together. I think I was one of the few people in the world who had known Taylor so well that I could remember her down to the last detail. It gave us a bond, but sometimes I couldn't handle it. Like tonight I was still reeling in the joy of the evening and I just didn't want to go down that road.

"This is so nice, what you did for your mom," she said, handing me a plate to dry.

"She seemed really happy," I said.

"Absolutely," she said. "You know, she is so grateful for you. She has a hard time expressing it, but she's working on it. And she really regrets leaving you."

"Really? She has never said that. She's pretty much told me the opposite."

"Well, it's complicated. I know you think she's selfish, and we all are sometimes. But women are *not* selfish when they should be and they really screw themselves. So in a way, your mom was kind of ahead of her time. But listen, she didn't tell you everything."

I really wanted out of that kitchen. I couldn't handle Tegan's vibe, and whatever my mom didn't tell me, well, she probably had her reasons.

"She had cancer," Tegan said.

"Cancer?"

"Yeah, this past year. She's in the clear now. Remission. Just fine. But she didn't want to burden you. I thought you should know, though. Just so you take it easy on her. She's still not one hundred percent."

The word *cancer* was still hanging in the air and I was no longer really hearing Tegan's voice. None of this made sense.

"I forgot I needed to go check on something," I said, and dashed out. I charged angrily out to the garden. Everyone was sitting around the fire pit and Andy was strumming the guitar, singing "Tangled Up in Blue." Marie was harmonizing. My mom's eyes were closed, dreamily. She was so beautiful, and so happy. Her bad haircut was pushed off her face and the reflection of the fire made her almost glow from within. I could see why so many women flocked to her for advice and comfort at the retreats, turned her into their personal guru. She had this magnetism and you just wanted to be around her, like she had all the answers. It was odd to realize how few answers she often had for herself.

I sat down and tried to sing along. My mom's eyes fluttered open and she looked over at me and smiled. She reached out a hand and I went over to sit next to her and she enveloped me under her arm. My heart, which had been too full earlier in the evening, was hurting now.

At the end of the night, I walked her to bed. She was a bit wobbly and the pathway stones were unpredictable. As we walked she watched Andy with Tom's youngest son, teaching him how to stoke the fire.

"You should do it now. He'd be the perfect father."

We got to her room and I tucked her in, brought her a glass of water.

"Have the baby now," she repeated. "You're not getting any younger."

She was right. I would be turning thirty-eight this year. I had to make a decision soon.

"What if I'm just at a crossroads, and I'm reaching for meaning and it just looks like a baby?" I said.

"So what? People do all sorts of things to find meaning. Especially have kids. There are worse reasons to have children."

"I feel like this is what Granny wanted all along, for me to have kids of my own. But I was never sure she was happy being a mother, so why did she think it was such a good idea for me?" The minute the words left my mouth I wanted to take them back.

My mom looked at me hard. Then she said, "Even when mothers don't seem happy being mothers, they still love their children. Most of the time. My mother didn't seem very happy being a mother and I think she did love me and Marie very much. Your grandpa, God rest his soul, was not a nice man. Our mother was stuck with him. It was hard to grow up in that environment. She tried the best she could. She made mistakes. But we all do."

"I guess it's hard thinking about being a mom when you aren't sure you've learned how to do it right," I said.

"I can see that," she said. After a pause she went on. "But you shouldn't let it be an excuse. If you are afraid to do something, the fact that you are afraid you might not be good at it, or might not have a good model for it, shouldn't hold you back."

I suddenly felt like I was in one of her seminars, but she wasn't wrong all the same. And even though my mom was still talking about having babies, I was thinking about Andy. I wondered if I was letting our relationship keep me from getting what I wanted. And if I wasn't going to get what I wanted from our relationship, was love enough?

"Ruth wanted you to have children, Missy, because she thought it would make you happy. I don't think she had another agenda. Not really. Well, okay, maybe she also thought it might put you more on the straight and narrow."

"Straight and narrow! She should see me now," I said.

"She might have surprised you. But we'll never know."

"I was so mad at Granny before she died; I always thought we'd make up, and then she went and died on the trip."

"You know, she had a plan," my mom said.

"What do you mean?"

"She left your father a note. A suicide note. She left a note for you, too, but he didn't want to give it to you. He probably still has it."

"You mean, I felt so guilty for so many years, and she always knew she was going to check out? She left us on purpose?"

"Yes, she planned it. It was a last act of control."

"That's so sad. It's so sad she got to the end of her life and couldn't rely on anyone to care for her."

"I don't think she thought of it that way. I think it was kind of bold, for someone who always conformed, was always afraid of not seeming normal and perfect. Honestly it was probably the one thing she ever did that I admired. She wanted to free herself."

I lay down beside her, like we did at the farm when the woodstove would go out in the middle of the night.

"While we are confessing things . . ." she said.

"Oh god, what else," I said.

"I was sick," she said.

"I know," I said, "Tegan just told me."

She looked at me and raised her eyebrows. "You knew?"

"But you're okay now? It's okay?"

"I'm going to be okay, yes. I think so."

"Why didn't you tell me?"

"Because," she said, "I was trying to be a good mother!"

She looked over at me and we both started laughing.

Larry walked in. "What's so funny, ladies?"

"Nothing, nothing," I said, leaving them for the night.

THE RV LEFT two days later. My mom whispered, "I'll fly out again for the birth. I'll stay for the first few months, if it doesn't work out with Andy, or even if it does." I whispered a *thanks* and helped her up the stairs to the RV.

I watched them drive away and then found Andy doing laps in the pool. I kicked off my sandals, sat down, and dangled my feet in the water. As I watched him swim, I thought about how he made everything in life stop when he put his hand on my arm. That feeling had been there even in Las Vegas years ago. But I had been afraid of it. I was afraid of what it meant back then. I'd had so many superficial relationships with cis guys, all out of fear. Even though Andy was the only person I wanted to be with, I felt like he'd helped me understand my queerness. Even if we couldn't be together, he'd helped me finally define myself, understand myself.

Andy swam over and wrapped his arms around me, soaking my dress, making me squeal and laugh. Then he said, "I've given this a lot of thought, and I think we should get married."

The moment was all I had ever hoped for.

"Don't you think?" he breathed, pulling me into the pool.

We kissed until I almost relented.

"I want you to be a part of my family," he said, and then I pulled away, splashed back, and hopped out of the pool, wringing the water from my dress.

"It's not going to work. If I say yes, do you know what will happen? It will be like one of those dumb rom-coms where the groom runs out of the church. You can't just ditch me, and then show up, and then make promises and ditch me again. It's been happening for months, and it hurts more every time."

"I'm sorry, I know. It's complicated. I'm trying to figure out why I'm like that. It's like I'm one of those dressers where one drawer can't open if the other one is closed. Sometimes the bad drawer opens and I just can't remember feeling the way I feel now about you, and then the other drawer opens and I can't imagine feeling like I don't want to be here. It's unpredictable."

"Well, then I'm always waiting for you to drop out of sight. I know when it's coming now, I can feel it. And I try to act like it's cool, like I'm cooler than I really am, about being dropped like that. It's like I'm walking on eggshells, waiting all the time. And maybe you're supposed to be with someone who never prompts you to open the bad drawer? I want to marry you more than anything, but marriage is not a solution to a problem. It creates more problems, we both know that. I need things I'm never going to get with you. I feel like I'm standing on the shore and you go in and out and it drives me crazy."

I GOT INTO the pool and we did what we always did best without question. And when I got back to the city, I cried for weeks and weeks. And of course, because I had pulled away from him, he showed up at my door unannounced, and we reunited over and over. I read books about attachment theory, and tried to solve our patterns over and over. But as soon as I was present and loving, he left, over and over. And finally I'd had enough of trying. I called Tom and said, "So, do you want to be an uncle?"

EPILOGUE

ON MY FORTIETH BIRTHDAY, I maneuvered around my party with difficulty, and eventually just sat in the cushy golden armchair Agatha had nicknamed the birthday/birthing throne. Finch placed a plate of birthday cake on my sizable belly, put a ridiculous tiara on my head, and took a photo. There's another photo from that day, with Tom, and when I look at it now, I see in his eyes he was absent. He'd descended into a sadness I couldn't help him with. The photo sits on the dresser Andy refinished for me as a baby shower offering, beside my nursing chair, where I sit most nights with Hazel, staring at her face and feeling the rotating thrill of about a dozen conflicting emotions.

My father came to the baby shower and brought the letter Granny wrote to me before she died. He said, "I was never going to give this to you, but I think it's the right time."

Missy,

I'm writing this to you, in the hopes that you are now well on your way to motherhood. And since I can't be there,

*I want to share some wisdom. I didn't plan to parent on
my own, but that's the way it mostly happened. There are
things you think are certain before giving birth but
afterward, very little is predictable. You will make
mistakes. Everyone does. Your mother did, of course. And
while I have a hard time with Carola as a person, I do
remember how hard she tried when you were little to be the
best mother she could be. I'm not sure what happened that
made her leave, but I did see how it affected you. I want
you to know that you won't make the same choices she did,
you're stronger than all of us, with your adventures and
your career. You are a determined young woman. And
you can do this.*

Love, Granny

It was what I needed to hear at the time. Most of the time
pregnancy made me feel like a superhero, like I could do anything. But in the third trimester, my fear became as unwieldy
as my body. What if I couldn't do it? I thought that a million
times a day. And I'd never felt more alone. I read and reread
her letter until I believed her words.

NOW I WATCH Hazel in Agatha's arms, as Emily delights in
being the older kid, and I'm thrilled, I'm ecstatic, unwavering. At four in the morning, I'm crying with frustration,
stressed out, covered in poop and disoriented and I feel regret, but a regret that can't be reversed, and thus it's mean-
ingless and momentary. I wake up and do it again. I don't
know how I'm ever going to get through the day. And then I

do. I get through several months of days that mostly look the same, but at the same time, she changes so quickly. I can't believe how much, from week to week. These are things all mothers say, but that doesn't make them feel less specific or profound to me, or true.

She squirmed in my arms at Tom's funeral, after he un-expectedly took his own life, crying out the way I wished I could, the guilt of not having known how much pain he was in consuming me. Still consumes me. It shook up my sense of myself, as someone who cares for her friends, her family, who is reliable. I was so obsessed with getting pregnant, with my breakup with Andy, that I hadn't been there for him. But I see him inside Hazel. She has the same smile, the same eyes. She pulled at Billy's long beard at the wake, as we talked about the old days, and I noticed every line in his face, wondering if everyone could see mine when I still felt thirty-two. She sat sleeping while Agatha cried over her split with Finch, and I gave her the same divorce speech Tom had given me.

I am single now, by definition, I guess. There won't be a wedding, at least not with Andy. After a few months of sepa-ration, he came back around and I reminded him that he couldn't offer me things and then keep taking them back. I had to look at myself and admit that the relationship with Andy didn't feel like a relationship. It felt like being addicted to the love he would give me, then take away. The high I got when he would come back around, there was nothing like it.

But now Agatha and I have a little single-moms club. We go to the park and watch Emily run around, while Hazel sits in her jumpy seat, wide-eyed and beautiful. She loves the big-ger children, and Emily is her favorite. Agatha will be with me when she takes her first steps. They will meet me at the hospital when Hazel gets a bad fever. Agatha says *It gets easier* when I need to hear that. We all go from day to day, and our future is undefined. But isn't it always?

I go on dates sometimes. Sometimes with Angus, who will hold Hazel in their arms wearing oversized sound-blocking headphones, as they both grin wildly while Agatha and I thrash around onstage. Later, teenagers flank the signing tables and proffer our vinyl reissues. And when they sing along to all the old songs, I never feel annoyed like I used to, because I know it's something to be thankful for.

EVERY MOTHER WILL tell you, baby in arms, that it was the right decision, and not only that, it was the *best one she ever made*. I often feel that way. I look at Hazel's tiny fingers and I'm in awe, and it's a new kind of awe I'd never experienced before. In other moments, I'm terrified. Some days I hold her, looking out the window of my house, watching the world go by, and I'm a type of bored that is too bored to fit the definition, and sad, lonely, and at odds with my skin and the outside world, more alone than I've ever felt before. Lonely enough to call my mother and beg her to visit. And she does. We sit like two old women in awe of the energy Hazel has all day long. And then Hazel throws up, and even that is funny. And when she learns to walk-stumble, the three of us go to the ocean and I take a photo of my mom holding Hazel up in the air against the light of a setting sun, a photo that Hazel will look at so much she will swear that she remembers the moment my mother let go and for a second she was flying.

ACKNOWLEDGMENTS

THANK YOU TO my agent, Samantha Haywood, for her unwavering support since day one, and to Andra Miller and Iris Tupholme for their patient editorial guidance.

Some of the facts from Ruth and Frank's experiences in 1922 in Turkey came from family diaries and letters, though their personal stories are fabricated. Thank you to my father, Keith Whittall, for gathering that information for me, and for showing me Bornova and Llija in person. Thanks to my mother for details about farm life and feminism in the 1970s.

Thanks to Gavin and Lisa for careful readings of the final text. To Matt and Allison for all of the pre-pandemic work dates. To Will, Angie, Paul, Dean, Courtney, Chase, Marcilyn, and Andrea, for friendship. JAWLZ forever. Thank you Torrey Peters, Ashley Audrain, Kristen Arnett, Iain Reid, Jen Sookfong Lee, David Bergen, Robin Wasserman, Ilana Masad, Alissa Nutting, and Jordy Rosenberg for their endorsements.

Zoe Whittall is the author of three previous novels: the Giller-shortlisted *The Best Kind of People*, the Lambda-winning *Holding Still for as Long as Possible*, and her debut *Bottle Rocket Hearts*. She has published three collections of poetry: *The Best Ten Minutes of Your Life*, *Precordial Thump*, and *The Emily Valentine Poems*. She is also a Canadian Screen Award–winning TV and film writer, with credits on the *Baroness Von Sketch Show*, *Schitt's Creek*, *Degrassi*, and others.